Don't you want to know?

Aron thought it was impressive that she hardly flinched when he set his hands around her throat. "I thought spies were supposed to be better at this," he whispered.

He could feel the breath in her throat, tight as she drew it inside the ring of his hands. "Did you?" she answered, trying to be casual, but there was a crack in her voice.

"Looking for something? Does my father know what you're doing this time?"

Aron wasn't quite expecting her to turn, slowly, inside his hands. She faced him, looking into his eyes, pressing herself closer to him. She was trying to manipulate him, he was sure of it, steadily pulling close until she slipped her throat out of his hands, but somehow he didn't find himself stopping her. He could feel her breath on his chin, he could see the crooked teeth as she opened her mouth to speak, and he listened to her. "No, he doesn't. But do you want to? Don't you want to know what he's doing? Don't you want to know what he's hiding?"

Also by Michelle M. Welch

CONFIDENCE GAME

THE BRIGHT AND THE DARK

MICHELLE M. WELCH

*thanks for reading
and supporting the library!*

BANTAM BOOKS
New York • Toronto • London • Sydney • Auckland

THE BRIGHT AND THE DARK
A Bantam Spectra Book / August 2004

Published by Bantam Dell
A Division of Random House, Inc.
New York, New York

ISBN 0-553-58628-9

Manufactured in the United States of America
Published simultaneously in Canada

OPM   10   9   8   7   6   5   4   3   2   1

Thanks:

To my editor, Juliet Ulman, for helping me get past a bit of a rough start.

To my friends who let me pick their brains: Leslie, Susan, and Kim for their medical knowledge, and Wes for his fencing expertise.

And—as ever—to Lejon, Brian, and Kim (again): my best support, my best critic, my best friend.

Biora

Kiela ❖

Kiana ❖

Sor'rai

Lake
Azin

Kian Pass

Kian R.

Azin R.

Alderstand

Riverside ❖

Seven Oaks ❖

**Western
Sea**

Cassile

Karrim

Manderan R.

Naniantemple ❖

Delton ❖

Great River

❖ Westin

❖ Kysa

Map of the Five Countries

Marlind

Straits of Marlind

Gayeth

Doss

Lithen

Aligh

Dahion

North
Water

6 5

Insigh

Azassi

Kerr

Vigtil

1 4
2 3

Tanasigh

Orrigh

Mt. Alaz

Anamaril

Siva

Mandera

South
Water

Iyla

Tristam

N

Ikindan Sea

Ikinda

Part 1

———◆———

BIORA

The dreams are too much. I never used to dream before, never. Sleep was black to me, empty, the only rest I was allowed, I suppose. I did not remember it and I did not think on it. That was solace enough. It was a moment that vanished from my memory, hours I simply ceased to exist; a passage that didn't even leave behind any trace of itself to tell me it was missing.

Tod was different—he dreamed. As a child he dreamed so often he stopped remembering the dreams, hiding from those little deaths. When dreams came to him later they meant something. There was the dream when he saved me when I was sick, and there was the dream he had when Loyd and Varzin were going to die. I don't know, though, whether he's had a dream since then. I don't know whether he's dreamed of me.

I've seen him. I have—they let him come here. Half-blind, he's no threat to them. He can't see the secrets of Sor'rai and carry them back to the people across the lake in the Five Countries or behind the mountains in Biora, those troublesome humans, and so the Magi allow him to come here. It is the Sages, of course, who bring him here, and they are not afraid of him. They wouldn't be; he's one of their own. So I can see him here, though he can't see me.

No, his sight isn't that bad, he can see bright and dark, contrasts, shapes against the light. That might not help him see me, though. I don't know, anymore, if I make a shape against the light.

It hurts, being here, seeing what they see. The dreams. I can't tell dreams from waking—the Sages are always dreaming. The passage is as subtle, its borders as thin, as the spiral of time that the Sages perceive. It is all time at once, no questions and answers, no cause and effect. I was a spy: I looked for my answers and evidence. None of that matters here. It is not time, it is not a line, it is not dreams or waking, it is nothing but IT IS. It hurt to come here. We're trained to withstand pain, spies, but it was not pain, it was nothing but IT IS. That pain has not dropped out of my head but sunk deeper somewhere, where I cannot see it, cannot feel it, cannot think of it or give it words, but only know it in that way that Sages know everything.

I do not know everything, though. My blood is not that strong; I am too much human. I have seen only images, shapes that barely stand out against the light. I have seen the boy but I do not know who he is. I knew Tod would find him but I could not have told Tod about it. I have seen Aron, and I know what he will do, but I cannot say what it will be. And I have seen sickness, a great shadow over a wide land that my sleeping eyes cannot penetrate. These are Sor'rai's real secrets, then, not the Magi moving the trees around, nothing that a human could see and go back and tell to the rest of the world, but the things that do not make shapes against the light. And no human, not even one who is only a little human, can see those things or carry them anywhere.

1

"WHICH SIDE ARE YOU GOING TO BE ON?"
The wind was high, the air drier than the leaves and brambles that crunched under Julian's feet. It was dry as fire, dry as the sun. Dry as drought—but Julian shuddered to even think the word. *Drought.*

"I'll be with the Dust," Davi was saying, his voice hardly carrying over the wind. "They'll choose me, I know it." He was up on the road, swinging a willow wand in his hand, whipping it around like a flail, like a scythe. He laughed, dry and dusty. "You'll be with the Water men," he shouted back at Julian.

"Then we'll have to kill each other," Julian answered, not listening, really, to his own words. One of the lambs was caught in the brambles and was calling Julian with frightened, mournful bleats.

Then Julian looked up at his friend. Davi should have replied by now, laughing him off or telling him it wasn't true. But Davi only whipped the branch, back and forth in front of him, cutting through the dry wind.

Branches and thorns caught Julian's knees, scratched him, bit through the windings around his legs. He wondered what made Davi talk about it, today, yesterday, almost every day for weeks now. Then he remembered, vaguely, like the smell of a rainfall just before he woke, that Davi's brother had gone only a few weeks ago. Who had taken him? Julian wondered. Dust? Water? He reached the lamb and sank his arms into the brambles, scratching bright blood onto his white skin.

"Or are you staying here?" Davi's laugh came whistling through the wind like the wand striking the air. "With the women and the girls? Tending sheep. Will you wear a dress and a shawl with your beard, like Telan?"

Julian spun around, wanting to chase Davi, race him, make him take it back. The branches caught his clothing and he couldn't move. He watched his friend stride down the road, distant, taller and broader, his copper-flax hair chopped blunt and short. He was nearly grown. He would be taken soon. Julian lifted the lamb over his shoulders and began to pick his way out of the brush.

One day, not long after that, Davi put a stick and a skin of water in Julian's hands, and they walked out from Kiela. They were going to see the men.

Kiela was a large town, larger than they knew. Its fields spread out over acres of land, even up to the mountains. Houses, pens with their crooked-ringed fences, fanned rows of plantings—it seemed to go on forever before they walked out of it. They mounted the feet of the hills and looked down on it, their home, the world of their childhood. How small it was there, distant in the vastness of the land.

They walked northward, very far, farther than Julian had ever walked. His feet began hurting him, he could feel every stone through the thin leather of his shoes, and he began to sweat inside his woolen tunic, beads of water slipping down his sides. Was it getting hotter? The land around him, beneath its tangle of scrub and brush, looked dry and sandy. It was spring, it should have been raining, the clouds heavy and thick. He looked up at the sky. The sun came out from behind the mountain in a blinding swell. Julian ducked, squinting, trying to shade himself with his thin hands.

Ahead of him, Davi laughed. "Is the sun burning you? Pretty Bioran boy. You should be brown, like me."

He wasn't brown, Julian thought loudly. The book-man was brown, although Davi would only laugh at him again for still going to see the book-man. Davi was honey-colored, wheat-colored. His hair wasn't even quite brown. But Aunt Ana said they were brown, and so they were. "We're all brown in Kiela," she would say, then she would smile at Julian, and say to him as if it were a secret, "except Julian."

When they neared the village, Julian did not at first see it. He saw only dark spots on the land, piles of sticks, scattered like a child's toy. Only when they came closer, and the spots began to grow, did he see that they were houses. Shacks, rough and broken, each so far from the next. There were no pens, no rows of grain. The land was unplanted and untended. Behind each house was a tiny scrap of a garden, stuck through with the drooping heads of tired stalks. Here and there an animal wandered, a mangy sheep, a bone-thin chicken. Women stood bent at their doors, and children sat in the shade and the dust beside their walls. Between those walls the dry land stretched out, barren.

And Julian saw that the faces on the one side of the village, where a few shacks were clumped near to each other, were brown, wheat honey and darker. On the north side, farther from them and across the rocky barrens, the women and their thin children were white, colorless as bone, and their hair was the same white cornsilk gold. It was as if they were not one village of Biorans, but two villages, two different peoples, foreigners to each other. Julian thought of the gatherings in Kiela, the Aunts and all the people together in a circle, and knew there were no such gatherings in this place.

"Look," Davi whispered then, and the whisper was lost in a distant rumble. "The men are coming."

They swept down from the mountain like a dust storm, like the heavy rains of late summer. They trampled the gardens and flooded the shacks. With the swing of knives the beasts were cracked in a bloodred blur. Tiny scurries of children ran into their shelters. In the clouded distance Julian saw one of the women, her pale hair flying, swing at the storm with a rake. From the mass of men one was singled out. He grasped the woman, pulled her into the house, and Julian saw nothing more of them. In the sound of chaos a narrow scream drifted, and was lost.

The boys pressed themselves behind the small shelter

of a hillock. "They're Dust," Davi breathed at Julian's side. "You can see the marks on their faces."

But Julian did not see the Dust men. On his back, low to the ground, looking at the sky, he only saw the sun. It stared down at him, hot and angry. Where was the Water, he wondered, or Davi said it. Where was the Water?

Then, as if summoned, they came. From the south, behind the hillock where the boys crouched, the Water men came, pounding the earth as they ran, tearing the air with their shouts. Their voices were so fierce and loud with rage that Julian would not have known they were human.

And beside him, Davi echoed their cry in a voice Julian had never before heard. He leapt to his feet, thrusting his walking stick out like a weapon, in the path of the Water men.

"Davi!" Julian tried to shout, but his voice was dust in his throat.

He saw one of the men then, heavy with rage, his dark face burning red, his hair like dirty flax. On his face was a mark, painted or cut or burned there, the curve of a line ending in an arrow. Julian wondered who the arrow pointed to. Then the man raised his weapon—what weapon Julian did not see—and brought it down where Davi stood below him.

Julian covered his face and rolled away.

Will I always be a coward? he thought. He did not look out to the field where the men were fighting, and he covered his ears with his hands. He did not know what the sound of it was and he did not want to learn. Eyes closed, trembling, he did not feel the change in the air or see the darkening sky until it was suddenly split with thunder, drowning out the noise of men. Julian opened his eyes. The storm clouds had come, heavy and angry. They opened and the rain fell, striking Julian's face and his arms, pounding on the earth.

In the haze of the rain he could pretend he did not see the men in the distance. The rain washed out all sound of them. Julian crept from his hiding place, going on his elbows, wormlike, until he reached Davi, and he pulled him away into the shrubs. There he hid until the rain was gone and it was silent.

2

THERE WAS RAIN IN THE AIR. TOD COULD SMELL
it, only faintly at first, just a hint. That was all he
needed, though. He could smell a coming storm cloud
from miles off, or at least he assumed that's where it was,
since he couldn't see it. But after that first scent of rain, it
would not be long before the light around him darkened
and he felt the pressure in the air change; then he would
hear the rain. It was something, he supposed—this sense
of smell in exchange for his sight.

It would be good to hear the rain, Tod thought. There
hadn't been rain in some time, which was unusual for
spring in Biora. The people were terrified of drought.
The children told stories of the ten summers of Light,
and when Tod first heard them he thought they were
nothing more than the tales children tell to scare each
other; but even the women, the elders of the community,
repeated the stories, and when they spoke it was with
gravity and warning. The ten summers of Light, Tod
gathered, were ten years of drought, when the clouds
that were customary in this cool northern country were
burned away by the sun and the rain did not come. Biora

was almost destroyed, to hear the elder women tell it. Tod couldn't imagine that there was really no rain at all, but there must have been a drought and it must have been serious. In his old and poorly remembered years of school in Dabion, he'd learned that Biora was once the source of science and philosophy, and Bioran scholars had traveled the Five Countries to spread their knowledge. That all ended hundreds of years ago, though— Tod couldn't remember which years—and since then Biora had been cut off. Something terrible must have happened behind those northern mountains, to undo all those years of learning. Tod had been in Biora for years and he had yet to meet anyone who could even read.

There was another sound outside. Tod looked up toward the window of his small shack. He could not see much through the window, but it was still a comfort to have it there, letting in the air and the light. He could see light, and contrasts and shapes, although much of his sight was gone. It had been gone for ten years, more or less. He found he didn't miss it so much. He could still work without what he'd lost, and that was all he needed to do.

"You are the book-man," Aunt Ana had said when she first met him. She had been so sure, so certain, that Tod had been unwilling to disagree or even ask how she knew.

Later, when he did ask, she'd said, "A Sage told me." Aunt Ana was the only Bioran Tod knew who had ever spoken to or even seen a Sage.

But she knew he was a bookbinder, even if she didn't

know at first what that meant, really, and soon the whole town knew. Aunt Ana was the closest thing Kiela had to a Lord Justice, or a mayor maybe, as far as Tod could tell. She told everyone he was the book-man, and soon they were coming to him with their books.

He'd never seen books in worse condition, what he could see of them. They had been stowed away in chests, hidden in basements that had been dug for shelter during the ten summers of Light. Their boards were gnawed, their paper was fragile, and the leather of the binding was flaking off like old frost.

"You can fix it?" Aunt Ana said as he pored over a worn volume.

This had been only shortly after Tod had come to Biora, shortly after he had lost his sight. He wasn't sure he could fix it; there was no paper in Kiela, none of the tools he needed, even if his sight had been good. But even then he wasn't willing to disappoint her. "Yes," he answered, and held the book up to the pale light, angling it in front of the window and trying to catch the shapes of the letters on the page. "What does it say?"

If he could have seen Aunt Ana's face, he might have said she raised her brows in a way that indicated the question was irrelevant. "We don't know," she said, and with that she was gone. Others came later to bring what tools and supplies they could offer, and Tod made do with them. He mended stitching and encased delicate paper in new covers. Tod Redtanner, bookbinder, was back in business.

So when he heard the noise outside his window this

humid spring morning, Tod expected that it would be one of the aunts or some of the children, maybe, bringing another armload of books to him. It was a surprise, then, when he heard the knock at the sill of his window and a voice, accented and uncomfortable with the distant dialect, calling, "Mister Tod?"

"Julian!" Tod cried, getting to his feet and picking his way to the door. He hadn't expected Julian to be here, so late in the evening, and he was doubly surprised that he neither heard nor smelled the sheep that the young man was normally herding. "Come in," he offered, holding the door wide.

Not that he needed to offer. His visitors seemed to think of his home as theirs. He was not part of their village, here at the foot of the mountains where the Sages who'd arranged his exile had put him, and he was wildly foreign and strange to them. Still, they seemed to take it upon themselves to care for him, to adopt him, since he had no one else. Every day, almost, someone was here, cooking for him, tidying his kitchen, tending his garden. Whether their attention was a gesture of generosity to someone in need or condescension to someone who obviously couldn't look after himself, Tod didn't know, but he didn't really care. He appreciated the company, blunt and insistent though it might be. Julian was through the door and into his kitchen before Tod had even pulled the door back all the way. Tod smiled in his own darkness and returned to his table.

As he got back to his work—sanding down boards for the new covers of books, a task he could do with only the tips of his fingers and no light at all—he realized that the sun wasn't the only thing missing. Julian, normally a cheerful boy, was unusually silent. He was doing something in the opposite corner of Tod's shack, blocking the small candle with his body. From the sound he thought that Julian might be patching a chink in the wall with some mud he'd brought from outside.

"The rain will be nice, won't it?" Tod ventured. "Is it already raining in the village? Is that why you didn't have to herd the sheep today?"

Julian turned toward Tod; he could tell by the movement of candlelight through the hair that hung on either side of Julian's head. Tod had no way of guessing the expression on his face, though, as Julian stood silently. He might have been embarrassed, caught shirking his chore. He might have been angry at Tod for prying. Or his expression might have been inscrutable, Tod thought, and this he thought more surely. As inscrutable as Elzith had always been.

Elzith—she would be able to figure it out. She would start analyzing the evidence: here was Julian, boy, alone, late, age about sixteen. Then Tod stopped as he pondered something. Julian was the only boy over the age of twelve who had ever visited him. In the ten years he'd been in Biora, even on those few occasions when he went into the village, he had never seen or heard a grown man.

"I had to take Davi to the herb-woman," Julian said faintly.

"Is Davi sick?" Tod searched his memory and tried to

find a boy called Davi, but it was hard to keep track of the children, coming and going in packs. Especially the boys. They usually came a few times and disappeared.

Julian mumbled something in response, but even Tod's sharpened hearing could not catch it.

"Well," Tod said in a voice he hoped was soothing, "tell him I wish him health."

A short laugh escaped Julian, and Tod thought it sounded mocking. He couldn't imagine why, and the young man said nothing that would help him. Tod wished he could remember Davi. He wished he could see Julian's face.

Then he sighed and turned his attention back to the boards, to the texture of the wood under his fingers. "I have a bit of work to do," he said, "I hope you don't mind." He picked up his knife, buried in the center of his table so he wouldn't accidentally brush it off the edge as he passed by, and began to carve the notches where the paper would be held in.

In his memory, long ago and faded, he saw himself sitting at his table in his cottage in Dabion, printed sheets arrayed before him, and across from him, Elzith. She'd complained of being bored and he had taught her to sew pages together. They worked together. It was the only time in his life he was not alone. He wondered where she was now. He knew where she was, of course, literally—she was in Sor'rai. He traveled there to visit her sometimes, a few times a year, whenever the Sages came for him. He didn't know why they came for him. They walked him through the pass into Sor'rai—a journey he couldn't see well and one that didn't seem to take as long as it should—and Elzith would be there waiting for him.

The first time he'd been surprised to see her. Ten years or so ago he was escorted into Biora, by a Sage who seemed so disturbingly familiar that Tod was glad he couldn't see his face. That man had left him near Kiela without telling him anything, just as Elzith had left him a day earlier when they reached Lake Azin, walking away without any mention of where she was going, and Tod had been miserably certain that he would never see her again. A year passed, and the Sage appeared at Tod's door, along with a female Sage who was certainly not Elzith, and they brought him with them on that too-brief journey into Sor'rai. Tod hadn't tried to ask them where they were going or why.

"What have you seen in the northern land?" the male Sage had asked Tod. Elzith had since told Tod that his name was Zann.

"Nothing," Tod had started to say, because his sight was gone. Of course Zann knew that, though, so he must have been asking about something else. Then the woman, who he'd learned was called Irisith, reached for his arm. He'd needed that support, because his feet at that moment had met ground that seemed much harder and more solid than it had a moment before. But he felt something more in Irisith's grasp. Something had opened in his mind and he had seen something through it: his small cottage, his books, the aunts and the children and the smell of rain.

"Peace," he had answered, strangely but knowingly. "I've seen peace."

And then behind him, another voice. "Well, that must be boring."

Tod had laughed. He would know the voice anywhere, though he couldn't see her, though he hadn't noticed her near him until she spoke. He had taken her in his arms and she had felt different, the tension in her gone and replaced by something strange, a weight that wasn't, a movement that was hard to measure. He'd breathed into her hair, now plaited in thin braids and smelling of leaves, "Restful. You should try it sometime."

"Unimaginable," Elzith had answered, with her familiar sharpness. "My constitution couldn't take it. I've got a hole in my gut, you know." Then she had spoken more seriously, gently, with some kind of pride in her voice. "Biora agrees with you, Tod, I can tell. You agree with it. But then, I think you could be content anywhere."

Tod nodded. That was the first time he'd known it was true. "And how are you?" he'd asked. "What have you been doing these days?"

"Well, this and that. Sage things. You know I can't tell you." She paused for a beat. "Just like a spy. It's almost like home."

Tod had reached a hand to her face, feeling the lines that had formed around her eyes. She was smiling.

For ten years he'd been visiting her in the same way. It gave richness to his contentment, to see her there, alive, safe. It lit the dimness in his empty cottage. He did not have to feel alone in the permanent shadows, because he knew he would see her again. But as time went on, she was no longer the same. She seemed thinner, not in her body but in her substance. It was harder to find her voice among those of the other Sages, although her words were still sharp. She put less scent on the air. And when Tod held her in his arms, even as he encircled her entire body, he wondered where she was. He found himself sleepless at night, afraid to dream of her death.

Tod sighed and picked up his knife again, realizing it had slipped from his unmoving hand. He had work to do, as he'd told Julian. In his mind's eye he could imagine Julian coming to his table, sitting down, asking Tod to teach him how to bind. He imagined himself telling Julian about binding law books in Dabion, about Keller the printer, about the memory book he'd made and had to leave behind before he could ever finish it. But he knew the real Julian was standing, maybe leaning against the wall, far away and not coming nearer. Tod sighed into the silence and dropped his head blindly into his work.

But Julian stirred and stepped forward. "You know what it says," he murmured.

Tod had forgotten that he'd left some of the old books, some of the tattered pages, lying open on his table. Julian had moved away from the candle and it now lit up enough that Tod could see him standing close to the table, his head bent. He was looking at the writing and wondering what it said. "I would know," Tod answered, "if I could see it."

Julian sighed through his nose, sounding forlorn and young. "I can see, but I don't understand."

His ears sharp, Tod could hear the change in the young man's breath, faint as it was, just a touch faster, more eager. He heard Julian catch several breaths, readying himself to speak but not certain how to say it. Tod had guessed before Julian finally asked, "Teach me."

So Tod put away his knife. He washed the glue from one of his brushes and dipped it in leather dye. He found a sheet of thin leather that had not yet been colored, pale enough that he would be able to see the contrast of dye on it. He felt Julian sit beside him at the table where he'd sat alone for some ten years. Then, in large bold letters that he could see in the wavering light of his candle, he began to teach Julian to read.

3

IT DID NOT RAIN THAT DAY AS TOD HAD HOPED, and Julian walked home through thick air and too-dry dust. The storm clouds hovered and rumbled and passed, reaching places like the distant village, but leaving Kiela untouched. In the morning Aunt Ana called a gathering for the rain.

In the center of the village was a wide dirt plain, and it was there that the people gathered. They sat on the earth as they always did, the women with their looms and their grindstones and the clay pots they shaped with their hands, the children with their toys, wooden blocks and dolls stuffed with straw, skin balls, sticks in the hands of older boys. Two or three boys would break away from the crowd to swing at each other with their sticks, shouting and hollering with the cheers and the clapping of the younger ones. Children would laugh and old women would tell riddles, young women braided each other's hair, and around them the small animals that went free in the lanes clucked and brayed. It was the same as any gathering, Julian thought. Except now, between their light words, above their laughter, their eyes drifted toward the sky. They turned their faces up toward the thin clouds that crossed the sun, and their faces were afraid.

Was it this way at every spring gathering? Julian could not remember. The children who sat in a ring at his knees shouted at him, tugged his sleeves. He'd been ignoring them, looking around at the other people. He turned back, saw them making faces and laughing.

"The Light wounds us and the Light blesses us," Aunt Ana was saying from across the dirt plain. The people echoed her words, murmurs seeping through the crowd like water. Her hands set the rhythm of the work, moving the cards that worked the wool, and the other Aunts pulled their shuttles in time, hands at the grindstones carrying the rhythm. The boys at the edges of the group struck their sticks together with it. Julian traced letters in the dirt to the rhythm, and the children laughed to it. "How do you write Light?" they asked.

Julian traced the L, he knew that. The book-man had taught him that. "This is *L*," he'd said, painting it out large, "as in light." Tod hadn't known what he was speaking of, Julian thought, when he said the word so casually. *A* had been "apple," but Julian didn't know what such a thing was.

Behind him Julian felt a hand on his shoulder. His mother sat behind him, spindle loose in her hand. Her eyes were warning. *The Light wounds us.* Letters were not to hold it. Julian brushed the figure out of the dirt with his hand.

"It will give the rain to us, if we give to It," the words

echoed in the gathering. It was spring, and there were always sacrifices in spring. Every spring, Julian thought. They must have spent every spring waiting for it to rain.

One of the young women finished braiding her sister's hair. "Dela has hair like the thick summer wheat," Aunt Ana said, and Dela smiled. Her hair was pulled back into the braid the women wore, tied back so they could work, and below the end of the braid her sister tied it off and severed it with her knife. The gift of the hair was passed around by the Aunts and they murmured over its beauty.

"Our sheep were full and fat this winter," Aunt Ana went on. Yiera carried the wool in her arms from the shearing. It was given to be carded, to be spun on the spindle, and the first part that Aunt Ana pulled out was for the Light. "Yiera led the shearing this year," said Aunt Ana, and the others crooned their approval. Yiera smiled and looked around her, until she reached Julian and she made a scowl. Yiera was a few years older than Julian and she thought the shepherding should be her duty. "What a waste to teach it to a boy," she would say, never speaking to him.

Aunt Ana saw Yiera's scowl. Julian watched her gaze at Yiera, disapproving and wise, but Yiera did not pay attention to her.

A girl of twelve or thirteen years rose from her loom and went to Aunt Ana, her bit of cloth shaking in her hands like leaves in wind. "I finished this," she whispered in her timid voice, and she held out the cloth, uncolored wool lined with a pattern of brilliant red.

Aunt Ana praised her in a bright voice, and then the other girls at the looms. She took handfuls of grain from the bowls of the women and sang to their craft. A crowd of small boys leapt up in a raucous dance and she praised them. "And Julian," she said, turning to him, "yet the white star in Kiela, beautiful like the old ones."

Julian smiled for her, and his mother and his Aunts murmured their praise. He plucked from his head, as he always did, one cornsilk hair. They were wrong, he knew. He'd seen others as white as he was, outside of Kiela. But they lived apart, and no one praised them. If his beauty was all he could give, he thought it wasn't much of a gift.

"Now what do the boys have for us?" Aunt Ana called, and all the older boys jumped to their feet. With shouts and fire they showed their arms, the fighting they had practiced. The women watched them, their sons who would leave soon and not come back. They were quiet, but the fear in their eyes that they tried to hide was for the sky.

Julian watched them, the boys that were his age. He saw his friend Macus, whose mother lived in the house beside his, wielding his stick furiously. Julian hadn't even seen Macus practice his fighting. Last spring he'd spent the gathering sitting here next to Julian, playing games with the small children.

The one Julian did not see was Davi. He was not fighting in the dirt plain. Julian looked around, among the houses outside the circle, trying to see through the doorways and the windows. Davi would be watching, Julian was certain, though his arm was bound and motionless until it healed. He would hate to miss the fighting. Only a few words had he said to Julian when he emerged from the herb-woman's shack, that morning before the gathering. "They were Water men," Davi had said, and his voice was strange and hard like the rock Julian had hidden behind. His body was not the same, arm fixed in a sheath of wood and strung on a sling that hung from his neck. His movements were not the same, slow and heavy with danger, like the great ram that Julian had watched Aunt Ana and the other women struggle with when he was a child, straining at its bonds. And his face, most of all his face was not the same. A red scar stretched brutally down the left side of it, pulling his eye and his mouth into some strange aspect, but it was in those eyes that Davi was the most changed. They were dark, cruel, and Julian did not want his friend to look at him. "I will go with the Dust," Davi had said, "and I will kill them." Julian had spoken no more to his friend since then.

The younger boys took sides, calling themselves Water and Dust though they had never seen any, never been close enough to see the men's faces or hear the noise of them, and they cheered or hooted for the fighting boys from the ground where they sat. The fighters who lost gave up their sticks, carrying them to Aunt Ana, dragging them along the ground with shamed faces, to be given to the Light. Those who won took their knives and cropped their hair short, so they might be seen as fighters. Julian saw Macus shear himself of his oat-colored hair and swing the rope of it in the air, triumphantly, as he carried it to the Aunts.

Julian's hand drifted up to his own hair, without thinking, hardly noticing it, until he felt his mother behind him again, combing through the white-gold with her fingers, as she had when he was a child. She was laughing. He turned to look at her. What was in her laugh? She was mocking him, or soothing him. He didn't know. At his knees the children were laughing in echo. They had drawn a picture of him in the dirt, his long thin face, curved lines of hair stretching over his boxy shoulders, a zigzag for the whiskers growing over his lip. Julian put out his finger and etched in antlers and a pair of wings, and the children rolled with joy.

"This is what I have," a voice said from among the women who worked their needles. Yiera's sister Reena stood, holding a garment in her hands. Reena was younger than Yiera, Julian's own age. Her work was very fine and the women sang with praise of it. Then another voice cried out, "Don't forget mine, Aunt Ana!" It was Telan, who sat among the women, and he waved a crooked length of twine in the air. All the women laughed then, as he got to his feet and sauntered toward Aunt Ana, his skirt swinging at his ankles.

Reena was laughing, and her bright face turned toward Julian, and her eyes shone. The sun was bright on her throat and moisture gleamed on her skin. All through him Julian felt the color in his blood, drawing him up tight, aching in him. His flesh felt soft and taut, hot and shivering with a strange chill. But inside all of it he felt the deepest sadness.

"Then it is time," Aunt Ana said. "We will give these things to the Light."

They stood then, in the dirt plain in the center of the village, and one by one the women brought pieces of wood in. They built their fire in the center of the plain, high and bright. They lit the wood and the flames went up, high and hot as the sky and the Light Itself. One by one Aunt Ana gave the things to the fire, and the fire gave them to the Light, the smoke of them rising into the sky. "So the rain might come," Aunt Ana said. "So we might live as we always have."

And in the crackling, the voice of fire and the voice of the people who spoke her words over and over, came Julian's voice, alone. "But why?"

The people were moving away from him. It might have been the heat, the fire growing too great to stand near any longer. Julian felt the breath of it on his face and his eyes stung. But the voices were quiet, no one answering him. Across the fire, behind the shifting flames, Aunt Ana watched him, but she did not answer.

That night the fire was quenched by rain from the sky. They heard it hiss as it died and smelled the sharpness of its last smoke. A few days later another fire was built in the dirt plain, because the men were coming.

Julian did not go to see the men. He never had before, though now he wondered where he had always been. In the fields with the sheep, he thought, or to the bookman's. He wanted to go there now, but first Aunt Ana had given him work to do in the village. She wanted the old books mended, and Julian had to bring them out from the cave cut below her house, where they would hide from the Light if It came back to punish them. Julian crept into the cave, trembling, as if he could feel the hands of the dead who had perished in the ten summers long ago, catching his hair, grasping at his ankles. He went through the books where they lay in their dust and rescued them, placed them in a barrow so that he could take them to the book-man.

He did not mind Aunt Ana's work so much. The more books he took, the longer he could stay at the bookman's house. He could stay late into the evening hours, and it was these hours that Julian waited for. The bookman needed the brighter time of the afternoon for his work, when there was light enough for his half-broken eyes to see; but in the evening, by the sputtering light of an oily candle, he would teach Julian the letters. The letters enchanted Julian. They were not so lovely and rich as the patterns that the women at the looms worked, and they were not like the figures in the blankets that some of the elder and finer weavers made, images of creatures that echoed in the mind and called up the sound of thundering hooves, warm and real. The letters were only shapes, less than the patterns that repeated and locked together across their clothing, weird like the bent knees of animals or dried and dead trees. But soon he would know them, and he would put them together, and then they would become real. Then he would know what they meant, and he would know things that not even the Aunts knew when they told their stories at the gatherings, the only words they had, echoing through the people over and over.

"Why are you digging those up?" the small children asked him as he climbed out of the hole in the ground with his arms full of old books.

"Aunt Ana told me to," he answered. The small girl nodded, so wise and solemn Julian nearly laughed, but the boy kept at his questions. "Why?" he asked. "Why did she tell you to?"

And the Aunts were there nearby, building the fire for the men who would come, and one of them said, "It is our history. Not many people have the luxury of looking at their past, it's hard enough living each day. But we are blessed, life is not so hard for us. So we can look at these things from our past and save them."

The Aunt smiled in her wisdom, although the children looked as puzzled as they had been before. "But why are we saving them?" the boy insisted again. Julian set his load on the ground and crept back into the cave, as the sound of the boy's eager voice hurt his ears. None of the answers you look for will mean anything, he thought, when the men come to kill you.

They came that night. They came every year, Julian knew, though he didn't remember it and had never seen it. First one side, then the other, never crossing paths. Aunt Ana said they were not allowed to fight in Kiela. The Dust men came first that year, and Julian watched them come.

They sat in their circle in the dirt plain, their fire burning in the center and drums rumbling among them.

It was the men who brought the drums, Julian realized. The women did not have them, making music with their voices as they worked in the fields, singing to the rhythm of their wool cards and their grinding stones. Children sang and clapped their hands, but the voices of the men were silent and their hands beat the drums that only they had. Julian knew the drums from every summer of his life, he'd heard them in his sleep in the warm nights, but he never knew what they were. The drums bled through the earth and shook Julian's feet where he stood in the shadow of his mother's house, in the ring at the edge of the dirt plain. Every year the boys were taken away to die, just outside his walls, and he'd never quite realized it.

Light from the fire lit the men in flickering waves. They squatted near the ground, their feet below them, ready to rise and strike at any threat. Those with the drums held them between their knees, like spiders clutching grotesque eggs. The men were clothed in vests and trews cobbled together from animal skins, and their legs were wrapped in sheaths of leather or wool and wound around the outside with lacings. Julian wore the same windings on his legs, all the boys did, and the women did under their skirts when it was cold. They were not so different. Julian shivered. The faces of the men were rough, crowned with blunt-cut hair, grown over with the scrub of their beards, and on their cheekbones they were marked with three circles, each one of them, the pattern stained into their skin.

The fire burned in the center of the circle of men, and

between the fire and the men, the boys fought. They were bare to the waist, showing their arms and the sinews of their bodies, striking at each other with their makeshift weapons, each one hoping to show himself the strongest. The men would take the best of them and make them warriors of the Dust. In the center of the circle, his arm still hobbled in its sling, Davi fought hardest, wildest, swinging his one good arm more fiercely than any of them. The fire cast shadows of the boys on the shacks around the circle, and as Davi fought his shadow crossed Julian, and Julian felt cold under it. He backed away, behind his house, where he could not see the recruitment.

"How old are they, do you think?" a voice hissed in his ear.

Julian froze, feeling the stubble of a chin pressed into hair, hot breath on the back of his neck. He could not answer. No one counted the ages of the boys—there was no reason to. The boys who fought were the ones who were ready to leave.

"They've heard that call," the voice went on, arms wrapping around Julian's waist. "Every boy does, they say. That call to go out into the world and fight. But not every boy does. I heard a different one."

Hands slipped along the folds of Julian's garment, seeking something in his chest, his waist, his belly. Julian felt the breath hot on his neck, and his own skin cold against it. Behind his back a heart thumped fast and eager, but Julian was still, as if molded of ice.

Then the hands released him and the man behind

him stepped back to arm's length. Julian turned around and met the face of Telan. The man held Julian's head in both his hands, peering into his eyes. "No, you have not heard that call, either," he murmured. Telan backed away into the deeper shadows, shaking his head. "What have you heard?"

"I don't know," Julian whispered, but Telan was gone and he did not hear. Julian was alone with the sound of the drums.

4

"LET US SPEAK NOW OF THE ELEMENTS OF MATTER," Julian said.

Tod looked up and smiled. The young man was reading; Tod could see the shape of his head bent downward and when he listened he could hear the rustling of paper. Julian had been reading a lot, every scrap, every page, insatiably. In the two years since Tod began teaching him he had read more than Tod had his whole life, he thought, while he'd had sight enough to do it. Julian read with enchantment and passion, so much that Tod himself was fascinated, and as far as Tod could tell, Julian even understood what he was reading. Tod couldn't have said as much for himself, when he was binding books of law.

"It has long been said that the elements are four: earth, air, fire, and water. But this definition in its simplicity overlooks much. The intricacies of earth, for example, are lost by naming it such. The earth beneath our feet and the earth of which our feet are made are so disparate as to be different categories of matter entirely, and yet they are the same. Such is the nature of humanity: at once of the earth and greater than the earth."

Tod shook his head as he ran his finger along the crease inside the fragile pages, feeling for the tip of the needle and drawing it through. He wasn't one for musing on human nature. It was enough for him that his fingers worked, that he could pull the needle, and that he hadn't once pricked himself, hadn't once stabbed his clumsy fingers with the razor point, since he'd lost his sight. That was enough greatness for him. "Who wrote this book?" he asked.

Julian's voice drifted from his reading without any pause. No interruption upset him, unlike most people Tod had ever met. He wished he could have had that kind of calm when he was eighteen. He might have thought that calmness was a trait of Biorans, if Julian hadn't already told him, in disturbing hints, about the wave of violence that crept through the country.

"Dal'Nilaran," Julian answered.

"Dalinaran?"

Tod heard Julian's easy laugh. He was glad to hear it. He wanted to think of Julian as a happy boy. He had the lingering feeling that boys in Biora were not happy. "No, like this," Julian said gently, and he reached for one of Tod's brushes to sketch the letters out large. "D-A-L, that's the world name."

"The what?"

Julian frowned, his brow casting shadows down his face. "His—his family name, you'd call it."

"Like his father's name?"

Julian breathed out another laugh, though Tod didn't understand why. "Father's name, I suppose. There used to be more world names. Maybe there used to be fathers to give them."

Tod dropped his needle, and felt it swing on its thread like a pendulum passing across his leg. There were no fathers, he thought. There were no men in Biora. Well, there were children, so of course there were fathers, but the men did not stay in the villages. They did not raise their children. They went out, Tod guessed, to fight each other in the country. No fathers? Tod thought with a small shock. Who would you rebel against? How would you know who to be?

"There are only two names now," Julian was saying, "world names, family names. The names of the men, the two sides. *Dal* is for the Water, they still use it. *Yor* is for the Dust. Davi is Yor'Davi now." Then Julian's face fell, and he was silent.

Tod looked up at him, the faint light from the window lighting his downcast face. Tod reached his hand out, trying to find the young man's arm, to pat it comfortingly, in the darker shadows of the room. But Julian did not see him, and before Tod could reach him, Julian raised his arm and lifted his book, and was reading again.

"*Now we come to the matter of light and its composition. There are those scholars among us who hold with the corpuscular theory, who yet argue that the manifestations of fire that are the source of light give off from themselves particles, such as seeds or pollen in the wind, and these particles, when they collide with objects of the earth, reflect into human eyes and create the perception of light.*

"It is the more convincing theory, however, that the nature of light is that of the wave, not unlike the behavior of water in a body such as a lake. In watching the movement of light around an object, one can observe how the waves bend, as when the waves produced by a stone dropped in a pool spread when they pass a stand of reeds."

"Waves," said Tod suddenly.

Julian looked up from the book.

"Waves, like water, like the Water men." Tod put down the pages he was working on and sat up straight. "And those other things, particles, they're like dust. It's the same thing. Water and dust, it's the Light Controversy. That's what ended Bioran learning, in the Five Countries, I mean. I learned it in school. It was—oh, I can't remember the year, it was too long ago. But the scholars fought about it. The Light Controversy, that's what it was!"

Julian didn't respond. After Tod had caught his breath he saw that Julian was nodding calmly. "The men," Julian said, "they fight each other. They each say they are right in following the Light, and the others are wrong." Julian nodded again, and was quiet as if nothing else needed to be said.

Tod sputtered. "But no one's an enemy of light. It's not a god, it's light! It's science! They're scientists, they're scholars. They're not warriors. It's an argument, it's a theory. They were scholars! How did this happen?"

Julian put down his book and reached out his hand toward Tod. Tod had lost his chance and the young man was comforting him now. "But that is Biora," Julian said. "That is life here." He patted Tod's arm like an aunt soothing a frantic child. "That is life here."

Julian did not remain sad for long. "It was lucky for you," he went on, "that you came to Kiela. It is not so bad here. There is no fighting in Kiela, the Aunts won't allow it. The men won't come together, they won't fight each other here. They won't come in and take what they want. The Aunts, they make them bargain. The women will give their grain, their meat, if the men pledge not to steal it. These days they must barter," the young man added proudly. "They can't just take the food now, they must give something for it, wood, skins. That was Aunt Ana's doing."

Tod believed it. Aunt Ana was a formidable woman. Could she stand up to an angry, violent man, though, who'd given up all the rationality of his forefathers? The idea made Tod shiver.

"They can't take the women, either," Julian continued, tranquilly washing dye out of Tod's brushes. "The women won't let them. They must negotiate that as well. The men do as the women wish, it is all chosen by the women, and the women offer themselves to the men, and the men give their seed. It's a ceremony, in the fall, at harvest time. The harvest dance."

Tod remembered hearing one of the aunts mention the harvest dance, though he hadn't known then what it was. He felt himself blush. "Have you been to one?" he asked.

"Oh, no," Julian answered. "None of the village boys go." Then Tod heard the breath of a shy laugh. "But there will be one soon. The men are coming, and the women are making their dresses."

There was a moment where neither of them said anything, but Tod felt the tautness of their breath, and at once they both let it out with a laugh of embarrassment. Tod wished Julian saw as little of him as he saw of Julian. It would be a sad sight: a forty-year-old man snickering like a schoolboy. He wondered, to distract himself, whether he really was forty. He'd lost track of the years recently; they no longer seemed so important. He wasn't sure Julian was eighteen, either. Now his mind was all muddled, and everything was very sad. Julian had gone back to his reading. Tod felt himself, sharply, slowly, missing Elzith.

Julian did go to the harvest dance then. He did not join the dance himself, of course; but he watched from outside the ring of houses around the dirt plain, as he had watched the boys fight in the summer, and he did not watch alone.

The men sat in the center of the plain again, but this time they were in half a ring. The women made the other half, standing, facing the men, watching them. The men beat their drums and the women gave their voices, singing in time with the drums, chasing them, matching them. There were no words that Julian could hear, and they needed none. In the center of the ring burned the fire, hot and wild and fast in the women's care. They would not let it spread too far. Before the fire, before the men, the younger women danced, those who would get a child. They moved and turned to the beat of the drums and the pulse of the voices, their garments fluttering in the heat of the fire and the passion of their dance. They watched the men as they danced, and when their feet paused they would make their choices, reach a hand to the man they picked. Over their shoulders the elder women would see, and with their voices they would grant their approval, and they would open their ring to let the woman and the man out into the dark fields beyond.

Julian was behind the men, watching the dance, and he could see the Aunts as they watched the men's faces, judging them worthy of their daughters or not. He could not see the men, though, and he did not know what it was in their faces that made the young women choose the men that they did, or what made the Aunts grant their blessing.

"How many have gone?" whispered a voice at Julian's side.

He turned, silent in the shadows. Reena was there. "Four or five," he answered, while his voice still could speak. When he saw her his throat filled up and he lost all breath for words. She was dressed for the dance, in the garments that the women had been making for weeks. It was not a dress, really, Julian saw. Some fine thread of a fiber he did not know had been woven into long thin sheets, scarves, layers of cloth as fragile as the wings of butterflies and as brightly colored. When the firelight caught it the fabric glinted like stars. When the breeze stirred it the layers whispered around her bare legs and arms.

"I can't go," she murmured, leaning close to him, folding her arms against her breasts as if she were cold, though the night was warm. "I'm too nervous."

His arms ached to go around her and warm her. "Can you dance?" he managed to say.

"I don't know."

Julian sank, slowly, to the ground, sitting on his heels, looking up at her. "Show me."

And Reena danced, stepping fearfully at first, covering her face with her hands and shaking with silent laughter. She put forward a foot and the scarves swirled around her leg, though she tried to hold them down. A rumble purred in Julian's throat. Then from the circle on the dirt plain the women's voices came up, calling, blessing, fierce with life, and the drums beat faster. Reena turned and her feet were loosed. She moved on the pulse of the drums that drove her heart. Her arms moved, her hips moved, her hair flowed with the swirl of the thin garments and they melted together. Julian swayed in the wind of her. She stepped toward him and he leaned back, his hair on the ground. He lay before her as she lighted upon him. The voices and the drums were the same, none louder than their breath and their blood coming fast. Her garments drifted over him, over his legs that were bare in the night's heat under his tunic, where he could feel the heat of her own skin. As he fell and sank and reached up into the depths above him, indescribable in all the words he'd learned, his mouth opened in a long cry, until she came down to him to silence it with her kiss.

5

"FORTY YEARS," THE MAN MUTTERED AS THE BLACK-suited wolves walked away. "Forty years I've farmed this piece of Karrim, and you'd take it away from me." The tax collectors did not respond to him. The farmer would never say the words loud enough to be heard. The Dabionians might evict him from his parcel for failing to keep up with the steady hikes in taxes, but they weren't going to make him disappear in some foreign prison for his words. He wouldn't raise his hands in some rude gesture the moment they were in their carriage, either, as his son would have. Once. The farmer turned away to gather his belongings from the ground where they lay in front of his now-padlocked door, to bundle them into grain sacks and haul them away.

But where was he to go? Who would take in an old man? The families around him could hardly feed another mouth, no matter how hard he worked. He paused as he stooped over one of his sacks, wiping his hot brow. He worked hard, harder than any man he knew, harder than his son had. His hand trembled as he tried to push back the hair that clung damply to his forehead. It stuck there stubbornly, and in a flash he snagged the strands up and tore them fiercely from his burning scalp. He still worked hard, as hard as he ever had. If he couldn't pay the tax, it was because the price of grain had gone down, not because he was old and lazy. When he'd started, forty years ago, prices had been so much higher, with the Manderans competing in the market. Bloody Dabionians wouldn't pay a penny more than they had to, barely enough for the farmers to live on. A man couldn't raise a family on their money. His son couldn't have.

His son had always had the devil in him, something wild and mad. Wanderer blood, the old farmer was sure of it. The boy's mother had been one of those wanderers, he thought, seeing more clearly now with age. She hadn't said it and she hadn't looked it, but she must have been. She'd seduced the farmer with whatever magic those madmen had, then bore him a son and left it with him while she wandered off again. The boy was gotten wild and was born wild, and he'd grown up wild, much as the farmer had tried to beat some sense into him. The boy was restless, always moving but never doing anything. No amount of scolding or whipping with a switch would make the boy mind. He ate off the table without ever putting anything on it. The farmer could not abide such irresponsibility. When the tax collectors came the boy would shout curses at them, and his father had to cuff him in the mouth to quiet him. It was a wonder the farmer hadn't been evicted years earlier, just on account of his son. Then, when the boy was seventeen, he wandered off. The farmer was relieved. He could get back to work.

But sometime later his son returned, with a girl in tow, fat with child. How was he going to feed all these people, the farmer had raged. He spent nights shouting at his son, stealing sleep from a day that began with early dawn. The girl, at least, worked. She cooked and kept the house, and when she'd birthed the child she tied it to her breast and went out to work in the fields, and when the child was big enough to walk it toddled along behind her, dragging sheaves of wheat. And the farmer's son did nothing, wandering in and out of the barn door, up and down the stairs, to the river and back, out of reach of his father's arm.

Then there was the season of the storms. The floods came and drowned half the crops, rotting them in their fields. Then the sun burned hot with drought and burned up the rest. That was the only time the taxes went down; all the farmers in Karrim would have been evicted if they couldn't pay and the Five Countries wouldn't eat. But the farmer could barely eat, either, and he couldn't feed his son and the boy's woman and their brat. "You take them," the farmer had demanded, seizing his son's attention with the back of his hand, "and you feed them yourself."

The next morning brought the first rain in a season. The farmer rose and went to his fields, expecting to see the woman out working already, but she was not there. From a distance he heard her voice, though, and he went to find her.

She was at the edge of the river, kneeling on the ground, her clothes and her hair wet as if she'd jumped in. "What are you doing?" the farmer shouted.

The woman pointed down river, sobbing and choked. "I couldn't save them," she cried.

Some distance farther the river bent and flotsam washed up against a cluster of rocks. There, clinging in the grasses, the farmer saw a scrap of blue, a piece of child's clothing. His heart had stopped. His son had taken the child and thrown himself into the river.

It was the branch of the river that ran out of Lake Azin, strange, wide, and uncrossable. The current was fast and the mist that rose as it tumbled over the rocks made the land on the other side hazy and impossible to see. The wanderers came from that land on the other side. His son had gone back to them, where he belonged. He had sent the boy away. Every night the farmer dreamed it, waking with a fever, hearing his son condemn him as he leapt into the current with the child in his hands. But that river seemed cool to the farmer now, as he dragged all his belongings in two sacks along the ground behind him. He was hot, sweat running down his brow. A fire in his skin tormented him, and as much as he scratched at it he could not relieve the burning. Only the water could, he was certain. No one would take him, an old man, an old tyrant. The river was the only place that would. The river would not scorn him, though he had beaten his son into madness, though he had caused his death and that of the child. He dropped his sacks on the ground and fell to his knees. He could not think in the fever. He tore at his hair, too hot on his head, warming his brain and burning the thoughts out of it. He had to get to the river, to cool his skin, scratched bloody now and still without relief. The river would not refuse him. The river would forgive him. As he stumbled to its banks he could hear it rushing and crashing, calling to him, calling him home.

Two wanderers watched the old farmer on the bank of the river, watched him waver, watched him tilt into its current. Then they clasped hands and strode into the mist that rose from the water. Sages did not have strong magic, not alone, not such as the Magi would call it, the ones who moved the trees to keep Sor'rai hidden, who worked spells great and small. Sages did little of this. They saw time and knew things. They could move themselves through space if there were several of them together, through time, and some of them could do more. One of them could reach into hearts.

That one was sitting on the grass on the other side of the river when Zann and Irisith arrived. "You didn't save him," she said.

"The river saved him," Irisith replied. She was a very old Sage, and she had wandered all over the land of the growing fields. She knew the farmer and his fever, but even she could not bring the end of it.

Elzith did not listen to her, and she did not stop questioning. "Could you have saved him? And the others—there are more coming, aren't there? The sick. Can you save them?"

"Can we?" Zann asked. "What is that? You see only his death. But you have seen the one who will save them."

"No, I haven't," the woman said, still too human. Her eyes were still too sharp, and they reflected the green of the grass and the sky and the things around her. "Your words make no sense. No one can save him now, and I haven't seen anyone."

"You have. You will. You do," said Zann, and he wandered through into the trees.

Elzith dropped her head into her hands. Irisith knew the dreams hurt her inside her head. She still thought they were dreams. "You will see him again," she assured the woman as she suffered in her humanness. "I see him. I birthed him once."

Irisith laughed at the woman's face. Humans always called Sages mad, even those with the blood of Sages. It was to give them understanding that the Sages mixed their blood with the humans, and they would understand and they would never understand. So it was with those who only lived once. Irisith watched the human-Sage press her hands to her head and laughed as she wandered through the moving trees.

6

<hr>

BEFORE A YEAR HAD GONE BY, REENA WAS WITH child. Julian had not gone to the dance again, but Reena had, he had seen her, her scarves trailing behind her as she walked past him, to the dirt plain. She had not seen him. The men came several times that autumn, and each time Reena went to the dance. Julian wanted to ask, he almost asked, which one it was, the Water or the Dust? But he could not speak the words.

"Well, why don't we let him come to the dance?" he heard one of the Aunts say, one day when it rained so hard he could not walk to the book-man's. They were sitting in his mother's house, baking bread at the fire pit. Julian did not grind, or knead, or bake, but they let him add wood and stoke the fire. "He's a lovely boy, with that white Bioran color. It's good blood. Why should we always look to the men outside? And he's old enough to do the business."

The women around him laughed as if he were not there. He leaned over the fire, feeling its heat on his face. Only his mother acknowledged him when he sat back, and it was to say, "Now don't be vain, with that color."

But she spoke softly and kindly, and when the women had left she took out her polished wooden comb and drew it through his hair, spreading it over his shoulders.

"They don't want me here," he whispered.

His mother said nothing, only running the comb more slowly.

He turned, making his mouth smile. "I know," he said. "I am not for here."

"You are," his mother said. "You are the old blood, Aunt Ana says it, fair as you are, rare. You are beautiful."

Julian shook his head, "Of here," he said. "But not for here." He held the comb still in his mother's hands. "I would have died long ago if I went out with the men."

She dropped her eyes, torn between love and shame. Her son was beautiful and disobedient and alive. "I have been lucky."

But when the rain stopped Julian went out and walked far into the fields. He looked up at the clouds in the sky and around at the living things in the earth. He looked at the brown of the earth beyond Kiela, harsh and dying. It was good here, he'd told the book-man. Things could be worse. But he would never give his sacrifice to the Light and ask it to remain the same.

When he came back along the wet roads he went to the pen to gather the sheep, now that the rain had ended and he could take them out. But he could not find them. He ran through the roads, went into the bushes behind Aunt Ana's house and tore his legs in the brambles. He was frantic, calling out for them though they would not hear. Then he went back to the pen and saw that the latch had not been broken after all. The sheep had not escaped. They had been taken out.

And looking down the road into the north field again, he saw them return, and it was Yiera who brought them. Julian turned before he could see what she wore on her face.

He sat in the brush behind Aunt Ana's house, in the thorns. She came to him without his calling her. "It was always to be Yiera's work," she told Julian. "You were never to have stayed."

Julian did not answer, and soon Aunt Ana was gone. As soon as he heard Yiera put the sheep away and latch up the pen and leave, he went to the foot of the eastern mountain and the book-man. He went without thinking of returning.

It was not long after that Aunt Ana came for him. He heard her outside the door of the book-man's house. Tod heard her too, and knew who it was before she spoke at the door. He heard her step on the earth, the grasses parting way before her feet.

"She hasn't come to visit for a while," the book-man said.

"No," Julian answered, and he closed up the books and arranged them on the table. "It's time for me to leave now."

The book-man knew what he meant. He looked up, sadness in his half-empty eyes. Julian went to him, hesitantly, holding out his hands but not certain what to do. There were no farewells in Biora. Girls did not leave, and boys did not say good-bye. Tod reached out, grasping for Julian's hands, and held them close for a moment.

"There are men in Kiana," Aunt Ana said to Julian when he came out of the little shack. "Men from outside. They want to see the books and they want to see you."

Julian nodded solemnly. No one would disagree with Aunt Ana.

She smiled then, warmly, and led him before her with a hand on his shoulder. Even at his height, he walked in her shadow. She walked him down the hard road southward, toward Kiana, giving him a bundle of books to carry, a skin of water slung over his shoulder.

Kiana was not as far away as he might have thought. It was south against the mountains, and at its outskirts Julian saw something he had never seen before. A pass through the mountains. Through the deep shadows of that cleft a new light shone, cast by a new sun on a strange land.

He was so possessed he did not even hear Aunt Ana's words. The men that she spoke to were dark like Tod, talking in accents he could hardly decipher as they spoke so quickly, though their dialect was the same as Tod's. There was land beyond, over their shoulders, another land. Julian felt drawn to it, as if it called him. He could tell Telan, though he would never see the man again—this was the call he heard.

"I think he will go," Aunt Ana was saying, and Julian turned to hear her. Her eyes were on him and he stepped forward to her command. She looked then at the men, the men from outside, and Julian saw that they were traders, their wagons loaded high with gear. She looked at them with eyes that said she did not trust them, not entirely.

Julian put his hand on the knife in his belt. It was Davi's knife, carved of bone. Julian had found it in Davi's room after he had left. He knew he would not use it, but he grasped it all the same. "I will go," he said.

Aunt Ana looked at him and he stood under her gaze. He did not know what she might see in his face that would make her grant her blessing. But then she nodded, the wise woman, and Julian climbed into the wagon of the traders.

Later, as he was being shaken painfully by the wagon rolling over the rough road through the mountains, he would wonder why the men were taking him. He would listen to their voices and he would hear them speak of him in the same words as those they gave to the books, goods they harvested from Biora like grain, goods they would sell on the market in some foreign city where there was use for them. Later he would grasp his knife more tightly, and try to imagine in his mind Davi's fight before the fire in the dirt plain, whipping his arm out to prove his strength, as if Julian could learn from that memory. But these thoughts were only very small in his mind. Before him, around him, beneath him was a world wide and unbounded by mountains, and the sun struck him as he passed through it as if Light were a blessing after all.

7

WHEN ZANN AND IRISITH CAME FOR HIM, TOD didn't want to go. They never came when the children were out at his cottage; the Sages' coming was like a signal that the children had gone home. He strained his ears on the breeze and tried to hear their voices, drawing away toward Kiela, singing their songs in high young pitches. As the Sages led him reluctantly to Sor'rai, Tod imagined that all the children whose faint voices he thought he still heard were girls, that they would never leave the village.

"But they will leave," a voice said. "They always leave, each in their own way. They are gone now." Tod did not know who spoke, disoriented as he was by the passage so he didn't know where or when he was. It never seemed to matter which Sage was speaking. The hands that held his drew him onto the grass—he could feel that beneath his feet, and he knew he had traveled some distance from the mountains. He was walked beneath trees whose leaves dappled the light, letting it fall onto him in patches that he could feel, that he could see in large hazy pieces of nothing. Light was a difficult deity.

"Why," he murmured, not expecting an answer. "Why do they leave? What happened to them that they became like this?"

"You know, you see it yourself. There is no peace. People collide, the humans, fighting for land and gold and words. There is peace. The humans survive, work the land. It is their way. They do as they must, as they know."

The voices of the Sages were like water, flowing and swirling in no direction, calming in their constancy. But this time Tod did not feel calmed. The circle of their words left him confused and desolate. Where is Elzith? he thought to himself. He knew they would hear him, if they wanted to.

For a time it was silent. Tod lay back in the grass, looking up at the leaves he could not see. If he'd known trees well when he'd had sight, he would look up and recognize them, be able to name them. He could pick up a leaf, like he did now, in his hand, and run his fingers along the edges, smooth or serrate. He could tell the shape of it and he would know the tree it belonged to. But the city he'd been born in had few trees, and when he lived in his cottage outside the city, the trees had been only scenery that he ignored outside his window. These trees were not his home.

"And what is?"

Tod shook his head. "I don't know. I thought Biora would be, but it isn't what I thought it was." He turned on his side, in the direction he thought he'd heard the voice come from, though he was no longer sure and he could hear no breath or movement to assure him. "Nothing is, I suppose." He laughed a small, thin laugh. "You told me once that I was content here. Am I still?"

"You are content and you are anxious, you are angry, you are full of love, you are full of peace. You are a master and you are an invalid. You cherish the morning and welcome the night, you mourn the night and dread the morning. You are broken and healed. You are frightened of everything and you are strong."

Tod sighed and turned onto his back again.

"And I am speaking in circles like a madman."

He tried to laugh again, at the sharp, un-Sage-like words that marked the voice of Elzith. There was a rustle and some garment of hers brushed his arm; she might have lain down beside him, but he could not bring himself to reach out for her, afraid she might dissolve. He did not feel any warmth of her body, did not smell any scent of her.

"I don't know why it bothers me so much, and why now," he said to her, speaking up into the sky. "I've lived there ten years, more than ten years. I knew what things were like. I had my cottage and the people took care of me, as much as I needed them, and what happened in their lives was outside of me, none of my concern. As if I could do anything about it, if it was. But now, now I can't bear to think of it. It wakes me up at night, I go to the window and wonder if men with weapons are going to come crashing in. Ten years I've lived in the same place and no men have been anywhere near me, I haven't even heard any fighting. Why this, why now?"

"You try to work the leather, your father's leather. You dress the skins, they are rough and wrinkled. You color them red and they are not red. You tell your hands to do what they should and they do not. You cannot control them. What can you control?"

"Nothing," Tod said. "I would have made Julian stay if I could have. I would have made him not grow up if I could have." Elzith gave him no Sage answer. There was no answer. "But why? Why did it happen?"

"What happened, you mean? What happened when and what happened after? As if I know history." She was silent for a long time, so that Tod thought she might have disappeared, vanished from his side and into the air. The light through the leaves began to dim.

"There is drought in the land," Elzith's voice said in time. "Drought in the summer, flood in the winter. Nothing will grow, people die, children are not born. Those still alive fight one another for what they can get, scraps to keep them alive. Fires take their history, they forget who they are. They fight old fights without knowing why. They fight one another, the pale ones who always lived there, the others who went away and came back, the dark ones who came with them. They fight one another, the wise ones who lost their wisdom. They fight because it is all they know, the only food they have."

Tod heard her breath, drawn in deeply, as if she'd spoken it all without breathing. Tod's skin felt thin and light as air moved over him. "How do you know?" he murmured.

Elzith moaned, or laughed. "I don't know," she said, hoarsely. "And you don't understand it."

"No."

"The scholars were sent back to Biora, fighting about light. That's not what they were fighting about, of course, it was only the excuse. The side that won the argument would get control over all the schools, the bodies in them and the land they were on. Quite a business, that science. They kept fighting when they got home, nothing else to do, since the country was in a drought. The Biorans who stayed didn't want them, couldn't feed them or the wives and children and foreign converts they brought along. The scholars went to hide in the mountains, until the dry trees went up in forest fires. All their books went up with them, and when the scholars got so hungry they started forgetting things, all that was left was the fighting. One side versus the other, and no one can remember why.

"Biorans were dying, while the scholars were fighting. Villages almost destroyed, crops decimated. The survivors fought each other for what they could find. Then the scholars, the men in the mountains who used to be scholars, came down looking for warriors to fill their ranks. They took the boys, taught them to fight. The women stayed in the villages, pure-blooded Biorans and mixed-blooded ones fighting each other, trying to grow enough to live, watching their sons being stolen away, watching their daughters being raped to give them a new generation. Then a new generation, and a new generation." Elzith halted and sighed a hint of pain. "It hurts, this thinking. History, one thing after another. Everything I used to think. But it is still the way you think, isn't it? You understand now."

"No," Tod murmured uneasily. His heart pounded in his throat. For a moment it had been Elzith's voice, the voice he remembered, fading in and out of the Sage sound. "No, I don't understand. How did Kiela happen? It's not the same there, that's what Julian told me. Why not? And why did Julian have to leave?"

Elzith spoke as if her lips were half-closed. She sounded very tired. "Good ground. It's more fertile there than most of Biora. The people could thrive there if they cooperated, if the pure-blooded Biorans and the ones of mixed blood stopped arguing with each other. So they thrived, and they became strong, strong enough to stand up to the men who came to rape them and steal their food. Then they made a bargain with the men: They would trade their goods, trade their bodies, peacefully, if the men stopped fighting in Kiela. And they did." Elzith moaned slightly. "Julian is blond, have you noticed? Like the pure-blooded Biorans. Some sort of throwback to the old generations. And he had to leave."

"What does that mean?" Tod cried. He heard the leaves above him rustle and wondered if the force of his voice had disturbed them. "Why did he have to leave? How do you know he had to leave? Why couldn't he change it, why was it his fate?"

In the echo of his voice he couldn't hear Elzith's breath. It was a long moment before she said, "I don't know."

"What happens to him?" Tod asked, more quietly.

"I don't know."

"You're not telling me everything."

There was another long pause, then Tod heard something that sounded like Elzith's laugh. "Don't you trust me?"

Tod did not say that he didn't, that he couldn't, because he no longer knew her. She knew what he was thinking already, if she looked.

"You should know, Tod," she said, "if the boy's going to die. Have you dreamed about him?"

"No. I haven't dreamed since I came to Biora."

Elzith made a small noise, a knowing murmur. "That's because you're content."

"I *was* content."

For a moment Tod listened silently for the leaves, the only companions he knew he had. Then something breathed on his skin, the back of his hand. Leaves falling, he thought, but it wasn't. Some slight warmth in the touch told him it was Elzith, her hand reaching for him. He turned his hand upward to grasp her fingers.

Then the earth beneath him shook. A terrible cracking thundered in his ears, and the ground tipped with a lurch. The leaves trembled violently and disrupted the light falling on him. A heavy scent of dust filled up his nose and his mouth, stinging his eyes and making him cough. His hands flew out, trying to shield his face, trying to grasp at some kind of cover. Then it stopped, leaving a deep boom that still echoed in the ground, and the dust and the shaking leaves. Elzith's hand was no longer there and he could not reach her. "What happened?"

"They're moving the trees."

He'd heard of that, Tod thought, but he must not have believed it actually happened. It was a story, like the fairy stories children were told in Dabion. Ten years he'd come here and he'd never heard the trees move. "Can you see them?" he asked, troubled. "The Magi?"

Elzith made a sound in her throat. "Yes, I always do."

"Every time? Does that mean you've bound them?"

"Every time?" Elzith paused, and Tod listened to her breath pass as she thought and he heard the change in her voice. "No, not every time. It can't be. It's all magic, everything they do, Magi. They move matter, that's their power, they move everything. Sor'rai is a small country. The Magi don't have what they need, there aren't many things here. If they need meat but they have bread, they make meat. If they have leaves, they make bread. They make fire and they make firewood. They move it so it changes. You've seen it yourself, at the Bioran gate. That pass used to be open, Biorans came through, they watched the Magi, and the Magi let them until they decided not to and they closed the pass. They moved the matter and closed the gate. There are Magi there now, holding the gate closed. Sages pass through it, they disregard matter, they disregard the Magi. The Sages don't tell the Magi they've seen them, and the Magi don't say they've been seen."

Tod was shaking, listening to the voice that no longer

sounded like Elzith's. "They're only words, then? They're not really bound? He could come after us, then. Magus."

He wasn't sure she would answer, but she did, and there was the faintest hint of recognition in her voice. She knew which Magus he meant and she remembered him. "He could. But he won't. He said the words, it was like casting a spell on himself. He's locked inside it like the rest of them are locked inside this country."

What? Tod wondered. What did that mean? The Magi couldn't leave Sor'rai? He wanted to ask her, he wanted her to tell him, whatever the answer was, because without those words he would have nothing else to think about but Julian's absence. He thought he might have spoken the question, but it was blotted out by the noise again, the trees moving, being torn out of the earth with a terrible wrenching sound. His fingers clutched at the ground as if he could hold on to the grass and steady himself. When the sound finally faded Elzith was gone. Tod knew it because Zann and Irisith were there.

They had come farther into Sor'rai than Tod had thought, and it took some time to get back to the pass. Each step hurt, the shock of it reverberating into his heel and up the bones of his leg, reminding him that nothing lay before him but his empty cottage, and sleep that might be marred by dreams, and contentment that he'd have lost. When the ground beneath his feet grew rocky and he knew he was coming near to the mountains, Tod said, "I want to see the gate."

The Sages didn't ask what he meant. A hand pressed

him between the shoulders and turned him in some direction, then pushed him lightly forward.

He could see the gate. He hadn't expected that, even if he'd had sight. But there was a ring of light that was too dense, too bright, and Tod could see it against the dimness of the rest of the day. He reached his hand out toward it. He could feel it. It was as if the lines of air had been picked out and changed into net instead, hanging like strands of spiderweb, floating across a stretch of air where they shouldn't be. It stuck and stung and repelled his hand. The smell of it made his eyes burn and his stomach sour. It was wrong.

His other hand was grasped and suddenly the ring shifted, there but not there, no longer perceptible under his fingers. The brightness was gone, the smell was gone. Tod couldn't even feel the ground under his feet. This was what it was to disregard matter.

"You have a question, human," Irisith's voice said in his ear, no breath moving his hair. "You wonder if this gate holds them in as it holds others out. And the answer is yes, it does hold them. But not always, not always."

Tod did not ask what she meant. They moved forward, breaking through the light that did not catch them, and they were gone from Sor'rai.

Part 2

——◆◆◆——

INSIGH

I have seen Aron, he is something I have seen. I see him in flashes and I know him from the inside, in pieces and in fibers, as if I were going through his blood. I cannot see the outside of him, though. Will I, later, when I know more, when there is less human in me? Will I be able to understand humanity better when I am farther from it?

So I have seen Aron, and I know him, and I know what he will do. But I do not know him, the lines of his hands and the shape of his fingers, and I do not see what the hands will do, what they will reach for, what they will take. I see the circle of the world and I see what is in the next curve of it, the arm of the spiral that curls beneath me, or maybe above me, and I see that Aron is in it, but I do not know what he is doing there. I see what is there but I do not understand it. I see pain and illness and death—what could I possibly understand more than death, having sent so many there with my own hands, these fingers that I can almost see through as I hold them up to the light, looking for their shape? But why are they dying? And is Aron there, in the feverish shadow that hangs over the unnamed land in my dreams? That I do not see, and the Sages will not tell me.

1

Summer, 776 C.C.

———◆◆◆———

OUTSIDE THE SCHOOL OF BIORAN SCIENCE IN Insigh, on top of a wall that divided the inner sanctum of the lecture buildings from the surrounding commons, two young boys sat. They were not at their lecture, though they were dressed for class in their dark suits, which mimicked those of their elders: jackets despite the summer's warmth and long vests studded with pewter buttons that were polished by the boys themselves under threat of punishment and added desk work. Their wigs were carefully combed, woven of hair bleached to a color not seen naturally in Dabion, fitted in miniature to their close-shaven heads at great expense. Their fathers, Justices of high degree throughout Dabion, had paid dearly for the privilege of sending their sons to the Insigh school.

The fathers of these two boys might have been dismayed at their sons' truancy. But it was not disobedience that drove the children to the commons during their lecture hour. All the students had been evacuated from the hall where they had gathered for the afternoon natural sciences class. In a far corner of the lecture hall, behind a

chair that had been broken and not yet repaired, someone had started a fire.

"I think it was one of the fourth-years," one of the
boys said, the smaller and slighter of the two. In the time
since its inception, the School of Bioran Science had
grown, moving from a small building on one of Insigh's
major streets where a handful of students went to hear
lectures, to a complex on the outskirts of town where the
fortunate admits lived for ten years of study. These boys
were in their second year, aged eleven, and they had just
come into a sense of superiority over their new first-year
peers only to be bullied back by older boys newly grown
into adolescent strength. The slight second-year boy had
lost one too many buttons to thirteen-year-olds and had
been chastised for slovenliness one too many times by
the professors.

His companion on the wall was a larger boy, somewhat darker and heavier in the face. The thick black of
his eyebrows argued fiercely with his blond wig, which
sat a little askew on his head. "They wouldn't dare," he
insisted. "Not Baran, not Nosselin." He paused, recon-
sidering his judgment of the cantankerous son of the
cantankerous leader of District Four. "No, not Nosselin
either. Not any of them. They couldn't have gotten in to
set it. It was set real cleverly, too. I saw it as we were going
out." The darker boy smiled appreciatively. He was sorry
to miss the natural sciences lecture; they had been going
to learn about fire and sources of light. "It was on a fuse,
someone lit it before we ever came in, and the fire came
up when Professor started speaking, like it was timed to

do. Real cleverly. But the fourth-years couldn't have done that. Professor wouldn't have let them in before lecture."

"So it had to be an older boy," the slighter one said. "Or one of the tutors."

At once their eyes tracked across the commons, where the older students were directing the younger boys to keep them from crowding curiously near the lecture hall. There, among the higher heads of the ninth- and tenth-years, among the graduated students who remained as tutors and apprentices to the professors, was the one who came to their minds, instantly, unspoken. No one would speak of him aloud, in the open. No one knew what he might hear, and no one knew what he might then do.

Kuramin was in his last year at the Insigh School, or so it was commonly thought. No one seemed to know exactly, although even the oldest students said he'd been there forever. The professors, every one that any outspoken boy had the courage to ask, refused to confirm his year or his age, refused to speak of him hardly at all. Some grew angry at the mention of his name; some were merely silenced, and wrinkled up their brows as if confronted by some mathematical enigma they could not solve. No one knew as much as his given name, or where exactly the Kuramin family might be from. Kuramin spoke little of himself, either—not that many students were willing to ask him. He was intimidating just to look at, taller than any of the other students, his shoulders slightly hunched like a bird of prey descending on some small fowl. His face seemed too dark, maybe not when people looked straight at him, but later, when they thought about him and tried to call his face to mind. Something was wrong with that memory-face: too strange, too uneven, too dark. "Dark as an Ikindan," the heavy boy whispered to his more timid schoolmate. Neither had ever seen an Ikindan.

"I heard he set the fire in the servants' kitchen," the slighter boy replied nervously.

"And the cook's knife went missing," his friend went on. But they uttered these dormitory rumors with tight voices, all the deliciousness of the scary stories sucked out. Now they had seen a fire, a real fire, themselves. Now they looked across the commons at Kuramin, at the face that looked normal in the crowd, with real doubt and with true fear.

"What are you doing here?" a voice uttered from behind the boys' backs.

They jumped with such shock it nearly threw them from the wall. Gripping each other's wrists for courage, they turned slowly to look for the speaker. "Sorry, Master Jannes," they mumbled together.

"Sorry," the tutor echoed. "Sorry for crossing school lawns during lecture hours, sorry for failing to attend to the direction of elder students." His mouth turned in the slightest cruel hint of a smile. "Sorry for sitting on the wall like a couple of cracked eggs in your nursery rhymes. How sorry would that be?"

They were not normally happy to see Aron Jannes. Tutors were assigned to catch and correct the mistakes of students that the professors at their podiums might overlook. Jannes caught far more than the normal errors in far more places than the classrooms, and he exacted punishments for them that the professors would not think of. He spoke not many more words than Kuramin, but those words were chosen carefully. With the specter of Kuramin not fifty yards away, though, the boys were relieved to see something familiar, even if it was a familiar threat. "Very sorry," they answered solemnly.

"Sorry enough to give up this week's candles?"

The boys looked at each other and sighed heavily. Without the candles for their desks, they wouldn't be able to study past dark. The wardens wouldn't give out any more than their week's ration, so if the boys fell behind, their grades would suffer and there would be nothing they could do. No one tried to argue with Aron Jannes, though. If he wanted the candles, he was going to get them. "Yes, Master Jannes," they obediently said. "That sorry."

"Good," Jannes said. Then, not needing to say any more words, he turned and eased away across the commons. The boys knew when to expect him to return for the payment, and they did not let out their held breaths until he had vanished from their sight.

"He should go after Kuramin," the darker boy whispered. "Jannes would keep him under thumb."

But his friend shivered and shushed him. "Don't say it, not even as a joke," he said. "Don't even say it."

Aron Jannes came for the candles that evening in the time between dinner and the late study hour, when the comings and goings of students made it difficult to track any unusual movement. He didn't really want the candles. The trick was to intimidate the students by taking something important. What most people thought was important was money, though the younger boys rarely had much of it, and Aron hated to take money anyway. You would have to do something with money. Last time he took some, from a loudmouthed fourth-year who was trying to be trouble, Aron just buried it.

Candles, though, had at least some use. He could light up his room—tutors, those graduated students who remained at the School of Bioran Science to work under the professors, were allowed their own private rooms, cramped though they were—and stay up past curfew. The dark hours were more interesting, free of tedious assignments from professors and bratty students who needed to be kept in line. If only it weren't so quiet at night, so close and isolated.

A knock came at the door and Aron quickly blew out the extra candles. Students were confined to their dormitories at this hour, so it had to be a professor. Aron had to put on a good face. He buttoned up his vest and returned the wig to his head, and went to the door.

"Good evening, Master Jannes," the higher mathematics professor declared. Always so formal, Aron thought. They were all such good actors in Dabion, always declaring and announcing, never speaking. "I hope the events of this afternoon have not been too taxing for you."

Aron murmured an appropriate reply and tried to smile politely.

"We have been asking the tutors to keep a careful watch on their students," the mathematician continued. "We are particularly interested in any suspicious activity that might have been observed. I trust that you will report any such suspicions to us, Master Jannes."

For a moment Aron thought of all the names he could provide. Suspicious students, yes, there were a few. Quite a few, every one who had ever scorned him, every one who had insulted him, who had stood in his way. He could implicate all of them. He could make them disappear. Aron's breath caught with the excitement.

"And, Master Jannes," added the professor, "we do wish to keep close watch on Kuramin. Have you seen anything out of the ordinary concerning him?"

The plans vanished from Aron's head. He had to work hard not to scowl every time he heard Kuramin's name. The student was strange, too strange, and he did nothing to hide it. No one else could get away with being so strange, such a misfit. Aron certainly couldn't; he'd learned that much. Besides, he was sure Kuramin was following him. "No, professor, but I will keep watch," he answered carefully, like he should.

The professor left and Aron shrugged out of his vest and wig. He relit the candles, sat at his desk, and tried to re-create his list of suspicious students. But no names came to him, not one. The ink in his quill dried and he scratched the paper mutely. There was no one who scorned him anymore, no one who insulted him, at least not to his face. No one would dare stand in his way. He had finished what he intended to do when he came to the School of Bioran Science. There was no more power to get over anyone. What power he had was dull, dry like the pen he scratched pointlessly over the blank page, back and forth, in circles that went nowhere. With tired eyes he watched the candles as they flickered and melted themselves away.

2

"A S I HAVE SAID BEFORE," LORD JUSTICE MARSAN repeated, "if we are not to regress severely in our pursuit of the ideals of Bioran science, it is imperative that we appoint Greater Justice Athal to the seat of Lord Justice of District Three."

Rayner yawned discreetly. There was an advantage to being perceived as old and frail, offensive as it was to be coddled and pitied by the Lord Justices beneath him. He could show his utter boredom and it would come across as nothing but the noddings of a senile old man.

"But Athal does not have the political experience that Zein does," said Nosselin, District Four's sour leader, with more than his share of irritation. Rayner would have fired him by now, had he been running things in name, rather than only in deed. Nosselin didn't have the subtlety to be a politician. But Rayner had to agree with his assessment of Bioran learning. "Are we professors or Lord Justices?" Nosselin demanded. His ridiculous blond wig lay in a heap on the table before him; Nosselin was as unwilling to wear it as Rayner was to wear his, unless protocol demanded it. Lord Councilor Muhrroh did not enforce such protocol in the meeting room of the Circle.

"Athal does have extensive education in the rational sciences," Marsan sawed away. "He is as able to manage the dealings of Justice as any of us. If you will allow me to remind you, I had little more judicial experience than Athal when I was appointed by you to replace the late Lord Justice Varzin of District Six. I did, however, have a great deal of training in Bioran learning, and it is that rationality that allowed me to transform a district that was plagued by superstition. Such rationality can only be a benefit to the Circle," he concluded, looking pointedly at Nosselin.

Now that was one of the more foolish decisions the Circle had made, Rayner thought, indulgently shaking his head—appointing Marsan to anything. That he'd had little more judicial experience than Athal was an understatement. He'd had little more judicial experience than a puppy. The other Lord Justices had only appointed him because of his, and their, obsession with Bioranism. They'd done it to win favor with Muhrroh. What a ridiculous irony it was that Muhrroh began to lose his interest in Bioranism almost immediately after Marsan's appointment.

"But what about the rational sciences?" the bewigged men crooned. Muhrroh nicely agreed that rationality was important, but put away his Bioran books, the lessons that were never resumed after the unfortunate death of the inept Justice Advisor Jereth Paloman. "But what about the lovely new Bioran school in Insigh?" the

Lord Justices cried. Muhrroh arranged for the appointment of several new professors, who dived into their pointless studies with all the passion of men who have no other power but that which they can create in the fictitious world of academia. The Lord Councilor, however, never visited the Insigh School himself.

"But what about our lovely wigs?" Rayner mumbled mockingly, hardly drawing the attention of the men in the wooden room. Of course they wouldn't give up their wigs. The absurd things were expensive. In a country that scorned the gaudy colors and jewels of old Mandera, wealth had to find new ways to be displayed.

"This argument cannot yield a decision," Muhrroh was saying. "We will come to no resolution if we are at odds with one another. Let us adjourn and contemplate the candidates on our own, in silence, that we might discuss them less heatedly at our next meeting."

The Lord Justices stood obediently and bowed their heads to the old patriarch, turning to exit the room with muted grumbles. Jannes and Frahn trotted out at Marsan's heels. Rayner would have thought they'd have realized that Bioranism was over by now, but the fools still supported Athal. Nosselin led the opposition, with Timbrel, who should have retired before he ever took the contested office, and Wirthir, who had replaced Hysthe in District Five three years before. Not what Rayner would have chosen for allies, but at least they didn't delude themselves with Bioranism. Yellow-haired scholars were not important. It was gold that was important.

District Three was in the southeast corner of Biora,

sharing mountainous borders with Azassi and Siva. It
was ugly and inhospitable land, particularly the Alaçan
region in the extreme southeast, and would be of no interest to anyone if a vein of gold had not been found in
the Alaçan mountains. Azassi claimed the vein as their
own and was anxious to send miners to exploit it. Athal
was of the narrow-minded rationalist school that called
all wealth wasteful and immoral, a holdover from the
evil years of Manderan dominance, and he was willing
to let the Azassians have the gold. Funny, Rayner mused,
that Athal still wore his expensively tailored suit and wig.
Zein had a much more reasonable attitude, though, and
he was an ally of Rayner's.

Rayner waited until the six Lord Justices had exited,
and the simpering secretary after them. They bowed
their heads to him politely, and Rayner gamely smiled
back. The secretary even said, "Good day to you, old father," before he and his overpolished shoes withdrew
from the room. Rayner could hardly keep from scowl-
ing. They only knew him as the retired Greater Justice,
Aln Rayner, who had been called to the Circle for advise-
ment. They did not know that he was the head of the Secret Force, even here, in the most exclusive chambers of
the government of Dabion. To the Lord Justices he was
merely an old man of eighty years, invited by Muhrroh
to sit at his elbow and humor the elderly Lord Councilor. He moved more slowly now, it was true, and he
spoke little, taking the excuse of his age to act as if he
were weakened, but his mind was sharp as ever. It was an
excellent cover for the head of covert operations. No one

in the room would have guessed that Rayner was the most powerful man in Dabion next to Muhrroh himself.

From outside the room came the voices and footsteps of the escorts who led the Lord Justices through the labyrinth and up to the ground level of the Great Hall. All those escorts were Rayner's, operatives trained in his barracks under his orders. The men who claimed to run the country would be lost in a black maze like helpless rats if not for Rayner. He held their lives in his hands and they didn't even know it. More servants came into the Circle to tend to the lamps and the chairs and whatever else servants did; they were Rayner's as well. Few of them had worked under him directly, though, and many did not know him as anything more than their bewigged betters did. Rayner knew each and every one of them, of course, their faces and their names and the names of their families, and as they meekly pulled out his chair and handed him his walking stick, they had no idea that he could eliminate them and everything they had if the mood struck him. He smiled with wide arrogance and they saw nothing more than an old man's mindless, gap-toothed grin.

Rayner nodded, very slightly, to the Lord Councilor before he took his leave of the room, and Muhrroh returned the nod in kind. Rayner's servants would not come for the old patriarch; Muhrroh employed his own personal guard, operatives nominally of Rayner's Secret Force, but controlled entirely by Muhrroh. Rayner wished he could linger in the Circle chambers to see the faces of some of these operatives; but he'd been dismissed by Muhrroh, and he would not make such a bluntly disobedient move.

Rayner needed no escort back to the surface. He knew paths through the labyrinth that no one else did except, perhaps, Muhrroh, and he did not have to rely on underlings to find them. No one followed him out or directed his steps. At the end of his passage he emerged into an outbuilding near the stables behind the Great Hall. This exposed him to the stench of animals, it was true, but no one would seek or expect to find him there. It was just as well that his olfactory sense was somewhat dimmed; if he had to be affected in this small way by age, when so many lesser men had been turned to infants, this was no real loss. He took a handkerchief from his pocket and shielded his face before opening the outer door and stepping into the stable yard.

Lord Justice Jannes stood before him.

Rayner frowned behind the cover of his handkerchief. "My lord—my lord Jannes, is it?" he said, acting out a confused squint as he gazed toward the sun.

"Yes, your honor," Jannes answered. "Forgive me for not addressing you by your proper title, but I do not know what the correct form of address is for one in your position."

No "old father" was forthcoming, Rayner guessed. He lowered the handkerchief and frowned freely. Rayner did not like Jannes. He'd been trying to kill the man for the past ten years and Jannes was proving infuriatingly difficult to catch.

"You have found secluded places to keep yourself,

haven't you, your honor?" Jannes went on. "Very strange places, but this seclusion will suit us now, won't it? I have learned something about you, something I doubt you would want widely known."

And I've learned things about you, Rayner could have replied in that same irritating voice. I've learned you're trafficking in alcohol, subverting justice, siphoning money from vice. I've learned you're a hypocrite, not that that's a surprise among the esteemed ranks of Dabion's judges. But Rayner would ruin Jannes's theatrics with that little monologue, and he felt like some entertainment. He raised his eyebrows provocatively and waited for Jannes to continue.

"Lord Justice Hysthe died under unusual circumstances three years ago, didn't he? The official reports gave no indication of it, of course, but the circumstances were unusual. I have finally discovered just what those circumstances were. I hardly think Lord Councilor Muhrroh will like to hear that the head of one of his own organizations arranged the assassination of one of his Lord Justices. I hardly think you'll remain long at the head of that organization."

Rayner let his mouth twist. This *was* entertaining. Jannes was more a hypocrite than Rayner guessed, handing him this virtuous babble. Muhrroh wasn't likely to care that Rayner had a hand in Hysthe's death. The Lord Councilor already knew that Rayner was seeking Jannes's death, and that he'd achieved that of Jannes's wife. What's more, he knew it even before appointing Rayner to lead the Secret Force. Muhrroh could very well know about the assassination of Hysthe already, if he was as clever as he was supposed to be. Why he would let Rayner continue in the position was beyond him, but Rayner didn't really care. It hardly mattered to him, and there were more interesting things to do than wonder what was in Muhrroh's head.

"I never liked you, Rayner," Jannes was saying still, going on with such seriousness that Rayner found it hard to hold back his laughter. "I never liked you when you worked in my jurisdiction, and I couldn't wait until you retired. You are the worst example of corruption I ever laid my eyes upon. I met you in my first four years as Lord Justice and I have seen nothing worse in all the years since. I hated the day you came back and we were forced to work with you. The Lord Councilor never should have appointed you, and I will see you out of that position."

Now Jannes was merely an idiot. It was stupid for someone who wished to take someone else down to give him such a warning. To be effective—assuming Jannes could be effective—one had to use speed and stealth. Showing off like this was selfish and offensive. Rayner thought briefly that he should kill Jannes here and now just for his stupidity. There was certainly some tool in the stable that would suffice.

But before the thought could become any more than a passing fancy, Jannes began to walk away, and a crowd of people who had been merely stragglers near the stable a moment ago thickened and formed a barrier between Rayner and his target. Rayner could not reach Jannes even if he were really motivated to do so. Jannes was protected.

That was obviously what the people were. They were too convenient to be merely servants, and they moved too much like soldiers in formation. They were spies out of Rayner's own service.

Rayner's eyes narrowed. Spies out of his own service, and not a single ugly, grubby face that he recognized. These were operatives from Muhrroh's personal guard. The Lord Councilor was protecting Jannes. Of course, Rayner realized, amazed that he had not considered it before: That was why Jannes was still alive. Muhrroh himself was the one who had stymied every attempt Rayner had made to eliminate Jannes and intercept his liquor business.

But why? That was a question far more intriguing than whether Muhrroh knew about Hysthe's assassination, an itch far more irritating than the authority Muhrroh appropriated by employing his own guard. Why was he using that guard to protect Jannes? Rayner would have to pursue the answer right away.

3

THE SCHOOL OF BIORAN SCIENCE IN INSIGH WAS
built on the grounds of what was once the headquarters of the Black Force. Some ten years before, when
Dabion finally outlawed Nanianism and the mystical,
slightly mad, somehow threatening followers of that
religion, the Justices undertook a massive effort to close
the monasteries in the neighboring country of Cassile,
the center of Nanianism. The Black Force was instituted
to guard the Justices as they went to Cassile to lend
firepower to the mission. A rumor had circulated that
a little too much firepower had been lent, and monasteries were destroyed in several embarrassing debacles
that wiped out a good number of the Black Force as well
as the offending monks. No troops returned to the headquarters from their stint in Cassile. Those who were still
alive after all the monasteries had been closed retired or
returned to less colorful police work in the Public Force.
The Black Force was disbanded, no longer needed.

By the time the buildings were emptied, Dabion had a
new use for them. Lord Justice Marsan of District Six
was an ardent supporter of Bioran learning, as well as

being surprisingly charismatic in his new jurisdiction, and soon there was a thriving new population of students looking for somewhere to study. The Insigh School was moved to the larger campus of the former Black Force headquarters, the barracks were renovated and filled with rows of desks, and the weapons warehouses were turned into libraries. The sole building that was not converted was a small storehouse at an extreme corner of the grounds.

The professors, apparently believing their students to be as scholarly as themselves, did not expect that there would be any interest in the dirty, dilapidated building. They certainly did not anticipate that the locks on the door might be picked.

The storehouse was packed nearly floor to ceiling with all the things the Black Force commanders saved from their ill-fated missions: old uniforms, broken pieces of wagons and harnesses, masonry pried from the ruins of Cassilian monasteries and confiscated from the guards who wanted to bring back some souvenir, boxes stacked with written records that no Justice had ever decided to read. There was barely a path through the mess, but in the back of the building, almost buried against the farthest wall, was a rack that still bore two short swords, three muskets, a pistol, and a horn of gunpowder.

The metal of the weapons was rusty with disuse, and the parts that someone might test would prove to be nearly immobile. Only one of the muskets still had its ramrod fixed to it. The swords' scabbards were discolored with water damage from a leaky ceiling, and the leather of the belts was cracked and dry. But the horn was untouched, somehow spared by the elements, and the powder inside was as good as fresh.

The powder made a nice line, poured from the plug in the small end of the horn. There wasn't much of it, and it didn't make a long fuse, but it was long enough to go from outside the doorway into the building, wind along the narrow path through the refuse, and make a lovely curve into a convenient pile of broken wood that used to be a wagon. It could be lit and left for several minutes before the fire was touched off, perhaps half an hour before it consumed enough of the mess to become apparent. An impressive amount of damage could be done before anyone came to put it out; the storehouse might even be satisfyingly unsalvageable.

Aron Jannes stood at the edge of the school grounds and looked out on the road that ran south from Insigh. It was at this time of the season, every season, that the Lord Justices met, drove into town in their carriages and pristine suits, made their official pronouncements, then rode back out of town to their home districts. They always left at the same hour, without fail, and, in the break between classes, Aron could reach the edge of the grounds and watch them go, three carriages starting at first together, in perfect file. They would pass the school, and just before they were out of sight, two would turn to the west on their way to Districts Three and Four, while the third continued south to Origh in District Two. That one would be his father.

Each season, on that same day and at that same hour, Aron came here, watched the carriages roll out, and tried to distinguish the southbound carriage from the others. The three were identical from this distance, polished black and flawless, as if dirt were an affront to justice, and the horses were always changed lest they look fatigued. Each carriage had the figure of the scales of justice painted on the doors. There were stories, Aron had heard, about carriages in Mandera in the days of the Ikinda Alliance, when the barons and dukes and whatever outdated nobility that existed back then drove around in carriages with designs painted all over them, family crests and granted arms in garish colors. The greatest accomplishment of Justice was that it had outlived the fall of Mandera, said the professors. Aron wondered if the Lord Justices could even see what hypocrites they were. They should be standing here, he thought, looking out over the road at the carriages rolling by.

When he first came to the edge of the grounds, as a tenth-year student with privileges to leave the dormitory, then as a tutor who did not need to attend classes, Aron had lurked under tree cover to watch the carriages. Now he stood out in the open, in the clearing between the trees and the storehouse. The Justices in their carriages could see him, if they looked. His father could see him, if he looked. Aron imagined that his father would be looking out the window, that he would catch a glimpse of his face, even this far away, and he would see his father's eyes widen as he recognized him standing in the clearing. One day—Aron told himself, his breath going cold—one day he would see it.

But this time, like every other, the three carriages went by anonymously, and the sun glinted on their windows and blacked them out. Aron turned his head as they went south, blurred in the distance, and parted from each other. Even if he squinted he could not see which one of the three remained on the southbound road.

But he did see someone else in the clearing. Kuramin was standing near the doorway of the storehouse.

"What are you doing here?" Aron snapped.

Kuramin raised his eyebrows. There was something wrong with them, Aron thought. They were too dark, almost muddy, like they had been painted on with a shaky hand. His mouth was somehow crooked as it turned in a strange smile.

"Are you following me?" Aron demanded, slowly stepping toward him with his shoulders drawn up, as he did when he approached younger students who needed to be taught more than the usual lessons. He was not used to stalking someone taller than he. "Why are you following me?"

Kuramin stood his ground, still smiling weirdly. "Aren't you going to run?"

Over Kuramin's shoulder, the glass in the storehouse window cracked and a tongue of flame lapped out.

When Aron was young, he used to fight, actually fight, lunging out with his arms and legs. He hadn't done that since he was ten years old, not since the only person who had ever respected him refused to respond to it. He had different arms and legs now, ones that had never lunged or struck or kicked. He had taught himself the posture of the student, the clerk he was being trained as, the Justice he was destined to be. It suited him to grow into that body and so he had. But in that instant, standing before Kuramin in the clearing, his arms and legs unlearned everything they knew, and he jumped at the intruder with all the fury his body had forgotten.

A woman was walking toward the Insigh School. She was approaching from outside the city, although she had come from Insigh at first, walking far out into the country before beginning her search. She did not take the road. Somewhere near the school, she'd been told, she would find the person she was looking for. She didn't know where. He could be anywhere in the fields outside the school grounds, and she had been looking for most of the day.

It was getting late now and she was losing light. The search would be more difficult in the dark, and she was getting closer and closer to the school. At least she wouldn't be seen in the dark, even if she had to get right up to the school grounds, right up to the road. That was probably where he was after all, she thought. Idiot. On the road or still on the grounds, like they'd told him not to do. She cursed under her breath. It was always like this, working with him, working with the rest like him.

Her foot caught in a rut in the ground and she almost

swore aloud. She bit the inside of her lip to stifle it. Her mouth was full of those bites, puckered bits of flesh that caught in her teeth. She sat on the grass and chewed, like a cow, until she tasted blood. The velvet-smooth fields and hills of Dabion were an illusion. Beneath the carefully groomed grass—so carefully, she knew just how carefully—the ground was broken and pitted. Keep the commoner off the grass, keep him in his place. Only the good people in their carriages who could go on the roads were allowed to come out. The woman stretched her leg out from under her skirts and rubbed at her ankle. She looked at the sky around her, the failing sun she'd had no time to see while she was searching the ground. And in the sky was a thick smudge of smoke. Something on the school grounds was burning. She laughed mutely, spitting blood. The man she was looking for probably had something to do with that.

Dusk brought out the light of the fire, and as the woman approached she saw the building, its walls and roof eaten up by the rising flames. Stiff black silhouettes stood in front of them, men in uniforms, Public Force who'd been called in to fight the blaze. The professors in their gowns and wigs would have been running around like madmen in front of the fire, not knowing what to do. She could imagine it, she could almost laugh. The Public Force had cut down the boughs of the trees that hung closest to the burning building, to keep the fire from spreading, and they were standing with their hands on their axes, smug. They did nothing else but watch the last of the smoke smolder out.

"Impressive, isn't it?" a voice said from behind her.

The woman whirled around. There he was, near the road, just like she thought, and he was speaking out loud. She shuffled toward him on hands and knees, scraping dirty scratches into her skin and her clothes. "What in hell are you doing?" she hissed when she was close enough to him that her voice wouldn't carry. "Someone will see you."

He was lying in the taller grass at the edge of the road, not easily visible but not caring to hide. His face was mottled with bruises and blood, looking muddy in the poor light. "It was lovely when it was born, bright, golden. Fire. It is not what they think it is."

"Madman," the woman hissed under her breath, not caring to hide it.

The man acknowledged her insult by smiling but kept on with his words. "They teach their children about light, they think they do. But they do not know what it is." He smiled again, his mouth weird and twisted. "You are called T."

"You know bloody well what I'm called." She tugged at his arm, pointlessly, since he refused to move. "Come away from the road."

"He doesn't know what it is, either. I tried to tell him."

She stopped at that, stared at him. She wanted to strike him, to muddy his stained face more. "You talked to him?"

"I tried to tell him. I asked him. He wouldn't listen."

On the school grounds the smoke was dying, and the guards were starting to leave. The woman hissed at her unwanted companion to follow her, and she crawled away toward the slight shelter of a tree, away from the road. Then she waited for him to reach her so she could scream at him. He took his time.

"What did you say to him?" she demanded, when he finally reached her and dropped carelessly to his stomach. "Answer me this time. What the words were. I've had enough of your evasions."

The man lay quietly as if nothing disturbed him. "I asked him if he was going to run. From the fire."

Frowning, the woman looked back at the traces of smoke. She looked back at the man, then she pounded her hands on the ground. "Damn you, that is what you said. And it still makes no sense. What about the fire? You're not going to tell me that, are you? Are you, K? I should have left you out here."

The man turned slowly onto his back, letting out a sigh of the pain that did not show on his face. "He did not know, he had never asked. I wanted him to ask." He opened his eyes and spoke patiently, as if to a child. "I challenged him."

"I don't care what you said," the woman muttered. "You provoked him. That's the point. You provoked him. You risked everything. You could have ruined the entire assignment. You probably did. Do you think you can go back now?"

"I do not have to." He smiled. "That is the point."

The woman dropped her head in her hands. "Madman. Bastard. Idiot. The whole lot of you. Why do I keep doing it?" She waited, watching the sun disappear behind some green hill, chewing the inside of her mouth. The school grounds fell silent as the crowds dispersed, the professors hiding themselves in their rooms, the Public Force filing by on the road. After the guards had passed, the woman rooted in the pockets of her skirt for the things she had brought. She lit a tiny lamp and opened a vial of a tincture, spilled a little of it out on a cloth and started daubing it at the man's face. She sighed heavily. "You can stop trying to fool me. I know what you really look like, and I can't see what I'm doing."

The man turned his face toward the light. The blood smeared it where he had passed his fingers, and thin blades of grass clung to it where he had brushed the ground. Then his face changed. The pigment bled out of it, draining like sweat rising to the surface and drying into the air. His mouth changed, losing its shape, growing thinner, and his face fell down to its bones like old age rushed to a horrible speed. He breathed out and the flesh on his body seemed to go with it, and his clothes hung on him awkwardly. The light shone through the fine-shorn hairs on his scalp and his skin looked red in the light.

"Ah," he sighed. His voice did not change. "I can breathe again." He looked up at the woman, his eyes shadowy with fatigue, one of them sunken with a purple bruise that stood out like it was painted. "It doesn't look so bad now, does it?"

The woman didn't answer. That little show was all in her own mind. The wanderer had planted it, like he planted the image of an olive face and dark hair in the heads of every student at the school. She knew how his so-called magic worked and she didn't like it one bit. She frowned at the damage. One blackened eye, a split in the lower lip, a puffy nose that had stopped bleeding and probably was not broken. "What's the matter, K?" she sneered. "Did he tie your hands up first?"

"Such fighters, all of you. Not for me to stop. I am going home."

"The man won't want to see you yet."

K shook his head. "He won't. I'm not going back to him. I am going home."

The woman stared again. "You can't leave."

"You can tell him." The Sage smiled. "It is time for me to go."

The woman balled her cloth in her fist, tore it out, ripped it. "Time for you to go!" Her teeth sank into her lip as she struggled to lower her voice. "Why do you think you know time? Why do you think you know where to go? Acting so wise, like you know the future." She shoved him with her hands, pushing the side where she thought a rib was cracked, trying to make him cry out.

But he didn't cry out. He sat up, then stood, smoothly and quietly. "But I do not know the future," the Sage said. "If I did, I could tell you the answer to your question, the one in your blood that you do not ask." Then he climbed onto the road, ignoring her objections as if they were only wind at his back, and began to walk toward the north.

4

ARON JANNES TOLD THE PROFESSOR WHO CAME to his door that he was ill. He soiled his fingers with soot from candlewicks and rubbed his eyes and nose until they grew red and watery with the irritation. He dampened a towel in his pitcher and wrapped it around his neck to simulate the sweat of a fever. The towel gave him something to sink his chin into, to conceal the bruise that lined his jawbone. Kuramin had not raised a hand to him, but Aron had struck his chin on the man's shoulder, or elbow, or something, he couldn't remember now. He didn't remember how the fight had ended, for that matter, or what spurred him to take cover until he could sneak away unseen. No one had seen him, Aron was sure. It would be three days, at least, until he could go out again.

Three days with no news. It was only by chance that Aron overheard some loud-voiced student outside his window, where Aron was watching through the smallest slit in the curtains so no one would see the damaged part of his face, talking to his peers about Kuramin's disappearance. The other students, being slightly brighter, hushed him quickly, so Aron had been unable to hear what sort of gossip was circulating about why Kuramin was gone or what happened to him.

Three days of rumors, with Aron unable to direct them. There was no telling what might be said about Aron in that time, and he had no access to the students who would tell him. He doubted three days would be enough time for any of them to lose their fear of him, not entirely, although the thought of it ran through his mind endlessly, hour after hour, each long dull hour that he sat in his room. Three days was time enough for him to go mad with boredom.

Three days with no fires. There couldn't be any fires, not without Kuramin to blame. A fire now would be proof that Kuramin didn't do it.

Aron was angry. Kuramin had ruined all his plans. Aron hadn't had to think until now, just follow the path he was on. It was easy until now. The path had opened up to him when he came to the school, when he was thirteen and the campus had just opened up on these grounds. He'd woken up after two years that he couldn't quite remember, like he'd fallen asleep for a long time, when one person was killed and another one left him. His father had sent him here, with the other Justices' children, since he wouldn't dare be the only one whose son wasn't at the school. Aron had gone without even thinking about how he didn't want to be there. Then he found the path, all the things he could do, laid out for him by the pathetic teachers who praised him for his good work and had no clue about what he was really doing. It was almost as if his father had handed it to him.

Third-year students learned the rules of logic. If one thing was true, that made another thing not true. If one premise in an argument was refuted, then the whole argument was wrong, gone, vanished. Find the wrong premises in the books and the books would disappear, under desks, in ditches, down latrines. Fourth-years learned the threats to rationality: power, wealth, superstition. Superstition was easy, tell a few tales, spread a few rumors. Aron knew scads of them and the younger students were gullible. Wealth could come or go. It was all power. Fifth year was law, and law gave him theft, almost too easy. Any bully could tear buttons off first-years' coats. Mathematics was useless, only good for impressing professors. Natural sciences were more interesting: propulsion and gravity, water and fire.

Fires were hard when he was a student; even the matches were rationed. Once when Aron lit one and dropped it into the rubbish bin behind his dormitory, the matches were taken away for two weeks and the students had to go to the housemaster every night to have their candles lit. When Aron dropped a candle in the bin, all the students were required to do their nightly studying in the common room, huddled together under lamps over which the professors kept close watch. Those professors only showed Aron the next step in the path. He had to build a better fire.

By his ninth year it became obvious what he would have to do. Tutors had freedoms that the students did not. They were not committed to classrooms, they could walk the grounds unquestioned, as if sitting those final exams turned an untrustworthy child into a near equal. Aron had to become a tutor, to flatter the professors enough that they asked him to stay, to be their apprentice. If he'd thought about it, the idea of remaining at the school even a day longer than he had to might have disgusted him. Winning the professors' hearts would have been as ridiculous and unbearable as trying to win his father's. But he wasn't thinking, he didn't have to. The path was there for him.

Now, though, it was ruined. Kuramin had appeared so conveniently. The aggressive strangeness that made him so irritating was the very thing that made him useful to Aron. He nearly screamed to be suspected. It was easy to blame him for the fires, and the thefts, the rumors, everything else that Aron had done since he came to the school. Kuramin had always been there, like Aron's bizarre, spying shadow.

"Blast him," Aron murmured to nothing in the room. His suspicions were correct; he realized it now that he was forced to think. Kuramin had been following him. Kuramin was a spy.

Aron crunched a paper into a ball and hurled it across his room, where it collided with the wall and fell into a pile of similar missiles. That was what had become of his latest tedious assignment: to score examinations for some professor. Aron didn't even know what the subject was. Kuramin had spied on him. Why? Who had sent him? Aron seized his hair in his hands, too short to grasp well. He had to get back outside. He shouldn't have had the fight, he thought, bumping his bruised chin against his knee. He was sitting in his chair with his knees drawn up like a child. He had to set another fire. Could he? Would his father see this time? Did his father know about the others—had Kuramin told him? Aron pressed his childish chin against his childish knees until the pain made his eyes burn.

Three days later he dressed, put his wig on his head, lit his last extra candle, and held it in front of the mirror. The shadows on his chin were thick and dark, the bruise yellow-gray against his white cravat, as if he hadn't shaved. He frowned over the candle. Then he blew it out and opened the door.

Before he was five steps down the hallway, before he had even passed a window letting in enough light that someone might see his discolored chin, one of the professors stopped him. "You've been called away," the professor said.

Called away, Aron repeated to himself as he packed his things. Expelled? Because the school wanted him gone, or because his father wanted him back? Aron laughed sharply at the mirror. Of course his father didn't want him back. Then he took the mirror down, the hand-sized square of glass framed in a thin border of wood. The school wouldn't waste any more money than that to supply vanity. Aron laid the mirror on the floor, amid the pile of crumpled examination papers. He lit his last candle again, tilted it to put three drops of wax on the mirror, then fixed the candle to the improvised base in the center of the papery kindling. Then he dragged his trunk behind him through the door, closed it, and turned the lock.

Part 3

THE FOREIGNER

So I see the boy, and I see Aron, and I know they will meet. I see them together in the curve of the spiral, at the end of what I can reach in my narrow vision, and I know they are there though I do not know why or what they have done, those actions and evidence, cause and effect.

I have asked the Sages—without the actions of these people, each thing they do, each time they reach out a hand and its narrow little fingers to take something or give something, how would the spiral turn? If they did not move, then time would cease to move. We must see their actions, those things you don't care about, those things I am not able to reach in this dim sight of mine. Of course, they say. It is all of time. You see. It is the Magi who don't. And then I dream again, and time moves me out of sleep and I do not feel it. Something is wrong in the fevered world and I do not know what to do.

I tell Tod about it, the dreams, the boy and Aron. He doesn't like it, this vision. Is it my fault, then, that the boy left? Did I make him leave by knowing he would do it? If I could see the steps they would take, would my thoughts steer them there? Could he stop the people in his dreams from dying?

I ask him again if he's dreamed. He has not. Does that mean no one else is going to die?

So the boy went out, to his fate, perhaps, as he was supposed to do. And Aron as well, walking the path he could not help but choose. That was my fault, I suppose, not by dreaming him on it but by leaving him to it. I left him with anger and that anger drove his steps. Tod doesn't like this, either. I can do nothing to change it.

1

I T WASN'T UNTIL JULIAN WENT OUT INTO THE WORLD
that he felt his life. In Biora he had lived without
knowing it, watching the days pass without seeing them,
breathing the air without tasting it. He had lived in a
small part of his mind, a part that filled up with words
once he learned to read them, but he had not known then
what the words truly meant.

"Light is the wave that reaches out from a source,
from the candle, from the sun," he murmured to himself. He could feel it now, the waves on his skin, moving
across and leaving hot pink burns in their wake. He
could watch it and feel it as he passed long hours in the
sun. He could lie back in the wagon and look up at
the sun, burning gold in the sky, giving off a halo of
waves when he narrowed his eyes or they became damp,
or when a cloud passed it, thinly, barely covering it. It
was there now. He could feel it.

He had wanted to learn to read so that he would
know things, words the Aunts had never dreamed of. He
had to laugh at himself now, short-breathed in the sun.
He did not know much at all.

The insects, though, were the same. They buzzed around him in the same way that they had in Biora, tickling his ears, tormenting him when he tried to brush them away. They bit and stung him and turned his already tortured skin redder and hotter and itchy. Sometimes Julian would catch them, find them as they were biting him, before they could fly away, and he would peer at their thin feathery legs and wings and wonder how something that looked as if the air would crush it could cause him such trouble.

The Aunts had stories about the insects, he remembered. Why are there mosquitoes, the children would ask, slapping at them in the damp summer. The Aunts always smiled, hardly scratching at their own red welts. Sometimes people start thinking we are the greatest thing in the world, their wise answer went. The mosquitoes remind us that we are only flesh and blood.

"Damned bugs," one of the men in the front of the wagon muttered as he slapped about himself. Julian still had some trouble with their accents, which were coarser than Tod's, but he was well familiar with their curses. "Cassile in the summer," the trader complained to his partner. "The whole country could fall into the ocean, and be better off."

Julian laughed a little inside himself, where the men wouldn't notice. They needed the mosquitoes most of all.

The traders were like light and dark, opposites to each other, water and dust. If they'd been in Biora, they would have fought each other to the death. One was a large man, a boulder of a man, his face dotted with pockmarks. The other man was thin and sharp as a knife, his chin and nose pointed, his elbows and knees protruding through his clothes like the angles of spider legs. They had paid Julian little notice in the time that they had traveled through the bright hot country whose name he'd learned through their repeated swearing. He sat in the wagon among bundles of wool and crates of old books, receiving no more attention than the goods did and little more food and water. Then, every few days, the weight in the air cracked and broke and the rain came down. If they were near a village, the boulder man and the knife man would drive the wagon under some structure, but more often they simply stopped at the side of the road and threw a tarp over their load, Julian and all, and outside of it he could hear the boulder muttering, "Damned rain, bloody summer in Cassile."

The air, at least, would be cooler, after the rain stopped and he was allowed to emerge from his leathery cocoon. He would be able to sit up and feel the breeze on his face, wind breathing through the weave of his tunic, traces of cool in his hair. It was that he would wait for, those few moments before the clouds parted and the heat returned. He would wait for them as anxiously as he had ever waited to visit the book-man.

Had he ever felt the rain, he wondered. Had he ever stood in the dry fields around Kiela, looking up into the clouds, until they released their treasures on his upturned face? He must have been out with the sheep when it rained; he remembered the scent of wet wool, but the feel of the rain on him was gone, forgotten or never captured.

At night they would stop to make camp, the men un-
rolling a tarp and sticking it up on poles to keep off any
rain that came, mounding rocks into a ring for a cooking
fire and unfolding their bedrolls to lie on the ground.
Julian had nothing to lie on, and they didn't offer him
anything. He sat at the edge of the rain fly, sometimes
outside it, looking up into the sky and the stars that were
lost in the clouds, swirled into them like whirlwinds of
dust. It rarely rained at night, though, and Julian fell
asleep on the ground and woke dry and hot to the sun.

Once the men pitched camp in a clearing where another wagon stood already, but the wagon was alone, no
horses hitched to it, and there was no fire lit nearby.
When Julian squinted he thought he could see a figure
huddled before the wagon. The traders looked in its direction as they put up their rain fly and made their ring
of rocks. Finally, the knife man was eaten up by the curiosity and strode over to the lonely wagon, calling, "Ho
there, trader, did your horses run off?"

The boulder man grumbled about losing his help,
struggled for a moment with fitting a corner of the tarp
onto the point of a long pole, and grudgingly called
Julian over to help him.

The knife ran back a moment later, his eyes wide,
long sharp feet cutting through the grass. "We can't
camp here!" he hissed.

"We're not moving now," the boulder answered, heft-
ing the pole upright and waving Julian away.

"We have to!" cried the knife, and he pointed back

toward the lump in front of the horseless wagon. "He's got plague on him!"

The boulder frowned severely and turned to unpack the cooking gear, muttering as he went, "There's no plague."

Julian watched the knife wring his hands frantically, but he was unable to move the boulder. He untied both horses and retied them to new trees, farther from the other wagon, and picked up each article of his own, his bedroll and his pack and the metal dishes that the boulder tossed out on the ground with a clatter, moving them to the farthest end of the space covered by the tarp. The boulder shook his head and frowned derisively at his companion. Julian looked over his shoulder at the man huddled across the clearing. A mist of rain drifted out of the sky, breathing a farewell to the daylight. Julian walked through it to the man at the wagon.

He was wrapped in an old blanket, his head half-covered and bowed to his knees. He might have been sleeping; Julian could not see his face. As he bent closer he heard long, shuddering breaths, and he saw that the man was shivering despite the blanket. Julian shrugged out of his woolen tunic and draped it over the man's back. The day had been hot and his undershirt was damp with sweat, and in the misted evening air Julian was finally cool. The tunic, though, was too small to fit around the trader, and it slipped from his broad body. Julian pulled it up again and wrapped the sleeves around his shoulders, and as his hand brushed near the man's face he felt the heat of fever.

Quickly he went back to the camp and fetched a cup

from the pile of gear to fill it with water. "Where are you going with that?" the boulder barked angrily, his hands busy with the cooking. "Go after him," he said to the knife, but the knife refused to leave his safe corner. Julian carried the water back to the huddling man unimpeded.

The sun was down by then and the moon was new, and though Julian pushed the blanket away from the man's head he could not see his face. Clumsily he tried to put the cup to the man's mouth and coax him to drink, but the lips moved in those shuddering breaths, unaware of the water. Julian leaned in closer. *Seven,* the breaths said, whispering over and over, *Seven.*

"Seven?" Julian asked.

The lips paused, parted, let a little of the water pass them. The man shivered hard and Julian set down the cup so he could press the tunic back around his shoulders. "Seven," he repeated, and his head sank farther.

Julian sprinkled a little water into his hand and lifted it toward the man's forehead, to cool his brow, but before he could reach it the man's head shot up again. "I killed seven," he said. His voice wavered like the flickering light that drifted over from the campfire. "Two Dabionian. Two Azassians. One in Biora. Two in Karrim." He swayed, once away from Julian, once toward him, and Julian felt himself lean backward so the man would not touch him.

How many men, Julian wondered, had Davi killed by now? He thought of Davi's knife, lying forgotten in the wagon, but knew it would do him no good. He would not use it to defend himself against a man who had killed seven. He made himself sit upright. "Drink," he whispered, raising the cup again.

"I had to kill the Dabionians," the trader went on, not hearing. His voice dropped some of his words, falling out of range, then wailing upward, and he had to stop between them to gasp for breath. "They were guards, I didn't have my papers, they would have arrested me. Prison. I would have died in there. Had to kill them. I told myself it was their own fault, two of them at that outpost alone, not even a village nearby. Dangerous. I had to. The Azassians, they made me angry. Tried to cheat me, wouldn't pay for what I sold them, looking down, laughing at me, up on their piles of gold. Had to kill them. Then it was easy, then it was easy. In Karrim, two traders, they had money and I didn't, they had goods and I didn't. It was easy, on the road alone. I killed them." His voice caught in his throat, and his hands flew up to his head, grasping his hair in fists. Julian heard a tearing noise and reached out to stop the man's hands. "Traders," the man wailed. "My brothers. I killed them."

The air was cold now, and Julian's shirt clung to him damply. "Biora?" he said.

"Biora," the man echoed, shivering. "I raped a woman in Biora. That's not wrong, is it? They're less than women there, like animals, they live like savages there. But the little boy saw me, what I did to his mother, he was going to scream. Who knows what they would have done to me? The lot of them, savages. He was so small, it was easy, that boy, so small."

Julian thought of the harvest dance, Aunt Ana and

the men around the fire. So many years had passed, though, Julian knew, before Aunt Ana made the dance and made the men follow it. He turned his head upward, toward the stars drowning in clouds. He'd thought it would be different here. He'd thought he might find something, outside the mountains. "Are you going to kill us?" he asked.

The trader's head swiveled toward Julian slowly. Julian could not see his eyes, they reflected no light, but he did not think the trader could see him. "What?" the man breathed.

Julian lifted the cup to his lips again. "Drink," he said, and the man drank blindly, like an infant.

In the morning Julian woke to see the trader lying on the ground, the blanket skewed around him. The cowl it had made around his head the night before had fallen away, and in the light Julian could see his face. Wounds and scratches covered it, uneven trails carved jaggedly across the skin as if by some strange claws, swollen and colored red, although the flesh of his face was white as ice. His hair was in clumps, patches of hairless wounds more numerous than the patches of hair. His hands, Julian saw, were scratched and scarred, the nails broken and stained with blood turned dark and discolored, and they were frozen in their rigor, clenching and clawing at something Julian could not see. He did not know whether the trader had seen it, or if he ever would.

"He's dead," Julian called to the other two traders, where they sat under their tarp cooking their breakfast.

They looked in his direction for a moment and turned their heads back toward their fire.

"We need to bury him," Julian called again. The boulder sat immobile, and the knife fretted about sharply but did not say anything. Julian reached for the straining hands and tried to fold them down, to stretch the man out flat and cross his hands over his breast. That was how the Aunts laid the dead in their graves before covering them up with earth. Julian laid the blanket over the trader and smoothed it over his body, though it was not earth. He sat back on his heels, silently. He did not know the burial songs; he was not a woman and so he had never been taught them. Then he shrugged his shoulders, which had gotten stiff in a night that had been colder than he anticipated. He eased his tunic from under the edge of the blanket and stood to pull it down over his head.

"He's putting that on!" a voice shrieked behind him.

Feet pounded toward him and Julian froze, his arms inside the tunic and his face buried. Someone snatched the neck of the garment and held it fast, so Julian could not move, and then tugged until his arms were finally pulled free. Julian flinched as strands of his hair were snagged out of his scalp, and he watched them float away, tangled in the wool of his tunic. The boulder stepped away, holding the garment at arm's length. "You're coming with me," he barked over his shoulder, and Julian hurried to catch up to him. The knife scurried away at the large man's approach, squealing as the boulder kicked the cooking stand off of the fire, and the boulder dropped Julian's tunic onto the smoking flames.

"Off with that," the boulder said, waving a hand at Julian's shirt without looking at it. "Burn it all. That man died of something." He did look, then, at the knife, who was covering his mouth as the tunic began to smolder, and sneered, "Something. Not plague."

Julian shrugged out of the shirt and dropped it onto the fire. He had left his shoes in the wagon, and in the warmth his legs were unwrapped, so he had nothing else to burn. He did not understand why the boulder was laughing in rough, rumbling breaths. "Naked as a dog," the man snickered, shaking his head as he walked away from the fire. "They live like damned animals."

In Biora, the boulder must have meant, as the dying trader had. Julian stood up straight on his two feet. He wasn't an animal. He was from Kiela. But the men would not understand what that meant.

A few moments later the boulder returned and threw a pile of fabric at Julian. He caught the pieces, the two of them separating in their fall, and shook out a shirt with enormous, sacklike sleeves and trousers with two wide legs. "Put those on," he grumbled. "Try to look like a civilized person."

The knife began to shriek again. "You're not bringing him with us! He stayed all night with that—that—" He shook a finger at the dead man, unable to utter words for him. "He's filled with plague by now!"

The boulder scooped the cooking gear noisily into its sack and hefted it over his shoulder. "There is no plague," he hissed at the knife as he stomped back toward the wagon.

Before nightfall the boulder called Julian down from the back of the wagon, where he had spent the day listening to the knife's thin whining and the boulder's stony silence. "Come here, boy," he barked. "Hold this horse."

Rain began to fall as Julian climbed out, drenching his hair, trickling into the wide neck of the men's shirt. It made him chilly and it made his hands slip as he tried to hold one of the horses while the men unharnessed the other. The horse was huge and strange, its head high above Julian's, snorting anxiously in the rain and stomping its hooves as the harness shifted awkwardly without the weight of the second horse. These horses were much larger than the donkeys they kept in Kiela, larger than any animal Julian had seen. Gingerly he put out a hand to touch the animal's muzzle. It snorted wetly at his fingers and lowered its head so Julian could stroke the velvety nose.

Behind him the men were swearing frantically. The second horse was stumbling, tripping toward a tree as if it were blind, nearly crushing the knife when he got between horse and tree. A rumble of thunder spooked the animal and it tried to lunge away, throwing the knife down. "What in hell do we do now?" he shouted.

"We can't lose any more time," the boulder said. "We'll haul the wagon to Alderstand and get a new horse there."

The knife spat mud from his mouth. "One horse can't pull the wagon. Who's going to wear the other half of that harness?" he scoffed, pointing at Julian. "Him?"

"I'll get this one back in the harness," the trader insisted. "He'll calm down."

In time the horse did calm down, too calm. The men managed to strap him into the harness but they would not let him walk on his own, and while the knife held the reins from the wagon box, the boulder walked at the horse's withers. Julian was ordered to walk on the other side, in between the two horses. The sick horse jerked and stumbled, pushing Julian against his mate. The animal's muscles twitched uncontrollably and he jolted at sounds. As they walked, though, through a day that warmed after the rain, the horse grew tired. He seemed hardly able to walk, his head hanging low, and Julian felt he would have to carry the animal's weight before they ever reached their destination.

When they arrived, people were waiting for them. From the fields around the village of Alderstand they had seen the wagon coming with its sick horse. Julian felt the traders and the wagon stop suddenly, but between the high shoulders of the animals he could not see what had stopped them.

He could not see who owned the deep, angry voice that spoke like a solid thing, like a gate that would not let them pass. "Go back where you came from," it said. "Take your disease with you."

"We're traders from Dabion," shouted the boulder. "We have license to do business in any town we need to, and if you give us any trouble, it's the Justices you'll answer to."

"You're not doing business here," the villager repeated. "The last time traders came through here, it killed half our livestock, seven children, and the blacksmith's whole family. You'll take those animals out of here."

But the traders would not take their horses away. "We need another horse," the boulder insisted, "then we'll leave."

The villager refused. "No. You'll keep quarantine. Then you can look for a horse. Then you'll leave."

So the sick horse was unstrapped from the harness and they were all led toward a building in town, the boulder grumbling and the knife fretting and the villagers pushing them along with sticks and rakes. The man who had spoken led them, the elder of the village, Julian thought. He wore a stole over his shoulders and he stared at Julian with dark and suspicious eyes. "Is that where the disease comes from? Up north? Does he have it too?"

But I'm not sick, Julian wanted to say, but fear caught the words in his throat.

It was the stables they were brought to. Julian was locked into a stall, the sick horse in the stall beside him, the other horse beyond, the two traders in the stall on Julian's other side. "You're lucky," the boulder told him mockingly, speaking through the slats. "The villagers didn't kill you, this time. They're just going to quarantine you. They didn't even lock you up with the sick horse."

A strange word made of strange letters, he thought. *Quarantine.* Even Tod had trouble spelling it. Julian had seen it once in an old book, a long book he never finished reading that spoke of the four humors, blood and bile and the others he couldn't remember. Illness was an imbalance of the humors, he'd read. Then Dal'Nilaran wrote another book that said this was wrong. Illness was caused by a carrier, an infected thing. Waves or particles, which was right?

"We're not lucky," the knife argued morosely. "Horse is already sick, that means we've all got it."

If illness was caused by a carrier, Julian thought, then the sick horse could kill the villagers. The traders could, perhaps. Even Julian could. He trembled, feeling sweat on his skin, and he pressed his hands to his face to feel for fever.

Through the slats on the other side, Julian could see the sick horse, locked up alone. The horse was so tired he could hardly stand or keep his eyes open. He could not keep his head up, and had to rest it on the gate of his stall. Julian imagined he stood below him and let the horse rest his head on his shoulder, that he scratched behind the drooping ears. But Julian could not get there. He was alone in a place where he could not go backward and did not know what was forward. He put his chin on his knees and trembled in the cold of his sweat.

"Sleeping sickness," the boulder said, watching the horse fall. "Not plague."

After the horse died, the villagers came to the traders' stall and let them out. They took their remaining horse and left without speaking to Julian. No one came to open Julian's door. He sat alone in the stable with his hands on his brow, unable to remember what it was supposed to feel like.

2

"SO, OLD MAN, ARE YOU STILL WAITING TO DIE?"
Cal Serinason grumbled at the voice that disturbed
him, the woman at the door of his cottage. He had been
waiting to die for most of his life. He shut his eyes tight,
knowing that would not dissuade the monk. She had survived the razing of the monasteries ten years before; one
old man's stubbornness was no match for her.

"It seems that the world has other plans for you,"
Sybel said, her voice hard and insistent.

"*The world is shifting sand on shifting water,*" Cal
quoted. "*Permanence is illusion. Illusion is vanity.*"

Sybel let out a small, dry laugh. "Yes, we did used to
say that, didn't we? You have a long memory. We wrote
those words a very long time ago, when all we knew of
the world were the things that troubled us. We didn't yet
know what real torment was."

Cal opened his eyes and looked at the monk in annoyance. She stood inside his door, uninvited, her hands
folded inside the sleeves of her garment. It was a sign of
her fortitude, or her madness, that she wore the loose
robe openly in the village of Seven Oaks, with no attempt

to conceal it or the head that she had shaven close to her scalp. It was a sign of her strength that the village elders, such as they were, would never think to turn her in to the Dabionian authorities who occasionally made an appearance in Cassile. Sybel essentially ran the village herself; fully half its inhabitants were followers of Nanian, their makeshift monastery strung together in a network of inconspicuous cottages. If Cal thought about how far they must have come, these monks, surviving violence and oppression, rising again in defiance of Dabionian law to pursue and spread their faith—but Cal did not like to think about such things. He didn't want to hear about what she had suffered; he had his own sufferings to think of. He frowned and turned his head away, toward the window.

He did not like his cottage. It was too bright, with its large window and whitewashed walls. The old monastery at Seven Oaks had been a real monastery: low stone buildings with dark walls, the sanctuary silent, the refectory dim, the cells of the dormitory small and only pierced with narrow windows. Penitents should lie on hard cots and meditate on the vanity of the world, not be distracted by its light and scenery. That was what Cal had been seeking when he came to Cassile some ten years earlier. That was what he found, for a single season, before the Dabionians came to close and dismantle the monastery.

Something had roused Cal that morning. Something had spurred him to run out and face the intruders, to fight like the cavalier he had once been, though he had no sword and his saddle was locked away and his horse was long dead. *Glory to old Mandera!* he might have shouted, or some such foolish thing. Doubtless, he looked like a fool, a harmless madman rather than any threat to the Dabionian Authority. The black-uniformed guards had laughed at him, then arrested him. Cal was sent to Karrim to serve ten years working the fields in a prison camp.

Why had he come back to Seven Oaks? It was a question he'd asked himself often since his return, though his reasoning had seemed unquestionable at the time. He'd thought it would be the last place on earth where anyone would find him, and Cal Serinason absolutely did not want to be found. He had not even expected anything when the villagers took him to Sybel upon his arrival. She could not be anyone who remembered him from his brief time in the monastery, he'd thought—all the monks were certainly dead, and he didn't know any of the villagers, in keeping with the old separation between village and monastery. When he'd seen Sybel he'd held in a gasp. But she was not a monk he knew; she'd come from Westin in the south.

She seemed to know him, though. "You're a Manderan," she'd said, examining him with a shrewd and very discomforting eye.

"Yes," Cal had croaked. The hair he had never cut, the beard he had never shaved. His country followed him no matter how far behind he left it.

Sybel had nodded like one accustomed to being

correct. "Those things we found in the storeroom, they must belong to you."

So his past followed him as well. In the ground below the old monastery there had been a storeroom where all the monks and penitents buried their worldly possessions. Cal had never imagined that his would still be there, untouched by the Dabionians. But for whatever reason, the storeroom had not been plundered, and the last items unclaimed by survivors or villagers were things that could only belong to the son of a wealthy merchant of Mandera: an armload of antique clothing, a saddle, two rusty swords, and a lute.

"It seems we were meant to find you," the monk had mused, almost to herself, still eyeing Cal closely enough to see all his unshriven sins through the thin layer of his skin. "Well, the world brings us what it will. Find him a cottage," she ordered one of her acolytes, and Cal was settled into the new monastery.

He'd lost track of the time since then; it might have been more than a year. It had been the most tedious year of his life. Nothing was waiting for him, he'd abjured the possibility of finding anyone, and he had nothing to do. Picking turnips in the Karrimian winter, that freezing and backbreaking work, was less painful than the too-bright quietness of life in the cottage. Some of the acolytes came to bring Cal food and keep his fireplace, but other than that there was nothing, day after endless day. Except, sometimes, there was Sybel.

She was still in his cottage, unmoved by his turned back. "What about these things?" she said, pushing with her foot at the pile of Cal's belongings, which lay on the floor in a corner. "They look rather permanent. Very dusty, very unkempt."

"I don't want them," muttered Cal.

"Hmm," the monk responded, the syllable heavy with meaning, and Cal began putting words to it. That was the response of a child, he thought: *I don't want them.* Fifty-eight years old and he was pouting like a child.

Then he thought, Only fifty-eight. "Not such an old man," he said aloud to himself.

Sybel smiled subtly and quietly stepped out of Cal's door. She had done her work for the day. It was very slow work, but there was not a rush. They would be alive tomorrow or they wouldn't.

Not such an old man, Cal continued in his thoughts, but such a life! No one could come through it whole. He turned to look at his things. His clothes—surely not the same clothes he'd worn at his first midsummer festival when he was sixteen, surely they would not fit him now. But he pulled the shirt over his head, the white linen yellowed slightly with age; he drew on the breeches, dark red like wine, the velvet thin and worn; he buttoned the heavily embroidered vest close around his body. Age had begun to wither him down to the size of a young man, for they must have been the same clothes. They even smelled, faintly in Cal's dimmed sense, of bonfires and roses, passion fruit wine flowing in the fountains of the city of Kysa. Mandera before the fall.

He unwrapped his saddle and mounted it over the footboard of his bed. His horse—he couldn't even remember its name. None of the horses survived the collapse of 742. When the trade alliance with Ikinda ended all trade into Mandera ended, until the Dabionians came later. They didn't come until Mandera was good and hungry. The horses had been slaughtered for food. But even that had not been the worst. Cal reluctantly drew one of the swords from its scabbard. He did not like to think of the years of the rebellion. At least, he thought with a lump in his throat, this had not been the sword he'd carried then.

And then the lute. He could hardly bear to look at the lute, or recall the song he'd tried so long to learn on it, or think of the person he'd gotten it from. He pulled it onto his lap and curved his body around its pear-shaped one, plucking tentatively at the doubled strings. Out of tune, the pair sang in a mournful harmony, echoing through the wood and into Cal's stomach. His shoulders sagged, his back curved farther, and he sobbed dryly.

Sybel found him sometime later. "Good," she said. "You're dressed. Put on your hat and come outside."

It was bright outside—what business was it of the world to be so bright? Cal squinted, trying to smooth the straggly feather that plumed his hat before lifting it to his head. "What am I doing out here?" he asked crankily.

The monk looked at him with a face that frowned and smiled equally, as if she had a lemon in her mouth and she found it amusing. "What are you doing out-side?" she asked in turn, and gestured outward with her hand at nothing in particular. "Why don't you ask the outside?"

"*Mystics,*" Cal muttered to himself. He made a dutiful

circle around the monastery complex and went back into his cottage.

"I would have thought that the study of economics would have made Manderans more industrious," Sybel mused dryly, visiting Cal again a few weeks later. "All that money, all that merchandise, all those *things*, I'd have thought managing them was a good deal of work."

"I was the youngest son," Cal answered, sitting at the fireplace with his back to the door. There was no fire needed on the sticky summer morning, but Cal stared at the empty grate very intently. "I never studied economics."

"I see. You spent your father's money and industry was not required of you. So it seems you need more direction." Sybel approached the fireplace, stepping into Cal's line of sight and brushing the dust off his mantelpiece. "I have a proposition for you. You have been here too long without achieving anything. I believe you need to spend a short time elsewhere."

"Proposition? That sounds like a command."

Sybel made her lemon-smile. "We found your things in the storeroom where worldly possessions were buried. You came here as a seeker. You came back, so you must never have found what you were seeking. Consider this an invitation to a quest."

"Quest," snorted Cal, coughing on the dust. "Doesn't sound like Nanian."

"Nanian was a seeker. He was seeking peace, an end to conflict. He believed he could find it within. I believe we looked too far within and forgot how to look without. I believe we paid for that error with our deaths. Now you..." she began, looking down at Cal again with her piercing gaze.

Cal did not wait to hear her analysis. He got to his feet and went to his door, only to collide with an acolyte waiting outside, holding a walking stick, a flask of water, and a map of the crooked road to the nearest town.

Why did he go? It was a question he asked himself repeatedly when the storm broke on his way to Alderstand. His poor clothes were soaked, water falling in a stream from the pinned-up fold in his hat. His battered old boots were coated in mud, and he found himself involuntarily thanking Sybel for providing the walking stick that kept him from slipping on the saturated road. When he reached the town he found it nearly lifeless, all its people having taken shelter indoors.

"Smart of them," muttered Cal, looking for a public house. No, not a public house; he wasn't in the mood to endure gibes at his soggy cavalier clothes. The company of animals would be preferable. He sought out the stables.

Alderstand didn't have very many horses. Most of the towns in this part of Cassile were velvet mills. Now that Dabion controlled the whole industry, Cal supposed, the townspeople no longer brought their own goods to market. And they no longer wove anything but black, Cal added with a snort. But that would eliminate their need for horses, so the stable stood nearly empty.

Nearly empty. The first thing Cal heard after stomping some of the mud off his boots and shaking the water out of his hat was a voice, very human, asking, "Who's there?"

Damn that woman, Cal said to himself, once his mind had cleared of the shock. She had sent him to Alderstand to find something, and here something was. Cal had had enough of people who knew things they shouldn't; he'd met more than one in his lifetime.

Locked up in one of the stalls, its door extended by a wide board nailed over the upper opening, was a youth. Cal peered through the slats to see him. A pair of shockingly blue eyes blinked back at him. Azassian? There was a red cast to the face, but the brows were not red and the whiskers were not red. The youth was blond—faintly sunburned, and blond. He was a Bioran.

"How in the world did you get here?" Cal asked.

In a thickly accented voice the youth replied, "I'm not sick."

Illness, danger. Someone wanted the boy confined, perhaps wrongfully. Cal could release him. It was drama, it was adventure. It was temptation. The youth was exotic, a legend in the dull world. For an instant Cal wished he had his sword, to pry the lock on the stall. For an instant his heart beat at a tempo he had not known in years. Then he laughed at himself. He was an old man. And then he looked at the stall door and saw that it was not locked.

"Hurry," Cal said. "Everyone will be out as soon as it stops raining."

3

A RON JANNES WAS DOING TRANSCRIPTION. HE HATED
doing transcription: the strained eyes from trying to
decipher the scrawled shorthand of the court reporters, the
cramped hands from hours of writing, the ink staining his
fingers with ugly black splotches as if he were some common clerk. I might as well have become a common clerk, he
thought, not quite awake enough to feel bitter. His father
had stuck him in a clerk's office in Origh, not even anywhere
near the Great Hall, but next to a lesser court building,
scribbling out the words of trials sat by some Lesser Justice.

> Donn Ironsmith, charged with setting fire in his
> father's shop. Devil's advocate argued that the fire
> was accidental and caused by a faulty bellows. Table
> of Justice declares the argument unreasonable.
> Ironsmith found guilty of arson, assigned to Prison
> 45 in District Four.

Transcriptions had to be made for the printers, who
would further translate these records into their metal letters, to print them up and bind them for the archives in

the Halls of Justice. Aron wondered why anyone would care about so many petty criminals with their boring thefts and riots and arsons. He wondered why the bloody printers couldn't learn shorthand themselves, to save clerks the trouble of writing everything out for them.

But what other busywork would old Filanar Jannes find for his errant son if he didn't have transcription to do? Aron petulantly stuck his inky thumb all over the paper, spotting it with whorled thumbprints. His father obviously didn't trust him with anything important, like annotations or indexing. Aron wasn't even allowed to leave the office and take the transcriptions to the printer. The printer's name was Blackletter, and the other clerks in the office said he was a cranky old bugger. Aron would have liked to meet him just for the entertainment. Aron would have liked to pass the printer's door and keep walking. But where, exactly, would he go?

> Marri Weaver, accused of stealing from her employer. Coins and silverware found in her bedroom. Devil's advocate had no compelling argument. Weaver assigned to Prison 16 in District Six.

An old clerk came in and dropped another armload of records on Aron's desk. "I see you staining that page," he said ominously. "The Lesser Justice is losing patience with your work. You can stay through your dinner break to recopy it if you insist on being so sloppy."

The old clerk hardly took his eyes off Aron when he was in the office, giving Aron very little time to make faces at him. He frowned at the spotty page. All those years of playing nice at the Insigh School had earned him nothing. *I shouldn't have bothered behaving at all,* Aron thought. He would have ended up here just like any Lesser Justice's brat, and the embarrassment to his father would have been worth it. Aron was destined for the clerks' office from the start. They had to give the inferior sons some sort of work; they couldn't send them all to jail. Dabion's population wasn't falling fast enough for that.

Tom Wheelwright, accused of burning an abandoned cottage outside of Origh. Prosecutors brought forth witnesses who identified Wheelwright at the event.

Aron scowled at the words as he wrote them out, carefully tracing the shapes of flames in the O's and the D's. Obviously his father was trying to tell him something. He had never confronted Aron about the fires on the school grounds, never said whether the spy had reported him. His father certainly never talked to him about why he had been recalled home. He'd hardly said a half dozen words to Aron before shipping him off to the clerks' office. But of the cases Aron had transcribed, only a few had been anything as interesting as thefts or beatings or prostitution. The vast majority had been arson, and while some of the less destructive and more mitigated crimes might have been punished by a period of short-term slavery working in the outlying villages or in Karrim, every arsonist was sent to prison, never to be seen in the open air again.

> Devil's advocate called forth Wheelwright's brother, Shaan, in an attempt to render an alibi. As Shaan Wheelwright is known to this court as a reprobate and a user of alcohol, his argument was discarded.

The point of Aron's quill broke and splattered ink in a thin shower across the paper. The old clerk raised his head from his own desk and frowned at Aron.

"I don't have any more paper," Aron complained.

The old clerk pulled a sheet from his desk and dropped it in front of Aron. "I've already planned to go out for more today," the clerk said coldly. "Did you plan this little accident to coincide? Was that your last quill, too? Should I have the stationer cut you another one?"

The clerk knew very well that Aron was forbidden to carry a penknife. Aron smiled pleasantly, baring only a little of his teeth. The old man grunted and stepped out the door, letting it slam sharply behind him.

For a moment Aron reveled in the sensation. He was alone. Of course there was another clerk in the office, a bent little rodent of a man who crouched in his corner, day in and day out, huddled over his work. Aron had never even heard him speak. Once, though, when the elder clerk went out on an errand and Aron got up from his desk, intending to stroll out the door, the rodent had sprung up with a dexterity Aron never would have imagined and was at Aron's shoulder, fixing him with a look of such intensity that Aron wordlessly sat down. When he was especially bored Aron would imagine what the rodent might do to him. As long as Aron wasn't moving, though, the huddled little clerk ignored him. Aron stretched his cramped hand over his head and looked back over the words he'd written.

... known to this court as a user of alcohol, he read. Shuffling through other pages of shorthand discarded in his overflowing wastebin, Aron hunted for other occurrences of the peculiar thick curlicue that represented alcohol. An illegal still closed down, a smuggler condemned for bringing the drink from Karrim, an old woman accused of giving out abortifacient herbs and unauthorized restoratives.

Restoratives, Aron had transcribed. The shorthand was the same as alcohol. Every time his father asked the kitchen servants to bring him a cool restorative, he was asking for alcohol. Aron laughed out loud. The high-and-mighty Filanar Jannes was no more than a common criminal himself.

But what could Aron blackmail his father for? Would the Lord Justice really free his son from the drudgery of the clerks' office on the threat of exposure? Aron didn't think he could get his father to listen long enough to even make the threat. Could he confiscate some of that restorative from the kitchen and turn it in? Turn it in to whom? The LJ's only superior was Lord Councilor Muhrroh. Aron would be stopped long before he got to him. It was a fine idea, but he had no plan. This new path required far too much thinking, and the business of transcription had wreaked hell on all his power to think. It was as if his father had planned it that way. As if that spy had told him all about it.

It was then, as Aron was stretching his neck, looking up at the ceiling and turning his head from side to side, that he caught sight of the window over his left shoulder. It was only by chance that he saw the woman standing there, watching him. He might not have paid her any no- tice—she was only a commoner after all—but he was curiously reminded of the girl he had run across in the alley behind his house, one night last week when it had finally gotten too dark to read and he was allowed to go home.

Funny to see that sort of woman in this part of town, he'd thought, the central district where the houses were square and painted white and the alleys were swept clean. Dabionian law scorned such illegal activities, of course, and according to the Justices all things carnal were probably invented by the Manderans. What the old men did to amuse themselves, Aron wasn't sure and didn't care. There was always Karrim, and his father cer- tainly wasn't the only one to travel so frequently to that country. At the Insigh School Aron had overheard a group of ninth-years concoct a plan to visit Karrim and its brothels on their summer holiday, and Aron had earned himself no small amount of praise from the pro- fessors by turning the students in. It was a ridiculous plan anyway. Thanks to the wigs and the hair that had to be shorn underneath, there was no way for a Dabionian of the ruling class to become anonymous. That left the holding cells below the Lesser Halls, where prostitutes awaiting trial—and a few other, sometimes cleaner women as well—could usually be talked into things that might or might not reduce their sentences.

It was extremely unusual, therefore, to see the woman out in the alley, in any alley, much less Jannes's alley. But when she called at Aron and offered him a price he happened to have in his pocket, he didn't waste any more time wondering. That would be a shock to the old Lord Justice, wouldn't it, Aron thought with a hot thrill, leaving a stain in the alley, maybe some shred of undergarments. The thought of it was far more exciting than actually taking the girl, which Aron found a little boring, and as he'd strained and waited for the business to finish, he'd stared with distracted repugnance at the whore's open mouth and the black gap in the front where a tooth was missing.

He wouldn't have recognized the girl's face had he seen it again, couldn't say what color her hair had been, and only had a vague impression of the shape and size of her body. But when the woman outside the window of the clerks' office turned suddenly in surprise to shout at an out-of-control horse that nearly dragged its carriage up on the sidewalk, Aron saw in that wide-open mouth the unmistakable gap of the same missing tooth.

The next thing that happened was another chance, a bizarre, absurd chance. From the corner of the room came the sound of the hunched clerk coughing, a sudden fit that bent up the little rodent even more than he already was and crippled him where otherwise he might have lunged at Aron to keep him in his seat. Not yet thinking about the woman at the window, how she knew where he lived and where he worked, or how she had arrived the instant the old clerk left, Aron was on his feet and after her.

The woman saw him and darted away.

It was stupid to think he could follow her, Aron eventually thought as his running legs failed and he had to stop for breath. She was a street woman, spy or no spy, and she knew every turn and every alley in this town. She'd have lost him even if Aron wasn't hunched over, propping himself up with his hands on his knees, gulping air and fighting a stitch in his side. He didn't have a clue where he was going. Pathetic, he thought, that a grown man of his class couldn't find his own way around his own city, having spent his whole life driven in carriages and led by guards and locked up in boarding schools. "They're turning us into little children," he spat at a passerby, some commoner out on an errand, who was watching him too closely. "Can't find our way without our chaperones." Aron laughed coarsely as the passerby jumped back a step, staring at this strange clerk and his strange behavior. Aron was in his shirtsleeves, and strapped to a buttonhole in his vest was the penner that would hold his quills if he'd had any and his penknife if he were allowed to have one. He did look like a clerk, except that his vest and breeches were black velvet and the buttons were polished silver. *Look at whose son I am*, the clothes said. "As if it means a damned thing," Aron answered aloud, and the passerby hurried away.

He could go to his house or he could go to the Great Hall. Those were the only places he knew how to get to, just like when he was a child and his father would take him to the Hall, and he would stand in the atrium and scream at the top of his lungs. Sometimes he wished he could do that again. He had nowhere else to go and the woman had completely lost him. He turned up some street he didn't know and headed for the Hall, its great height visible from anywhere in Origh.

Origh was an ugly town, Aron decided by the time he got to the Great Hall. All square streets and order, white-plastered, as the Justices liked it. It was just as well that he'd been withdrawn from the Insigh School, Aron thought, or he'd be stuck here, working in some courtroom, or a professor pinned to some campus. Then he laughed bitterly—where did he think he would go? He'd already established that there was no way his class could achieve anonymity. Farmers and prison camp workers had more freedom than he did; they could run away and hide in the next village, at least. Aron had nowhere to run away to. He was pinned as much as the Justices and the professors, with a penner strapped to his vest to tie him down more. Clerks could be arrested if they forgot to carry the case that held the chains of their profession. Aron had to wonder whether, if he ever were arrested, his father would bother freeing him.

When Aron was small this would have made him angry. He would have shouted and kicked. Now he was twenty-two, tired, his feet sore, his breath short, and he was only morose. He felt frozen in place, as if it would be too much effort to move, like he'd felt on those days when he looked at the things he'd extorted from the younger students at the Insigh School and decided they weren't worth anything after all.

So frozen there, in the shadow of the Great Hall, stalled at the steps and looking at the door to the servants' tunnel underneath, he saw the woman again, slipping into that lower door.

Aron lunged forward, pushing through the traffic that blocked his way, men with deliveries of papers and wood and meat and women with baskets of linens and all the things Aron never paid attention to, all loud and clear to him now as he tried to fight through them. The woman's hair tossed in the distance, loosened from its kerchief, receding down the tunnel. He couldn't lose her again. The tunnel turned and weaved and Aron found his face to closed door after closed door, tripping over other people as he doubled back and hunted for the kerchief again, the loose hair. She started up a row of stairs and Aron stumbled up after her. Down a corridor she flung open a door and shut it sharply behind her, only steps ahead of Aron, who collapsed on it, huffing and cursing.

Then he turned his hand on the knob. The door was not locked.

He threw it open, shouting, "Who in hell are you? Why are you following me?" But his breath was cut short. In front of him stood his father.

Aron panted, his voice wheezing in his throat, staring at his father and at the woman who stood behind him, her back turned toward the door, only a little profile of her face showing around her disheveled hair. The teeth, Aron thought, he had to see the teeth.

His father's hand was sliding into his pocket; he was putting something into it. An envelope, Aron wondered. A purse? He stared at his father's hand, just in line with the woman's hand, as if she'd handed the thing to him, whatever it was, and he'd put it into his pocket. But what could she have given him? Men paid whores, not the other way around.

"Go home, Aron," Filanar Jannes said.

Aron found his voice in a gasp of anger. "I'm not going anywhere. Tell me who she is!"

"Go home," his father repeated, with dangerous slowness. "Now."

Aron looked up and saw someone he did not recognize. Looking into those cold, serious eyes, Aron realized he did not know them. He'd never before met his father's eyes. His father had never met his. Aron wasn't sure he ever wanted his father to meet his eyes again. The woman still did not turn around. The Lord Justice would say nothing else. Aron backed out of the door and it was shut and locked in his face.

The operative known as T was angry. She was angry at this assignment, having to watch Aron Jannes. He was moody and unstable and impossible to predict. She was tired of impossible people, impossible like the Sages. The whole business was K's fault, she was sure. K was supposed to watch Aron, keep him out of trouble—that was why Muhrroh had assigned one of his best Sor'raian operatives to Aron, to keep him out of trouble. That fire was proof that K had failed, wasn't it? Aron got in trouble and his father pulled him out of school, then K left and T had to watch Aron. It made her very angry.

She was angry at the LJ. She'd told Jannes they should meet somewhere else, not under the Great Hall, where there would be dozens of witnesses at any time of the day or night. Somewhere inconspicuous, that's where you met for transactions. Somewhere public, that's where you watched someone, where you'd just be a face in the crowd. It would have worked if she hadn't been instructed to follow Aron so closely, even up to his door, to the alley behind his house. When he came up on her suddenly, in one of those Origh alleys that didn't even have any refuse in it to hide behind, she had to do something quickly to distract him. So he got close enough to see her mouth, then she was sent to follow him again, and he recognized her. And he tracked her, because the LJ told her to meet him at the Great Hall, the first place anyone would look for him.

Madmen, all of them, and the worst ones were the ones who thought they were sane. She was angry at Muhrroh, putting her on these assignments, making her work with the Sages. Being angry at Muhrroh made it easier to forget that she herself had told Muhrroh she would work with the Sages. He found out she could talk to them; he made his offer and she took it. She'd agreed to work with the madmen. But it wasn't her fault, she insisted to herself, bitterly. She had to get some sort of control over the madmen. It was the only way she could prove she wasn't mad herself.

Once K asked her to guess his real name. She should know it, he said—seventeen letters, he'd help her spell it. He was making fun of her, her poor spelling, her difficulty reading. She'd learned to read too late. Names didn't matter anymore, she'd told him. They only kept their initials so Muhrroh could keep them straight every time they changed aliases. T was just as glad to forget what her name used to be.

So she waited in the little room under the Great Hall, counting to one hundred after Jannes left. She chewed the inside of her mouth and invented curses for him with each number. When enough time had passed she could walk out and the servants who passed by would not make note of the two of them together. Then she could leave the public place for better, more secret passages, and leave the insane people for better, shrewder ones. She was going to Insigh.

4

RAYNER DID NOT NORMALLY ATTEND MEETINGS OF the Circle when someone he'd summoned would be there; those people might ruin his cover as a harmless old man by recognizing him as the one who had briefed them. This time, though, Rayner couldn't resist. Kerk had found quite a prize for Rayner this time. Rayner counted himself lucky to have such a fine assistant, his right-hand man in the Secret Force, his local director in Insigh. Rayner wished he could have replaced all his local directors with Kerk; the lot of them were irritating, squabbling parasites. Kerk could probably do all their jobs. He was Rayner's best. Rayner paid him well to be his best.

It cost a pretty penny to keep Kerk on his side; indeed, it had been the prime motivation behind Rayner's installing Wirthir as the head of District Five. Gaining control of the main road out of Azassi meant he had control over all the money coming out of the country, and this was at a time when the Azassian chieftains were demanding an entry into the economy, a market for their gold, to replace the business they lost thirty years ago when Mandera collapsed. Rayner had been personally responsible for establishing the pressing of the new Dabionian currency out of Azassian gold, and charging the Azassians for the privilege, of course. Kerk only worked for the highest bidder and Rayner was determined that the highest bidder would continue to be he.

Rayner's investment had paid off beautifully this time. Find me something that will convince the Circle to support Zein, Rayner had said. That was all the direction Kerk needed. Fortunate, since Rayner had no further leads. For nearly a year he'd been trying to get the Circle to reject Athal for the replacement in District Three, and making very little headway. He'd paid off Wirthir and Timbrel a long time ago, but Nosselin was too uncooperative to be bribed. Frahn had been the one behind the opening of the Bioran School in Insigh, so he was hardly going to be swayed away from Athal, and no amount of cash was going to make Marsan abandon his darling. Buying Jannes's sympathies was, of course, a lost cause. Nearly a year of negotiations, with the date of Timbrel's retirement looming ever closer, and no consensus could be reached. Timbrel was likely to change his mind with or without Rayner's money, if the decision kept dragging out, and there was no way of knowing which side Nosselin would turn to if he got irritated enough. Rayner was fairly certain he could keep Wirthir's loyalties, but Muhrroh had the power to override the vote of a single Lord Justice in order to obtain a consensus. Something had to tip the balance in Zein's favor, and it had to happen soon.

If the Circle couldn't be swayed toward Zein, then Athal had to be discredited. Dirt needed to be dredged up. Kerk was the man to do it. Rayner dispatched his best operative and waited. An awfully long time, in fact, so long that Rayner began to wonder if some Azassian gold miner had turned Kerk against his old master. Rayner wasn't too far off the mark, as it turned out. Kerk returned, from Azassi, with a little extra gold in his pocket from some job he'd done on the side, and a certain special prize for Rayner.

So it was with delicious anticipation that Rayner awaited the Lord Justices, watched them as they entered, squinting, from the maze outside the Circle chambers, adjusted their foolish wigs, and took their seats. Rayner sat in his chair at the Lord Councilor's shoulder and let his eyes shine with a mad glint. The Circle was seated, the Secretary took his place, and the meeting began.

"It has come to the attention of the Circle that a visitor has joined us," Secretary Bint began from his podium at the feet of the U-shaped table. An odd bird, Bint, thought Rayner. Easy to spy on, very predictable, but hard to buy off. The idiot actually fancied himself a man of integrity. "It seems that this visitor has a recommendation for Justice Athal in his candidacy for the seat of District Three."

Bint stepped aside and the door to the chamber opened again. The Lord Justices turned their heads, all six blond-topped arrogant heads, to see who the visitor was. And all six mouths dropped open in expressions of complete shock. Through the doorway, his small blue eyes blinking with the sudden light, came a young man in a grayish suit of rough-spun stuff, whose flushed red-pale skin branded him an Azassian of the purest pedigree. On his head was an authentic, long, blond, curled, horse-tail wig in Dabion's finest Bioran style.

Rayner cackled in the stunned silence.

"My lords," Bint announced, his own smooth cool voice sticking a bit, "may I introduce to you Unther r'Gayeth."

The Lord Justices still sat there like six stuffed pigs, invisible apples in their mouths gagging them dumb. Muhrroh was the first one who could speak. "Welcome to the High Council of the Five Countries, Mister Gayeth," he said, only the faintest hint of shock burring his gracious tone. "We are pleased to see that the spirit of Bioran learning has spread so far."

"Pleased," croaked Marsan, "quite pleased. We had no idea any of the Azassian households were pursuing Bioran scholarship."

The young red man nodded eagerly, himself a little stunned. Probably never been this far away from his hovel, Rayner thought distastefully. "Of course," he said. "Our chieftain, Erril r'Gayeth, is a great supporter of your schools." The boy's accent was distractingly thick, and wisps of his bright red hair stuck out from under his wig. "He hopes to lead our country in Bioran learning. He hopes to emulate your greatness." Unther dragged out the vowels in the unfamiliar word, *ee-myoo-late.* Rayner cringed with laughter.

"But tell me, Mister Gayeth," asked Frahn, who had finally found his voice, "how did you get started on this path of learning?"

It was the question Rayner was waiting for, the one he had planted. They should have known the answer if they hadn't all been too stunned to remember how the Azassian had been introduced. Even now Rayner could see the look on some of their faces, Nosselin, Wirthir, as they figured it out.

"It was your great peer, Justice Athal. He came to House Gayeth and taught our chieftain the first lessons."

There was little more to be said in this meeting with their visitor, who had come all this way to speak on Athal's behalf. Secretary Bint thanked the young man and showed him the door. All the Lord Justices sat wordless in the sound of shuffling feet and gulped water.

"So Athal has been," Marsan began, struggling, "influential. In the cause. Of Bioran learning." He swallowed. "Abroad."

The Circle was quiet, trying to accept that statement. Then Rayner spoke, from the perfect standpoint, just a senile old man rambling incoherently. "Erril r'Gayeth. Ah, yes, I remember. The one with the armies."

It wasn't Erril, but his ancestor, Byorn r'Gayeth, who had led the armies that brought his country to civil war in the year 510. He'd led those armies all the way across Dabion, decimating everything in his path, almost as far as Biora itself. And the striking point of his war was Bioran learning. House Gayeth had lost control of the mines and Byorn had been desperate to regain some sort of power. Learning was the power he went after, just as bloodily as he'd fought for gold. The names of Gayeth and Biora could never be spoken together easily again.

And Rayner knew it. Just the simple error, saying Erril but meaning Byorn, as every man in the room knew, was enough to bring down Athal.

"Strange that you never mentioned this interest of Athal's," Nosselin barked at Marsan, nearly jumping up out of his chair but unable to keep the nervousness out of his voice. "Is there anything else we should know about your candidate? Any reason why he singled out Gayeth to convert to the miracle of Bioran learning?"

Marsan was white as a sheet. "No," he said weakly. "I had no idea he'd been to Azassi."

"No idea?" Wirthir asked, with measured incredulity. "That seems strange, especially what he stands to gain, leading Azassi and gaining entry to the Circle through your influence. That seems like a lucrative proposal, one you must have seen the benefits of."

The accusation hung heavy in the room. Rayner shook with mirth, looking like he was having a fit of palsy. He couldn't have planned anything more perfect. Athal wasn't merely being discredited for contracting with the household that spawned the greatest threat to come out of Azassi. He was also being accused of trying to take a share of Azassi's gold. Wirthir was a genius, planting a suggestion like that. Rayner couldn't have done better himself.

The suggestion was doubly ironic. Rayner had put Wirthir into the seat of District Five just for that sort of lucrative proposal, to gain control over the trade out of

Azassi. And while House Gayeth, as militarily inept as they now were, stood no chance of ever regaining control of their mines, Zein had every chance of gaining control of the Alaçan mines, if Athal's discrediting cleared his way to the seat of District Three.

Rayner left the meeting of the Circle in a fury of joy. He laughed aloud as he wandered back to his chambers, with such satisfaction and conviction that the servants who saw him might have doubted that he was the dotard old man they thought he was. Rayner had not even had to put up with Jannes as he left, hadn't had to watch Jannes fix him with a look that was supposed to be intimidating, reminding him of the threat he held over Rayner. Jannes had been holding on to that threat all summer; Rayner wished he'd tell Muhrroh about Hysthe's assassination and be done with it. Jannes probably thought he was gaining some sort of control over Rayner, making him nervous by dragging it out this long. Jannes had a lot to learn about the cat-and-mouse game. But even thoughts of Jannes couldn't spoil Rayner's mood. Gaining his chamber, he sat down in his chair, raised his feet onto his desk and leaned back luxuriously, closed his eyes, and imagined he had a glass of spirits to toast his own luck.

It was a disappointing shock to Rayner when he found himself waking up. He had not planned to fall asleep; he had not even realized he had fallen asleep. It was the fault of imagination, he was certain, closing his eyes and thinking of things he didn't have. Imagination was a waste of time—only action was of any value. It was unacceptable and it would not be allowed to happen again. But the most unacceptable thing was that his unplanned slumber had been punctuated by a dream.

The dream had been of failure, a frustrating and haunting failure: his own. When he had first accepted leadership of the Secret Force, he'd had hopes of discovering the identity of Muhrroh's preferred successor to the infuriating Loyd, someone who was both missing and undoubtedly valuable. For several years Rayner had attempted to track this person, examining every known member of the Force, sorting through every scrap of paper that could be found with their names, searching for any evidence of an exceptional relationship to Muhrroh. Rayner found nothing. Muhrroh had very little respect for written documents; there wasn't even a list of all the active operatives. That was one of the things Rayner had changed at once, noting the spies with appropriately coded names, of course. When Rayner had first come into his position, the only way he had even known who the spies were was to be introduced to them, personally, one by one, by Muhrroh.

That was the form the dream had taken, an old frustration cast large like actors upon an illegal stage. Rayner was standing before a long line of men clothed in black cloaks, paraded before him by Muhrroh, each with his back to Rayner. One by one Muhrroh turned them around so Rayner could see their faces, and not one of them was the man Rayner was seeking. Rayner frowned as he remembered the dream. Dreams were a sign of a disturbed mind, and Rayner did not have a disturbed mind.

He'd wasted time looking for the preferred successor, as it turned out. No single man had stood out from any of the others, and Rayner's hopes for entertainment and profit had died. He hated wasting time. Undoubtedly Muhrroh had taken some effort to conceal the successor from him, and Rayner did not like to have things concealed from him.

He had never liked it, not since his father disappeared when Rayner was sixteen, only to reappear twelve years later on Rayner's doorstep. He gave no explanation, confessed nothing about those twelve years, spoke no words to his son. It was as if he had shown up merely to taunt his son, now the governor of Prison 15 in the godforsaken reaches of Dabion, to see if Aln Rayner would have the nerve to imprison his own father.

Rayner had, of course. The man was a criminal, after all. He did not speak a single word to the man after that day, when he commanded his guards to take the prisoner below. He had not wasted a single thought on the man for years, but still the bastard had made an appearance. In Rayner's dream, the last cloaked man in the line, the one Rayner had known in his dreaming mind was the man he was looking for, turned around to show his father's face.

The knock that came at the door was so utterly incongruous with the fragments of the dream that still stuck in Rayner's head that he actually started, cracking his knee against the bottom of his desk. Entirely unacceptable. He would need to do something at once to prevent any further disturbances. "Come!" he shouted to the intruder at the door.

Opportunity had a way of presenting itself, Rayner thought. The person at the door was Tanie. "Come in, my dear!" he said.

Tanie stepped inside quickly and closed the door firmly behind her. For a woman, Tanie was surprisingly competent, and she always brought him the most interesting news. The pain in Rayner's knee subsided at once, and the irritating dream went easily to the back of his mind.

"I have news," Tanie reported coolly. "Muhrroh arranged a transaction today."

"Did he? With whom?"

She waited a beat. She was good at this game; Rayner kept thinking he should hire her officially. She'd been working for him exclusively, not for the Force at large, for almost six years. "Lord Justice Jannes. To send him money."

"*Did* he?" This was interesting. Muhrroh really was protecting Jannes, and now Rayner knew why: Jannes was supplying him with something he needed, something he was willing to pay for. Rayner savored the idea with a relish, running his tongue over the inside of his teeth. Then he frowned. Tanie was telling him nothing else about this meeting. She did not know why Muhrroh was paying Jannes. The question began to needle Rayner like an itch. Muhrroh was hiding something again. What could the Lord Councilor need? He had the position of highest power in the Five Countries. He had more money than anyone since the Manderan barons. What could Jannes possibly give him that he did not have?

"Tell me why, Tanie," Rayner hissed, sitting up intently, grasping the girl by her arms. "Find out, and tell me why." Muhrroh was hiding something again, but he was not going to keep it hidden. Rayner was no nervous child from whom secrets could be kept. "Find out, Tanie," he demanded. "I need to know what Muhrroh is paying Jannes for. Find out for me. It is very important."

But Tanie pulled away from him. There was something strange in her eyes, a little fear at Rayner's unusual urgency, and something else. She had plans of her own; Rayner could see that. She wanted something from him, and this was the way she thought she could get it. Rayner would have to watch her, and watch her carefully.

"Of course," Tanie murmured, turning toward the door. "Anything you want." She smiled a little then, one of the few times Rayner had ever seen her smile, and in her slightly and carefully parted mouth he could see the gapped line of her teeth.

5

THE TRADERS WHO BROUGHT JULIAN TO ALDER-
stand were unlucky. When they finally returned
with their new horse and went to the stable to claim their
wagon, they found the Dabionian authorities waiting for
them.

"Yes, these are the two," the elder circuit clerk said to
the younger one, his eyes turning from the rocklike
trader to the narrow, bladelike one. "Remember them,"
the clerk directed his protégé. "We've revoked their trad-
ing license—how many times now, gentlemen?"

The traders declined to answer.

"Three or four times, for underreporting earnings
and failing to pay taxes. And they keep coming back to
these villages, raiding Biora, carrying their loads across
to Azassi, threatening the locals. Told you they were going to turn you in to the Justices, did they?" the circuit
clerk asked the village officer, who stood in the barn with
his prisoners.

The man in the stole nodded grimly. "Frightened my
villagers," he confirmed, "and threatened us with the sick
animal they brought in."

"Sleeping sickness," the younger clerk said helpfully. "Bred by mosquitoes from the marshland between here and the Kian Pass. That's what the horse that died had, I'm sure of it."

"Kills people as well," the Cassilian added. "It has before. I can't imagine why it hasn't killed the two of them yet, or that boy they brought with them."

"Boy?" the clerks asked, puzzled. "What boy?"

"The Bioran," said the Cassilian, narrowing his already glowering eyes as he stared at the traders. "We never let him out. We let the traders out—we never should have—and after they left, we found the Bioran was gone as well. I wonder what they did with him."

The traders mumbled, the skinny knifelike one fretting and the rock shushing him. The elder clerk's hand went self-consciously to adjust the wig on his head, and the village officer answered to his gesture, "Yes, blond as those. Blonder. White as milk. They were taking him to Dabion, to sell him off as a curiosity."

The younger clerk blinked at his superior. He had only just realized the purpose behind the hot, scratchy, flea-ridden wig he'd been compelled to purchase, at no small expense, on his promotion to the circuit. If he was to work for the Halls of Justice, and not just for the printer in Kerr who called him clever despite his humble origins, he would have to look the part. It had never occurred to him that looking the part meant looking like a Bioran. There was a Bioran school in Insigh, one he had daydreamed about going to, if only he'd been born a Justice's son. The schools were modeled on Bioran learning.

The government was based on Bioran logic. But the clerks of the Cassilian circuit were ordered, among other things, to prevent traders from bringing goods out of Biora, despite the apparent demand for them. Something about *unauthorized traffic*—it was very confusing. There must have been something frightening about actual Biorans. The young clerk scratched discreetly at his scalp under a flap of his wig and wished he were in Kerr setting type.

The older clerk cleared his throat and looked around the stable, wondering to whom he should address his question. "And where is the boy now?"

But unlike the traders, Julian was lucky. He and his new companion cleared the village before the rain of the previous afternoon had stopped, and were back in Seven Oaks before the village officer of Alderstand even noticed Julian's absence.

"So this is what you found," said the woman with the robes and shaven head, eyeing Julian as he stood at the doorway of her austere cottage, rain dripping from his hair.

"It is," the old man answered gruffly. He had spoken very few words to Julian during their walk, with the rain running into their mouths and drowning their words, but Julian thought that the old man did not care for his company. "Now what was the end of this quest meant to be?"

The monk smiled, a tight smile that frowned at the same time, like the oldest of the Aunts in Kiela, one who still remembered the time when the men did not trade but took. "It is your quest, Cal Serinason. What *is* the end of it?"

Julian followed the old man back to his cottage, where the woman had ordered a pallet to be laid out on the floor for Julian to sleep on. Cal grumbled at the sight of it and took his place in the only chair, pulling it close to the fireplace with his back to Julian. Julian sat down on the pallet and peeled off his muddy shoes, looking for something to clean his feet with. In the corner of the room, near the foot of Cal's bed, was an old pile of unfamiliar objects. There was a curved form of leather, fixed with straps and dull metal buckles and rings. In a book of mathematics, Julian knew, was a formula that would describe the shape of that curve, and an alchemical text would surely name the metal. Such fascinating words, in those books, so full of promise, so full of anticipation of the unknown world. Julian once thought the words would give him the world. Now Julian had come outside and seen the world, and knew it was little different than his own. The two long bars of metal, flattened thin and pointed, were swords, Julian knew, though he did not want to admit it.

What he did not know was the source of the music that the old man was playing. He leaned carefully to the side, trying to better see the instrument Cal had placed across his lap. Its bent neck held two rows of screws, to which were strung ten strings, and Cal was plucking at them with the hidden fingers of his right hand, slowly and tremulously. His head was bent forward in concentration, his eyes closed, and Julian was able to creep close enough to see his face better. He was dark like the traders and the villagers, but his gray hair hung over his shoulders, almost as long as Julian's, and his mouth was framed by a beard and mustache, all carefully combed. His clothes were old but brilliant, like brightly colored birds whose feathers were touched with dust, and he wore boots of black leather that rose high up to his knees. At the end of his melody he paused, sighed, and opened his eyes. They were sharp and bright, the brown of them polished with gold. He looked directly at Julian. Once he was beautiful, Julian thought. Now he was worn and weary and bitter.

"What is your instrument called?" Julian asked.

The gold-brown eyes sparked with irritation. Cal was about to call Julian an idiot—Julian knew that look from Davi. But the old man swallowed his words to take a longer breath and shook his head. "Look at you," he muttered. "You can see the light right through you. A strong wind would throw you off your feet. And you're the most feared thing in the Five Countries. They fought you out, years ago, afraid you'd tear the world apart. This whole religion was made to fight you—they wanted your science gone, so they preached it out of existence. And here you are, looking like a porcelain doll. You don't even know what a lute is."

He sighed his resignation and turned away, putting down the lute behind his bed where Julian couldn't see it. Then he reached for his hat, swept it onto his head with a broad and unconscious motion that scattered raindrops around the small room, and walked out.

Later that night a monk came to bring the evening meal, a tray with two bowls and two drinking vessels. "He's gone out, hasn't he?" the man with the cropped hair said. "Sometimes he walks in the woods around the village. He'll come back. Sybel knows he will." And with that, the monk was gone.

The monks paid as little notice to Julian as they did to Cal, the two unbelieving foreigners in the cottage together. Sybel had given them leave to remain and so they remained. They did not touch the lives of the faithful. Sometimes Julian saw Sybel outside the door of her cottage, watching him, but she rarely spoke to him. She knew what needed to be known, Julian thought. He did not question a wise woman.

Cal spoke to him even less, almost nothing at all in the days following his outburst about the lute. He would be asleep when Julian came in at night, moving carefully so as to not wake him, and he would be gone into the trees in the morning when Julian woke. During the day Julian washed Cal's dishes and swept his floor, and once Cal made a *humph* of recognition, but that was all.

The other villagers of Seven Oaks paid Julian slightly more notice, but they watched him from a distance, this lonely visitor. "From the land up north," one would say to his neighbor, who might ask, "Up north? Where?" They knew Biora less than they knew Dabion, and they only knew Dabion from the clerks in the black suits who came to take the goods they made and the tax money every season. Seven Oaks was far off the road that ran out of Biora, and most of the villagers had never heard of the scholars who had brought science out into the world, those many years ago.

"There are mountains up north," a well-traveled herder might say. "Must be he lives at the top of one, where it's cloudy and cold. Higher up than the sun even. Must be they're all that pale."

Not many villagers had the nerve actually to speak to Julian. He was more interesting as a rumor. Once an old woman was walking away from a mill filled with rows of velvet looms, her basket loaded with folds of heavy new fabric, and she called to him to help her carry it before her frail arms dropped it. He did so cheerfully, but when a few of the farming men approached him, trying to judge whether he was strong enough to push a plough, he shied away from them like a frightened horse. An odd creature, they said. No plots to plough on top of that mountain up north. Best to leave him alone. So they did, except for the girls.

Julian spent most of his time with the trees, not out in the woods around the village, where he might interrupt Cal and his solitary walk, but in the center of the village, where the seven tall trees that gave the place its name stood in a ring. He could stand at the base of one of the oaks, looking up into the branches above him, and his restlessness would be stilled. He could look up and see the life in the tree, centuries of life echoing in its leaves, and he could think that this was all there was, no avaricious traders, no men fighting each other in the dry Bioran dirt, no deity called Light.

Then he would hear laughter behind him, shaking

him from his reverie. He would turn, brushing his chin on the ancient rough bark, smelling the old dry richness of it as it rubbed into his skin. Behind him a cluster of girls gathered, watching him, laughing.

His mother and the Aunts were not alone when they called him beautiful. The girls in the village had begun watching him as soon as he came to Seven Oaks, and once their fathers declared him useless but harmless and so allowed him to stay, they watched him as closely as they could. He was fascinating to them, with his fair skin that had faded to warm gold once the sun's burn had healed, lighter than the pale skin on the palms of their hands, smoother than the palomino-colored horse that the miller owned. The monks had given him a razor and his face was clean, his features perfectly drawn. His hair was long and a shade more fair than his skin, loose and tossed by the wind. His eyes were a blue dark as the sky at dusk, and when he smiled at the girls they shone. The girls laughed, enchanted. The weather was beginning to turn cool again and he wore his clothes loosely to take in the air, not buttoned up to shield himself from the sun as he had in the late summer when he arrived in Cassile. His sleeves were rolled back, showing the long lines of his arms, strange and thin and strong, and the wind blew the fabric of his garments close around his body and his limbs.

The first girl to speak to him was one called Beth, shy around her friends but bold enough to find Julian when he was sitting alone behind Cal's house one late afternoon, the dusk-blue of his eyes echoing in the sky. She came to him with a basket in her arms, asking for company as she went to the stream to do her washing. Julian was on his feet at once. His heart stirred the restlessness that slept in him and beat it out into his blood. As Beth leaned over the stream, pounding linens with river rocks as the strand of her hair that had worked its way out of its knot skimmed the water, the soft shape of her breasts pressed against her bodice and escaped the neck of her blouse. Julian leaned close into her, mingling the strands of their hair and their breath, and touched the skin of her throat.

A fury of noise crashed out of the trees. Beth's brother and a mass of his peers rushed down to the stream and jumped on Julian in a mound.

It was with some surprise, as Julian picked himself up once the boys had withdrawn and spat out the mud from his mouth, that he saw Cal standing near him, the scuffle having drawn him from where he lurked in the nearby trees. He seized Julian's arm to steady him. "You didn't fight back?" he said.

Julian had swallowed his voice—Cal had clamped his hand on a bruise. "No," he mouthed, shaking his head gingerly and watching the sky blur.

"Why not?"

The cut in his lip made a crooked line as Julian tried to smile. "I'm a coward."

Cal stared at him, unable to answer. He pulled the boy's sore arm over his shoulders and limped him home, where he lit a lamp and stared at him more. Julian asked hoarsely for water and washed his wounds, and a faint painful smile colored his face all the while. In the morning Julian woke to ringing in his head, and outside the window he saw Cal there, scraping the rust from his swords.

"Boy your age should know how to defend himself," Cal said shortly. He had no other words until he was done cleaning the blades, then he put one in Julian's hand and began to teach him to fight.

The sword was heavy in his hand, its length dragging his wrist down though he tried to hold it even over the ground. "It's not balanced as badly as that," Cal scolded. "Do you have any strength in those stick-arms of yours?" The old cavalier stalked back into his house and pulled his chair out onto the grass. "Can you even knock that down?"

Julian smiled through the swelling in his mouth. Sheep were not small creatures, and he'd handled them all his life. There wasn't a doubt in his mind as he struck the chair with the flat of the blade and threw it two yards across the grass.

Cal nodded in silent approval, kindly ignoring Julian as he rubbed his wrist. "Good," he said as he retrieved the chair. "Now let me show you how to hold it right."

By the time Julian's bruises had healed, his wrists were no longer weak. He spent hours in the day holding each of Cal's rapiers in his hands until he could hold them steady, until his hands were black from the metal of the hilts and Cal found gloves for him. The old man would search for his gear in the morning and find that Julian had it out already. "And this is a coward?" he mumbled once, blinking in an early light as he watched Julian practicing on the grass.

Julian smiled.

"Don't try to hand me that charm, boy," Cal said grumpily at Julian's bright eyes. "Your stance is all wrong."

While Julian practiced his stance, counting through the positions of his arms, rocking and lunging first on one foot, then the other, Cal rigged a post from a supple branch of wood. He fixed an acorn to the top of it and stood it in front of Julian, pushing it so that the branch swayed in the wind. "Hit that," he said, pointing at the acorn that bobbed at shoulder height.

Julian lunged, holding his arms and his legs as Cal had taught him, aiming the point of the blade in his strong hand. The acorn dodged him. Julian broke into laughter. Cal only shook his head.

After three days Julian hit the acorn. An hour later he struck it such a precise blow it shattered. Cal blunted both rapiers by folding strips of leather over the tips and wrapping them close, then faced Julian on the grass.

The monks were drawn to their windows by the clash of steel. They watched with worried eyes as the men struck and parried, confused by the numbers the old Manderan called out, puzzled more by the bright laughter of the young man that rang even when he was hit. In time they were satisfied that this was not violence, and they chanted their prayers for ease and composure, and closed their shutters.

The other villagers found the swordplay more interesting. They came out of the mills and their plots and gathered around Cal and Julian as they practiced, in numbers that grew as the news spread. The smaller children started dividing themselves into two groups, each cheering for one fighter, although they could not follow the fight. Julian saw them and caught their eyes, and he began acting for them, falling in a dramatic heap on the ground when he lost, waving his arms victoriously when Cal allowed him a hit. The children jumped and shouted in delight. Cal shook his head and frowned, but Julian noticed that the cavalier's arms began to move in wider arcs, with an old and unconscious flourish.

When the parents came to collect their children from the show, Cal would work Julian more seriously. Julian could wave his arms with as much flourish as he wanted when he was practicing with his target post, dancing with the shifting movement of the acorns he fixed to it, lunging and diving with the swish of the metal in the air so that even Beth's brother and the other older boys watched him with fascination. This wasn't the challenge, though. The movements by which he won or lost in a duel were slight, precise, earned with a skill that Cal possessed but Julian could only imagine. He would lunge proudly and Cal's blade would slip in for a hit that he could hardly see to parry. The bruises from Julian's fight with the village boys were replaced by the fierce round dots of Cal's blunt across his shoulders and under his arms, and when he undressed at night he saw the red marks of them standing bright against his white skin.

They did not have many spectators for their real

duels, but when Cal retired to his cottage to rest, Julian stayed out on the grass, swinging his blade with arms tired as water. There would always be someone to watch him practice, the boys, or the girls.

One afternoon when most of the village was out in the fields for the harvest, Beth came to the cottage. Julian was lying on his bed on the floor, his arms outstretched and the bruises dark on his bare skin, and he sat up when she came to the door. He called to her and she let herself in. Her hair was tied with a thin ribbon and she loosed it when she lay down beside him, letting it spill over his chest.

What was the call, he thought later—what was that call he heard? Was it Beth's voice, her soft and wordless cry? In her arms he could think so, but in the chill of her leaving the call would echo in his ears and it would not be her voice. Was it the ring of steel, his blade and Cal's, or the laughter of the children watching them in their circle? Was it the whistle of wind through the leaves of the oaks? It was, he would tell himself, drifting to sleep on his pallet, waiting for Cal to return and play the shimmering notes of his lute. But in dreams the music was different, and the call still tugged at him. *I am not for here,* he whispered in his sleep, every face in Seven Oaks becoming that of his mother, not telling him good-bye.

6

THE OPERATIVE KNOWN AS T WAS WATCHING ARON Jannes, again. She was not happy. But the Lord Justice had told Muhrroh that his son had tracked them, that he had seen the transaction, and that he was upset, and Muhrroh wanted Aron watched so that he didn't do anything rash.

"You can simply watch him this time," Muhrroh told her. "You needn't make him follow you."

The men in the black suits always talked like that, never saying what they meant. *Say it!* she wanted to scream. She hadn't made Aron follow her. She'd messed up and Aron saw her and that's why he followed her.

"She has nothing to fear," another, unexpected voice added. T felt her back tighten—she hadn't noticed that anyone else was in the room. Once she saw that person, she knew she should have. Standing against the wall of the tiny courtroom office, against a range of dusty bookshelves and doing her best to disappear into them, was a female Sage. One of Muhrroh's operatives. T frowned. She should have felt the scraping on the surface of her mind as the Sage made her think she was a row of books.

"She does not," Muhrroh agreed indulgently. He was never far from his Sor'raian operatives. He seemed to have one with him all the time. T thought the Lord Councilor of Dabion was a little cracked. "Certainly you do not," he added, addressing T. "I have the utmost faith in your ability, Thessa."

Her breath fumed in her and she clenched her teeth tighter. She hated when he used her real name.

But she returned to Origh and did follow Aron Jannes, waiting for him far up the street from the clerks' office, watching for him to come out the door at the end of the day. She knew him from that distance by his walk: slightly hunched, slightly wavering, but his head raised and alert, like a cat seeking out some creature to torment. A hurt cat, she thought. She kept the same distance as she walked behind him, hiding herself among the other people in the street, jostling them when they blocked her view of him. When they came to the street where his father lived she stepped into the alley. A girl in a servant's clothes was not to walk in front of the Justices' houses. She had to look between the fences to see him pass, catching only snatches of his dark clothes, to make sure he went as far as his house and did not appear on the other side of it. Once he was inside, she had to look in the windows to watch him.

Behind Jannes's house there lived an old, retired, cranky, and rude Greater Justice called Umbrin. The old GJ lived alone and the rooms on his second floor stood empty. Only one servant lived with him, since no one else could tolerate him: He lost kitchen help after half a season at the most. It was easy for T to hire herself out to make a few dinners for him to get inside the house. Umbrin shouted insults at her when she brought the food she made, and she rifled through his spice jars wondering what looked enough like poison that she could smuggle some in. But soon after he'd eaten he fell asleep, and after she let his ugly, stinking manservant push her over the kitchen table and satisfy himself, he left her alone as well. She spat blood into the cook fire as she stood up, trying to hold back the bile. Men were easy to con, that's why she did it. They were so easy they made her sick, every last, stinking, grunting, disgusting one of them. But now she was alone.

The upstairs bedrooms were locked even though they were empty, but the locks were easy to pick. One of the rooms had a perfect view of Jannes's rear yard and every room on the back of the house that had a light in it. Tonight Aron was in the yard. T sat in the deep sill of Umbrin's window, pushing the curtains against the darkened glass and peering through the split in them. She didn't have a spyglass. It was a foolish name, she thought, spyglass. It sounded too forbidden, too exciting. She only wanted it to save her eyes from the dust, so she could sit farther back from the curtains. And so she could see Aron better. He was in the yard, she saw him, in his shirtsleeves with his wig off, and he was doing something, but she couldn't see what.

She wished she could leave, sometimes, like K, Kuramin, whatever his name was. But she didn't know where she would go. She had no home country like

Sor'rai. She'd been born in Dabion, in one of the villages in District Four that existed only to tend the grass so the Justices had something pretty to look at when they went around in their carriages. It wasn't her home, though. Nothing wanted her there, and her grandfather was six years dead. He was the only one who'd ever been sweet to her, and even he had never saved her from the scorn of the village women and the abuse of the boys. Even he had never defended her or her mother from the rumors, the chants that the children sang about Thessa Wood-bridge and her mad old mother who walked barefoot in the snow and lifted her skirts when the men in carriages drove by. Her grandfather only grinned toothlessly and tried to recall the name of the Justice who was supposed to be her father. Old, toothless, helpless, and dead. That was her memory of home.

So she was here, in Origh, working for Muhrroh. She followed his insane orders, talked to his mad Sages, and sat in the dusty window watching Aron Jannes. She had to. She had to stay close to Muhrroh because Rayner needed her to, and she needed to stay close to Rayner. She needed it more than anything she had ever known.

Then she saw what Aron was doing. In the corner of the yard a small bush was going up in flames.

Fire! she screamed in her head.

Aron watched the fire, going backward a step at a time as it grew. When the flames threatened the tree above them he hurried into the house.

A few streets away there was a squad of Public Force guards, marching in lines as they went to do some kind of business. One of them broke away from his rank and turned quickly up the alley. He ran to the wall behind Jannes's house. From another street came a woman dressed as a washermaid, faster than she should have. In the alley behind Jannes's house they joined hands, and then they did what only T was able to see. They crossed through the wall and blew out the fire. Fire did not matter to them and they made it vanish as completely as the wall did in front of them.

Then they broke hands, and the man in the uniform hurried to rejoin his squadron. Mad wanderers in the Public Force—it would kill the Justices to think of it. How many asylums could they fill if they caught all the Sages? T made a short coughing laugh at the thought. But she doubted the asylums could hold them. They were out in the world, after all, in the city, in the streets, though she was damned if she knew why.

Then the washerwoman turned, for an instant before she disappeared from the alley, and gazed straight up at the window in Justice Umbrin's house.

T fell back from the window, cursing under her breath. The Sage had seen her. T bit her lip in a fury. She was supposed to talk to them, not the other way around. She was the one who conveyed the orders. She was above them, the one in control, the sane one. They were not supposed to speak to her. The Sage in washerwoman's clothes was not supposed to look up at her and say, clearly and loudly in her head, in answer to her unspoken question, *Why do you think we are here? Have you learned what we tell you? Do you see that you owe your life to our blood?*

7

"SO, BOY, WHAT HAVE YOU LEARNED?"

Julian had been called to Sybel's cottage, the first time he'd been inside, the last time he would be. He wondered sometimes what the monks' cottages were like, and wished he could have gotten a better look inside Sybel's door that first rainy night. Cal described the old monastery as four square walls and little within, dark and dim and cold. Julian imagined there would be books lining the walls, certain that monks would be like scholars, but those who studied what could not be seen. Cal told him, in fact, about his mother's book, a book of prayers that came from the monastery where she had fostered as a girl. Sybel's cottage must be full of similar books, if it was full of anything.

So it was a surprise to Julian to enter Sybel's door and find himself surrounded in green. Everywhere there were pots, large and small, on the floor and fixed to the walls and suspended from the ceiling, and every one held a plant or a flower or a vine. It was the forest caught in a handful and transported inside. Julian was so captivated, looking around at the foliage, that the monk had to repeat herself. "What have you learned?"

Julian turned toward her, looked at her shorn hair and earth-colored robes, her round face in the center of the green, and felt the sorrow knotted in his chest. "This place is not mine."

Sybel raised an eyebrow. "Is that what you were seeking, then?"

"I couldn't stay in Biora."

She nodded, raising her eyes to look at the past over his shoulder. "That was what we thought. We couldn't stay here, we were forced out of our homes, when the men came to kill us."

Julian nodded fiercely in agreement. She understood.

"The world moved us despite our attempts to escape it. We were lost, forsaken; our faith had abandoned us. Many of us were willing to die, eager to die, in fact. Almost every monk who survived the closure at Westin went to Naniantemple, all my brothers and sisters, the last of my family. They went there to die. And they did— they found what they believed they were seeking. But I doubted them. They scorned me, they condemned me for clinging to life. When I found other survivors, so many of them were praying for death, wishing they had not lived. We were not to remain in the world. But I believed that was wrong. We were alive, and it was for us to learn why. It was for us to discover who we were." Sybel paused and brought her gaze back to Julian, strong and deep-reaching. "Who are you, Julian of Biora? Who are you other than the blond one, the one with the cavalier's sword, the one the girls tell stories of?"

A small tremble moved inside Julian's throat. "I don't know."

Sybel smiled her frown. She had known the answer, of course. "I gave the old man a quest, although I don't believe he has completed it yet. Perhaps you will be more successful. This is not the place for you to find yourself. You are too distracted by the world here. You should go east. It is not as safe there, but no place is, really. Go to the bridge across the Great River, and you'll find Rett. He was one of the survivors but he couldn't bear to come back to the monastery; he keeps the bridge now. Give him my name and he'll let you cross. On the other side—if you turn south you'll come to a settlement. You might be tempted by that: attention, people to watch you. I think you should go north, toward the lake." The smile again. "But you will make your choice."

That was it, Julian thought. He was going away. Somehow this scared him more than when he left Kiela. He was wiser, now, about the unknown. North, toward the lake—it frightened him. A settlement was something he knew.

"Will you say good-bye to Cal Serinason?" Sybel asked then.

The knot tied itself up in Julian's chest again. He had not learned how to say good-bye. "No."

But Cal was there when Julian went back to the cottage to collect the few things he had gathered in his life at Seven Oaks. The old man sat at the fireplace again, just as he did the first time: his back to Julian, the lute in his lap, only this time there was a fire, crackling softly. Julian stepped backward, trying to withdraw without being heard.

He was too late. "Take the rapier," Cal said suddenly.

"What?"

"Take the rapier. You'll need it, looking like that. Take the rapier."

Julian bent carefully to retrieve the sword from the floor, trying not to scrape it against the boards. Cal did not speak again. Just as Julian was leaving, closing the door silently behind him, he heard Cal sing for the first time, the words that went with the music he had struggled so long to play, a song about a river.

Cal couldn't play the lute. He hardly knew how to tune it, and he had to skip the strings that seemed horribly dissonant because he couldn't remember their tuning at all. The notes he picked out were few and halting, and the words he remembered fewer. It was not music, no matter how it managed to impress the boy. Julian had never heard music; he had never heard a true bard, a true minstrel, working the strings as if she could draw magic from them, spinning a tale true and heartbreaking from her lips with a voice so pure and moving it hardly seemed born of a human throat. Julian knew nothing of it.

Julian hardly knew beauty at all. It stood to reason: Beauty itself was shortsighted. He couldn't even see himself if he looked in a glass. Cal knew how it was; it was how he had been. What others had seen in him was a world away from what he truly was. The cavalier, the gallant, the son of Baron Serinason. Songs were sung of his exploits—Cal wrote one of them himself. They were lords of the world, his brother Wenn once told him. At one point in his life Cal acted the part. He wore his elegant clothes and carried his sword with a swagger, seduced the daughters of barons and took the courtesans' quarter by storm. And after 742, he joined the rebellion, following the ringleader Sever Enilan in what Enilan called a righteous fight against the Dabionian invaders who wanted to ruin Mandera. None of them saw that Mandera was already ruined.

Twenty years later, after Enilan had been assassinated, Cal came back to Kysa. Twenty years later, the ruin was evident. Cal's father and Wenn were long dead. Kysa's statues were crumbled and its fountains overgrown with mold and weeds. Cal stood on the steps of what had once been the house of a baron, looking at the walls that had been stripped of their paint and ornamental columns and the door that was missing its stained-glass panels. It was now the house of Olen Serinason, Cal's oldest and only remaining brother, a manager for Dabion. He opened the door to Cal and frowned at him, the prodigal brother who was not welcomed home. Olen only tolerated him because Cal could relieve him of things that had been stored in the house, things from the old years that Olen was tired of hiding from the Dabionian inspectors. He loaded the claret velvet clothing, the saddle, the swords, and the lute into Cal's arms and shut the door on him.

Cal went to Cassile then, not to the monastery where his mother had fostered, but to Seven Oaks, the farthest he could find. He put the things he did not want into the penitents' storeroom and prepared to face a cold death. But then the Dabionian guards came, and Cal did not die. The things he did not want were rescued a second time. So Cal had the clothes that fit him again, the swords he did not need, and the lute that never let him forget.

He did not need Julian to remind him. He knew he had been beautiful; he knew he had been blind. He did not need to be captivated by the art of the boy's movements, the passion and grace of his fighting, more like dancing than defense. He did not want the sight of Julian and the young woman he courted, glances caught through the trees and stolen through the slats of the shutters, the richness of the girl's flesh and the long beauty of the Bioran's limbs calling back an old longing, one he had pursued everywhere, knowing no source, knowing no bounds, knowing no satisfaction. He did not need to be reminded of the one he had pursued most fervently, the one he had lost.

The lute was already there to remind him. He thought his incompetence with the instrument would blot out any memory of the woman he'd gotten it from, his clumsy fingers slow with age and so unlike hers. He'd thought leaving it, burying it, would make it go away, but twice it had unearthed itself and brought itself back to him. His past followed him. It had come with him through all the destruction and all his failures, always reminding him of one failure, one thing he had destroyed. He only had the lute because he had failed so brilliantly with the woman who had played it for him. He would give anything to take back that mistake, to have never hurt her, to have never gotten the lute and had it follow him and call him and force him to play it, only a pale, pitiful echo of her music. He would give anything to not be there in the cottage that Julian had just left, plucking hopeless notes to drown out the noise of the boy's beautiful footsteps, waiting for Sybel to come once again and ask, as always, the unanswerable *What have you learned, old man, what have you learned?*

8

LORD JUSTICE JANNES DID NOT NORMALLY MEET with Muhrroh outside of the Circle. Their personal transactions were of too sensitive a nature for the relatively public setting of the Great Hall. The Lord Councilor had been shrewd in making this decision, Jannes thought, shrewder than he knew. It was impossible to know how deep Rayner's subversion ran. With Rayner's operatives in place, even the chambers of the Lord Councilor might not be secure. Jannes would have to warn Muhrroh not to articulate any plans he might devise aloud, lest Rayner be alerted to them.

If Rayner was alerted to this meeting, there was nothing to be done about it. Jannes had waited long enough to report his discoveries to Lord Councilor Muhrroh; he had to act now. Rayner's manipulation of the Circle against Athal could only be the first step in a new sinister plan. It was time for Muhrroh to put an end to it.

Jannes looked around him as he ascended the steps to the Lord Councilor's chambers in the uppermost floor of the Great Hall. The corridor was wide and white, more like Jannes's own house in Origh than the rest of the Hall. The Great Hall in Insigh had been built long ago; it had been started even before the arrival of the Biorans in the second century, and curiosities like the underground maze that led to the Circle chamber were relics of that earlier time, the years before order and rationality. The upper level had been added far more recently, creating a contrast of light and purity with the older parts of the Hall. Jannes felt his apprehension ease just by walking between the clear white walls. No villainous agents could be hidden here.

"The Lord Councilor will see you now," a servant said quietly from within Muhrroh's door, and Jannes was admitted.

He walked through an antechamber lined neatly with the works of the old Justices, shelf after shelf of the revered tomes. Windows of the clearest glass overlooked the capital on both sides of the building. Tables and chairs of clean square lines stood about the chamber for those who might be invited to read from the Lord Councilor's personal collection. Then the servant opened the door at the far end of the antechamber and Jannes was surrounded by a strange darkness.

"My lord?" he called tentatively through the gloom.

The curtains in the room were pulled fast, darkening Muhrroh's chamber like night. Strange lamps burned around the chamber, blue flames hovering on the surface of a liquid fuel that filled small metal bowls fixed to the walls. In the midst of these faint lights sat the Lord Councilor, a large book open on his knees and two guards shadowy at his sides.

"Lord Justice," Muhrroh beckoned. "You must have news of great importance."

"I do, my lord," replied Jannes, dismayed to find a quaver to his voice. As he cleared his throat his eye was caught by one of the guards. For an instant he was positive that the man was one who had worked as a bodyguard for him, but when he looked more closely at the man, his face seemed entirely different. "It is a matter of grave danger. Your servant Rayner is working to place Justice Zein on the seat of District Three, in ways that are extremely suspect. I must warn you that his motives cannot be trusted. I have discovered that he does not work toward the protection of the Circle; indeed, he has already acted in violence against it."

Muhrroh's face was obscured in the dimness and Jannes could not read his expression as he related the evidence that linked Rayner to the assassination of Lord Justice Hysthe. The Lord Councilor was silent as Jannes spoke, making no interjection. Such news would shock the most garrulous of men mute, Jannes thought. The silence continued at the end of Jannes's declaration, as the echoes of Rayner's betrayal hung on them in the dark room.

But Muhrroh remained wordless. "My lord?" Jannes was forced to prompt.

"Yes, Justice Jannes?"

Jannes was stricken. He had expected horror, righteous rage, even a cold condemnation in the Lord Councilor's regal voice. These words, the simple confirmation that a speaker was heard, as if Jannes were speaking of nothing more grave than the weather— It was unthinkable. "My lord!" he cried in a whisper. "Did you not hear me? If Rayner arranged the death of one of our own, then none of us is safe."

Muhrroh smiled then, indulgently, the pale shine of his teeth barely visible in the dimness. "You need not fear for yourself, Jannes. You have a certain importance to me and I shall continue to protect you."

"But my lord!" Jannes continued breathlessly. "There is an assassin in our Circle. Even you are in danger!"

One of the guards poured fuel into a new vessel and set it alight. The spark, the odor, snagged Jannes's senses. He had a certain special importance to the Lord Councilor. Jannes stared. He knew what was burning inside the silver bowls.

The guard with the match turned in the new flare of light and winked at Jannes. His face was once again that which Jannes had thought he'd seen a moment before, his former bodyguard.

"No, Lord Justice," Muhrroh said, his face suffused with the blue glow and an unnatural calm. "There is no danger that can touch me."

Jannes found himself in the white corridor without realizing he had exited the room. The Lord Councilor was mad, Jannes was certain: entirely, utterly mad. His orders meant nothing. His promise of protection was meaningless. Jannes stumbled toward the stairs and grasped at the railing to keep from falling.

From the level below a footman called up to him. "Your carriage is ready, my lord."

Carriage, Jannes thought, as slowly as if the man had spoken some Sivan word. He was due home. The carriage was waiting for him. He had to return to Origh, to his house, to face the damage of which he'd been notified, the aftermath of the fire set by Aron.

The Lord Justice flew down the stairs in horror. He was not safe. His family, then, was not safe. His son was in danger. He would have to arrange protection for Aron, and not only from Aron himself.

Jannes did not notice that he was being watched as he flew. Only when he had passed did the watcher extract himself from the shadows at the foot of the white stair. The classical architecture of the upper floor was conducive to rationality, they said, and not at all conducive to espionage. Rayner hated it. The common servants of the Great Hall would let him pass anywhere, of course, but Muhrroh's personal guard would see him in the annoyingly wide and square antechamber and would not let him through.

The whole business made Rayner sour at the mouth. He should not have to do this spying himself; he was too important for such menial tasks, and that was why he had people working for him. He wouldn't use Kerk in the Great Hall, though, and Tanie had left Insigh. It never occurred to him to assign anyone else to the job of watching Muhrroh. He couldn't be sure who was his and who was the Lord Councilor's.

But he could get no farther than Muhrroh's door. He pinned that door with his eyes, tracing the dull geometric patterns carved into it in neat squares, boring into it with his mind as if anyone could really move things that way. If he had some of those Sor'raian operatives that the older, more superstitious spies immortalized in their rumors, maybe he could see what was on the other side of that door. He would not be outside, halted, stuck.

He scoffed at himself. Superstitious. He had never been superstitious, even as a child. If anyone heard Rayner thinking this way, they'd be justified in calling him a senile old man. Believing in magic was as bad as dreaming.

Still, he could not move away from the door. Muhrroh had him trapped there. Merely by lingering inside with the door closed, Muhrroh had trapped him. Rayner frowned. He had never allowed a man inside locked doors to control him; he would not allow it now. Rayner moved to stand, to turn his back and put the door behind him. He tried to stand. In a fury he smashed his hand against the marble banister and hauled himself upright. His knees were not arthritic, he insisted coldly. He was not weak. He would find what Muhrroh was hiding.

9

"YOU'VE GOT TO SEE THIS," ONE OF HIS FELLOW indentured servants called to him.

Aron sat back on his heels and looked up. People were heading west, toward the riverbank, a fat flock of them, so something was definitely going on there. It would give him a chance to get out of the dust, at least, to roll down his sleeves. He was tired of digging up broken spade blades and other things lost in the dirt. His peer started walking out of the camp, calling over his shoulder, "You coming?"

They weren't really indentured servants, of course; that would imply there was freedom at the end. The work camp was full of those petty criminals who weren't dangerous or interesting enough to put away in prison; they were sent to Karrim for a year or a few to work the criminal out of them. Someone had to run such camps, and this one, in a remote corner of Karrim, was where they trained the aspiring guards. Aron had been shuffled off here when his father came home, after he'd lit the fire in the yard. He'd been here for most of the autumn season. Funny that the criminals could look forward to their freedom, but the guards—not likely.

Early on, Aron had done as little as possible. There was one veteran camp guard who shamed the others into working, going out into the fields and making the lethargic prisoners do something. That was until he stumbled in a gopher hole and cracked his ankle like a twig. The Dabionian authorities wouldn't waste the expense of replacing him in any hurry, though. The condemned prisoners and the guards in training were left to run things by themselves.

The workers kept at their work, sluggishly, for a few days, until a wheel on the wagon that they used to carry the harvested grain from the field to the mill broke. The grain piled up and the mill stood unused. "What in hell are you doing?" one of Aron's peers demanded, seeing the condemned sitting on the ground doing nothing.

"We can't work," they said. "No cart."

So they didn't work, and the guards did nothing either. Aron spent at least a week lying on his back, looking at the sky and twisting grass strands between his fingers until they fell apart into little bits. Then the stores ran out and there wasn't anything to eat.

"What are we going to do?" someone asked. They were all sitting in a circle, guards on one side and workers on the other, watching each other with eyes that drifted around and around the circle but didn't find anything. Aron cringed as each pair of eyes fell on him. He hated the directness, the staring, the challenge. *What are we going to do?* each pair of eyes asked him. No one had ever looked straight at him and he didn't like it.

That wasn't true, though. The girl in the street outside the clerk's shop did, looked straight at him. And one other person, a long time ago.

But not everyone in the circle looked at Aron. Some of them looked at nothing at all, as if they couldn't be bothered to lift their eyes away from the ground, as if the effort were just too much for them. Left alone, with no one to tell them what to do, they might sit there and stare at the dirt until they starved, until they toppled over and fell in the dust and died.

"Idiots," Aron said suddenly, jumping dizzily to his feet. "We're going to fix the bloody thing."

That was how Aron found himself working. He picked up an axe and chopped wood until his hands blistered, then frowned at the pieces when they weren't the right shape. He grabbed a piece in his reddened hands and pulled at the ends of it, trying to make it bend into an arc, and behind him he heard one of the workers laughing dryly.

"What?" Aron demanded.

The dusty criminal yawned, and said, "That's not how you do it. It's the metal that's the problem anyway. Tire's warped. You need a blacksmith."

With a large step Aron was standing nose to nose with the man, face to his dirty face. "Are *you* a blacksmith?"

The criminal let out a puff of sour breath. "Before they sent me here I was."

Aron closed his hands on the shard of wood until he felt the splinters bite into his flesh; the pain the only thing that would keep him from putting his fist through the man's lip. "*Then*—" he hissed, "*fix it!*"

Dabion had left them to manage by themselves. They would only manage—Aron discovered, despondently—if he herded them through it. The wretched wouldn't do any more than they had to; they'd proven that well enough. So Aron was left to make sure they worked, to see that things were fixed, to dig up broken spades for repair since no new ones were coming. Aron was as dirty as the workers, more so than some of them, with his velvet breeches so covered in dust they looked like leather or burlap and his shirt more brown than white. He had abandoned his coat and his vest and gotten rid of his wig a long time ago. Only his cropped hair was left to distinguish him from his tangled-headed servants, and as time went by without the services of a barber, even that distinction started to fade.

He was even dirtier than the guard who called him with that "You've got to see this." The other guards didn't spend as much time on the ground as Aron did. Instead they strutted around, preening themselves like birds, whining about the dirt under their nails, as if they weren't all the dregs of their class, the rotten sons who weren't cut out for polite work in the city. Stupid bastards. "You coming?" his fellow guard called again, and headed off toward the riverbank without waiting. Aron watched him go, looking at his ears, which were bright red in the cold. The man had rather clumsily applied his razor to his scalp, trying to keep the top of his head as neat as his chin. Aron hadn't shaved in at least a week.

Then he looked back across the camp grounds. The camp was almost empty, everyone having gathered to see the unknown spectacle, and Aron's hair was long. He had accomplished what the rest of his class had failed: He looked like a peasant. He could be anonymous. He could run away and go into hiding, leaving the camp and the lazy workers and the worthless guards to starve without him.

He got to his feet, dropping his spade. He looked over his shoulder at the open road out of the camp. Then he rolled down his sleeves and headed for the riverbank.

Aron did not expect what he saw. He could not see it completely, since the ring of workers and guards around the spectacle was fairly thick, but he did see a tall head in the center of the ring, standing above the other people, and the head was crowned with white-blond hair.

"Jannes!" shouted a few straggling voices as he came near. "What do we do about him?"

Lazily the bodies shifted aside to let Aron move closer. The weird, tall, white-headed figure in the center was weirder still: he was holding a sword. A real, shiny, steel, old-dead-Manderans-style sword. Aron coughed out a laugh.

It took him a while to determine that the utter apathy of the workers was not just carelessness in the face of death. The man with the sword did not seem to be actually attacking anyone, though he was swinging the sword around in the air and striking it against sticks and the butt ends of pitchforks that the people were waving at him. Someone dropped a stick, or it was knocked out of her hand, and she went down on the ground, and the blond man only laughed. He lowered his sword and no one took advantage of the lapse to beat him or jump on him. He held out a hand and helped the woman worker to her feet.

In the pause a few more people bothered to look at Aron, and they went quiet. Some of the workers dropped their sticks or tucked their tools under their arms and wandered away as if they might go back to work. As the blond man began to lose his audience, he turned his attention to Aron.

"What in hell are you?" Aron asked.

The man smiled again, a small, irritating smile, and slid his blade into the sheath where it belonged. Aron wanted to kick his long thin legs out from under him and knock him on the ground.

Someone in what was left of the crowd said, "He's a Bioran."

Aron was not impressed. "There are no Biorans."

The man looked a little surprised. "Don't you have Bioran books?" he asked, in an accent that made Aron's ears ache. "The traders who took me to Cassile said everyone had Bioran books, and everyone wanted more."

In the schools, maybe, Aron thought. Out in the rest of the world, even in the clerk's offices, no one talked about Bioran books. It was a conceit for professors, that rationality and logic. There wasn't any rationality in the rest of the world. They certainly didn't talk about books in the work camp. The closest thing to a scholarly debate that had occurred among Dabion's lesser sons was when a few of the guards started telling stories about sick people they'd seen on their way through Karrim, and one who'd studied a Bioran book on diseases said they didn't know what they were talking about, because the symptoms they described didn't match any known illness. Aron couldn't have cared less about Bioran books, himself. The one thing he thought as he looked the foreigner up and down was that his hair was too straight. The wigs that all the classically trained Dabionians wore were blond and curled.

"So what can you do," Aron asked him, "other than wave a sword around?"

The Bioran, who called himself Julian and didn't offer any surname, was a useful worker at least. He didn't do anything particularly well, but he had a strong hand and he wasn't lazy. He didn't expect anything to eat until he had worked. He didn't stop working until the end of the day, when it was too dark to get anything done. When the other workers scoffed at him he only turned half a glance to them, and smiled his small, irritating smile.

"Is everyone in Biora insane?" Aron asked Julian, watching him eat alone one day.

Julian half smiled, and answered, "Most are more so." Then he fell silent and kept eating.

Aron wrung his hands and stomped his feet. He didn't like being ignored any more than he liked people looking him in the eye. "What are you doing here?" he prompted.

"Going east," Julian replied, unaware of how ridiculous an answer it was. "I was told to go east. I started in Seven Oaks, then went to the bridge at the river. I could

have gone north toward the lake, or south to a settlement. I went south. I came here."

Aron shook his head. No one could really be that simple. "So you were run out of Seven Oaks," he said. "What
did you do? Swing that sword at the village officers?"

"No," Julian said with no sense of irony. "But I don't
suppose they liked my having it. The fathers of the
young women didn't like me much, either. But they're
not the ones who sent me away."

"Fathers of young women," Aron interrupted. Without the bragging and leering, Aron wasn't quite certain
he'd caught Julian's meaning. "Young women you
tossed, you mean. Women you tumbled, rolled, got on
their backs, sharpened your stick on, sowed like a field in
spring. That's what you mean? Their fathers ran you out
of town because they didn't want you getting any more
bastards?"

Julian looked at Aron, his head tilted, his mouth
turned at the corner. He wasn't smiling, but he was looking Aron in the eye. Aron flinched away. He was the son
of a Justice; he was the one who passed judgment. Others did not pass judgment on him. But the Bioran's expression showed as clearly as a writ of law that Aron was
being judged, and it was not favorably.

"All right," Aron said slowly, to keep his voice steady.
"Why did you come *here*? And why did you leave Biora
in the first place?"

It took some time for Julian to answer that. He looked
up at the sky, around at the boring brown landscape and
the endless rows of crops in the fields. *My* fields, Aron

thought. He was the one who made sure they were planted. The Bioran had better not judge them harshly, he thought.

"It was not mine," Julian answered finally.

"What in hell does that mean?"

Julian faced him again, eyes steady and calm. "Do you think?" he asked. "Or do you just spit out words?"

Aron fumed silently.

The Bioran looked at the sky again, like some mad wanderer. "Biora was not mine," he repeated. "I came here to find something that was."

"Stupid," Aron uttered under his breath. He got to his feet and walked off somewhere else. But Julian's words were stuck in his head, like a riddle he was supposed to figure out. *Was not mine, was not mine,* echoed in his ears, that accent driving him mad. He couldn't sleep that night, trying to solve the riddle, though he had no idea what the question even was.

In the morning the Bioran was there, up early, the first one out in the fields. Aron wanted to march out through the corn rows and demand the answer from him, *Did you find it? Did you bloody find it?* He stood at the edge of the field and tightened his blistered hand on the handle of a hoe.

At the mealtime Aron felt a shadow over his shoulder and was startled to find Julian there. "So what is there to the east?" he asked.

"Are you going east?" Aron said. "You'll have a problem. This side of the river people don't just come and go as they please."

Julian nodded, looking into the distance where the monotonous fields blurred into the horizon. "You'll have to show me what to do, then."

"*Show me what to do,*" Aron mocked under his breath. Ignoring him, Julian sat down behind Aron and leaned against his back. That was how the workers sat in the fields: back-to-back, leaning against each other for want of chairs. Aron grumbled and hunched forward so that Julian was not touching him, but he did not go far.

10

THE SEASON WAS TURNING. WINTER WAS COMING and it was growing cold. Julian felt it in his bones when he woke, on the hard bunk in the dormitory where the workers slept. There were not enough mattresses or bedclothes to go around, and the bunk Julian had been given was broken, fetched from a trash heap in a dusty corner. He had to be careful when he lay down not to capsize it and throw it off its cracked leg.

The guards brought out their coats, black and matted, all made the same with long sleeves whose cuffs were folded back and buttoned, and long bodies pleated in the back to spread out a wide swath of fabric. There were more buttons down the front of the coats, all of them silver-colored with a tinge of gray, and if Julian looked close he could see figures carved into them, but he could not get close enough to see what they were. Only the guards had coats. The workers did not, and they huddled close together in the chill.

"We're running out of firewood," Aron said. He always sat apart from the other guards, as Julian sat apart from the other workers, on a rock at the edge of the camp. The others were sitting against the walls of the barn and the dormitory, on the side away from the wind. Aron sat out in the air, the wind tugging at the skirt of his coat and sweeping through the fringe of his hair. "A week, maybe, and what we've got we need to save for cooking. Don't expect to see Dabion come out to bring us more."

At the end of the day Aron went back into camp, to the dormitory and the kitchen where the meal was being made, to watch that the workers there were not wasting wood. The camp's two women were in the kitchen. One stood over the stove, and the second sat near it, on a bench fashioned from an empty barrel, trying to warm herself by the fire inside the smoking black furnace. She was pregnant, and she would run her hands over her belly, trying to soothe the infant through her thin garments, before putting her hands back out toward the stove to warm them again.

Aron kicked the barrel beneath her. "You told me you couldn't work," he said. "Only workers in the kitchen."

The woman struggled to her feet and went out into the wind. Aron did not give her his coat. Julian had none to offer her.

When Aron turned to glare at him, Julian went to the pile of wood against the door, busying himself by chopping the pieces into smaller bits. When he watched Aron, he saw in the darkness of his hair and skin and eyes the face of Davi. They saw nothing around them but the darkness, his friend and Aron, nothing but the fight. They saw only their own element, buried in it, choking on it like the dust. They could not see they needed the water, that the water needed the earth. Julian could only hope that Davi was sitting, as Aron did so often, on a rock out in the air, looking over Biora's fields as the wind buffeted him. More likely he was where the wind would never again touch him.

Aron went around the kitchen, looking in pots and barrels, peering in the one where the woman had sat to make sure it was empty before tossing it out the door for Julian to chop up. "No water, either," Aron uttered as he passed the open door. "If it weren't for the river here, they'd be leaving us to drink our own piss."

It was with surprise, then, to Julian and Aron both, that they watched the men come from the east, on a morning that met them with frost. "Here they come," one of the guards said, shading his eyes with a hand that was purple with cold as he looked at the silhouetted figures coming out of the sun, "the clerks of the Dabionian sodding Authority."

Aron looked back at Julian, standing in the doorway of the barn. The Bioran did not look scared, he did not cry out in fear, and he did not plead with Aron to hide him. He would have to hide, Aron knew. If the Dabionian Authority found him, they'd take him. If anything was unauthorized in the Five Countries, it was Julian. And Julian knew it, Aron was sure, as he watched Aron with those steady eyes, calm and weirdly blue, waiting to see what Aron would do.

Aron ran for the barn, and Julian anticipated his lead and vanished inside the barn doors.

Outside Aron could hear the heavy wagon rolling to a stop, the clerks asking who was in charge, someone saying it was Aron Jannes. Inside, Julian was looking for something to hide behind. The camp had no livestock and the stall panels had been pillaged for firewood. The hatch in the floor that led to the storeroom below had been padlocked, to keep the food inside rationed. Julian had nowhere to hide.

Aron felt in his pocket for the keys to the padlock. As his fingers closed around them he saw himself pushing Julian below, locking the door over his head, turning him in to the clerks outside. Thoughts of winning his father's praise were certainly exaggerated, but he would earn his way out of the prison camp, he was sure. Turning in Julian would have to be worth Aron's freedom—it would have to be.

"Jannes!" a voice shouted behind the thin panel of the stable door, and it began to swing open on its creaking hinges. Aron tore the ring of keys from his pocket and flung it across the room to Julian.

If he didn't catch them—Aron would remember thinking as the keys hung in the air—if he dropped them, if he stared at them like an idiot, then Julian deserved whatever he got. But he did catch them, and he opened the padlock in an instant, and he was through the hatch before Aron even had to block the clerks' way.

There were three of them, the clerks, bundled comfortably in gray wool greatcoats over their black suits, hoods drawn up over their heads. Their faces were not burned red with the wind like those of the people of the camp. They had a wagonful of gear: firewood, water, salt meat, hay, seed, moth-eaten bundles of threadbare jackets and old blankets. They brought two new inmates and took away three whose terms had ended. "And take this one," Aron told them, handing over the pregnant woman by the elbow. "I don't know why you even send women out here, you know what's going to happen to them."

The lead clerk nodded, yawned, and made a lazy note in his ledger. "Take the grain down to the storeroom," he said in a bored voice to one of the workers.

"No," Aron interrupted sharply. He looked back through the doorway at the unlocked passage below. Julian had pulled the padlock in with him. He hadn't left it on the floor, to announce his presence like a shout. He'd taken it below with him. Aron nearly felt a flash of pride. "Put the sacks up here, against the wall," he ordered in a surly voice.

The workers outside were sorting through the old clothing, pulling on every garment they could get their hands on, layer after layer of them. Two of the men grabbed for the same shirt and tugged at it, threatening its seams. *Are you that stupid?* Aron wanted to shout at them but didn't. He couldn't watch them anymore. He walked toward the other building, the kitchen and dormitory, hoping to find someone he could scold for breaking into the new store of meat.

Before he got there, he smelled it. He didn't recognize the smell at first, though he felt like a fool once he did.

The scent should have been as familiar as the sweat on his own shirt.

He couldn't see it yet. As he turned back toward the barn he noticed that the workers didn't see it either, not that they noticed much beyond their own noses. They probably didn't even smell the smoke, the harsh sweetness of burning wood hanging like blood in the air.

Aron wondered who'd set it. For a second his breath caught—he stared at his hands and searched his pockets. He didn't know if he had matches. He didn't know whether he'd struck one and dropped it inside the barn door, while his brain stepped outside of him and closed its eyes until he had finished. But it must have been one of the workers or the clerks, and it must have been an accident. When the dry wood of the barn, fueled by the fresh shipment of grain, shot up in a sudden flame so massive that people nearby fell on the ground, Aron was sure it had been an accident. No one would have sacrificed so much on purpose. He was almost certain he wouldn't even have done anything as mad as that.

Around him people began to realize what had happened. The goods they had waited for so desperately, the bulk of their food and their seed for the coming seasons, all that would keep them alive, was gone.

Somehow this woke the workers from their apathy. Somehow they decided they did not want to be forced to starve by fire. They jumped to their feet, shouting and waving their arms. They shook fists at the clerks, and some of them even began to clumsily rake away the dry grass between the two buildings, to keep the flames from spreading from the barn to the dormitory and kitchen. But Aron noticed none of these things, because he was walking toward the barn.

The door was thrown open with a blast, the fire gorging on air. Aron stepped into the gaping hole. He looked up at the flames rising over his head, lapping the roof. The sacks of grain were already gone. Such a terrible waste. Such a beautiful waste. He could never have planned such miserable destruction, not after all the work he had done, tearing his fingers and dragging the whole camp behind him and forcing them to stay alive. But life was nothing compared to fire. He felt the flames move around him and longed to eat the desperate heat of them.

Then in a shock he felt something throw him down, roll him away from the door. Dirt clouded his eyes. He had forgotten Julian so completely that he didn't know at first who was on top of him, bony limbs spiking his body.

Aron blinked furiously. "What are you doing?" he hissed. "They'll see you!" He kicked Julian off of him, tore off his jacket, and pulled it over Julian's head.

The expression on Julian's face, glinting orange in the fiery light, was so close to pride, thankfulness, love, that Aron could not stand it. The Bioran didn't know that Aron had almost locked him inside the barn. He grabbed at Julian's wrist fiercely, not looking at him. "Run, you idiot!"

The barn was gutted now, its thin walls gone, the fire gnawing still at its skeletal beams. The people had fallen back, shouting, crying, running for shelter. The black-smith was confronting the clerks, face red as he demanded that they go for help, that they leave one clerk behind as collateral, to ensure that they would come back to evacuate the workers and not leave them to starve. Aron did not stay to hear it. He was running toward the river. The guards were shouting about water, rooting in the kitchen for all the pots and pitchers and basins they could find, anything that they could use to pass water up from the river, anything that had not yet been chopped up for firewood. They argued with each other about trying to put out the barn, arguing that it was a loss, that they should wet the dormitory and the ground in between to keep the fire from spreading, that there weren't enough pots or pitchers anyway. Someone shouted at Aron to find the bridge keepers at the river, to press them into helping. They had great barrels and wagons to carry them; they were called on to fight fires in the region, and they could save what was left of the camp.

Aron did not hear them. Julian did, and when he caught up to Aron he would tell him and they would summon the bridge keepers, and they would halt the fire at the barn. But before that, for a few moments, Aron only ran. The fire was behind him and the water was before him and his thoughts could not run fast enough to catch him. Julian was following, and they ran on the riverbank like children.

11

THE HEALER TOOK THE MAN'S WRIST IN HER HAND, feeling the flutter of his blood in it. She had done little more than that in the three days since he had been brought to her, and each time the pulse flew a bit faster, a bit weaker. She could do little more than that: hold his wrist and watch in fear and weakness.

Had the others been there still, she could have asked them for their help. It was rare that Healers traveled together; they normally wandered in isolation, going from place to place where their hands were needed. The ring of tents that had stood in this farmer's field until three days ago had been an unusual sight. The last time she had been in such a gathering had been some years ago on the west side of the Great River, in the land of the monasteries, when there were monasteries. That time, as with this time, it had been the Sages who had called the Healers together.

Sages, those wanderers, knew the Healers, though the Healers did not know them. The Sages could call them by their names, names they themselves had forgotten. The Healers listened to the Sages when they called them, when they drew great numbers together because they were needed, because some terrible illness was coming. So seven Healers had come and stood their tents in this field, and for days the farmers and their children had come to them with fever. But it was only fever, and most were healed with a pass of the hand over the forehead. The others wondered why they had been called, why the Sages had drawn so many of them for such a small thing, when there were greater hurts elsewhere. They took down their tents and went away. The woman stayed, though, one Healer left to treat the last few fevers that might come, thinking she would stay only a day or two, then move on herself, wondering what the Sages had truly meant when they spoke of the coming plague. She did not wonder whether they had been wrong.

The day after the others left, a young man came, leading and half-carrying, with great difficulty, a man with the plague on him.

"My ma's said just as well," the youth said, panting and nervous. "It's th'estate manager, see, and he's always been real cruel to us, taking th' taxes out of our livestock when we've got none, wouldn't let my sister marry 'cos she had no dowry, then has her whipped when she runs off with the boy. Just as well, ma's said, let him get sick, let him get fever, let him die of it." The youth gasped and dropped his eyes shamefully. "But I couldn't let him, I couldn't, not like this."

Helping the youth lower his burden onto the ground in her tent, the Healer looked at the man, so full of fever she could feel it radiate from him. But it was no fever she had seen before. The estate manager was much further gone with it and he was delusional, crying out at images that attacked him from the shadows within his head, flailing his arms and fighting at things he could not see.

"Thank you, son," she murmured to the young man, and he was only too happy to take his leave and hurry away, leaving the Healer to watch her patient and wonder what she could possibly do for him.

The fever did not subside at her hand. She gave him water steeped in herbs to drink but he spat it out. The second day he tore at his hair, scratched the skin of his face and his neck with his nails. The Healer tried to hold his hands still but he fought out of her grasp. When she tied his arms down he wailed in horror and misery.

On the third day the wounds he had torn in his skin flared with infection, angry and red as fire. She could not touch them without his pain bleeding through into her, and she could not reach her senses below the surface of them even to try to heal them. Carefully she dabbed at the wounds with a bit of ointment, a thimble to douse the inferno.

Only once, before the infection grew so great that her senses could not penetrate it, did she reach into him to touch the illness from inside. Once, for a brief instant, before she fled from it in such terror that her body fell backwards and her physical throat let out a cry that echoed in the air. Now she sat beside the man's body, watching it burn away, chastising herself for being so afraid that she did not try harder to reach him.

"You have seen this before," a voice said at the door of her tent.

The Healer did not turn to see who had come. Only Sages were brave enough to walk so boldly into the place of Healers. "I have," she answered, not knowing how.

"You have seen it and you have forgotten now, but you recognized it when you touched him."

She shivered as she tried to escape the memory of it, what she saw in his body, the shape that the plague wore. She knew it like the name she had forgotten, like the land she had been born in and did not know anymore. "It was west of the river before. Long ago."

The Sage came closer, crouching over the sick man's body. She was a woman with long dark hair, and the Healer realized that it was strange even to see a Sage's hair. Hers had not been colored and wrapped so thoroughly as was usual among the wanderers; only a few leaves had been woven into the braids. Her clothes were different as well, and under the riot of colors, the garments shredded like ribbon, she wore what was recognizably a black shirt, its sleeves split to bare her arms. "Do you know how to cure it?" the Healer asked her faintly.

The Sage looked up. "I know how it will be cured," she said, looking close into the Healer's face. "But it is not time. I know you."

"I do not remember you," the Healer answered, dropping her head and reaching for a cool cloth to pat her patient's face, futile as it was. "I do not remember Sor'rai."

"No," said the wanderer, "it is not that. I knew you

later, you healed me. It was west of the river. I was human then."

The Healer looked into the woman's eyes again. She
did not have Sage wisdom, but she could see in the shadows of the visitor's eyes—not as turning and changing as
Sage eyes, not as clear and touched by age as human
eyes—that the woman had lived one life and now lived
another. "You can remember?" the Healer asked. "You
can remember that life?"

The Sage woman nodded.

In the far distance of her mind, the Healer could look
down into a well, the great strange depths of it, deep and
cool and dark. She could not see what lay at the bottom of it, but she could hear the echoes of water. "Is it
worth it?" she asked as she sat in the dry earth. "Remembering?"

The Sage's face turned in a wry twist, a smile drawn
from bitterness that magic could not touch. "I remember. I remember the plague and what will cure it, I remember it before it comes. I cannot do anything. Is it
worth it?"

At their hands the estate manager sighed in his agony.
They looked down, braved the searing pain to touch his
arms as soothingly as they could. His eyes fluttered
open, he murmured lost words, and then, for an instant,
he looked straight at the Healer with lucidity. His voice
rasped. He said two words, his last: "Forgive me."

The Healer tended to the body, cleaning it and wrapping it. She did not know the nature of the infection or
whether she could clean it from her tent and her clothes.

When she emerged from the tent, she found that the Sage had already begun building a pyre. The Healer moved her donkey a distance away and covered its eyes so it would not be frightened by the fire.

As the fire burned she asked the Sage, "Will he be forgiven?"

The flames shone gold on the women's faces, and beyond them figures gathered to watch from a shadowy distance. "I cannot see that," the Sage said. "It is not our world. It is above us, and none of us can see it, none of them can see it. I see this world, this spiral, and that is all." She sighed with a great weariness. "And it turns, and I go elsewhere." The sun had fallen, and as the Sage walked away from the fire she was hidden in the darkness.

12

THERE WAS NO HIDING JULIAN ONCE THE TRANS-
port came to evacuate the work camp. They came
sooner than anyone expected, the two clerks who were
allowed to go for help fearing for the safety of the third,
perhaps. An enormous wagon pulled by four tired-
looking horses arrived at the camp only two days later.
The clerks were bundled inside, along with half a dozen
Public Force guards and their assortment of weapons.
The guards in their gray uniforms filed out of the
wagon, gazing disapprovingly at the black remains of the
barn and the condemned workers who did not look suf-
ficiently intimidated by their pistols. They didn't recognize how greatly the fire-induced threat of starvation
overshadowed any fear of gunpowder.

"I don't know why they're evacuating all of us," Aron
muttered. He was hanging back in the dormitory, kicking at bunks. The Public Force had neatly relieved him of
his leadership, ordering the workers and guards into
queues, leading them out of the building and ushering
them into the transport. Aron was once again a discarded lesser son, barely a step above the prisoners he

had supervised. "They have to rebuild the camp. They're going to send out a crew to build a new barn. They have to store all of us somewhere until it's done. Why don't we build the new barn? Why don't they let us *do* something, other than just sit here, eating and shitting, running around in circles? We just work to keep ourselves afloat out here, that's all. What kind of pointless work is that?"

In the bitter cold Julian had almost completely covered himself in too-large garments, and these disguised him enough that the Dabionian crew had not yet taken any notice of him. He trailed Aron quietly, almost idly, straightening out the bunks that Aron kicked out of place. "What else would work be for?"

"Is that it?" Aron growled, throwing a savage kick. The blow missed its mark, his ankle jarred against wood, and he swallowed a cry of pain. "That's how you're going to be the whole way back? I'll throw you out of the wagon if you keep talking like that."

Julian paused to lean against a crooked bed frame. "You're angrier now than you were before," he mused. "Why?" He watched for a moment as Aron paced back and forth across the room, limping, then he smiled. "You're angry because they're taking the camp away from you."

"See what you know," barked Aron. "I'm angry because they're sending me back to my father!"

And as soon as he said it, that was all that filled his mind. He was being sent back to Dabion. The others might be relocated to work camps in other parts of Karrim, but Aron was going back home. No matter how he tried to get away from that white square house, from his worthless fate, from his father and all the questions he wouldn't answer and the eyes that did not know his son at all, Aron was always going back. His hands closed into fists and his dirty, broken nails bit into his palms, but that was the last move he was capable of making. Anger and dread filled him so thoroughly that he was paralyzed.

Somehow he got into the wagon and found himself sitting on a hard bench, facing Julian. The wagon was large and uncovered, and the frigid wind pushed at the people roughly. Snow had not yet started to fall, fortunately. The Bioran's head was bent under a blanket that he held closed at the neck like a cloak, only a shadow of his face visible. Aron watched the wind pick out a white-gold strand of hair and blow it around. *It was not mine,* Julian's voice said in memory. *I came here to find something that was.* "What does that mean?" Aron would have demanded, but his throat was full of bile and ice. *Anger,* the only word he could form. He saw the white house in his mind, the Hall of Justice, the clerks' office. *Anger.* He saw the shape of his father, tall and black in his suit, the absurd blond wig showing the back of his head, always turning away, always leaving. His father, his mother, Elzith—*anger.* He saw the yard where his mother had died, while his father sat in his office and never once came to tell Aron what had happened, how she'd died, if she'd been killed or if they'd caught the killer. Ten years and more and he had never once asked if Aron missed her or said he missed her too. *Anger, anger.* He couldn't feel his chest, couldn't feel air in his mouth, could barely hear the rush in his throat as he sucked in a panicked breath. Across from him Julian lifted his head, throwing out some kind of sympathy from under the blanket that shadowed his face. Aron did not want to see it. He blew the breath out in a cloud of mist and shut his eyes.

After a blink of time he found it was snowing. The wagon had stopped; the drivers were unwilling to go uncovered in the storm. Aron's eyes drifted open through no effort of his own. In his anger-frozen mind he could not think clearly enough to complain about the cold or to ridicule the sight in front of them. They had come to the drab cluster of a farming village: a few houses and outbuildings, a rickety exchange hall where the farmers would bring their shares for the tax collectors. The wagon had pulled up in front of this hall and the passengers were being unloaded into it. Aron's eyes passed over the sagging roof and badly gapped walls, and he did not wonder how they would keep the weather out. He did not laugh at how the shelter was hardly better than the camp they had just left. His eyes dropped shut again, frosty lashes weighing them down, and the picture of his father reappeared in the darkness there, and he trembled with cold and fury.

It was as if in a dream that he heard the gunshot.

One of the Public Force guards was a veteran of the closure of the monasteries ten years before. A lank, gray, nervous man, his heart had never beat the same after recovering from the diphtheria that destroyed Monastery 74 on the west coast, and he had never stopped jumping at shadows. He had been trained to shoot on sight but never learned why or what he was shooting at. Orders from his superiors and rumors made by the young men from his barracks—they were all young men, once—created in the guard's mind a terrifying vision of bizarre magic wielders, anxious to cast fearsome spells upon him if he hesitated to kill them.

This guard had no idea what magic workers might look like, although he was sure that they would not be the skinny, shaven-headed monks that his unit was ordered to shoot. Shadows of the grotesque faces he had imagined still haunted him in dreams, peering at him over long crooked noses, slavering from mouths crowded with razor teeth. When he reached for the arm of one of the workers disembarking from the wagon, pulling askew the blanket he was wrapped in and exposing his head to the icy air, the guard was convinced that the pale face he saw was that of a wicked demon, and the gold hair that suddenly flew in the wind was a host of tentacles whipping out to attack him.

Shouting, the guard pushed the pale intruder away. The force of his movement threw them both to the ground, and the guard fumbled for his pistol. Badly primed, hastily loaded, somehow it still fired but it missed its mark. Behind the wagon the listing door of the exchange building cracked with the bite of the wayward bullet.

Aron opened his eyes blearily at the sound. Workers, guards, and Public Force were crowded in a ring, and Aron would not have been able to see anything if he hadn't been still sitting in the wagon, above them, and if the ring were not widening as the people warily stepped back. The guard with the pistol sprawled on the ground, thrown by the kickback of his shot and paralyzed by some sort of fear. Facing him, now on his feet, was Julian. Obviously he's never seen a gun before—Aron thought, the words forming slowly and dryly in his mind—but he'd figured out that it was dangerous and the guard was trying to harm him. Julian's bag was at his feet, an oddly shaped thing Aron hadn't paid attention to before. From its oblong shape Julian had drawn the rapier.

Through the noise of anger Aron heard himself think, *Oh, no.*

Guards were shouting now, raising their weapons, positioning themselves in front of Julian. I should do something, Aron thought. He needed to stand up and raise his voice and stop them, tell them Julian wasn't dangerous, tell Julian to drop his sword. Aron was the only one who could do it. No one else would. Aron was the only one who could stop them. If he stayed silent, if he did nothing, if no one did anything, the guards would attack. Julian would not stand against them. Julian would die.

From deep in his throat Aron heard a thin, pained sound. It was blocked there, the picture of his father holding his mouth shut, holding his arms tight against his body, not allowing him to move.

But then came a crash and clatter, steel striking the ground. Julian had dropped his sword and the guards were swarming over him, trying to push him down or tie him up, a few gingerly reaching for the blade as if it might spring at them like a snake. Aron remained in the wagon, gathering snow on his shoulders, forgotten. Even his fury could not stand up to the cold and it left him, and in its wake came a fierce trembling. Aron could not steady himself and he did not know why.

The Public Force left Julian propped against the side of the building, bruised and bound, until they had gotten the workers settled in their leaking new home. They walked past him in a wide arc, not looking at him, as if they hoped the strange figment, now disarmed and quiet, would conveniently disappear.

"We should take him to the local authority, now," one anxious guard finally said.

"He can wait," another disagreed. "There's seventy prisoners that need relocating. The foreigner isn't going anywhere."

"The local authority won't know what to do with him. He needs to go back to Dabion. This parcel is under District Two. We should send him straight to the Lord Justice."

"I'm not taking him to Jannes," more than one guard said at once. "We'd never get him through, we need someone with authority to get him into Origh, straight to the Great Hall. We'll lose him on the roads, to the clerks if not to the commoners. One of them's too greedy to let him pass, the other's too superstitious. They'll call him a witch or an elf, he looks like it."

"Take him to parcel eighteen, there's a circuit clerk there now, they can take him back."

"The road's out with the weather, we can't get there from here."

The guards were silent, eyeing each other. Then, "There's a Jannes on the manifest."

The Public Force had commandeered one of the farmhouses, and once Aron was found under his shawl of snow and identified as the Lord Justice's son, he was sent there with Julian, separated from the rest of the camp's refugees to await special transport to Dabion. Aron was given a seat in front of the fire to thaw out; Julian was banished to a dark corner. Aron stretched his fingers out over the flames and tried to feel something other than the tremors that still would not leave him.

A nervous, hunched little woman sidled up to Aron and gestured at the pot hanging over the fire. She would not meet his eyes, of course. Dropping a crooked curtsey, she reached in and ladled the soupy contents into bowls. One she handed to Aron with another curtsey and a slightly rusty spoon, shaking as if she were afraid of accidentally meeting his hands, and another she took to Julian. Still bound tightly at the wrists, he raised his hands up to receive the bowl. The farm wife shook even more fiercely. She did not give Julian a spoon. He wouldn't have been able to use it. He smiled and thanked her with a sincerity that seemed terrifying to her, and she hobbled away.

"She's sick," Julian hissed from across the room.

Aron looked up from his soup. The woman had

crossed the room to her bed—the farmhouses were so small and crude that they had only one room to act as kitchen, parlor, and bedchamber—and her husband was motioning for her to lie down. He laid a hand on her forehead, his face contorted in an expression of worry. "Why do you care?" Aron murmured, turning away.

He should not have looked at Julian; he knew what expression to expect from him. "Why don't you?"

That night Aron slept fitfully, no bed but a blanket at the hearth, his dreams filled with the vision of Julian, raising his sword, facing the gray-uniformed guard, and being shot, over and over. Time after time the rapier flashed, the gun exploded, and Julian's chest cracked open in a wave of red, and time after time Aron's voice caught as if he were being strangled.

He woke with a metallic clatter: the guards and their guns coming to collect Julian into the special transport. Aron blinked at the light that flooded through the open door and wondered when it had gotten to be morning. The farmer was gone to work, and a huddle in the bed indicated the wife still sleeping. Julian vanished through the doorway and a guard's voice announced that they would leave whenever Mister Jannes was ready.

Ready? Aron laughed. When would that be? He looked down at the luggage that had newly appeared at his feet. Someone had made him the unwanted gift of a newly cleaned suit, scratchy and too small for him, a pair of barber's scissors, and his recovered wig. Grumbling, Aron searched for a mirror, but there wasn't even a glass window in the farmhouse. He had to cut his hair blind.

All this to make a good show for my father, he thought, snipping angrily. And at the thought of his father his hands froze again. All this, all this... His hand clamped on the scissors blade until he felt it bite into his flesh, and he pictured his father, black suit, cold eyes, looking down on his son and saying...

"I'm sorry!" a voice wheezed. Aron jumped and dropped the scissors, their point stabbing the worn wood of the floor. In her bed the farm wife was tossing in a feverish delusion, her eyes wild, staring at Aron as if she knew him. "I'm sorry!" she cried.

Aron shoved the wig onto his poorly trimmed head and darted out the door.

Outside he found a small, closed carriage, two guards on the box and one inside, guarding Julian. The Bioran looked up as Aron climbed in, and stared as if he'd seen a flying cat. "Your hair," he mouthed.

Aron laughed shortly. "You're who we got it from, aren't you?" He positioned himself on the seat and tried to feel comfortable, wishing there was a curtain to pull so he wouldn't have to watch the road dwindle down to Origh. "Do you feel honored?"

Julian shook his head absently, his face a puzzle. "Why?"

The driver shook the horse into motion and the noise of the wheels obscured Aron's reply. "Devil only knows."

Part 4

THE SPY

Time turns in circles that spiral back on itself, turn and speak themselves again, so it is everything we know because we know it again. There is nothing new, everything comes again, and we see it, and we know it all.

But that is Sage talk, and Tod does not understand it. The Magi would not speak of it that way. The Magi keep calendars and record the dates, and in their calendars they've marked the date when they left the land between the river and the mountains, to return to their homeland behind the lake. Under the lake they gather, the Magi in their council, walking under the water without drowning, to look in the mirror at the bottom. They look in the mirror and it shows them the land they left, the land that we came to call Dabion and Karrim and Mandera. The Magi don't care what the names are now. They do not listen to the humans who now live on the land and have for so many years that the human calendars don't record them anymore. The Magi watch to see how the land fares, though they will not spread forth their great powers to protect it. They will not touch the humans. They stay behind their lake and under the lake and will see nothing but water.

The Magi do not understand their countrymen, mad-

men and cripples, the Sages and the Healers, who did not wish to abandon the humans. They do not stay in their homeland, safe behind the spell-walls that protect them from the dark outside, but go out into the old land, as if it is their duty to help those creatures that now trample the earth between the river and the mountains. The Magi do not understand what even a thin-blooded broken half-Sage like me knows. Their calendars have put all of it so far behind them that they cannot see what is to spiral around again.

And then I see the plague, a black spot staining the curves of the spiral, here and there. I have seen it in the dreams, I have always seen it, in the dreams I never used to have, and I did not know what it was. But it is huge and dark and terrible, the blackness and emptiness that my sleep always used to be.

1

ARON WAS TIRED OF THE PEOPLE, THE CROWDS, the noise. His father's house was packed with them, had been every day since he and Julian had arrived. It was his father's plan, he was sure, to keep Aron from ever being alone and able to get into trouble. The house was so crowded he couldn't even get to the front door. The people spilled out into the rear yard, sitting there for hours despite the chill that still lingered in the early spring, waiting for their turn to see the Wondrous Bioran.

That was what Aron had taken to calling Julian, the Wondrous Bioran. He said it to Julian's face, and the idiot didn't even become insulted. He did nothing but laugh, even when Aron said it fifty times in a row like an irritating ten-year-old. Aron was the one who would get tired of it and stomp from the room, leaving Julian to the poking and prodding of clerks and Justices and the odd lucky merchant who managed to worm his way in. If it had been he, Aron would have taken a dive from the window by now.

"The Wondrous Bioran is fawned over by millions,"

Aron recited, fanning out a newspaper and pretending to read from it. "His Munificence brings with him the wisdom of the ages, peace in the provinces, and the cure for the cancer."

Julian leaned toward him over the small table in Aron's room where they retired for a few moments' quiet while eating their midday meal. He reached his arm out, and for half a second Aron imagined that Julian was attacking him with the butter knife. But the Bioran was reaching eagerly for the newspaper.

"I'm making that up," Aron said irritably.

"I know," answered Julian with his usual infuriating calmness. "What sort of book is that?"

"It's a newspaper, you idiot. A daily. It's where the men in the suits tell us what we're supposed to know."

It wasn't the brightest thing to say in a house full of those men in suits. When the door opened and Aron saw his father's head appear, he was sure he'd been heard and was due for some new punishment. He couldn't imagine what other miserable job in what rotten corner of the world was left for him to do. But he saw something else, over his father's shoulder, a face he had not expected. It was the girl from the alley, from the street outside the window of the clerks' office.

Aron half rose in his seat, fire caught in his throat. His ears were clogged with it and he couldn't hear whatever his father uttered to summon Julian back to the crowds that awaited him below.

The door closed. Aron shouted and jumped to his

feet. By the time he threw open the door the girl had disappeared down a hallway.

She was in the house now, though, and he would see her again, every day that he was trapped in the house with her. She wore a cap on her head and kept her eyes lowered and her mouth closed, serving nectar to the visitors and washing porcelain cups in the kitchen. She did not follow Aron; she didn't have to. The house was too small, too crowded with the people who were there morning to night for Aron to hide from her. He supposed she stood outside his door while he slept to make sure he didn't sneak out to light any fires.

"Her name is Toria," his father said the next morning, pausing for twenty seconds in the hallway to speak to his son, "and she has been sent by the Lord Councilor to provide additional security while our guest is receiving visitors. One would not wish him to come to any harm at the hands of men who might fear those who are unlike us."

"Of course, that's why she's here," Aron said, spots of fury forming in front of his eyes.

His father ignored the sarcasm and continued down the hallway.

Toria, as his father was calling her, was everywhere. Aron found her in the kitchen, on the stairs, at the door of the rear yard. She would keep her eyes down as if she didn't see or recognize him, and he would growl at her until she flinched her head away. The suited men went around, taking their drinks from her and handing their coats to her but taking no note of her, too busy with seeing which Justices were in the house and making sure those Justices saw them. Julian was too busy with his admirers, Aron assumed, to notice the girl, either.

Then one day she was gone. Aron went downstairs, into the morning's gathering crowd, but the girl was not there. He looked in the kitchen and couldn't find her. She did not lurk at the back door or at the front playing gatekeeper. Aron ran back up the stairs, turning the door handles of all the empty rooms, sure he would find the one she was hiding in. A rustle ran behind him like the passing of a skirt, but when he turned the runner was gone.

"Did you see that girl?" he demanded when Julian came back to his room to eat that night.

Julian shook his head, his mouth full. He ate with a knife and a spoon, never touching the fork, as if they didn't have forks in Biora. "Haven't seen anyone but the visitors. Justices? Greater Justices? How do I tell them apart?"

"You don't tell," Aron grumbled, watching the Bioran push greens on his spoon with the knife. "You *know* them. Barbarian."

Julian looked up then. That expression of his made it absolutely clear which one of them was the barbarian. "Who is this girl, then?"

Aron growled. "I don't know. She's following me."

"Hmm," Julian mused. "Why would she be doing that?"

"Don't ask me, ask my father." Aron kicked his chair

back from the table and stood, leaving his dinner untouched.

As he left the room and walked out into a house that
was finally almost quiet, he heard Julian say behind him,
"Your father's gone out."

From the corner of his eye Aron saw a figure dash
down the stairs, dark hair moving under a cap. Aron
jumped after her, two stairs at a time, tripping at the bottom. When he recovered he looked up, turning to each
side to find where the figure had gone. There were shadows in every direction, moving in the dark hallways.
Voices came from the kitchen. He stepped toward them,
trying to recognize the sounds: the cook, a scullery
maid, someone else? Behind him was the squeak of a
door. He spun and leapt to the corridor that held his father's rooms.

The first room was the library, and the door was
cracked open. Aron leaned against the jamb and peered
in. He didn't breathe. A long row of open shelving divided the room in a line parallel to the door, and there
was no one in front of it. Aron eased the door open just
enough to pass through it. He stepped close to the
shelves, quietly, rising on his toes until his feet cramped,
and peered over a row of books. He couldn't see anyone
on the other side.

Something hit the floor where he couldn't see it.
Aron's throat seized up and he froze. The pain in his feet
ran up through his legs. Slowly, achingly, he moved to
the end of the row, trying not to huff with noisy breath.
Another sound startled him, but he recognized it as the

rustling of pages. He looked around the end of the shelving. On the other side the window was open, and a gust had blown a book down. It lay now on the floor, the wind riffling through its leaves.

Aron went to the window and looked out. The yard on the side was small, hardly large enough to walk through, and the wall that separated it from the house next door was so tall it was impossible to see over. It was a ridiculous waste of land. Aron thought if he leaned out, he could reach the side wall with his hand.

When he did lean out, he saw a flutter to his left. A curtain was blowing out from another window, open to the room next door.

Aron climbed unceremoniously through the library window and crept through the narrow yard like a crab, keeping his head low. The open window with the fluttering curtain was in his father's office, and his father's office was always locked. Someone had wedged a piece of wax into the track so the window could not close all the way, so that it could not latch. Inside the office someone was shaking at the drawer handles. His father always kept them locked. When Aron raised his head, only a fraction, to peer over the sill, he saw Toria yanking on the drawers in frustration.

It wasn't he who was followed now. Aron watched Toria wherever she went, hiding behind doorways when she turned, looking down on her from the banister above. He watched her take a file to the lock on his father's bedchamber, one night after the household had turned in. He crept in after her, watched her plunder the drawers of his father's bureau. She was looking for keys to the office desk, he thought, though she wouldn't find them there. Now Toria was on her knees, reaching under the bed skirt, searching for any chest that might be stored there. Aron moved close to her, his feet no longer unused to walking on his toes. He hid himself behind a tied-back bed curtain while Toria's head was buried in fabric. She came up coughing with the dust, and sat at the edge of the bed, her back to Aron, her head lowered.

Aron thought it was impressive that she hardly flinched when he set his hands around her throat. "I thought spies were supposed to be better at this," he whispered.

He could feel the breath in her throat, tight as she drew it inside the ring of his hands. "Did you?" she answered, trying to be casual, but there was a crack in her voice.

"Looking for something? Does my father know what you're doing this time?"

Aron wasn't quite expecting her to turn, slowly, inside his hands. She faced him, looking into his eyes, pressing herself closer to him. She was trying to manipulate him, he was sure of it, steadily pulling close until she slipped her throat out of his hands, but somehow he didn't find himself stopping her. He could feel her breath on his chin, he could see the crooked teeth as she opened her mouth to speak, and he listened to her. "No, he doesn't. But do you want to? Don't you want to know what he's doing? Don't you want to know what he's hiding?"

He cursed her under his breath as he left the room

and went up the stairs, calling her every name he could think of—loudly enough, apparently, that Julian heard him. He saw the Bioran open his door and peer out, bleary-eyed, his hair white in the dimness and tangled. Aron ignored him. He went to the farthest room in the upper corridor. The door was not locked, but it was never opened. It had not been opened since his mother died. Things were kept there just as she had left them, her clothes, the basket of her embroidery, and her set of keys to all the rooms in the house and all the furniture inside them.

Aron went in, straight to the wardrobe. It opened with a creak, sticking in its frame, unused for so long. There was a drawer in the bottom, Aron remembered. He pulled it with some effort and looked in, but it was too dark to see. With his hands he rooted around, and gasped as something stuck him sharply.

"What is it?" a voice asked behind him, but Aron didn't hear it. He'd found the pieces of the mirror he'd broken when he was ten.

"Aron," Julian whispered, so suddenly close that Aron flinched and spun to face him. "What is it?"

The light behind Julian, framing the white halo of his hair, made him look like a ghost. Aron sidled away from him and backed out of his mother's door. Not until he was in the hallway, swaying on his feet, did he find the keys in his blood-smeared hands.

"Money, of course," Toria said, crouching at the desk in the office and going through each key until she found the one that fit. "Muhrroh's paying him off. What I don't know is why. What's Jannes giving Muhrroh?"

Aron swallowed. "Is that where he's gone tonight?"

Toria shrugged, looking up at him with wide eyes. "I don't know," she breathed, leaning toward him. "Can you find out?"

I can find out, Aron thought. He knew about his father's liquor—he would find a way to use that. The scratches on his hands stung, making his hands tingle like they'd been numb. Anger blotted his vision and throbbed in his ears, but this time he would not let it paralyze him. His heart jumped as the lock gave and the spy opened the drawer to his father's secrets.

2

IT WAS THE SAME DAMNED SAGE WHO CAME TO HER when T called, the one disguised as Public Force, one of the two who had put out the fire Aron had set in the yard. She knew she should have found someone else to deliver the message, a normal operative or even a street urchin who could be bribed with a penny, but she needed someone she could trust and she needed someone fast.

He came up to her with a smile, like they were old friends, finding her in the alley behind the barracks. She refused to tell him how relieved she was that he'd done that, sparing her the trouble of going to the door and meeting all those other guards and probably having to bend over for at least three or four of them. She was too mad at him even to think about her relief. The first thing he said to her was, "Why are we here, Thessa?"

"Stop it," she hissed. "It's not my name!"

The Sage smiled easily, going on as if he hadn't heard her, and as if no time had passed since he had seen her last. "Why are we here? You thought I would ask why *you* are here, Toria. Did she ask you, the Sage? Do you know whose blood you have, Tanie?"

T was about to shout at him for wasting her time, but his words caught at her, those mad words she ignored so often. *Why are we here, Toria? Tanie.* Her ears rang with the sudden pounding of her blood. He knew she was double-agenting. Muhrroh would find out. Worse, Rayner would find out. Her hands went cold and she forgot why she had called the Sage. But Sages were mad, she tried to reassure herself. They were all mad, every one of them, mad enough never to put two and two together. If her message would be safe, she would be safe; no one else knew what she was doing.

She rarely even admitted to herself what she was doing. The two of them, Muhrroh and Rayner, had recruited her at the same time. She might have chosen one if only one had approached her. It wasn't her fault that they both took notice of her, when she came to Insigh six years ago and started asking questions. Kerk had spoken to her first, of course; he cornered her in the public house, but she didn't know he had a reason to notice her. She hadn't known who he was, she'd thought he was just another man who would buy her a bowl of mush if she picked up her skirt for him. But others had been watching her as well, the Sages, Muhrroh's Sor'raian operatives in Insigh. She might have heard them scratching at her mind if she'd stopped asking questions long enough to listen. But they felt her and they knew she could hear them, and they told Muhrroh.

Muhrroh sent someone for her the same day, fetching her out of the public house where Kerk had left her moments before and taking her to his own rooms. He needed her, he said, from across the room where he sat in a chair and didn't even try to touch her. She could speak to the Sages and he needed her. It was unimaginable that anyone could need her for that. She'd spent her entire life pretending that she couldn't talk to them, that she couldn't hear them, that her mother hadn't been mad enough to be one of them. Now Muhrroh wanted her to speak to them intentionally. It was outrageous, yet the thought of it pulled at her. To command them, to control them—it would prove she herself was sane, wouldn't it? And Muhrroh said he needed her. He would pay her and shelter her and treat her like his daughter, *his very daughter,* if she spoke to them for him.

When she got back to the public house Kerk was waiting for her. He didn't know where she had gone and was upset about that. He pulled out a purse filled with silver coins, more money than she had ever seen in her life. He spilled it on the table casually, no one left in the tavern at that late hour to see it. It could be hers, he said, if she worked for him, for his employer. Then he told her who his employer was. She almost stopped breathing. It was the same man she'd come to Insigh looking for.

"Don't worry," the Sage in his gray uniform said. "Our old man won't find out."

"Muhrroh," T uttered, feeling her hands go cold again. Speaking in her head, and now knowing what she was thinking. They weren't supposed to do that, to read her like she was one of them.

"Muhrroh," the Sage echoed, rolling the R's. "Muhrrrroh. These humans have no sense of music, not even when they name themselves with it. He won't know about the other one. He will not call you again. You are going east with the boy."

T chewed her mouth until she could spit blood at him. He was making her angry. "What do you mean he won't call me again? Answer that, can you? And if you know so much, you must know why I called you in the first place, don't you? I shouldn't have to tell you the message."

The Sage nodded with a laugh. "All the plans are in place. The sun turns and his life ends, that is all he sees. He is almost right, almost. Why do you want to spy on the boy?"

T pushed the Sage, feeling through the oversized jacket the thinness of his bones. They never fought back. "Just send Rayner the message," she said, and stomped away before he could tell her anything else.

Rayner answered her the next day. There was a knock at the kitchen window, and she turned to see Kerk there.

"How did you get here so fast?" she demanded, when the household had finally turned in and she could go to the rear yard unseen. It was a day and a half from Origh to Insigh, one way. A rider might make it in a single whole day if he could get fresh horses, but even the fastest rider couldn't get to Insigh and back in a day. The Sage she'd stolen from his usual assignment must have spoken to another one, and him to another one, across Dabion in a chain of insane telepathy. She wondered who was at the end, and if Rayner knew one of his messengers was a madman.

Kerk scowled and did not answer her question. "He

told me you had a proposal. He's behind me, riding in a carriage. He'll be here tomorrow. He sent me to get you."

In the dark streets T recognized that they were heading for the Great Hall. Kerk knew the way well; Rayner must have worked there before. "It's not private here," T complained as they entered the deserted Hall. "I've been followed here before. And what will the LJ do if I'm missing in the morning?"

"He'll fire you," Kerk answered in a bored voice, leading her through a twist of tunnels and down a stairway into a corridor where T had never been before.

"But I have to stay in the house! The bloody plan won't work if I'm not!" T shoved at Kerk's arm, her wrists jarring as it did not give. "I'm always following you, going where you tell me to go."

They came to a door and Kerk swung it open so fast she didn't see it. He seized her elbow and wrenched it as he swung her inside, closing the door hard and pushing her against the inside of it. With a hand under her chin he lifted her head back, wedged a knee between her legs and pushed her higher. He pressed his face to her throat until it cut off her breath, and she felt his teeth on her skin. "Yes," he hissed. "Yes, you are."

Then he stepped back and dropped her. She couldn't get her feet under her, and she landed in a pile on the floor.

Rage burned sour in her mouth and she imagined him strangling her, raping her, biting her throat out like a dog. But he left her where she lay on the floor and sauntered to the old desk across the room, sat down, leaned back with his ankles crossed on the desk. He made no other move on her at all—he'd never done it once. Every other man had, the younger ones, the commoners. The only ones who hadn't were Rayner, Muhrroh, the LJ. Kerk thought he was up with that sort, the ones who wouldn't dirty themselves on a street girl, and T hated him even more. If he would just put her on her back like every other man, she could get the upper hand with him, at least for a minute. She'd get the upper hand on Aron Jannes that way, she knew it. If she could get Kerk that way, just for a second, it would be long enough to cut his throat. She screamed in acid frustration and pounded her feet. Kerk only looked at her, sneering. There was a stone on the floor beside her, a piece of masonry worn out of the wall, or something, she didn't see what. She just picked it up and threw it at Kerk as hard as she could. He snapped up then, fast. She couldn't even see if it had hit him or missed him. He reached her in a couple of steps and struck her on the head and she couldn't see anything.

"I'm disappointed in you, Kerk," a voice was saying blurrily when she woke up. "It's not like you to lose your temper like that. The poor girl doesn't have too many ideas. It won't do to knock them out of her."

She tried to groan her anger but her head split in pain with the vibration in her throat.

The figure that crouched in front of her finally began to look like Rayner. It took longer for T to figure out he wasn't crouching but sitting on the chair, and she was lying on the desk. A door slammed, pounding in her head, and she winced.

"Yes," Rayner's voice soothed. "My terrible assistant is

gone. I *am* sorry, Tanie. He will be punished suitably. I will have to find some way not to pay him."

"I know why Muhrroh paid Jannes," the girl croaked.

Rayner paused then, looking at her with interest. Without his voice her head could almost stop ringing.

"Jannes is smuggling alcohol."

"Trafficking, my dear," Rayner corrected. "He isn't carrying any of it himself, only arranging for its transport." He smiled at her with large eyes, like she was an idiot or a cripple. "But I know that already. You didn't bring me all the way down here to tell me that."

T pounded the desk with her fist, her head lurching as the surface jolted beneath her. "That's what—" she growled through clenched teeth, "he's giving—*Muhrroh!* He's smuggling the alcohol to Muhrroh, and that's what Muhrroh is paying him for!"

She had never seen a face actually look like light was dawning on it. Rayner was amazed, and finally silent. And then he did exactly what she hoped he'd do. His forehead began to furrow, and one finger on his hand began to shake. "But why?"

And that was when T answered, Thessa Woodbridge, the girl from some tiny village in District Four that existed only to make the Justice's fields pretty, who had come to the capital of Dabion when she was eighteen, knowing no one and nothing but a name, the name her grandfather struggled to remember, the name of the Justice who'd gotten her on a madwoman. The man who gave her her sane blood. Thessa had finally found the one thing that would bind her to him, the thing that would prove her value, the thing that would make her *his* daughter and not the mad-woman's. "I can find out," she said. "I can find out why Jannes did it. I've got hold of his son."

A slow smile crept slyly across Rayner's face. "You can spy on Aron Jannes?"

T nodded, her brains shaking painfully inside her head. "I got him to find the records for me himself. There's got to be more, letters or something, an order from Muhrroh. We can find it."

Rayner almost beamed at her, almost looked straight into her eyes and smiled, but his gaze was pulled away by some other thought. "You can get Jannes's son on your side. Then you can get him on my side?"

T nodded furiously through the pain. She could do anything for Rayner.

"Good. I have a use for him." He stood then, too fast for her to sit up and stay level with his eyes. "Stay close to him, Tanie." Then he slipped a hand into a drawer on the wrong side of the desk, some hidden panel, and took out a fold of something. "You'll be going back to Jannes's house now. I'll make sure you can get in, I'll send some-one to explain your absence. Take something back for me, won't you? Put it somewhere the Lord Justice will find it."

T sat up unsteadily and unfolded the thing with shaky hands. It was a piece of fabric stuck through with stitches, and by turning it around she could make out the shape of some flower, some weed, the likes of which she'd spent the first eighteen years of her life pulling out of the Justices' fields.

3

THIS PLACE WAS NOT HIS EITHER, JULIAN THOUGHT, and that was odd. The place seemed to live for him, breathe for him. If he was not in it, the rain would not come. When he woke in the morning it became alive, and when he went to bed at night it curled up under the trees and slept like the creatures who hid from winter. He looked out the window one night and saw nothing moving, nothing at all, and the house was silent around him.

One night, though, he had heard Aron in the halls. Aron did not sleep, either. Something haunted him in the shadows. There were many shadows in the house, Julian was learning. Even when it was full of sun and light and awake with the people inside, there were still shadows lurking in the corners, around the visitors' legs. Julian thought they brought them in under their coats.

What had the house done before he'd arrived, Julian wondered. Had it been asleep?

Still, the people were interesting, though he was careful not to get buried in the black of their coats. They stared at him with their large dark eyes, peering at his face and into his ears, pulling at his hair and squinting at the roots of the strands they plucked out. They poked at his skin with their fingers, scratched it lightly with their nails. They brought tapes to measure the width of his neck and his skull and the length of his limbs. They watched him eat and waited for the results in his chamber pot. They would have watched him sleep if Lord Justice Jannes had not turned them out at night, and if they'd been able, they would have lifted his lids to peer in at his dreams. They were fascinated by everything he did.

No, Julian thought, not by everything he did, because he did nothing. They were fascinated by the hairs on his head, by the skin he was born with, like the Aunts. It was still no offering to speak of. They did not care what he could do. They never asked about the rapier that was taken away from him in Karrim; he never had a chance to say it was something he could do, a skill he'd been taught and he'd learned and he was good at. He was proud. But his pride meant nothing. His ability with the sword was worth as little as his ability to read. Both had failed him. The men in the black coats only wanted to see the color of his hair, which he couldn't have changed if he tried.

The Lord Justice, Aron's father, was not often present. He was in the house, Julian saw him, and he watched each man who came in like some bird of prey, or one that feared being preyed upon. Nothing passed in or out without his seeing it, but he was never there when the visitors bundled into the parlor to examine Julian. Once he left the house and did not return until the next day, but Julian hardly noticed he was gone. Aron was never in the parlor, either. At mealtimes Julian found him sulking in his room, and when Julian went to bed in the room next door he sometimes heard his friend pacing sleeplessly.

Julian would have helped him if he could have. If there had been a rock he could pull Aron behind, he would have, but the shadows that haunted Aron were not so solid as a warrior with an upraised sword.

One visitor he liked. After Julian had been thoroughly measured and cataloged, after every hair on his head had been counted three times over, a man in a very fine black suit with a collection of guards in uniforms behind him came to the Jannes house. He was Lord Justice Zein, he said, and he smiled calmly and asked if he could speak with Julian. He sat down and asked a kitchen servant to bring tea and two cups.

"A rare thing, this tea," Zein said. "We've made our common tea for years from flowers and leaves, but this sort is made from spices native to Marlind. They came into the Five Countries centuries ago, with the Alliance traders. Manderan traders, of course, and their taste in tea was terribly scorned when the Alliance failed. But some of the Justices had gotten a taste for it by then, and they started growing it here, on one small parcel in Kar-rim. You've worked in Karrim, haven't you?"

Julian smiled and nodded. The sound of the man speaking—speaking to him, as if he had ears that could hear instead of ones that were just two inches long with disconnected lobes—was a beautiful sound. And Julian saw something in the man as well, very clearly, as if it were an object one could wear like a hat or a wig. The Lord Justice was not home here, no more than Julian was. There was a restlessness in him: lonely, aching, searching for the place that was his.

Zein wanted to talk to him about books. Did he have books in Biora? What did he read? Were there schools? Julian was sad to tell him that there were no schools, that he was the only one he knew who read at all. Seeing the disappointment in the Lord Justice's face along with the homesickness there was enough to bring tears to Julian's eyes. But he told Zein about the books he had read, about Dal'Nilaran and the elements of matter, and the Lord Justice lit up like Julian himself was the sun.

"Is that what he said?" Zein asked. The longing in his voice was the same as what Julian felt when he was first learning to read, the hope that soon he would know something that would take the pain away. He couldn't bear to tell the Lord Justice that his hope had failed. "Those were Dal'Nilaran's words? The elements are the same, earth, air, fire, water, all of the same matter? Fascinating. What else was there?"

Julian thought about light, the waves and the dust and the wars that came of it, but they were too terrible to speak of.

Others interrupted them then, other visitors with their tapes and books fat with notes. They bowed to the Lord Justice uncertainly, then went about their work. All the words Julian had spoken, all the things he could do and the things he knew, broke up in the air like smoke in wind.

There were a few other things that Julian could do,

though. Some of the Justices who came brought their servants with them, women to fill the kitchen and prepare food for the many visitors. As Julian stepped into the kitchen one morning, earlier than he expected to find anyone there, he saw one of those servants, a young woman with strands of dark hair that were already pulled out of the knot under her kerchief and strewn about the damp skin of her throat. The warmth of the early kitchen fire that she was stoking burnished her skin with a coppery glow, and when she saw Julian in the doorway, watching her, the color grew still deeper.

The elderly cook that Jannes employed shouted to the young woman to go draw water, not looking up from the table where she was working. The young woman stooped to pick up the buckets, showing Julian the rich curve of her breasts as she leaned toward him, and as she rushed out to the rear door, she caught Julian by the wrist. They crossed the small yard to the gate that let onto the alley behind the house, where dawn-going wagons had laid down piles of firewood and filled the water cisterns. Julian would not go through the gate, into the alley where he might be seen, but he watched her through a narrow opening, and pushed it wider to let her back through when she returned. She rewarded him with a kiss. He took the water from her hands, carried it to the door of the house, and set it on the step, then with his hands about her waist he led her under the shade of a tree growing close to the wall. She linked her arms around his neck and leaned against the building, an arm's length from the window where they could hear the cook muttering, "Fool of a girl, what's taking her so long?" The girl laughed, and Julian covered her mouth with his to quiet her. She drew her legs around him and he raised her up against him, lifted her clothes, swallowed her gasp and her light cries. The restlessness in his blood rushed out of him and for a moment, his heart was still. But the moment ended and he had to let her down, and she laughed as she ran back to the door, took up the buckets of water, and disappeared inside.

As he passed through the halls he was followed by the chime of female laughter. He saw faces watching him through doorways, eyes lowered with shyness or shining for a second before they turned away. They all watched him because of his beauty, he knew; but those few who followed him into quiet corners, pantries and closets, shadows under trees, he thought they followed him because of what he could do. He had a few skills, and some were appreciated. That was something like home. Those moments when he held a woman in his arms and tried to breathe her in and soak her up through his skin were something like peace. He remembered the women in the villages in Cassile between Beth and the river, how he had found quiet barns and empty fields in which to lie, where he could watch the women above him and see the colors of their skin and the shape of their breasts and the fall of their hair over their shoulders, the length of their necks as they tilted them back and the contours of their faces under the light of the sun or the moon. Here in the house in Dabion there was no time for undressing, and Julian could only drink the scent of the women at the curve of their necks, never seeing them, never touching their skin with his. Then he had to let them go, and they hurried away, leaving him with the echo of their laughter and the gorgeous sadness knotting in his chest.

There was no harvest dance in these countries; here the dance was always in secret. Once, though, when he led a girl upstairs and down the hallway, near the door that was never opened, Aron saw him. Julian was kneeling on the floor, facing the length of the hall with the woman across his lap, and when he finally opened his eyes as he surfaced from the moment's depths, he saw a door open by a crack. The woman rose and left him, not seeing, but when she was gone the door opened wider, and when Julian rose and went to it he saw Aron standing within.

His friend's face wore a mocking sneer that nearly covered the hunger on it, and he spoke with a breath of contempt. "You're such a dog."

Julian raised his chin, drawing himself up so that he looked down on Aron from a greater height. He knew Aron hated that. But Aron could not accuse. Julian himself had heard cries from the room next door, late one night; fearing something was wrong, he'd hurried out and seen a woman leaving Aron's room. She was one who worked for Lord Justice Jannes and was always in the house, and Aron did not seem to like her. "For you she's a guard," he told Julian, "but for me she's a spy." Julian had not understood that. When the woman saw Julian in the hallway that night she stopped with a small shock, but then she stepped to the banister of the stairs nearby, and she leaned over it so her back was to him, and she raised her tangled skirts to bare her legs. Her hair hung down into the vault of the stairwell, but through it Julian could see a trace of her face, and it wore the same terrible weariness of the women at the work camp in Karrim. Not once had he touched those women, and he would not touch this one. He reached for her skirt and let it back down, and he turned away as she watched him in confusion.

"And Toria?" Julian said to Aron's challenge.

Aron spat through his teeth. "She's a whore. They know what to do." He waited for Julian's ignorance to show itself in the blankness on his white face. "I'm not leaving bastards around. The women you're sowing don't know any better. They're getting stuffed with your babies, and their proper suit-wearing employers will throw them out to save themselves the embarrassment, and your pretty little women and their squalling bastards will starve in the streets. Those that aren't drowned like unwanted puppies." Aron rolled his eyes then, batting his lashes in a female parody as he sang in a high voice, "Oh, but it was worth it, just to be blessed by the cock of the Wondrous Bioran."

Julian backed away, and when he closed himself in his own room he found he was shaking.

That night he dreamed he was a dog, a bitch lying on his side as he nursed a litter of puppies, and one by one they were taken from him and thrown in the river. Each one had the face of Davi.

When he woke he hurried to the kitchen to find water to splash on his face, trying to wash out the pictures from his dream. The laughter that came from behind him was the same laughter he'd heard all through the last few weeks, the high chime of women's voices, but now he heard a hollowness in it, less like true laughter and more like the mocking giggle of Aron's parody. When Julian raised his head and looked at them they turned their eyes away so he could not truly see them. He thought now that they did not truly see him, either.

He listened to their words in the halls, heard them whispering to each other outside the door of the parlor where the visitors continued to map him. They spoke to each other of his beauty, how he looked like the kings in the old legends, the fairies on the shores of the lake. Taking his hand they could step into the tales and out of the square white walls. He would be crowned, certainly, some of them said, in the voices of children. The Justices would recognize him as the long-ago king returned, and they would give him a palace, and he would marry the women and take them away.

You are beautiful, his mother's voice echoed from a great distance. He had clung to his beauty when his faith in the books was taken away from him, when his sword was taken away from him. Beauty had always been his gift. A worthless gift; it was then and it was now. It had failed him and his passion had failed him, as all his other skills had. He was alone and restless and without a home.

When one of the Justices did come to him, leading his young handmaiden by the elbow, it was not to give Julian a crown. He brought Julian and the woman both to Jannes's office, demanding to be seen though Jannes never wanted to see anyone. "Your guest has wronged me, my lord," the Justice said angrily. "He has gotten my servant with child. I am not going to suffer the scandal of a ruined servant, and I am certainly not going to bear the expense of raising a fatherless child in my household. I demand reparation."

The Lord Justice looked at Julian, shaking his head very slightly, and his mouth turned in the faintest echo of the sneer his son had worn. Then he sat upright, looking up at his subordinate Justice as if he were looking down at him. "Your honor," he said, "I believe you have perceived this event incorrectly. You and your peers wished to examine every physical characteristic of the Bioran, and you have succeeded. Nearly. Your assessment cannot be complete without examining his venereal functions. That he has impregnated this woman is proof of this function. Fruit of this union can only give you more opportunity for scientific research. I recommend you do keep this woman in your household. I even offer her to you, along with her offspring—which, you will see, is rightly my property, as its father is my guest— without demand of payment. If you fear scandal, you can suggest that you arranged the union for purposes of scholarship. My guest will not contradict you." Jannes glared at Julian as he said these words, and Julian bowed his head meekly to express that he would not contradict. A sickness welled in his stomach, hearing the men speak of the property they were exchanging. He could not be a father, he did not know how. He was Bioran. The sickness in his belly was the only echo he would ever feel of the child that grew in the woman's belly, the child of his own blood.

Jannes dismissed Julian to his room and Julian saw no one else that day. The next morning he did not want to rise, and he buried his head in the bedclothes so that he could not hear the people calling for him. Someone came in, though, and Julian looked out to see Lord Justice Zein.

"Forgive me for waking you," the Lord Justice said gently as he took a chair beside Julian's small bed. "I was told you were feeling ill, but I did not wish to return to Tanasigh without saying good-bye."

"You're leaving?" Julian murmured, sitting up in the bed and wrapping the linens close around his body with a self-consciousness he had never before felt.

Zein nodded, the bobbing of his wig throwing sad shadows on his face. "I am to spend one more week in Insigh to complete my investiture, then I return home."

He fell silent, and Julian heard the emptiness that echoed around the word *home*. "What is Tanasigh like?" Julian offered.

"A fine city," the Lord Justice replied in an official tone. Then he looked around to make sure the room was still empty, and leaned in close like a whispering child. "But it isn't really home. You're from a mountainous land. Do you want to know a secret?" He smiled eagerly and sadly. "So am I."

4

L ORD JUSTICE JANNES HAD NOT BEEN HAPPY THE
first time he saw Zein on his doorstep. The newly
appointed Lord Justice of District Three was apparently
making his rounds, doing what all good Justices did and
making sure everyone saw him doing it. At the moment that was coming to Jannes's house to examine the
Bioran.

Jannes hated the crowds. They were a burden and an
inconvenience, eating his food and dirtying his furniture, demanding attention that Jannes did not have time
to give. Worse, they could easily hide a spy or an assassin.
Muhrroh had offered the services of Toria to protect him
from this threat, a dubious offer. Jannes doubted that
she would be much use against any sort of armed at-
tacker, and he was concerned that Muhrroh was reas-
signing the very courier who had always brought Jannes
his payments. At the moment, the exchange of purified
alcohol was the only thing that gave Jannes the least
hope that the mad Lord Councilor valued him enough
to try to keep him alive.

The best thing would be to get the Bioran out of the

house. Jannes had no interest in Julian himself; he had only affected an interest in Bioranism while Muhrroh had, and Muhrroh demonstrated that interest no longer. The boy was nothing but a liability, attracting crowds and scandal. Jannes was almost afraid that Rayner would make an appearance to view Julian; instead, he sent his puppet.

"Do not think you can fool me," he'd said upon Zein's first entrance, after ushering him into his office and closing the door. "I know as well as you that your master is not the harmless idiot he seems. He may do his best to trap me but I will not let you do his work. You are dancing for the wrong puppeteer."

"My master?" Zein asked, with more weariness than artifice.

Rayner had never shown outright support for Zein, but in the matter of District Three there was gold involved, and where gold was involved, Rayner was involved. Jannes had favored Athal for the appointment simply to oppose Rayner. Not that it had done any good. Rayner had manipulated the vote and Zein had been invested on the first day of the new year. "Your master," Jannes repeated. "The one to whom you will pay the tithe from your first delivery of Alaçan gold currency."

Zein nodded, making no attempt to deny or evade. "I am grateful to Justice Rayner for his support," he said, "inasmuch as he has helped me attain my office. I am not bound to him, though. I owe him nothing, and I would never make the mistake of trusting him." His face was so open, his voice so clear, that Jannes could almost believe him. He allowed him entrance to his house and access to the Bioran, and he was one of few visitors to whom Jannes granted permission to return repeatedly. He was an interesting man, this quiet, sad Lord Justice, and Jannes wished to watch him more carefully.

He needed to watch Zein more carefully. It was important to prove that District Three was entirely safe from Rayner's influence before Jannes proceeded with his plan.

Jannes was long in the habit of sending Aron away; the farther, the better. The boy was unable to avoid trouble, and Jannes was unable to tolerate him. Something had gone wrong. Jannes did not know what had happened, but the infant he had once seen drowsing in its mother's arms had turned into a screaming child, then turned into a troublesome student, then turned into an adolescent who set fires. Distance did not solve the problem; Muhrroh's operative Kuramin had reported on his last, most destructive fire at the Insigh School, and Jannes had reluctantly decided to bring the boy home for closer keeping. That decision was only followed by another fire, and Jannes responded with greater distance. He was assured that the fire at the Karrimian work camp had been an accident, sparked by a poorly extinguished pipe falling from the pocket of a supply clerk. Jannes almost believed it. But he did not like having Aron in the house, lurking sullenly in the corridors, his anger a palpable cloud weighting down his head and shoulders. What was he angry at? Jannes was stymied in the very asking of the question. He had never been able to ask Ciceline. He had never asked the Black Force guard—Kar was her name, he thought, Edith Kar, Elzith Kar—who had taken care of Aron for a short time some years ago. She had gotten the boy under control, Jannes remembered vaguely. She might have been able to penetrate the mystery of his anger.

But Jannes's paternal discomfort was no longer the only issue. There was danger in Jannes's house, danger that only increased as Julian remained, and Jannes was running out of places to send Aron. Cassile, Mandera, Azassi—those places were outside Jannes's realm of influence, and where he had no influence, he could not watch for Rayner. Siva was the only place remote enough that Rayner was unlikely to have any reach, and Jannes shuddered at the thought of his son in the heat of that desert, at the mercy of tigers and savages Jannes could not imagine. The shelter had to be closer. The best remaining option was Mount Alaz, a small and unimportant city in the extreme corner of District Three, in the mountains of the Alaçan region. That was to say, it had been unimportant, until Zein's appointment became an issue, and with it the Alaçan gold.

So Zein had to be watched. If he was the sole manager of the gold that came from his mountains, untouched by Rayner until the newly minted currency reached Insigh, then Mount Alaz might be safe. Jannes could easily make the excuse that he was sending Aron to foster in the Alaçan city and apprentice to its master, and that he was sending Julian to the mountainous environs because the sunny valleys of Dabion were having a poor effect on his health. Most of the Justices would dutifully accept both lies, despite knowing the rumors of Aron's complete unsuitability for any sort of work, despite having examined the Bioran. One did not question such things openly. Rayner would doubtless question them, but if Mount Alaz was safe, then Rayner would have only Jannes as a target for his malice. And Jannes would have only himself to worry about.

When Zein came to Jannes's office and asked for his leave, Jannes was not willing to let him go. "You are not due in Insigh until the next meeting of the Circle," Jannes insisted. "That is two days away. You should stay in Origh, ride up with me. Yes, send back that hired carriage. I will recommend you to my own outfitter after the meeting. You need a carriage and a team that suit your station."

"I have already bidden Julian farewell," Zein uttered, somewhat dazed by Jannes's sudden show of attention.

That indicated questioning, Jannes thought. It indicated mistrust. Who would be more likely to mistrust, Jannes wondered, a man who resisted Rayner or a man controlled by Rayner? "Premature," he answered. "The boy begged illness? Nonsense. I will have him roused and dressed. You may take him to the library. There are texts there you will wish to discuss."

Zein relented, Jannes gave his orders to a servant, and he retired to his bedchamber with a sigh of relief. He had bought himself more time. There was little enough of it to spare. At his basin he removed his wig and splashed cold water on his face. His nerves were wearing thin, quite thin. When he looked up from the basin and eyed himself in the mirror he was dismayed at the heavy circles beneath his eyes. He could not afford to lose his wits, not yet. It would happen soon enough.

That morning he had opened his desk, the locked drawer where he kept his private records of the business he managed in Karrim. On top of the books that would mean arrest, banishment, or the heathen gods knew what if they were found, Jannes had seen a strange bit of fabric. His blood had gone cold even before he recognized it. It was a square of embroidery cloth, yellowed with age, where a few flowers of some sort had been stitched. It was unfinished; a once-red thread hung loose from the open outline of a petal. Ciceline would not have left her work in that state. She would not have, and as Jannes reluctantly recalled, she had not.

It was thirteen years ago that he had last seen this piece. No, he corrected himself, he had not actually seen it. He had seen the hoop in which it had recently been fixed, still in his wife's hand, empty. She was sitting on a chair in the yard, her basket of thread lying on its side, its contents strewn and stamped in the grass. Ciceline would never leave her things in such disarray. Jannes frowned as he approached her, not listening to the hysterical weeping of the servingwoman who cowered in the kitchen, covering her ears with her hands. He didn't recognize any of those things as the clues that they were. When he stood beside his wife, seeing her body slumped and her head bowed, he did not realize what had happened, not until he saw the empty embroidery hoop clutched in her icy hand, and the needle that her thread had been torn out of, stabbed through a finger that no longer bled.

"What's wrong?"

Aron wedged himself closer against the desk, bowing his head over the papers that were spread out on the floor and pretending he didn't hear Toria. He had read everything he could find in his father's desk, emptied every drawer they had a key to, rifled through every file and ledger. He knew every detail about his father's trafficking of alcohol, every hidden still on every parcel in Karrim. He had read chart after chart listing bushels of grain and gallons of product and costs and profits, until he was swimming in numbers. At the end it was all worthless. The numbers were meaningless to anyone but Jannes. The names and the parcels would do Aron no good; he had still found no way to report them and no one he could report them to. In so many days of hunting through his father's office, he had found nothing he could use. The very idea had been ridiculous.

"What are you finding?" Toria pressed. "Why aren't you reading?" She fretted and inched closer to him, cornering him against the desk. Each time his interest seemed to flag she got frantic and tried to lure him with another drawer, a new cabinet. It was no longer working. Aron had seen everything already. "What is it?" she crooned, changing her tone, and she leaned close against him in a clumsy attempt at playing the seductress. She was determined to snare his attention, one way or the other.

That was the problem with this anger, Aron thought. It had gone too far beyond heat. Inside his father's house with its expensively burning hearths, he felt as cold as the snow in Karrim. Toria's offer did not even touch him. When he threw an elbow to back her away from him he hardly felt it meet her in the stomach, and the yelp she let out was almost inaudible. Spots formed in front of his eyes again. He was stuck. He could do nothing. His mad passion for secrets had gone nowhere. His father, he supposed, was to blame, and it only made him angrier, and the anger only froze him more solidly.

It took Toria's dramatic gasp of breath for him to realize there was a noise at the door. The lock was turning. His father was coming in.

Let him come, Aron thought for an instant, the words chiseling themselves slowly into his mind. It would save him having to move. But Toria grabbed his arm and pulled him toward the open window. They tumbled through it onto the grass, and Aron struck his head on the ground.

It was like rotting from the inside. Aron was certain, if he lay there long enough, his mouth shut firmly against the air, the anger would hollow him out. If only time would stop and let him rot. Toria crawled ahead, toward the library window and their escape, and hissed at Aron to follow her. He lay in the grass, listening to his father's rustling of the disheveled papers inside his office. Time moved forward; something had to break. His father would discover him and the world would crash down on him, or he would blow open on the force of the anger. His heart wavered, loud and unsteady in his ears.

Then a noise from Toria, a very strange noise. It shocked Aron into movement, turned her into the thing he was angry at, the source of the sound. He dragged himself forward on his elbows until he reached her. She was crouched below the library window, her head raised just over the sill, squeaking out her noise.

"What?" Aron hissed vehemently.

Toria did not turn her head, and Aron followed her eyes in through the window. Someone else had entered while they left the sash open. Lurking against the dividing row of shelves, shielded by it from the door, was a figure where there should not have been one, a man dim in gray, holding a knife behind his back.

Aron dropped to the ground, dragging Toria with him by the shoulders. "Who is he?" he seethed. "Did you leave the window open for him? Who sent him? Who do you work for?"

But Toria could not answer, muted by shock. Her head bobbed as Aron shook her like a limp doll. He could do nothing else. Fury at her pricked him this far but would carry him no further. The thought of stopping the assassin could not even reach his mind.

Then, inside, there was a noise, a body falling with a crash. Aron and Toria stared at each other, then looked over the sill.

The assassin, perhaps, had not expected anyone to enter the library. Whoever his target might have been, he was unprepared for the appearance of Lord Justice Zein. As the Lord Justice came around the bookshelf, the assassin hesitated. That moment would have been his failing. Julian came in a step behind Zein, and at the sight of the raised blade he did not hesitate. When Aron looked in he saw the Bioran standing above the gray figure on the floor, his hands still clutching the long rod that held the wick used to light the lamps in the room, hanging at the end of its arc and vibrating from the impact. Lord Justice Zein leaned against the wall, his face blanched and his hands absently seeking something to steady himself. Julian's brows were knitted in determination while at the same time his mouth was open in astonishment. The man on the floor did not move. Toria continued to move her mouth soundlessly. Aron could not stop staring, could not duck his head, not even when the door was pushed wider and his father walked in on the tableau, summoned by the noise.

5

LORD JUSTICE ZEIN HAD ALMOST COMPOSED HIM-self by the time Jannes called for him. In his borrowed room he watched himself in the glass, seeing the reflection adjust the wig on his head with hands that he willed not to shake. The hands obeyed him, at least in the dim reflection. Whether they shook in actuality he was not certain. The yellow curls, carefully and stiffly formed, hung down along the sides of his face, and he could not quite feel them there.

He should not feel distress at the business of assassination and covertness, he told himself. It was what he had been born to.

He walked down the corridor with acute consciousness, down the successive small and treacherous cliffs that were the stairs, into the Lord Justice's office, his second visit of the day to that room. He did not think that he looked troubled. Jannes did. The Lord Justice was in his vest and shirtsleeves, his cravat undone, his head unwigged. Before him on his desk were a glass and a decanter, mostly drained of their contents. But Jannes was a Lord Justice, a Dabionian, and he too composed himself when he spoke.

"My lord," he said evenly, fixing Zein with an uncharacteristically sharp eye, "I should offer you apologies for having endured such turmoil in my house. There is not time for such formalities. In fact, I owe my current resolve to the incident. Without having witnessed the surprise and fear you displayed at the sight of the assassin, I might have concluded that you were responsible for his presence."

Zein could do little more than nod. His connection to Rayner was showing its liability once again. Mistrust was inevitable when gold was involved. Rayner had assured Zein that support for the Alaçan gold was nearly universal among the Justices, barring a few myopic objections from the most devoted followers of Bioranism, and he further assured Zein that he would continue to work toward acceptance, in exchange for a small portion of the proceeds, of course. Certainly Dabion as a whole preferred to mine and circulate the gold itself, rather than leaving it to Azassi. There was a good deal of discontent among the Justices about the recent adoption of coins made from Azassian gold, which might prevent Azassi from becoming overly rebellious because of a poor economy, but which was still regarded as dancing with the devil. That assessment was ironic, Zein thought. He felt that he was himself stepping a bit too lightly around that particular demon, but his devil was not Azassian.

It did not in the least surprise him to see blame for the attempted assassination placed on Rayner's shoulders. But no, Zein had not known about the assassin, he had not helped Rayner arrange for his arrival; and he had indeed been so distressed by the invasion that he'd entirely forgotten a lifetime's training of secrecy and concealment of emotion.

"It is not safe for me to retain my son and the Bioran here," Jannes continued. "I must find new residence for them. The incidents of today make it clear that I cannot delay the decision. You do understand me."

What a rare thing candor was among the Justices. In the fragmented dreams of Zein's deepest sleep, he lived in a place where lies were unnecessary. Jannes's shockingly open accusation, the first day Zein arrived in Origh, made him nostalgic for the impossible. *Do not think you can fool me,* Jannes had said, and Zein had responded with like honesty. It must have been Julian. The presence of the Bioran changed the atmosphere of the house.

So it became even more difficult for Zein to keep his face still, his reactions concealed, as Jannes made his request. A lifetime of training, generations of scheming, and Zein could so easily destroy it all, simply by doing what he longed to do: to respond to Jannes's earnest plea with the truth. Mount Alaz was no safe place; it was the most dangerous place Jannes could send his son next to Rayner's own chambers.

Very few in Dabion knew the history of Mount Alaz; it was regarded by many as merely the largest hamlet in a region of primitive, destitute mountain dwellers. The Justices were fond of rewriting history. According to the books of the Justices, Dabion and the rest of the Five

Countries might have come into existence with the arrival of the Biorans in 200 C.C. It was known, of course, in the common history that was preserved in children's tales, oaths, and aphorisms, that the law of Justice had not always been the governing force in Dabion. Law was once decreed by the words of kings. Before the Five Countries had been named and drawn together in their uneasy coalition, the world was made up of kingdoms, each fighting each other for their pieces of land.

The piece of land that covered the southern range of mountains between what was now Dabion and what was now Azassi, named the Alaçan region in a tongue that had been obliterated when the Common Language was instituted, had been home to one of the last known kings. Officially, the king had never surrendered to the authority of the Justices five centuries ago, although this fact was likewise not included in Dabion's books of history. Tanasigh, the capital that Dabion had built, largely ignored the Alaçan region. Its people contributed nothing to Dabion's economy, and its nominal king posed no threat to Dabion's authority. The Alaçans rarely ventured out of their mountains. Tanasigh could go about the business of Justice without them. But things changed when the gold was discovered.

According to the books written in Insigh, the gold had only been discovered recently, within the last year or two, coinciding—fortuitously, for the likes of Rayner— with Lord Justice Timbrel's announcement of retirement. The Alaçans had discovered it fifty years before.

The Alaçans themselves ignored the gold for the first

few years. Too soft for making tools, it was useless to a community so small and self-sufficient that it had no need for moneyed transactions, so myopically poor that it had no desire for ornamentation. Their children amused themselves by digging bits of it out of the dirt and hiding it from one another. Then a circuit clerk on one of his rare patrols to the area happened to notice what toy the children were playing with.

Immediately the clerk—a gray little man as he was always described by those telling the tale, *a tired and gray little man*—leapt up with a shout, suddenly full of fire. He began spewing forth words, *spewing them forth* said the tale, though his precise words were not recorded, and the words filled the people with terror. They remembered the people of the other regions, in the memory that lives across centuries; they remembered the kings of old, the many kingdoms below them and the battles they waged. The mountains of the Alaçans were sacred, they were safe, and that was how the people survived these many years, while kings were overthrown below them. Now the gray little man would bring the armies of all the kingdoms into the sacred mountains. He would bring them to take the gold.

The Alaçans remembered new stories then. It was the gold that made the mountains sacred, the gold that protected them. If the gray little clerk brought the men who would take the gold away, the mountains would be destroyed. They could not let the man go. With the silver-handled knife that the kings themselves had forged, described so clearly in the tales though no one had ever seen it, the throat of the little man was cut.

Then more men came: ten, fifty, a hundred—the number varied according to the teller of the tale. Tanasigh investigated the disappearance of their clerk. The Alaçans buried the gold in the thin dirt of the mountains, which grew thick and impenetrable as leather, and eagles came down from the heavens to bear away the body of the clerk so it would not be discovered. The very earth was giving of her powers to help the Alaçans. But for a reason never explained in the stories, the son of the king feared this would not be enough. He left his father's side, the silver-handled knife in his hand. He went down from the mountains and journeyed to Tanasigh, seeking the Lord Justice called Athagar.

Zein would not express doubts about the authenticity of the tale in his own voice. It was a tale that had become a favorite of the Alaçans in recent years, though it had never been told when he was a child. Athagar only died in 759, less than twenty years past. Zein had read accounts of his death, where no known cause was recorded. He had also read accounts of a certain clerk called Guerit, who had come to Tanasigh from the southeast, and who had been charged with the murders of various Justices. All of the victims had been rivals for appointment to the seat left vacant by Athagar, or supporters of those rivals. Remaining alive were Timbrel, the weak leader who was given the position, and those who favored Timbrel, presumably because his weakness would leave them free to pursue their own ambitions.

The new Lord Justice definitely left the Alaçans free of further investigation. Such stealth in concealing Athagar's murder and in taking steps to ensure his successor suggested an operative far more steeped in Dabionian politics than an errant prince with a knife in his hand. It suggested that the practice of sending Alaçan students to foster in Tanasigh was an older practice than the tales recorded.

For after the king's son sacrificed himself to keep the Alaçan gold a secret, the stories said, the old king himself came out from his shelter under the mountain. Generations had been born who had never seen the king, but all saw him then. He was old and frail, but he was shrewd. Violence would only draw the attention of the people below, he said, and they would come faster and in greater numbers to the mountains of the Alaçans. The people of the mountains must court the approval of the new world, the old king said. They must show them that the Alaçans gave them no cause to fear. Only then would the Alaçans be free.

By the order of the king, a city was built in the mountains. Mount Alaz was at the northernmost peak, its city walls visible from the roads below, its buildings made in the style of the new world. The sons of the city were sent out to be educated in the schools of the Justices, and ambassadors were sent out to Tanasigh. Mount Alaz was added to the Dabionian maps and the rolls of the cities of District Three. Tax collectors came, a station was established for the Public Force, and the Alaçans were assimilated into the new world.

Only then would the Alaçans be free. That was the difficulty of folklore: exact words were lost or changed, their meaning muddied over time. It was not clear what the king meant by his words, what freedom he promised his subjects. The path that the Alaçans found themselves upon now might bear no resemblance to what the king intended. The old patriarch, who died before the city was completed, might never have sent his sole remaining heir, the son of the son who vanished in the courts of Justice, down the road upon which he now found himself.

In the year 760 and at the advanced age of twenty-eight, Zein was admitted to the School of Justice in Tanasigh. Zein advanced rapidly in his scholarship, performing so highly that he earned the recommendation of every lawmaker he worked with, and within only five years he was appointed Lesser Justice. In five more he was a Greater Justice, and one of Timbrel's chief advisors. When the Lord Justice began talking of retirement, he took Zein even more closely under his wing, making it clear that Zein was his first choice as a successor. But with such great favor came great scrutiny. Zein's lineage, never before the subject of inquiry, became the greatest question among the aspiring Justices of Tanasigh. It was with great interest that they examined Zein's first name, Guérite; determined that in the southeast region to which he denied connection, the family name preceded the given name; and discovered that this family name was the same as that of the fabled Alaçan king.

It was then that Zein chose to pay the greatest cost

imaginable. The Alaçans would be free. That was the
problem with folklore: an educated man could no longer
believe the magic of it with blind faith. The Alaçans
would not be free unless he fought for their freedom. A
great strike was necessary to distract attention from
Zein's lineage and win his continued favoritism. He revealed the presence of the gold.

The Alaçans now had something to offer District
Three, and all of Dabion. Rayner's interest in the gold,
painfully transparent and mercenary as it was, gave Zein
an advantage in the race for the seat of Lord Justice. It
was the final act necessary to complete the maneuvering
that had begun when Zein's father left home when Zein
was a child, solidified when his father's name passed into
legend as the savior of the secret of the gold, and became
irreversible when Zein's grandfather ordered the building of the city of Mount Alaz. It was the role he had been
groomed for by the efforts of the aunts who raised him;
it was the name he was born to. But it was not the end of
his task. Now in the position of greatest power in District Three, Zein was compelled to use that power. And
his plans for it would make Mount Alaz a very dangerous place.

None of this could he reveal to Jannes. To betray the
impending fate of Mount Alaz would be to betray his
entire people. Zein had to mask himself with the pleasant smile of deceit and tell Jannes that he would certainly welcome Aron, Julian, and the operative assigned
to guard them to District Three, and he would arrange

for the most comfortable accommodations to be found in that rustic city in the far corner of his home territory.

At least, Zein thought, trying to salvage some scrap of hope as he begged leave to depart for Insigh immediately, he might be able to see Julian again. In one of his covert visits to Mount Alaz, he might make contact with the Bioran without drawing attention to himself or the numerous secret transports of goods that were beginning to arrive. Zein liked Julian; the boy was utterly without guile, unable to lie. He came from the world that hid in Zein's dreams. His childlike innocence reminded Zein of the days of his very early youth, long ago and nearly lost, before he knew what he had been born to.

6

THEY WERE ALMOST THE WHOLE WAY TO DISTRICT
Three before Julian finally said something.

The ride out of Origh was nearly unbearable. They had set out in the middle of the night, Aron, Julian, and Toria crammed into a small, unmarked carriage driven by two men who didn't wear Public Force uniforms but did carry the pistols. Aron's father sent them off with no explanation; he didn't even speak to them again following the scene in the library. Nothing about Aron's snooping outside the window, nothing about the mess that had been in his office and the obvious signs of his son's spying. Aron was so insignificant to his father that he didn't even merit scolding, no more than a disgusting mote of dirt. He growled under his breath and ground his fingernail along the grooves scratched in the glass. It was a very cheap carriage. The glass was so old and damaged that it couldn't be seen through, which was probably desired, since there were no curtains or shutters. The windows also didn't open. It was unseasonably hot for a spring day and Aron was starting to sweat.

There was no one to share his complaints with. Toria was doing her best to pretend to sleep and had done so since the first night. Aron imagined her back was nearly frozen into that fetal curl, after so many hours of slouching against the inner wall of the carriage. They had traveled almost without stopping, not allowed outside when the horses were changed, only permitted to step out and relieve themselves when they were in barren territory. Aron had to laugh at that: A season in the muck of Karrim had proven its worth by training him to piss like a dog. The drivers hadn't even spoken to tell them where they were going. Only the movement of the sun, spilling blindingly into the curtainless carriage from one angle, then from another, suggested to Aron that they were headed east, and if they were headed east it must be Tanasigh.

Julian, though, Julian was also uncharacteristically silent, and that bothered Aron. What he wasn't sure of was whether it bothered him more than having to speak to Julian would. He thought Julian might ask questions that Aron didn't want to answer.

It was jarring, then, to hear Julian finally say something, just as the sun was going down and the carriage was starting to slow, probably as it approached the border crossing. The Dabionian border towns, Aron groggily recalled from his years in school, all had prosaic names like 2 East 1, named for the district and the direction of the border and which town it was at that border. They probably *were* passing 2 East 1, in fact, Aron thought; there probably wasn't more than one town on the eastern border of District Two, since District Three couldn't possibly attract enough traffic to require another road and another town to maintain that road. Straining to hear something interesting from outside, Aron instead heard Julian's voice, sounding oddly mournful. "I think I killed him."

Aron turned reflexively toward the voice, but in the dimness he saw only the faint pale glow of Julian's hair.

"I think I did. When we were sent back upstairs, I went out and watched through the banister. They carried him out. He was covered."

Julian didn't need to tell him. Aron had watched out his window after having been banished to his room, and when dusk fell he had seen a large, sacklike form hurried into a wagon, the guards moving quickly in hopes of not attracting attention from onlookers on the street. Aron had hoped, though, to remain in willful ignorance of the contents of that sack.

"Cal Serinason, the cavalier, he told me I needed to learn to defend myself, when he was teaching me the rapier." Julian paused and his voice thickened. "I didn't realize what that would mean."

"What did you expect?" Aron snapped suddenly. "He was an assassin. He was going to kill someone. If you hadn't done something, it might have been you. No one else was going to save you." Then his own voice thickened in his throat, blocking the air. No one else was going to do anything, not even Aron. *I am a bastard,* his voice uttered in his airless throat.

Toria stirred then, unexpectedly. "What does it matter?"

she spat. In the half-light her eyes glinted as they stared angrily, turning from Aron to Julian, then closing again.

And the carriage came to a jerking halt with a sudden barrage of shouts.

Julian reached instantly for the door, trying to fling it open, but it was locked from the outside. Even crippled by distress, his instincts were intrepid. Aron found it frightening. Toria was rubbing on the window with her fist as if she could clear it to see through. "We're being attacked," she uttered. "Robbers."

"Robbers?" Aron shouted. "I'm the Lord bloody Justice's son!"

"In an unmarked carriage!" Toria returned. "It's night, we're an easy target. The drivers are as stupid as you are."

"But we're right at the border. There's border guards everywhere."

Toria spat out a laugh. "And they're as devoted to the Justices as the villagers who starve to keep their roads clean."

Aron's mouth hung open with the realization. There was a world of injustice he had never dreamed of. In the face of millions of villagers and prisoners, the destitute and the forsaken whose faces he had never looked to see, his anger was very small. The carriage rocked with the force of people battering against it from the outside, and he hardly noticed it.

Then one of the drivers fired his pistol, and the horses were spooked.

The carriage lunged forward, lurching erratically in

the wake of the runaway horses. A cry shot off to the side, a driver being thrown. The other guard must have climbed down or been pulled down. Inside the carriage, like fools, Aron and Julian and Toria pounded at the doors as if someone would hear them and rescue them. Then everything tipped to the side. The right wheels of the carriage slid off the bank of a creek none of them had known was there. The shafts cracked with the strain, the traces snapped, the horses ran free, and the carriage tumbled into the water.

Darkness made the fear stretch longer, more slowly. It took a very long time for Aron to realize that the carriage was on its side, that he was on top of Julian and Toria, and that water was streaming in through the gaps in the poorly fitted door.

The windows wouldn't open, he knew that, although it took him countless minutes of trying for him to remember. He struggled to wedge himself against the left window, almost horizontal above him, and drive enough force into it with his arm to break the glass. Something from a physical sciences class scratched through his mind in a brittle shard, something about the pressure of water. But the creek couldn't be that deep, he thought; there was no large river so far east. Was there? Fear was an infuriating enemy. He shouted fury at it and drove his fist through the window, shattering the glass, ripping daggers of pain into his hand. Water gushed in and Julian and Toria screamed. Aron thrust his head into the air—no, the creek wasn't deep, and reached back to grab the people he couldn't see. They clung to his arms, they climbed out of the water.

A half-moon lit their three wet heads as they looked around. A thick growth of vegetation sheltered the banks of the creek. The horses had disappeared. The mob they could hear distantly was not visible; the carriage had been dragged far enough away that the robbers had not caught up to it yet. Aron held little hope that they would lose interest in it, though. "What now?" he said.

Julian faced him, a twist of smile illuminated on his face. "I don't know. What will you do now?"

Idiot, making fun at a time like this, Aron thought. But he was the one who had to answer. He was the one who knew they were going east, and east meant Tanasigh. He rounded on Toria, who was clinging to the upset carriage like a rock to keep her head above water, and demanded, "Do you spies know how to read stars?"

She sighed heavily and the moon picked out the shape of her head turning upward. "Yes."

"Then where in hell is east?"

Her arm extended outward, pointing down the stream. Aron seized her hand, grimacing as his torn fingers closed around her wrist, grasped Julian's arm in his other hand, and waded in the direction of the nearest bank with his charges trailing behind him. "We'll follow the tree cover, then," he uttered. The last thing he saw before they sank into the murky darkness of the foliage was Julian's face, widely smiling, teeth lit by the moon.

7

RAYNER WAS NOT HAPPY. THE MESSAGE HAD COME to him, only a few hours before it was announced to Dabion at large, that Lord Justice Jannes had rid himself of the presence of his son and the mob-attracting Bioran. The boys were going, improbably, to Mount Alaz, for the absurd reasons of studying civil management and accommodating poor health, respectively. Just when Rayner thought Jannes had already made himself as insufferable as possible, and just as Rayner thought he'd found the sweetest move in the game, the Lord Justice rudely snatched it from him. Rayner would no longer have access to Aron Jannes.

Rayner frowned over the missive, reading its words yet again. The sheer audacity of them suggested that they were false, written with vanishing ink that would soon fade to reveal the true message, or conjured by the delusions of a madman. Rayner, though, was most certainly not a madman. The words, therefore, had to be true, or as true as their writer wished them to be.

Another message, coming to Rayner through less official channels, suggested an alternate reason for the

movement of the boys. Jannes's motivation had been
that of the simpleton, the child, the beast: fear. Someone
had sent an assassin to his house.

It was a fool's move. The site was too public, too full
of witnesses. Chances of success were slim, and those of
identification great. It was even likely, considering the
number of Justices fluent in schemes and subversion,
that the contractor of the assassin would be traced by the
overly curious. Rayner shook his head in disapproval,
watching the paper tremble in his hand.

And his disapproval turned to unfamiliar dismay. His
hand was trembling in some unbelievable weakness. His
entire right arm, in fact, was gripped by a strange numbness, as if he'd lain on it when he was sleeping. That must
have been it, Rayner thought. He'd lain on it while sleeping, though he had risen from his bed hours ago.

He turned his thoughts back to the matter of concern. The assassin, doomed to failure. But the assassin is
expendable, Kerk had said. He need not succeed; his
presence would be sufficient to frighten Jannes. And the
girl Tanie. Interesting, Rayner thought, watching Kerk's
face darken at the very mention of the amateur operative's name. Why would Kerk so passionately despise
Tanie? Was it some deep-seated hatred of women, en-
gendered at the hands of an overbearing mother? A
tremble of laughter shook Rayner at the amusing image
of his best assistant cowering in the shadow of an apron
and a broom handle. But Kerk had arranged for the assassin, had he not? Rayner had no interest in killing
Jannes at this stage in the game; it would be far more sat-

isfying to use his own son against him, the option that Tanie had offered. Such rivalry between Rayner's two operatives put him in mind of siblings, competing with one another to win a father's praise.

Well, of course. All such dysfunctions were the result of parents. But this was not a topic to be pursued, either. Rayner glowered at his hand until he felt the numbness leave it and threw the paper back on the table.

Then, a thought, a vision, clearly in his mind where it had not been before. Kerk was there, telling Rayner of his plan, the assassin, expendable. Did he want to send the man? Kerk could send him right away—he was waiting only a few streets away from Jannes's house. Did Rayner approve? Did he favor Kerk's plan over Tanie's, the one child over the other?

And himself, so clearly, agreeing. Rayner gave Kerk leave to send the assassin. Rayner ordered the fool's assignment that lost him Jannes's son.

How could he have done it? He stared at his right hand that had so recently betrayed him. How could he have made such an incredible error? It was unthinkable, it was impossible. It could not have happened. Only someone suffering from the mental deteriorations of age could have made such an abominable mistake, and Rayner was not an old man.

He thrust himself back from his desk and rose to his feet. For an instant the world swung; the directions lost themselves and Rayner did not know where he was standing. Like an invalid—it was impossible. His vision cleared and he rushed from his room.

Since he had returned to Insigh he had lurked outside Muhrroh's corridor each day. Strange things were going on in the Lord Councilor's chambers. Servants were coming and going, men carrying casks down the pristine white corridors. Rayner watched them with relish from his hiding place at the foot of the stairs. The alcohol. Other visitors would follow, surely, everything that went with the liquor: thieves, prostitutes, smugglers. The evidence that would cut the regal master of Dabion down to the petty mundanity of every other criminal in the world. Rayner lurked in the shadows at the mouth of the corridor and watched for them to come.

But they did not. Each day since he'd returned to Insigh Rayner had watched, and no one came. No smugglers went by with bottles hidden under their coats, no fleet-footed couriers with coin jingling in their pockets. No one went near Muhrroh's chambers except the usual servants and their unusual deliveries. And then there were the strangers.

Stranger men Rayner had never seen. They were guards and servants, dirty beggars, urchin children with bare feet. Rayner cringed back from the smell of them as they passed; how had they even gained access to the Great Hall? And their faces were wrong. He caught sight of them only as they passed, in that last instant before they disappeared into the antechamber, where they turned their heads a little as the door was opened. They had eyes, noses, and mouths, certainly; but something was still wrong with them. Rayner could never get close enough to see just what it was, not without revealing his position. Then the wanderers came in: unmistakable, tall white bodies and rags and dirty hair, weird eyes casting all over the plain straight corridor as if there were something to see there. Maybe it was the eyes, Rayner thought, that thing in the faces of the others that looked so wrong. It must have been.

But that would mean there were wanderers in the streets of Insigh, in the corridors of the Great Hall. Twenty, thirty, who knew how many of them, in disguise and living among the people. It was preposterous; it was impossible. Such a thing could not be happening. It was outrage enough that the Lord Councilor of Dabion was entertaining such sorts in his private rooms.

Then a guard in the uniform of the Public Force walked in, up the marble stairs, into the long white hall. Rayner raised his head very slightly. This would be interesting, he thought: to see whether the guard was loyal and would take the law to the matter, or if he was another canker in Dabion's corrupt body, soaking up his share of liquor and profit.

Rayner saw neither. He saw the man's face change.

The lank brown hair, the dark face, were gone. Where the face had been was a strange white visage, pierced by water-colored eyes, and the hair fell around it in a tangled mess of braids. Rayner felt the wall press hard against his back as he fell; he might have rubbed his eyes, doubting them, even thinking—madly—that age was ruining his sight. Had he been a superstitious fool, he might have regarded this as proof that the wanderers were magic workers. In a moment a satisfactory answer formed in his head: Wanderers were conjurers, workers of the mechanics of deceit, like those performers of sleight of hand in the provincial areas, who distracted the crowd with cards in their sleeves while knaves picked the pockets of the audience. This man in the corridor was putting on an act, for what reason Rayner had not yet discovered. Rayner was well hidden and the wanderer could not know he was being observed, so there was no need for conjuring. It was proof of—if anything—only the madness of the wanderers.

Suddenly the pale madman turned his steps, circled back toward the stairs he had just climbed, and hunched down. He spoke to the shadows behind the pillars at the base of the handrail. "What's wrong with your eyes, old father?"

"Nothing's wrong with my eyes," Rayner hissed.

The wanderer made an infuriating smile and turned up toward Muhrroh's antechamber once more.

Rayner pushed himself away from the wall. It was some kind of sorcery, certainly, that paralyzed his joints and prevented him from getting to his feet, that caused him to cower along the floor like an insect for moments before he could stand. But he did not believe in sorcery. His choice was between magic and infirmity. Neither was acceptable. When he reached his feet he left the accursed corridor behind him, as fast as he left a prison behind him in the wasteland of northern Dabion.

8

TANASIGH WAS LIKE ORIGH AND IT WAS NOT LIKE
Origh. Julian wondered, as he listened to the questions that the Justices here asked him, whether men in Origh had been as dark as the ones he met here, whether their faces had really been as full of secrets and unspoken things as Julian now saw. I am older now, Julian thought.

The questions were different in Tanasigh. They did not look at his hair or his face or his fingers; they did not bring tapes to measure him. "I'm sure the news has gotten here already," Aron said from the corner of his mouth. "I'm sure the Justices were falling over themselves to be the first one to tell the rest of the world." So there were no questions about Julian's nature, and there had never been questions about what he could do. There were only questions about what he knew and what he could tell them.

Was this Justice or that Justice present at the Jannes house, they wanted to know. Who came with whom, who spoke with whom? Julian remembered few of their names, and the men asking him the questions were not pleased when he failed to answer. He offered that Lord Justice Zein had been there and he told them about the books they had discussed.

"Is there so little sun in Biora, then," one of the Justices asked, "that you are all so fair?" This Justice did not wear a wig. There were many in Tanasigh who did not, and it only made those who did look even more strange. "Why is it that such debates arose over the nature of light, if it was such a rare occurrence?"

"Perhaps it was the cause of such debate because it was rare," a companion said, his eyes bright beneath the shade cast by his wig. "And the matter, the matter of light is what is important. Like a particle when it moves in a straight line, and like a wave when it crosses through another material."

"But light has both qualities," Julian murmured. "Can it not have the nature of both things?"

Even the bareheaded Justice, who seemed so unconcerned with the discussion, stared at Julian in astonishment. "How can a thing be two at once?" he scoffed, and the scholarly one echoed him. "Think of light itself: It is either there or it is not. Bright or dark. It cannot be both wave and particle. Absurd."

Julian smiled at them. They did not know.

Then came the ones who wanted to know about Biora: how many towns there were, how large they were, how many men, whether they had armies. Julian laughed, dry and hollow. They did not know, they could not imagine.

"I wouldn't answer them, either," Aron said when they had left. "I wouldn't trust a single one of them. All schemers, the lot." And he grimaced as Toria, clinging to him, squeezed his broken hand.

Aron had been restless since they reached Tanasigh. It had taken only a day of walking from the attack at the border to find the city—a fortunate thing, as they had no food. They stumbled into the Great Hall at nightfall, hungry and footsore, Aron's hand mottled with dried blood, greatly startling the Justices who received them. The journey had indeed been planned in secret. But the Tanasigh Justices escorted their visitors to the chambers vacated by Timbrel's retainers, bound Aron's hand, gave him a draught to drink against the pain, and told him to sleep. Aron did so for some twelve hours. Then he woke, and had been sleepless and irritable ever since. He was starting to chew on his lips as much as Toria did.

He eased open the door to watch the departing Justices vanish down the corridor, then announced, "Let's go out."

Outside, Tanasigh was very unlike Origh. The streets were not square and white—they twisted through a labyrinth of merchants and printers and grocers and animals. There was a slaughterhouse in Tanasigh, where there had not been one in Origh. There was a stable of horses with their sounds and smells. The men who worked in these places wore gray and brown with their sleeves rolled up, and their dark hair hung about their ears and blew into their faces with the wind.

Aron plunged forward, dragging Toria along behind him in his wounded hand. He did not linger to see his surroundings, did not meet the eyes that regarded them. Julian turned to watch alone.

There were people who stared at him as he went, and those who ignored him. A group of old women ducked their heads and whispered as he passed, and another gray widow stepped by him with her eyes only on the heavy basket she struggled to carry. Two young men laughed at him, five children stopped in their games to stare with hanging mouths, and an ancient man covered his eyes and chanted something about evil spirits. Near the garrison in the middle of town the guards of the Public Force stood and squatted against the wall, watching him. "We're being invaded," one laughed to his fellow. "The fairies have come for real," another answered. "Hide your children or they'll become changelings." Other men, leaning on the butts of their long guns, yawned. But an older guard turned his head to the side, dizzy with suspicion, and uttered, "They shouldn't be out here," and his companion knitted his brow and took a menacing step forward, his fingers drifting automatically to the powder horn that hung at his side.

Those guards were what Aron finally saw. "We've come the wrong way," he whispered.

Then Toria jumped ahead of him, taking the lead. "This way!" she urged, and with Julian trailing, she dodged into a maze of side streets and narrow alleys, navigating the city with the nose of a hound. For a few blocks, Julian saw the guards over his shoulder, giving chase, but soon Toria lost them.

With panting breath she pulled them up near a large, drab building in a remote corner of town, and once near this shelter, Aron snatched back his bandaged hand, and snapped, "Quit dragging me!"

"I'm the one who got us away!" Toria cried, red-faced.

Julian drifted away from their argument. This would be that strange Dabionian custom called marriage, he thought. In Biora, surely there would be blood drawn. He approached the building and circled around the side of it, where there was a large yard encaged by a fence of rusty bars.

It was an orphanage. A door opened in the dark building and a line of children was ushered out into the yard, gray of face and slow of movement, shepherded by several frowning women in caps and aprons. The children milled listlessly in the yard, and the women kept their distance. A net was stretched between two poles and two children popped a ball over it with rackets, but most of them were too thin or weary to do anything but stare between the iron bars of the fence into the street. One child, a small girl, stood at the fence with her hands on the bars. Julian approached her with cold in his stomach, as if watching a desperate prisoner trying to escape, but when he neared her he found that her eyes were quite calm, and that they were the strangest shade of green and gray and colors he couldn't name.

"We don't know where this one came from." One of the women crossed toward the bars where Julian stood, a hungry interest glowing on her face. "Mostly we get them when the parents die, or sometimes girls in trouble come here to birth them so they won't be found out. This one just turned up on our doorstep, not even in a basket." The nurse did not touch her charge or take her hand to lead the child away from the fence. "She's fair like you, though. Maybe is she yours?"

And Julian's breath froze inside him. These would be his children, their father disappeared, their mothers shamed. Aron was right. Lamely he said, "I haven't been here that long."

The nurse laughed broadly. "Of course you haven't! I'm teasing you. We all know just when you got here, there's no one in town who doesn't. The child was left by wanderers, no doubt."

But Julian did not stay to hear the story of the girl with the strange eyes. He wanted to go back to Aron, his dark friend, and tell him he was right.

Aron was not going to stand still and listen, though. "Come on!" he shouted when he saw Julian appear from around the other side of the orphanage. "We've got to get back before they send the whole damned Public Force looking for us."

Julian lagged behind when they returned to the Great Hall, letting the squabbling voices of his companions fade ahead of him in the twisting corridors of that old building. Tanasigh was an old city, Julian had heard, built by the kings who ruled Dabion before Biorans ever set foot on the land. The Great Hall was built on the foundations of an old castle, and it was heavy and dark, full of shadows. Julian lost himself in them. It was quiet there, quiet as if Julian had never seen anyone and never would. He closed his eyes and wished he never could.

But a sound roused him, as it must. A servant passed

through the corridor where Julian was hiding, a young woman who kept the upper floors where the Justices lived. She saw Julian and she smiled, ducking her head as she did in shyness, then looking back at him more boldly. She did not come any closer to him, as Julian imagined she might. Across the distance between them he could smell the scent of her, the sweet mingling of ashes in her clothes and the crushed flowers she used to perfume her skin. In Julian's mind he could touch that sweet skin. He could reach for this woman, put his arms around her, draw her close and drink the sight and feel of her. He could hide from the very loneliness that he had sought a moment before. He could find in her what all his restless blood was seeking, if only for a moment. His body ached to go home. But it was Davi he thought of, the child born unwanted. He wished he could have saved him from that as he wished, hopelessly, that he could have saved him from the Water man's weapon. His mouth moved reluctantly, his lips wanting to touch her even as they formed the words, "I can't."

Her eyes met his for an instant, puzzled. She did not understand his words—did not understand his accent, perhaps. It was just as well. She shook her head and let out a breath of laughter, then hurried on about her work, leaving the corridor with the fading sound and scent of her.

When Julian reached the rooms he shared with Aron, he found they were not empty. Lord Justice Zein's clerks had come for them. "The carriage never reached its next stop," they said. "We knew something had happened.

The Lord Justice sent us to bring you the rest of the way to Mount Alaz."

"Where in hell is Mount Alaz?" Aron asked grumpily.

Julian took no note of his friend, instead watching the clerk who stood closest to him. His head hung low, his breathing was labored, and he passed a shaking hand over his brow.

"He's sick," murmured Julian, when the clerks had left them to gather their borrowed belongings.

Aron snorted. "Well, if he was waiting on the LJ in Origh, he might have crossed the border to Karrim, to stop in at the brothels there. That's what ordinary men have to do, ones who can't get away with seducing every female servant in the house."

"Or keeping their own?" Julian asked.

Aron narrowed his eyes and hissed. Julian thought he might have gotten very angry, but the twist of his mouth resolved itself to something like a smile of self-derision. "At any rate," he uttered sharply, "there's a fever going around in Karrim. Clerk probably caught it there."

Julian peered back through the open door, trying to catch a glimpse of the clerk disappearing down the hallway, but the man was gone. The only thing Julian could see was a face in his own mind, the face of the assassin, graying as he lay on the floor, his nose cracked upward into his skull. "It's going to be bad," he murmured, breath cold in his mouth.

"Why do you care?" Aron snapped. Then he sighed, very heavily. "Never mind. I know what you're going to tell me."

9

NOW REMEMBER," CARRA SAID AGAIN, TRYING TO be more insistent, "there will be five more people in the household, so we need more loaves."

The baker's wife smiled distractedly over her shoulder. Carra hated dealing with the baker's wife. The baker himself was difficult enough, constantly stalling when Carra came to collect the taxes for the Dabionians, bickering every single time she came to make an order, changing his prices arbitrarily. His wife, though, was almost hopeless when it came to business. She could sell a bun—usually at too high a price—but when Carra came to settle their account the baker's wife couldn't even tell her how much the Guérite household owed.

"Don't worry, dear, I'll be sure he knows," the woman said, hurrying Carra to the door. The older woman actually patted Carra's head like she was a child. Carra was twenty-five years old, some years younger than the baker's wife, to be sure. But she had been the mistress of Guérite for ten years already, and with the household went the management of the entire city. Carra cast an eye over the older woman's bodice, which was laced so tight she could have set a tankard on her bosom and drunk from it. Obviously she had no time for things like Carra and her account; she had some important tryst to conduct before her husband returned.

Carra's mother and her great-aunts had always warned her away from associating with people like the baker's wife. How, exactly, she was supposed to go about her business without associating with such people was unclear, but her female kin had been most insistent, up to their deaths. Carra could be corrupted merely by standing near them. There was an elaborate ritual of purification prescribed for cleansing one's blood after such contact, handed down through long tradition and involving many days shut up in a closet with burning rushes and cups of vinegar. Carra had to wonder why the warnings were given to her so direly. Another old tale told of the king's niece, whose blood was so pure that when her uncle lay wasting with disease, she pricked her finger and let a single drop fall upon his lips, and the illness left him immediately. Apparently that purity did not hold true for all king's nieces, only the ancient ones.

It must have been the Dabionians, Carra thought as she left the baker's shop. She had been a child when the city of Mount Alaz was built and the government of the lowlanders sent their people into the mountains, but her young memories told her that the Alaçan people had been terribly worried that their kingly blood might be sullied. The words of her mother and her great-aunts must have been to warn her against letting herself be seduced by a foreigner. Well, they had done their job quite well enough. Carra wasn't about to let herself be seduced by anyone.

Honestly, Carra didn't think the Dabionians would try. They did not know what to make of her. She had stayed at home, of course, and had not gone to Tanasigh to learn how to mimic the Justices, as her uncle Zein and so many others did. That was man's work. The Dabionians expected women to remain at home and were not surprised by that when they arrived in Mount Alaz. They were surprised to see Carra completely manage business in that home. Man's work was to go out in the world; the household was governed by its mistress, and the mistress of Guérite governed half the business in the city. Dabionian tax collectors looked at her in puzzlement when she handed them the coffers and records, visiting circuit Justices tilted their heads as if they couldn't understand what she was saying when she gave them reports of disputes she'd resolved, and guards in gray uniforms stared at her when she walked down the street. Several of them were staring at her now, leaning on their guns and murmuring things to each other in voices that they were wise enough to keep low. They weren't the ones who were summoned when someone reported a theft.

"Mother give me your patience," Carra sighed as she passed the garrison. Dabionian men would be the death of her. The courier who had arrived a few days earlier, bringing news of the five new people coming to the household, had not even spoken the news to Carra, but had gone out of his way to find a man in the room to speak to. He didn't work for her uncle, she thought; Zein's closest retainers were Alaçans. The courier even told the man—a butcher making a delivery of meat for the household—that he should keep a careful eye on Carra. "One of them that's coming," he stressed in a slightly lowered voice, "the yellow-haired foreigner, he's been thrown out of Dabion for getting children on the Justices' wives." Carra couldn't imagine that the rumor was true. Dabionian wives, as far as she could tell, weren't allowed far enough out of their own houses to encounter any foreigners.

The blacksmith's shop, when she reached it, was buzzing with noise. One voice emerged above the din when Carra appeared, the speaker waving his arm to get her attention. "I'm not stealing horseshoes from the smith!" the man shouted, the ostler. "I can't pay for them! It's his boy stole my purse!" And he pulled the blacksmith's apprentice behind him by the ear.

"He did, did he?" Carra scoffed. The boy was red in the face and wide-eyed, but it was not for any guilt. Biel was as innocent as a lamb. "I'm not sure I believe you. I seem to remember you've failed to pay your rent—what? Two, three times? You begged me not to evict you because you had no money, you hadn't sold a pony in so long. But then all of the city saw you walking down the streets in a velvet coat, bought from a Dabionian trader."

The man's face bunched up like someone had tied a drawstring around his mouth.

"Will he take back his accusation?" the blacksmith growled.

Carra raised an eyebrow. "Will you?"

The man let go Biel's ear, and muttered, "I'll take it back. But I won't pay."

"What will I do with the shoes?" demanded the smith.

"Sell them," Carra decided. "The ostler will sell his ponies without shoes, and take the cost off of his price. Then he'll send the buyers here to get them shod. And if he doesn't," Carra said, narrowing her eyes at the ostler, "then I *will* evict him."

Frowning heavily, the ostler slunk out of the shop, and the smith noisily went back to work. Biel struggled to catch his breath and stop his hands from shaking. "It's all right," Carra soothed. "I never believed him."

The boy looked at Carra with hugely pleading eyes. "He bought goods from the Dabionians," Biel whispered, his voice full of horror. "It's evil to court the enemy."

It was easy for the young, she thought, to be so certain. Biel knew the story of the king's niece and her pure blood, Carra was sure, and all the others besides. She patted his shoulder, her brow pinched, and turned her back to him.

Returning to the household, she found a large wagon crowded into its small courtyard. The five visitors, she thought, but instead it was a single driver with a tightly covered load. "Mistress," he said urgently and quietly, "the Lord Justice sends the first of his goods."

Lord Justice, Carra thought. What odd titles, the names the men of the lowlands made up for themselves.

She wasn't expecting Zein to start sending the goods so soon, though. Now she had to make room for them, somewhere, sometime. She sighed. "Mother save me." At least the visitors were delayed—it would give her time to deal with the shipment. But it was strange, the visitors being late. She wondered where they were.

It would be several days before she found out. She was in the storerooms under the household, directing every able man she could find to build shelves and racks. Three clerks—one more than she'd been told—came in behind her and coughed. "Where have you been!" she exclaimed.

One of the clerks was not Alaçan; he stared at Carra and at his two fellows who bowed and deferred to her. "There was an attack," one of them said, and Carra listened as he reported the loss of the two original guards and the recovery of the other three visitors, nodding absently. The last of the clerks needed her attention more than the man who was speaking. He looked terrible: pale, trembling, and when she laid a hand on his brow she found it was burning.

"Sweet mother!" she whispered. "What happened to you?"

A tear leaked out of the man's dry, reddened eye and slid around his nose. "Forgive me," he rasped.

She left the storeroom to the workers and took the sick man to the closet off her kitchen that served as an infirmary. For hours she tried every herb in her collection that might prove a remedy, and the man's fever only burned hotter. Finally, she left him, able to do no more than lay a cool rag on his forehead.

"Mistress!" one of her cooks said when she reappeared. The old woman wrung her hands and gestured over her shoulder with her chin, unable to come up with words to announce the surprising arrival of visitors in the kitchen.

One of them was the son of another Lord Justice, the courier had warned her—the courier had warned the butcher, at any rate. Some of those Justices wore wigs, Carra had heard, and the cloudy-faced young man had his hair clipped short, apparently for just that purpose. Some of the Justices didn't have any courtesy, either, she thought. The Justice's son didn't bow or take Carra's hand or even say a single word of greeting, but stood with his arms crossed and his mouth frowning. The woman standing at his shoulder didn't look any more pleasant. She looked Carra up and down and snorted through her nose. What was that about? Carra wondered. The woman turned away, so as not to look at Carra, and the profile she showed was hunched, the expression left on her face when the flash of hostility had passed dejected. Of course, Carra thought. She was a Dabionian woman. It would have to be unpleasant to compare herself to a woman who was strong.

And then there was the third of them, the yellow-haired foreigner. He was taller and slighter than the Dabionians, his hair very long and fine, his skin pale in color, and his eyes were as blue as the clearest sky. Carra thought about that—blue as the clearest sky. She sounded like a lovesick girl. She shook her head at herself. The idea of lovesickness had left her a long time ago. When other girls were plucking flower petals to find out who their true love would be, and the boys were following them through the streets and trying to steal kisses in alleys, Carra was listening to the last orders that her mother was giving from her deathbed, preparing to run Guérite. The boys were all married now, the girls busy with their own children, and Carra was too old to be courted. It was just as well; she was the mistress of the household and Zein's niece, and she had no time for husband or children. Romance was for adolescents. Then the yellow-haired foreigner smiled, and Carra's heart fluttered.

"Well, you're finally here," she said, clearing her throat awkwardly. "Now there's work to be done, that's what we do in Mount Alaz. It's downstairs with you, until I can get your rooms made up."

She thought the Justice's son might have said something, that he might have objected, but after twisting his face in a wry smirk, he pulled at the woman's arm and headed for the stairs. The fair man followed them, and as he passed he looked back over his shoulder at Carra, and his lips curved again. He moved smoothly as water, lightly as air. Carra shook her head to scatter an unexpected blush. The courier was right to give his warning, she thought—he just wasn't warning her about the right thing.

10

AFTER THREE WEEKS IN MOUNT ALAZ, THREE OF the most deadly boring weeks since the clerks' office, Toria came to Aron, and said, "I can show you what they're doing."

What they were doing seemed to be rearranging the entire contents of the keep, that weirdly ancient-looking building in the middle of town. They'd spent days clearing out the storeroom underground and building shelves in it, then they had to build a new shed to house the things they'd cleared out. The reason for all this was unclear. Aron had worked for weeks on the ridiculous project and had no idea what they were going to store or why.

Not that he'd really been able to work. His right hand was still splinted and bandaged; Carra, who was the local healer in addition to all the other things she had her hands on, had looked at it and declared it decently treated, for lowlander medicine, and healing nicely, but still broken. Aron had to learn to wield a hammer, not only for the first time, but in his off hand. He did not like it. He was clumsy and weak, constantly in danger of breaking yet another bone in his right hand as he tried to steady a nail in the fork of his fingertips that stuck out beyond the bandage. He put more dents in the walls and shelves than nails. Once he became so maddeningly frustrated that he took furious aim at the shelf he'd struggled with fruitlessly for half an hour, pulling his left arm back as far as he could, throwing it forward fast, only to be interrupted jarringly in the middle of his swing. Julian was there, stopping his blow and pulling the hammer from his hand.

"You can work later, friend," the Bioran said.

"Bastard," Aron replied, settling for delivering a kick to the wall.

But the project was soon done, and Aron was put to work as a packhorse. Julian loaded sacks and barrels into his arms to carry to another room. Aron obediently neighed.

"Better than a pony," Julian said, laughing cheerfully.

Aron rolled his eyes. "That's all I can bloody do around here. I can't even do peasant's work, I'm reduced to a damned horse."

"You can only do what you can," said Julian, "wherever you are." Then he smiled to himself, radiating light out of that milk-white face of his. "That's true. I think that has been my problem."

"Being annoying is your problem," Aron growled.

"I suppose it's rubbed off on me."

Aron made a frown but could not help laughing through it.

When they were done moving the stores, though,

they were dismissed. Whatever was going into the newly cleared storeroom, they weren't going to see it. Aron climbed up to the keep's highest level and sat at the parapet, swinging his legs as he looked down, watching Julian try to follow Carra around, and wondering what was being hidden from him. The idea of it was almost infuriating—something was being hidden from him. When he was in school, maybe, he would have pursued the secret with all his energy, to find it, to use it. But he probably would have failed.

Julian—he would say it wasn't important. He would tell Aron not to be angry. Julian had something to do, though. He had a reason not to be angry.

So when Toria came to Aron and said she knew what was going on in the storerooms, he didn't ask her where in hell she'd been for three weeks, and he didn't tell her to go away. He climbed slowly to his feet and followed her.

Where she'd been for three weeks, apparently, was exploring the keep. She led Aron through an impressive network of passages and corridors, down narrow stairs and even through a hidden doorway. At the end of the convoluted path was a wall—"This is the big secret?" Aron muttered when he saw it—but through a gap in the boards came a shaft of light. Toria covered Aron's mouth and pushed him forward to peer through the gap.

Behind the wall was the storeroom where Aron had failed to build shelves. Inside, men were opening crates and unloading their contents: barrels that reeked with the unmistakable tang of gunpowder, small heavy boxes of shot, and row after row of guns.

"That was in the first wagon," Toria hissed in his ear as she pressed close to him. "Another one came last week. The men are saying it's only the start." She twisted herself around Aron to look into his stripe-lit face. "Only the start. And they're hiding it from you. They don't want Dabion to know. That's what you wanted, isn't it? To know what they were hiding? Like your father hid things?"

Aron's eyes were possessed by the scene and his breath was taken away, but something he heard in her voice jarred him. His father—Toria spied on his father. He tore his eyes from the gap in the wall and stared coldly at her. "Why are you trying to manipulate me?"

Toria began to shake, her eyes going wide with panic. "You—you want to get your father!"

"As if I can do anything about him now," Aron said, his throat beginning to tighten with anger. "Here in the east end of nowhere."

Toria grasped him by the elbows, jagged nails biting through his sleeves, and hissed, *"I can get you back to him!"*

That he had found all his father's secrets already and they had done him no good, Aron had forgotten. That the woman was setting up what sounded suspiciously like a trap was only a little more clear in his mind. What filled Aron's thoughts and throat and blood was the memory of being frozen, crippled, paralyzed: anger at his father smothering him and burying him alive. He could not let that happen again. He was struggling to breathe already. He needed to get away from Toria and the madness she was trying to manipulate in him. Clambering to his feet, he stumbled back the way he had come, blind in the hidden corridors.

The city was too small, too close. He needed to get out of it, where people wouldn't see him, where Julian wouldn't come and try to help him. Julian would help him—Julian *would* help him, but Aron couldn't bear the thought of pleading with him, shaking like a child. Aron spiraled down the mountainous slope of the city until he came to the gates, and slipped out into the empty world.

Mount Alaz was some distance up the tall northern peak of the mountain range, dirty trails below it, rocky heights above it, ugly brown and scrub brush all around. Whatever was green in Dabion was a haze on the distant horizon. The summer sun burned mercilessly on Aron's high, unprotected face, although in the shade the air was strangely cool. And some way down the slope, off the poorly made road, several figures picked their way through the rocks.

Aron had no reason to follow them. He did. As he came closer he saw the ragged dirtiness of their clothes resolve out of the ragged dirtiness of the landscape. They were wanderers. Of course, Aron thought. No one was trying to put them in asylums here, so far from the Dabionian Authority. There were two of them, a man and a woman, nearly identical to one another in their rags and weirdly dressed hair. They took no notice of Aron, as far as he could tell, staggering down the slope as he trailed them, stopping to look up at the sky or crouch on the ground, to talk to the beetles, maybe. Aron gained on them, wondering what he was going to do when he caught up to them. Then he saw there was a third one, lurking on the downhill side of a large boulder, sitting still, watching very sharply as Aron approached, waiting for him. He would not have guessed who she was, until she spoke. It was a voice he had not heard since he was a child, one he heard more clearly in his dreams than even his mother's. "Did she tell you who she works for?"

He could not answer. He would not have answered her question, had he been able to speak. The words trapped in his throat were *Do you think you can come back, now? After leaving me, you think you can just come back?* But rage choked him and he could say nothing.

"But I don't think you would recognize the name, even if she did tell you," Elzith continued, the unmistakable voice, harsh and cutting, coming out of the strange, dirt-streaked, braid-framed face. "No one ever told you who killed your mother."

And the dam in Aron's throat cracked, splintered by an agonized scream. He dropped to his knees, bruising himself on the sharp rocks of the mountain's slope. The pain was not enough. Fiercely, he seized his right hand in his left, clenching it as he would strangle a throat, wringing the fractured bones inside until the shooting pain blotted out everything else.

11

WELL, THIS IS ALL I NEED," CARRA SAID, SEEING them approach from the corner of her eye. "The city's crowded, shipments coming in every week, people complaining of the heat, handsome foreigners to deal with, and now I've got another injury to tend." She wiped her hands on her apron and turned to face them. "You again? What have you done now?"

Julian had found Aron outside the city walls, crouching on the ground, dirt on his clothes and fresh blood staining the bandages around his hands. He had gotten to his feet with his eyes averted, shamed into silence. Julian did not know what had happened. Aron still had not said a word to him as Julian brought him to Carra's kitchen.

"Mother above!" the house mistress gasped as she undid the bandages and examined the new wound. Aron had cracked the splint and driven the wood into his hand, and a bone had been forced out of its setting, a jagged edge of it piercing his flesh from inside. "Did you try to feed it to the wolves? Were you breaking windows again? What did the windows do to you?" She went to a cupboard and took out a bottle, directed Aron to sit on a table and took the chair before him, set a bowl in her lap and uncorked the bottle. Looking up at Julian, she formed the voiceless words, "Hold him."

Julian jumped to her advice when she poured the fluid over Aron's hand, barely catching him and holding him steady by the shoulders as he began to struggle violently.

"You couldn't just scream, could you?" Carra said, calmly blotting the wound as Julian reached around to hold Aron hard by the elbow and stop his arm from moving. "No, you hold on to it. Can't let it go, can you? You'll just keep struggling."

"Bitch," Aron hissed. "What do you know?" But after Carra had cleaned his hand, pressed his bones back in place, splinted and bandaged him again, the pain had stripped out the last of Aron's anger. He slumped backward against Julian and did not fight the arms around him.

"What happened?" Julian whispered, trying once more to ask Aron. Then Carra found a piece of root in her cupboards and gave it to Aron to chew against the pain, and with his mouth occupied he refused to answer.

"Is he always so angry?" Carra asked, beckoning Julian to her after he had laid Aron out flat on the table to rest.

"He was," Julian said sadly. "I thought he was better. I thought I'd helped him."

Carra scoffed. "If he was that charming when you met him, why did you try?"

Julian did not have to think long. "He's my friend. We can't choose friends. Their paths cross ours and we take them in." Then he did think. He had traveled across three countries trying to choose his place, when what he needed to do was whatever he could, wherever he was.

Carra was watching him. The light must have broken on his face and she was taking in the glow of it. Then he smiled and she turned away with a flutter she tried to conceal. Something warm grew in Julian's stomach. "Well," she said, "that sort of anger will make him sick on his own. Can you try to help him again?"

"Of course," Julian breathed. There was nothing else.

"Well, then," Carra replied, and straightening her apron, she looked around the kitchen for something else to give her attention to. A scullery maid unknowingly obliged by spilling salt. Carra darted away to shout at her, calling back over her shoulder, "And you, off with you, stay out from under my feet!"

Julian laughed. He wanted to turn and dance, but there was a weight in his limbs that would not let him. Then he saw the table where he'd left Aron, and Aron was gone.

There was pain that was brief, sticking in one place for an instant, a slap of cold air on the face or an elbow thrown carelessly into a doorjamb. There was pain, then, that sank into the bones, bled through the veins into every farthest part of the body, pain you breathed out and back in again, pain you dreamed about when you slept. You could not relieve it, and if you tried to distract yourself from it by biting your tongue, you only invited the pain into that new part for it all to pulse together.

It was like being drugged with laudanum, Aron thought, swimming under it, the drug flooding the pain but not taking it away, washing out your senses so they looked at the pain but were too tired to feel it. He was ten years old when he'd had the laudanum. It was the last time he'd seen Elzith.

"Don't go," he remembered saying, in his silly, thin, child's voice. He remembered crying and throwing his arms and legs and whatever else he could get his hands on, he remembered asking if his mother was really gone, although he did not actually remember hearing his father's voice telling him she was dead. "Don't go," he'd said to Elzith, though, and he remembered that very clearly. It was the last thing that was clear before the laudanum.

But she did go. She went and she left him and never told him why. Now she thought she could come back. Elzith had always thought Aron would listen to her, she was always so confident, never bargaining with him or trying to manipulate him like others did. Then, just once, he asked something of her, hoping she would listen. But she did not; she left him. Now she was back and she expected him to listen to her again.

"You're the one who broke your word," he shouted at the air as he stumbled out into the pressing crowds, not caring who heard or what they thought. He could not go far before the pain would trip him up, forcing him to crouch on his haunches and hold his throbbing hand to his chest. He ignored the people who brushed past him, until one came and stopped there. Julian had followed him.

"How did I guess?" Aron rasped. "Not back with your new sweetheart? What are you waiting for? That closet off the kitchen is empty now, you know. The clerk died a week ago."

"I know," Julian said. "I think I know what killed him."

Aron moaned, angry at the dampness that blurred his vision. "Why do you care?" he asked again. "Why should I care?"

"I have to talk about something. You won't tell me what happened outside the wall."

Reluctantly, Aron looked up. "I'm going backward, aren't I?"

Julian nodded.

"There's not a river around here to rescue people out of."

Julian laughed. "Or a work camp to run. You can try Carra's kitchen, but I don't think she'd let you." Then he offered his hands to help Aron up, carefully grasping him around the forearms.

Aron swayed on his feet. He was exhausted. "I'd rather go backward," he said, but he let Julian lead him back to the keep.

There was a new commotion when they arrived. Lord Justice Zein had come to visit.

"Mother save me!" Carra exclaimed to one of her

cooks as she hastily chopped vegetables for an unexpected crowd. "No warning, he says he can't, must keep things secret, but he sent the Justice's son and the Bioran, didn't he? And that girl, where has she gotten to, and those clerks. Why can't he just say he's visiting them? These men and their secrets. Half a dozen retainers, try hiding them on the roads. And more mouths to feed. He could be sending me more meat, not just weapons and millet." Then the cook hastily shushed her, because the foreigners had come in.

Julian was a wrinkle she had not anticipated. Her uncle, the king's heir, was engineering the freedom of the Alaçans, and all Carra could think of was the Bioran. She could not take her eyes from him. He was full of brightness, his skin and his hair lit even lighter by his passion for everything he saw. He walked like a dancer, moving lightly on the earth like he weighed nothing, like no trouble could burden his shoulders. He would see her and smile, and it was as if he'd woven a cord from his white-gold hair and wrapped her up in it.

"What a silly fool I am," she complained to a scullery maid, "acting like a little girl, acting like you." Carra slapped the maid on the cheek with a towel and the girl giggled and darted away. There was no reasonable advice coming from that quarter. Carra could see Julian from the corner of her eye; she could see him everywhere in a single glance. "Now I can't remember what I was doing," Carra huffed aloud, staring at the mound of vegetables around her. She would have to try to ignore him.

Then she got an unlikely rescue. Aron spoke to her,

not Julian. "I think someone's calling for you from upstairs."

It was Zein's head clerk. Carra hurried up to the main hall to find the half dozen retainers who had come up from Tanasigh gathered in a circle. One of them lay on the floor where he had suddenly fallen, fretting in a fever.

The sick man was carried into the closet vacated by the last feverish clerk. Carra looked down on the new one, lying in the same cot, in the same fever. She had no idea what to do for him. The last man had burned and fought with delusions for more than a week, crying out things that Carra could not understand, and when his fever finally broke he began to tear at himself so violently that the butcher had to come in and tie his arms to his sides. Carra spent more time outside the room, trying to quell rumors among her staff, than she did at the sick man's bed. Then he died, and Carra did not know what from. She could only hope that this second clerk did not have the same thing. She sighed and began pouring medicines, trying to find something that would work.

Hours later she was sitting at the table in the kitchen, hanging her head over her arms, when a voice spoke from behind her. "I was worried about you."

Carra raised her head to see Julian's face, smiling gently. He carried a bowl of soup in his hands. "You had nothing to do but wait outside?"

Julian sat the bowl in front of Carra. "What's wrong with the clerk?"

Carra shook her head. "I don't know. I'll have to watch him and see if the fever breaks." She pushed at the bowl with her finger, not feeling hungry. "Is this part of your act? In case the women don't fall at your feet just because of your pretty face?"

Julian smiled as the color came up in his cheeks. He smiled even when he was being embarrassed, and it was even more enchanting. "You won't let me rest," he said, laughing.

"Rest? What makes you think you have rest coming to you? You'll rest when you're in the ground."

A cook who walked past nodded and gave Julian a look of sympathy. Carra made a face at her. Julian smiled again, and Carra's stomach fluttered with more than hunger.

Carra did not leave the kitchen much over the next few days. She watched the sick clerk but the fever did not break. She crushed herbs and made elixirs and nothing seemed to comfort him. Julian met her each time she stepped out of the closet, always holding a bowl or a cup, and she let him bring his offerings and sit with her at the table. She drank slowly, closing her eyes. The fever would not pass and she did not know what to do. Once she pulled the scarf from her head and rubbed at her temples, trying to ease the pain. She flinched when someone touched her; she hadn't realized Julian was now standing behind her, and he was stroking her head with long touches.

Her throat stopped up. "You'll want to sit back down now."

Julian leaned over her and she could feel his breath in her hair. "Why?"

Carra pulled away from him. "No, I'm not letting you do this," she said, flustered and tripping over her words. "You're not taking me in, I'm not listening to your— your—this—I'm not a silly girl. I'm not one of those women all you outsiders are looking for, I have work to do here, I'm not letting some man interrupt it, ruining me, getting a child on me, making the others think I'm a whore. I'm not." She sucked in a breath and pressed her mouth to the cup to quiet herself before the servants heard her.

Julian sat down, across the table from her. He folded his hands under his elbows. When she looked at him again he wore a slight and sad smile.

"Do you know that was not even what I meant?" he said to her after a few moments. "You tend to others constantly, I only wanted to tend to you."

Carra looked sideways at him. "That's not what you meant," she repeated dryly. "Really, that wasn't even in your mind. You never thought of it."

Julian's face went a little blank.

"Aha," Carra said. She could handle him; he would listen to her. "You look so shocked. Is this innocent face you're making part of the act as well? How many women have melted at the sight of that innocent face?"

For once Julian did not smile. "No!" he insisted, his eyes flying wide with frustration. "That's not—oh!" He pressed his hands on his face to cover it up, fingers splayed white over the red flush. "This is not what my face is saying. I *am* shocked, it's not an act. You've seen through me, you've torn me in two. I cannot pretend around you, I cannot fool you, not even when I've fooled myself." He dropped his hands and stared at them, derision turning his mouth at the corner. "Do you know I swore to myself I would not touch another woman?"

Carra spoke shortly and loudly, so she would not feel the ping of sadness in her stomach. "And how long ago was that? A few weeks?"

Julian looked offended for an instant, but did not reply, because Aron entered at that moment. "You wanted to look at my hand," he said in a babyish voice, holding it out to her. He sat obediently on the table in front of her, blocking Julian with his back. "Does it need more medicine?" he said. "Can I have what the clerk has been getting?"

"Hmm," she said, silently grinding her back teeth. "I think this has set crooked. I might have to crack it again to straighten it. And then you can go check on the clerk, I think he'd like your company."

Aron frowned severely. Julian, apparently, had not gotten far in ridding him of his anger.

But Aron was accompanying Julian every time he came to the kitchen. There was some bond between them, something that tempered the insults Aron spat out, something that held Julian to him. They argued over the kitchen table while Carra tended to the clerk. She found them waiting for her whenever she came out, serving melodramatic abuse with the soup. Once a housemaid came in to tell Carra that her uncle had called on her, needing her help in some matter at the garrison, and since he couldn't find her he'd gone ahead by himself.

"Do you see what you've done?" Carra snapped at her visitors, turning to Julian especially. "How much time have I wasted here with you? The city could have burned down while I've been sitting here. But you can't give up the attention, can you? You're the center of the world and you'll see to it that we all spin around you."

Julian tried to laugh. "I am not," he started to protest.

"Oh no," Aron chimed in. "You don't look for attention. You went around with that sword thinking no one would notice you."

"I don't need your help," Carra snapped at Aron, and he shut his mouth sullenly. "But I suppose you were quite dashing with that sword," she said, turning to Julian again. "How many women thought so?"

Julian let out a laugh that sounded like a whimper.

"That means a lot of them, doesn't it? They liked the dashing stranger. As if you needed to do anything to make yourself stranger. You catch eyes everywhere you go and you wouldn't give it up for anything." Julian sank back in his chair and Carra stepped closer. "You wouldn't. And for all your swearing that you've given up the attention of women you would go back on your oath in an instant."

Julian leaned forward across the table. "Yes," he breathed. "You know it, you see right through me, you always have. You are wise and frustrating and wonderful, you are the rarest thing I have ever seen. I wish I could drink you in just to reach it, that—that—" He threw his hands in the air, the words impossible to find. "You, to reach you, to reach what you know. And I would lie with you, I'd pull you to me, I'd pull you around me, just trying to reach it. I want you more now than I have ever wanted anyone. But that only makes me a fool. It only proves you right." He leaned back again, his collar falling open to bare his throat, his hair brushing his shoulder. The smile on his face was ironic and rueful. "It makes me a fool and you know it does."

Carra caught her breath. She turned away from Julian, the gold hair against the ivory of his skin, the shining blue of his eyes, and when she turned she found herself looking at Aron. He leered at her and traced his teeth with his tongue. She could not look at either one of them, and the kitchen was empty for the end of the day. "I—" she murmured, "I have to find my uncle."

As she hurried up the kitchen stairs she heard their voices fading behind her. "You should have taken her," Aron was saying, his teasing turned to acid. "You're thinking it means more than it does."

And Julian answered, "You're thinking it doesn't."

Carra did not have to go far to find Zein. He was in the keep's great hall, where a knot of his retainers and the highest-ranking Alaçans had gathered, but Zein was not near them. He sat at the far end of the hall, in the dark. The great throne of kings, worn and battered by time and neglect, dwarfed him as he sat in it, a man with cropped hair and a foreigner's black suit. His eyes were heavy as he looked up at his niece. "You remember the story of when the gold was found?" he uttered.

"The gray little man," Carra answered. "The silver-handled knife."

Zein nodded, his face desolate. "Why can't they forget?" Then he took a deep breath and raised his voice so that the others in the hall could hear. "The guards sent by Dabion discovered the stores. There was a confrontation at the garrison. The guards were killed, all but one of them. We can't let him go. We can't let the Dabionians come back into the city." His voice stuck in his throat, the voice born of Alaçan kings. "It is time."

12

RAYNER HAD COME AGAIN; HIS VOICE WAS AUDIble from the antechamber outside Muhrroh's door. "I put you into this position," he was growling to the guard at the door, "and I can take you out of it. Now let me through." In all his years of service Rayner had not changed. Muhrroh had appointed Rayner to head the Secret Force to keep him close, of course, as one should do with one's enemies, but the Lord Councilor had also borne the hope that Rayner might learn something in his later years. The effort had kept Jannes alive, certainly, although it had done little for Lord Justice Hysthe, one of Rayner's unfortunate victims. Rayner still loved politics too greatly. He had failed to grasp peace in life, and he would not die a good death. Ultimately, politics was of no consequence in the face of that final end.

It was no surprise, then, that Rayner entered the Lord Councilor's inner chamber with an expression of bafflement. His eyes, unaccustomed to the dimness, blinked blindly, and with the thin gray crown of his uncovered hair, gave him the appearance of a mole. Rayner had also failed to grasp his own mortality. He looked around the

chamber, at the vessels of purified alcohol that illuminated the room with their small blue flames, squinting
hard at the two Sages lurking in the shadows at the far
end. The scene was unfathomable to him, of course. He
could form no other words than, "What on earth..."

"The way of the world is gain," Muhrroh began,
knowing his tutelage was not likely to be heeded. "That
is what we were always taught. We are of an age, Aln
Rayner; do you not remember? All is gain: to gain power,
to gain wealth. We are not so unlike the Manderans in
that, do you see? We strive to gain power over Mandera,
over Azassi, over gold, over learning. All is gain, but we
forget what we have lost."

"My lord," Rayner said uncertainly, the tone of his
voice wavering between protocol and temper.

"It is one of the greatest faults of our age that we
rewrote the histories of the past. Such knowledge was
lost to us, in our effort to quiet the people. Our prede-
cessors, the ancient peoples, had wisdom that we cannot
imagine. How different the course of civilization would
have been, had we read their books instead of those of
the Biorans."

"The ancient peoples were illiterate, my lord," Rayner
replied shortly.

"Ah!" Muhrroh exclaimed. "That is where you are
mistaken. That is where Justices have been mistaken for
centuries. The kings who lived in this country before this
country was Dabion were literate, and they left their
writings behind." With a hand he gestured toward a dim
wall lined with shelves, and toward the scrolls that filled

them. They were fragile things, poorly preserved, not made to withstand the passage of years, but Muhrroh had found and recovered them. With great difficulty and in secret, he had commissioned a corps of scholars to examine them and translate them; that had been the work of ten years, while others were slaving over Bioran texts that lacked the greatest of secrets. Many of the scrolls were still untranslated and would remain so, but Muhrroh's quest was finished. He had found what he was seeking.

Rayner hardly spared a glance at the scrolls. "What are they doing here?" he demanded, abandoning his pretence of decorum as he thrust his chin toward the Sages.

"The Sor'raian operatives?" Muhrroh asked. "You never did appreciate their potential, I'm afraid. You managed them quite poorly, in fact. But it is not surprising. When your predecessor came to me with his offer of their service, he had little hope that I would agree. No—that is not true; he had every hope that I would agree, because he had seen it. Loyd could see the future, you know.

"You do not believe me," Muhrroh observed, smiling at Rayner's dumbfounded expression. "It was a mad chance, of course; I could not fully believe until I had seen it, but imagine the possibilities! Spies who can see the future, spies who can read minds, spies who can alter your perception of their appearance. Loyd offered me all this, if I would but save some of the Sages from the asylums. He had witnessed the abduction of his family when he was a child, you understand. His family—they

were Sages—they were imprisoned. Loyd was an idealist
in those days; it was a shame you did not meet him. His
goal was to save his people, and I accepted his bargain. It
was not until after his death that I learned his bargain
was moot. Sages cannot be imprisoned, it seems. A re-
markable number of them have escaped their asylums; I
need not have hired them into the Secret Force to protect them. But by that time I had discovered a new purpose for them."

Made docile by astonishment, Rayner watched as
Muhrroh drew one of the scrolls from the shelf and un-
rolled its crumbling parchment. "See this," the Lord
Councilor breathed. "The records of the court of King
Harald. You know his name? You will have heard it in
nursery rhymes and fairy stories, if you remember them.
The entertainers in Karrim still sing ballads of his ad-
ventures. But he was no mere creation of fiction, no
myth. He was a king who lived, and lived long. See, here
it is written. *A wise king must surround himself with
elixirs, the most potent being spirits purified. The flame
of these spirits is greater than any lamp, shedding not
light alone but the fire of life. A wise king must also surround himself with men of magic, for they are the oldest
children of the earth. It is by these means that the king
shall gain—*" and here Muhrroh paused, savoring the
breath with which he would articulate his greatest desire, "*—immortality.*"

Rayner looked up from the indecipherable script and
stared at Muhrroh. "That's what the alcohol was for?" he
stuttered. Then he drew his brows together and gathered

his anger, saying, "The spells of these magic men aren't very effective. Where are the old kings now?"

Then one of the Sages, one who could move without being noticed, appeared at Rayner's side, startling him. "But he has not told you why we stay," the man murmured. "Do you know of the plague? Do not worry, it's not what you will die of."

Rayner reeled away from the Sage's words, words he would undoubtedly dismiss as insane. Fumbling in his pockets, he pulled out a match, hoping to strike it and drive the Sage away with its flame. Three times he tried to strike it, but the grasp of his right hand was too weak. The fourth time he moved the match to his left hand and thrust it into the blue flame of a vessel of spirits. It caught in a violent blaze, and Muhrroh took a smooth step backward to preserve his precious scroll. The Sage only smiled. Grumbling like a beast, Rayner went around the chamber to light all the neglected oil lamps, brightening the room like day.

"Look at yourself!" Rayner shouted when he was finished, throwing the match on the floor and stamping it out as it began to burn his fingers. "You don't even know what's happening in your own country! There's revolution in the Alaçans. Zein has deserted his post. Mount Alaz has shut its gates and declared secession. This is what I come to tell you, and I find you here—locked up like a wanderer in his prison, raving like a madman!"

"There is nothing mad about the quest to evade death," Muhrroh uttered.

Rayner shouted wordlessly, unable to reply. He could

not move the Lord Councilor with his furious stare, and he relented and withdrew. The uneven pounding of his gait sounded his exit.

"He does not recognize his own weakness," Muhrroh said to the Sages. "He might fall. Do follow him and watch him."

"He will fall," the second Sage answered, one who could see the future. "But we cannot stop it." But the men obeyed the word of their master and followed Rayner through the anteroom.

Alone, Muhrroh wondered what the answer would have been, had the Sages given it to Rayner, had the avaricious Justice asked. Why did the Sages stay? But it was not a question to be answered. Muhrroh looked around his room, seeing it brightly illuminated for the first time in seasons. His books, his law records—the things that had once been so important to him—and the discreetly kept items of comfort, woven tapestries and elaborately carved woodwork, they all seemed strange and superfluous now. Then he saw a thing that he had truly given no thought to in those seasons of pursuing eternity: his mirror. It stood in the corner, draped with a cloth of deep green velvet that was at least as old as the mirror itself. Muhrroh unveiled it and positioned the glass. Framed within the gilding was his face, crowned with its costly wig. Slowly he lifted the wig from its resting place, keeping his eyes steady on the revelation of evidence. His suspicions were correct.

It always struck him as strange that so many Justices continued to wear wigs, even those who had never

espoused Bioranism and those who had become es-
tranged from the study as Muhrroh himself had. They
wore the wigs, doubtless, simply because Muhrroh did,
disregarding the Lord Councilor's waning interest in
Bioran science, and never knowing, never suspecting the
true reason that the leader of Dabion continued to cover
his head.

Not that he should take the loss of his hair as a sign that
the ancient prescriptions were not working, Muhrroh
told himself. At the age of seventy-nine, he had far outlived his father and his grandfather, both of whom had
succumbed to the cancer. He need not fear any swelling in
his abdomen, he was certain, but the loss of hair signaled
age and age signaled corruption. Even the powers of the
magicians of Sor'rai were vulnerable to the effects of politics. To be healed, Muhrroh resolved, he would have to escape Dabion. He would have to go closer to the source of
the power.

13

THE MURDER OF THE PUBLIC FORCE GUARDS drove Zein to a decision he had hoped not to face until much later. His position at the head of Dabion's District Three had given him power, of course, and some measure of autonomy; there were few who could examine his movements closely enough to discover or challenge the shipments of food stores and weapons he had begun to send to Mount Alaz. But there had not been enough time. Zein had been invested on the first day of spring in the year 777; it was now only summer of the same year. Two seasons were not enough to outfit the city as he had hoped. But legend required strife and great deeds, and so his people had murdered the Dabionian guards. Now Dabion would investigate. Twice before Dabion had investigated, and twice they had been distracted: first with political alliance, then with gold. The Alaçans had nothing else to offer. The time had come. The Alaçans would be free, and freedom meant rebellion. The message was sent, Zein having relented and decided to release the sole surviving guard to bear it: Mount Alaz declared its independence. The walls of the city were closed, and the Alaçans prepared to withstand a siege.

This news would be met with puzzlement by Insigh. The clerks who intercepted the weary and lame-footed guard would listen to his words and be certain that he suffered from heatstroke, walking too long through the summer sun, and his words were nonsense. Lord Justice Frahn—summoned in the place of Lord Councilor Muhrroh, who could not be found—seated the guard in his chambers and fed him a great quantity of water and nectar, making him repeat his words over and over, writing them down to be sure he had them right. "A siege?" he asked repeatedly, unable to believe what he heard. He told the guard to rest, allowing the man to sleep in his own rooms in the Great Hall until he recovered his senses, while Frahn sent his clerks to the archives to research this archaic term. It was just as Frahn thought. The siege that the guard insisted upon, even when he woke with no greater injury than a sunburn and the distress of having seen his comrades slain, was a thing of the old kingdoms, older than the Common Calendar, older than the Justices and the Biorans. It was a thing of war.

It was no easy task to find books on war in the Dabionian archives. The Justices in their wisdom had revised the old books, eliminating words that were no longer appropriate and replacing them with those that were true. What little the clerks did find only filled them with more questions, and they puzzled over accounts of siege engines and catapults and trebuchets. At Frahn's order they hunted for more words to describe these unknown things, the weapons they must use to fight the rebellious Alaçans. They read of ladders hoisted up against castle walls and great arms flinging fiery loads over them. They read of archers hidden in narrow slits in the walls and holes in overhead archways that released boiling oil on the heads of trespassers. The clerks' eyes widened with repulsion. Insigh could not be contemplating such things. It was absurd. They looked askance at each other and tried to hide the ancient books.

When Frahn came to the archives and demanded to see what they had found he was no less bewildered. He did not even know how to raise an army. There had never been an army in Dabion. There had never been a war in all the years counted by the Common Calendar. The Biorans discouraged war as an affront to reason. The Five Countries would be united in the peaceful pursuit of knowledge. If there were any dissenters, the Public Force would quiet them, but the Public Force was hardly a military. Even Azassi did not truly have a military, only bands of dirty ruffians who stirred up trouble with rival clans, and when Byorn r'Gayeth led his would-be army in the only incident that had resembled military action in the history of the Five Countries, he was forced to draw from the discontented peasants of Dabion and Karrim in order to build a viable force. The concept of the numbers needed to stage a military campaign was staggering. It would be more than the Public Force, more than the Black Force when it had been active, more even than the ranks of criminals sitting in their prisons in the hidden hills. And campaigns were not always a success. Frahn remembered the losses associated with the closure of some of the larger monasteries in Cassile, and those monasteries had not been well armed, stocked, walled, and prepared to withstand a siege. Frahn pressed his fingers to his aching temples and tried to imagine an answer.

At that same moment, several levels below Frahn in the chambers designated for an elderly retired Justice, Rayner was also pressing his fingers to his temples. His was no simple headache, though, but a massive pain that filled his head so profusely he felt it might split his skull because there was no room for it all. The pain blurred his vision and he could not see where he was. It was extremely upsetting. He shook his head, trying to dislodge it, to clear his vision and focus again on the letter he'd been reading. There, in his right hand—but it had fallen to the floor. What had it said? He leaned over the arm of his chair, the shifting of his balance throwing his head into a new fury of agony, and strained to make out the smear of words. Then he remembered. It was not good news. Jannes was gone; he had left Origh without even taking leave of the Lord Councilor.

Had he been one for such empty words as curses and oaths, Rayner would have spat out every one he knew. While he had been wasting time pursuing Muhrroh, a chase that had yielded less than nothing, Jannes had gotten away. Kerk was looking for him but had yet to find any sign of the man. Tanie was away in Mount Alaz, a move Rayner had initially approved of, since it would sustain his connection to Aron Jannes. If Tanie could gain Aron's confidence, it would give Rayner a way to locate the errant Lord Justice. Surely the father would contact the son, if he could. But then Muhrroh, the madman, let the Alaçans get away. His neglect allowed Zein to abdicate—Zein, the one Rayner himself had supported. Zein had deceived him, betrayed him! It was unimaginable. And now the walls of Mount Alaz were sealed, Rayner's greatest plans locked within them, unreachable—

A noise jolted him. Kerk had returned. *Did you find Jannes?* Rayner wanted to ask. Surely that was what he had done: sent Kerk to find Jannes. But he could not recall, and he could not speak the words.

"I found something very interesting," Kerk said, leaning casually with an elbow propped against Rayner's desk. He was a well-trained little dog, Kerk was. He expected Rayner to jump up immediately and dole out his payment from that desk. Rayner frowned and sat still, and Kerk sighed and continued his story.

"Your Lord Councilor has been getting quite lax with his records. He's keeping some, that is. Writing things down, probably so he won't forget them. I'm afraid the country's headed for hell. Anyone could walk in and take over his office, I think. It's certainly easy to rifle through and find out things about his operatives."

Rayner narrowed his eyes. Get on with it, he thought.

"Your Tanie," Kerk went on. "That's not really her name, did you know? Thessa, or something like that. Thessa Woodbridge, from some peasant family in District Four. I thought that was interesting."

Rayner did not think it was interesting. Tanie was a spy, and no one assumed that spies were telling the truth. People changed their names all the time. If he'd been more shrewd when he first came down to Origh from his family's land, years ago, Rayner might have changed his own name.

Kerk was setting his head on its side and looking at Rayner quizzically. A well-trained little dog, now he looked like a stupid one. "You need me to go on, really?" he asked. "Thessa Woodbridge, your Tanie, is in Muhrroh's rolls of operatives. She's been paid by him. She's one of his spies. She's been working behind your back, working against you, deceiving you. She's a double agent."

The words rolled in Rayner's head, slowly, like the pain was straw batting slowing them down. Double agent. Tanie was working against him. Working for Muhrroh, deceiving Rayner. Used him, as Zein had used him, stepping on him like a ladder, to climb up and leave him behind. "She tricked me," Rayner said. "She won't get away with it."

That was what he thought he said. In his voice he heard an infant's babble: *yeeee-eee-ee*. Kerk still stared at him like a puzzled dog. Rayner tried to reach out his arm, his right hand, but it would not move. "God's teeth," he shouted, absurd criminal's words seething in his mind, "bastard, whoreson!" But none of it came out, nothing but *gaaaah maaa oooh*. Furious, Rayner stood, but his legs shook beneath him and his right leg would not hold. Kerk's damned dog face was the last thing he saw before his vision went black and he fell to the floor.

Part 5

THE TRIAL

And have I moved them by knowing their moves, Tod asks me. Once asked, has asked, asks still. Have I turned their steps by seeing their path? Can he stop the people in his dreams from dying?

It doesn't matter, he told me, about his dreams. They will die with or without his dreams. The dreams only tell him what he should do.

So I see the boy. I know him from the inside, blood through his flesh. He is without guile and he is without deception. Integrity is in his very breath. He could not turn from the path I see him on even if my dreams were wires that moved him like a puppet. And I see Aron. And I see the path that Aron moves on, the arm of the spiral curling back beneath me, and I see who will meet him on that path. The other Sages have seen as well, they have seen the humans with their battles, so small and insignificant to Sage minds. They have seen who Aron meets on that path, and they know the men better than I do. But it means little to them.

It should have meant little to me. As a human, as a spy, I would have stilled the emotions I denied having, and I would not have been moved. As a Sage I should have turned my eyes toward greater things. This human matter would not draw me out from the land behind the lake. But we have come out already, to see the plague. I tell Zann and Irisith of my plan and they shrug their tattered shoulders. We have done what we do, they say. We have laid our stories and our seed and our blood. The humans will listen and they will not, they will die and they will not. What more would you do? Can Tod stop the people in his dreams from dying?

Still I see Aron, hazily with these Sage's eyes, and I see who he meets on his path. He will come to a choice and he will not see it. He will move past it as if his feet are not his own, as if he cannot choose. He will lose himself as I lost myself the day I forsook Tod to save my own life, when I tore out my heart and sacrificed it to the game. And I cannot let him do it.

Zann and Irisith watch me, with those eyes that are not human. And they nod. Then we will find him, they say, and we will move him.

But what will his choice be?—that I do not see. If the Sages do they do not say it. Can I save him, though I could not save myself? What is this sight worth? But if Tod cannot stop the people in his dreams from dying, neither can he stop having them. And we have done what we do.

1

I FOUND A WAY OUT."

Aron looked up. He wasn't expecting to see Toria; she hadn't been around much. It was no easy thing to hide in such a small, crowded city. He assumed she must have been well buried under some other men's sheets. "You found what?"

Toria grabbed his hands, jolting the splints. "A way out!" Her nails dug into his wrists so he couldn't pull his hands away, and Aron let out a short noise of pain. Toria was not a careful person. "We can leave."

"Why would I want to leave?" Aron answered. "It's been such a lovely place to spend the summer." The truth was he was desperate to leave. Everyone was. Rumors of a fever were spreading as the season dragged on and the days grew hotter than any summer that anyone could remember. People were walking through the streets with their hands pressed to their foreheads, hunting fearfully through their hair looking for lesions on their skin. Whenever someone fainted from the heat they were rushed to the kitchen by neighbors who tied scarves over their faces so they wouldn't breathe the infected air. No one actually wanted to go into the kitchen where the clerk still lay raving and dying, so they gathered outside the door. Aron found himself stationed there handing out ladles full of water, because that was where Julian was, and Julian was there because that was where Carra was. A few gulps of water and the patients were usually healed. Aron thought they looked a little disappointed when they stumbled away. With no plague to worry about, there was nothing else for them to do but look out over the city walls and wait for soldiers to arrive. "And I don't believe you," Aron said. "How could you manage to find a way out?"

Toria shushed him angrily, trying to keep others from hearing their words. "Do you want to know or not?" she hissed under her breath. "Do you want to stay here, or do you want to find your father?"

There it was again: the trap. And the trap brought him to the terrible paralysis that always came with his father, the struggle to breathe, the need to escape. And escape brought him to Elzith. Aron's throat closed. "I don't trust you!" he hissed.

Toria began to shake. "You have to!" she cried, pushing at him with her hands. When he did not move she growled in frustration and turned her back to him, running up the stairs. He watched her disappear around the curve in the stairwell, dirty ankles bared by the skirts she had tucked up at her waist.

I could follow her, Aron thought. It would keep him away from the kitchen. Up was a trap, down was sickness. Aron scratched at the wall next to him, wondering if he could dislodge a stone and go through. But Julian was downstairs, and that was where he went.

The Bioran was quiet, which was strange, and he was not smiling. "The last one they brought in," Julian said, after a few minutes when he sat not saying anything, "did have the fever."

Aron snorted, too loud, too glib. "Of course. The clerk was in the kitchen, so were all the cooks, so was all the food. The first one was, too. That's two cases. What did they think was going to happen? Of course the fever was going to spread." If he kept talking, Aron wouldn't have to consider that first clerk, the one who had ridden with them from Tanasigh to Mount Alaz. He wouldn't have to think about the air they had shared in the carriage, the air that could have carried the fever from him to Aron, to Julian.

"The second clerk died," Julian said. His face was drawn and dark. "He wounded himself, did you know that? He had lesions on his face and his arms, the rumors were right about that, but he tore them himself, when he was delirious. We finally heard what he said then. He was naming his sins."

"You heard him?" Aron asked, his voice beginning to shake. "You were there?" He clenched his left hand around the immobile right one, fighting the urge to touch Julian's forehead and pray that it was cool.

Julian was nodding grimly. "It is a terrible thing. We must fight it."

"Why *we*?" Aron stammered. "It's not even your city!"

Julian looked up at him, that judging expression.

Aron was making a choice and it wasn't the right one. "Who else will? And it is not only here."

But Aron would not stay to face the accusation. He was on his feet, fleeing the sickroom air of the kitchen, but he could go no farther than the kitchen door. He leaned against the door and closed his eyes, then ground the heels of his hands against them to blot out the terrible images he saw there.

The clerk had to be buried. No one else wanted to touch him, so Julian helped Carra carry his body to the upper slope on the far side of the city, where the peak of Mount Alaz joined the range behind it and the wall ran out, no longer needed. They dug a hole in the slope, laying the second clerk next to the first one, and when they came back down and walked through the streets the people gave them a wide berth.

The blacksmith's apprentice had the fever on him now. "Biel!" Carra cried when they brought him in, and she'd been in the closet tending to him since then. Her other duties went neglected, the household budget, the rents, the taxes. There were no clerks to collect the taxes and no one from whom to buy goods for the household. Any servants who brought their squabbles and complaints were stopped at the kitchen door by Aron. He was getting desperately sick of hearing them. Then the baker's wife was brought in, her husband carrying her in a sling fashioned from his floury apron, and she had the fever.

Carra came up from the closet at the end of one long day and sat at the table, staring into a cup of boiled ale.

"How many barrels do we have?" she asked the servant who brought it to her, although she was past figuring the rations. She bowed her head toward the table and Julian ran a hand over her sweat-dampened hair. There might be enough room in that closet, Aron thought, for Julian to have done her, especially if they did it on their feet. The sick people were probably far enough gone that they wouldn't even notice. Aron screwed his face up as if he were disgusted by something, and realized it was himself.

"The baker's wife is delirious already," Carra said. "She's crying out about her sins, the women she's gossiped against, the customers she's cheated, making a cuckold of her husband."

"You could hear what she was saying?" asked Julian, surprised.

Carra coughed out a little laugh, gallows humor. "You hardly need to. Everyone knows everything she's ever done. She's a fantastic gossip but she's a terrible liar. Make out a few of her words and you can put it together."

"Then what has the boy done?" Julian mused, seriously, as if plague could really rise out of one's sins. Aron scoffed aloud but silently he pleaded, *It's not our city.*

Carra shook her head. "I've known Biel all his life. He's innocent as a baby. He hasn't done so much as lie his way out of trouble. Once his brother stole a melon and he made himself sick trying to keep the secret."

They were quiet at the table for a moment. The kitchen had grown nearly deserted, half the servants too afraid to come to work, most of the population of the keep going elsewhere to eat their meals. The only sound was the terrified voice of the sick woman in the closet behind them.

Who else will? echoed Julian's voice in Aron's head. He clenched his eyes against it but it did not fade. "The baker's wife was here two days ago," he gasped, "complaining about her oven. She'd hired the blacksmith to fix something about it and she wasn't happy with the job he did. She brought the apprentice with her, dragging him by the ear. I guess the blacksmith himself was avoiding her. She was raving, she was shouting, tearing her hair. There was a scratch on her face and it was bright red."

Carra stared at him. "She was already in the delirium. She'd torn her skin."

"I just thought she was a little cracked," Aron said, trying not to sound like he was apologizing. "I thought that was just how she talked."

"She had open wounds and the infection was on them," Carra said, taken up in her thoughts as if they were fever themselves. "The apprentice was with her then. That's how it spreads." She rounded on Aron. "Where was the baker's wife when the clerks came?" she demanded.

Aron's mouth fell open dumbly.

"But the clerk didn't have the wounds yet when he arrived," Julian interrupted eagerly. "She would have had to encounter him later."

Carra jumped in her seat. "She came to the kitchen to

deliver bread three days after. I placed the order the day they came, and it took that long for the silly goose to bring it. She sat here at this table for four hours gossiping with the cooks. No doubt she was snooping through the closets, looking for something to talk about."

Aron watched them pick apart the plague with the zeal of black-robed professors dissecting a mathematical formula. But you're not in a lecture hall, he wanted to shout at them. You're in the same kitchen where the baker's wife sat gossiping, you're in the same closet where she caught the plague from the guard, and you're there day in and day out. Unnoticed by Carra and Julian as they talked eagerly about death, unwilling to fight it with them, Aron slunk away.

"All right," he hissed when he found Toria. "What do you want from me to show me this way out?"

Toria looked at him hungrily. Food was already being rationed; Aron wondered if she would eat him, given the chance. "Come with me to Rayner."

Who in hell was Rayner? Aron shook his head. "I don't think I trust him. Find something else for me to do."

"Then I'll go to him," she pleaded. "Just find something for me to take him. Find out something about your father. Please. I need to know."

"You mean Rayner needs to know."

Toria nodded deliriously. Maybe her escape was coming too late, Aron thought, but she hadn't been anywhere near the kitchen, the bakery, or anyone as innocent as the blacksmith's apprentice. "Fine," Aron agreed. "Wait here."

He thought she might have followed at his heels like a starved dog. She did whimper like one as he walked away, afraid he was changing his mind.

He needed to find Julian alone, without Carra. He had to wait in the kitchen for almost an hour before Julian emerged from the closet.

"What are you doing here?" Julian asked. "It's late. You should rest, keep your strength."

Aron growled in frustration. "She's right, you know. Every damned thing you do calls attention to yourself, even when you're trying to be generous. Be selfish for once, will you? Be a bastard like the rest of us."

Julian laughed as if it were a joke. "What do you mean?"

Aron wanted to grab him by the collar and shake him; he almost did, but his hand stung in its splint and would not clasp. "You've been living on top of the plague," he whispered fiercely, rising on his toes to hiss in his friend's ear. "Keep at it and you'll die of it yourself. Keep with her and she'll let you. I've got a way out."

"A way out?" Julian asked innocently, shaking his head as if he didn't understand.

"I'm leaving! I'm leaving the city. I'm getting away from this plague. And I'm taking you with me."

In the whiteness of Julian's face it looked like light was breaking, a light that cast more than understanding. It was the light of some wisdom that mortals like Aron would never reach. "I can't go," Julian answered simply.

Aron pushed at his chest. "Are you mad?"

But the brightness of Julian's face was not without clouds. There was no innocence in it, no naïveté. He was staying and he knew what it meant. "I cannot go," he repeated.

Aron shouted and pushed him again, but he only threw himself backward. "Can't leave her, then? Don't think you can find yourself another tumble? You can stay here then, you and her and all the rest, and you're all mad. You can all hide inside your walls and starve yourselves, and hope the plague gets you sooner." He sounded like a maniac. He wanted to say something else, to say something more, but instead he turned and ran out of the keep, through the streets, twisting his ankle as he skidded down a slope to the place where Toria stood waiting for him, still whimpering like a kicked dog.

2

T HE WAY OUT WAS THROUGH THE MILDEWED, dilapidated shack inhabited by a tinker in what was the bad part of town in Mount Alaz. In a city so small the bad part of town consisted of not much more than his shack, the land around it, and the makeshift tents set up by the city's few beggars. Two feral dogs growled at Aron as he picked through the rocks on the unleveled ground, dancing near his ankles and trying to bite at him. Aron growled back at them and they skittered backward, hovering and watching him warily.

The tinker's shack contained, incongruously, the entrance to a tunnel under the mountain, the ancient passage that was rumored to run directly from the old king's underground castle, a place no one had actually seen. No one was seeing it now, either. That part of the tunnel was sealed up, the tinker said, and the whole passage was supposed to have been sealed up as well, to prevent enemies from finding a breach during a siege. The tinker had other plans for the gate he kept, though.

"Who's he?" the man said, pointing his chin toward Aron, his voice even more wolfish than the growls of his dogs. He was lanky and unshaven and his teeth were worse than Toria's. "He's not paid."

"I paid for him," Toria argued with an ugly frown. "He's with me."

The tinker shook his head and crossed his arms over his chest as if he could make himself more intimidating that way. Aron could have lifted him and thrown him over the wall if he'd been willing to get close enough. "You paid for yourself. Everyone else pays in copper."

"You're selling the way out?" Aron laughed out loud at that. "You're stuck in the middle of a fishbowl. What good will money do you?"

The tinker frowned but didn't answer, reaching for Toria's arm.

Aron felt a pinch of anger but could not tell why. "If you know how to get out," he asked the tinker, "why don't you just leave?"

The tinker looked offended. "Alaçans don't leave," he said. "Outsiders leave. Alaçans stay." Then he dragged Toria to his fence and, without any concern for Aron's presence, bent her over it and pulled up her skirt.

The woman was a known prostitute, Aron said, defensively, in his head. He had paid for her services himself. There was no reason for bile to rise in his throat, watching the tinker's handling of her, as if someone close to him were being violated. There was no reason to feel ashamed that he stood there and did nothing. Accusations of the sort he got from Julian were something he was leaving behind in this devil-cursed city.

"Don't you get tired of doing that?" Aron asked Toria,

trying to sound unconcerned, as they made their way down the muddy slope of the tunnel a few minutes later. The tinker had thrown back a few floorboards in his one-room shack and ushered them inside, not bothering to give them any direction or light. Toria had brought a stub of a candle in her pocket. Aron thought this was uncommon foresight on her part.

She was not amused by his question, though. She stopped dead in her steps and nearly dropped the candle. "Don't you criticize me!" she shouted. "You don't know what I think, you don't know who I am! You haven't lived through half of what I have in your pretty black suit!"

Aron took half a step back. "That means yes, I suppose."

Toria did not answer. He heard the huffing of her breath, and a shaky hand threw the light around the mucky tunnel, lighting up cobwebs and frightened spiders. A minute later she walked again, and Aron followed her light.

They walked for a long time through the stifled air. Which would be more unpleasant, Aron thought to himself, starving or suffocating to death? He decided the monotony of the walk would be what killed him. Only now did he wonder whether the tinker was honest, whether there was a way out after all, or if he had simply devised this clever way of killing off the outsiders and earning himself some coin—however useless—in the process. Aron would have walked right into it. The irony of the very thought made him laugh in a dusty cough.

This was the trap that would get him. Toria threw a half-lit glare of annoyance back at him, but Aron only laughed more. He would expect such stupidity of Toria, but he would have thought he was smarter. He must have been wrong. Everything must have been wrong.

He was laughing so hard he didn't notice when the light began leaking in. There was an end to the tunnel after all. Hysterics were cutting off his breath. At its mouth the tunnel narrowed, and they were forced to go on hands and knees, and finally to slither through the mud toward an opening that was barely wide enough for their shoulders to fit through. Toria went through first, snake-like, but Aron found himself caught, still shaking with uncontrollable laughs, and he couldn't breathe. He was stuck. Toria shouted at him to calm down in a shrill voice that was painfully funny.

He would not remember finally getting through. He found himself in a puddle at the foot of the mountains, a stinking, stagnant leftover from some downpour of late-summer rain. The air was humid and mud covered Aron's clothes and face, caked in his bristly hair, stuck in his ears, and itched. Toria was already trudging ahead onto the plain before them. Aron looked up at her, then past her.

There was an army on the plain beneath the mountains. At least, it was what would pass for an army in Dabion. Public Force clumped together in their dull gray and waved muskets as tiny black-robed figures tried to impose some sort of order on them. They had nothing, as far as Aron could see, that could possibly breach the walls of Mount Alaz. It was one of the most pathetic spectacles he'd ever witnessed.

He didn't think that for long, though. The army was not much of an army but they were well able to spot two people on foot, uncovered on the open plain.

"Get down, you idiot!" Aron shouted at Toria in a whisper, not that it would do any good to hide now. Guards were already moving toward them, their guns primed and aimed. They might capture the escapees and interrogate them, or they might shoot as soon as they were in range. Aron did not like the idea of dying in the mud; he could hardly even laugh at it.

Then he heard a voice, to the side, among the shrubs at the mountain's foot. When he heard it he did not know whether to run toward it or toward the guns. "This way."

When the blacksmith's apprentice was two more days gone, the delusions began. Carra stood at his bedside and watched him with mystification as he tore at his hair and scratched deeply at his arms with cracked and bloody nails. "What could he possibly be seeing?" she breathed. Exhaustion was showing in her face, and the basin of tincture tilted in her hands. Julian took the basin from her and sent her out to rest. As he crouched beside Biel to wash the wounds on his arms and fingers, he lowered his head and tried to hear words in the long, thin, horrified cries that issued from the boy's parched lips.

"What is a banshee?" Julian asked Carra later, when they went to the well to draw fresh water. They went only after the sun set, as the other people of the city would not let them come near, and so they could not go to the well when others were about.

Carra looked at him from a corner of her eye, too weary as she carried her heavy buckets to turn her head all the way. "A spirit, the death harbinger."

"What does it mean when you kill one?"

Now Carra stopped and faced him. "What?"

"That's what Biel has been saying. He killed the banshee, and now she's coming after him."

"It's a story," Carra said. "A legend. If you hear the cry of the banshee, someone close to you will die before the night is out. The boy in the story killed the banshee so he couldn't hear her, so his mother wouldn't die." She lowered the water to the ground, unable to carry it any longer. "But it's only a story. Biel would have heard it in his nursery, as a child. No one has seen a banshee since— oh, maybe never. Maybe all the stories are lies."

"So the plague attacks the guilty," murmured Julian, "and if they are innocent, it will make guilt for them. It wasn't meant for Biel but because the infection came to him, it made him guilty."

Carra stared at him. "That's mad," she said, but the thought did not let her rest as she lifted her burden and carried it back to the keep.

Over Julian's shoulder he saw movement in the street. He looked, he had to, though he knew it was not what he thought. It was not Aron out there, walking silently in the shadows on the other side of the street. It was not Aron and it would not be Aron. He was gone. He had left the place, he had to leave it, even if it meant leaving Julian behind, never seeing Julian again. This was not his home and Aron did not know how to make it his.

I know now, Julian thought. He had spent his life letting the wind and water push him where they might, hoping they might send him to a new home. And Carra was right when she said he needed the attention of others. He had used that attention, surrounded himself with it, trying to build a home, decorate it, and make it his own. If the people around him noticed him, if they saw him so much that they thought he belonged there, then perhaps he would. But it was not true.

It was by chance, of course, that he was here. The wind had carried him up the mountain and closed the walls around him. But now it was different. He did not belong here because others saw him here. Others hardly saw him at all. He belonged here because he was needed here.

Carra was the only one who did see him. When she looked at him now, though, it was not his face she saw, the fair perfect lines of it or the frame of his hair, the shape of his body and his movements, the things she had seen at the start. When she looked at him now it was with all her hope and despair, with solidarity, and with thanks.

They reached the kitchen and filled the cistern from the buckets, splashing themselves and their clothes. Carra's hands slipped and she dropped her bucket. It rolled across the floor and struck a tower of shelves stacked with crockery. The tower jolted and collapsed like rows of dominoes. Her mouth fell as she watched the crockery cascade to the floor.

"I don't think everything broke," Julian said hopefully, when the crashing noise subsided.

Carra stared a moment longer, her eyes wide with horror, then she laughed. She leaned against the cistern and laughed. "I'm so tired," she said breathlessly.

Julian smiled and brushed the damp hair back from her face. He watched her laugh out all the weariness she could, but he had to hide a tear in his eyes. Under his hand, her forehead was hot as fire.

3

"WHY ARE YOU FOLLOWING ME? LEAVE ME ALONE!"
Aron shouted recklessly, not caring that the approaching gunmen were only strides away. Let them shoot, said the thought that flew through his mind. Let them take out this woman who betrayed him and this girl who used him, let them take him out, he didn't care, let them put an end to it, now.

But the guards did not shoot. Toria pulled at his sleeve, vainly trying to stop his shouting, staring in horror at the guards. Then she stopped pulling, her hand caught in his sleeve like a thorny branch. "What?" Aron started to growl.

But Toria's face had changed. At her other side, someone had taken her arm, two wanderers standing with hands linked. "Huh," she said, then looked back out at the guards. When Aron tried to pull his arm away she seized it more tightly. "Hold on, you bastard," she said, with a caustic laugh in her voice that Aron did not understand.

He followed her eyes over the plain. Four guards stood there, looking around like they were lost. They pointed their muskets at things like scurrying rabbits and scrub rustled by the wind, but they did not aim at the people standing only twenty yards away. One lifted his head and stared straight at Aron but did not see him, looked right through him like he was glass.

"Yes, hold on," a voice said at his other side. Elzith had caught up to him and clasped his right wrist above the bandages.

Something jolted as the chain was completed, something resonating under his feet. Aron stumbled though his feet were not moving, and anxiously he rounded on Elzith. "Why are you here?" he tried to shout, but it only came out in a rasp.

"To save your skin," Elzith answered. Her voice was as casual as it had ever been, and she set her head at a careless angle, just as if she were telling him that if he cheated at cards it would come back to him, or that he should apologize to his mother, or any of those other things she'd told him. All the things that were lies now that she had left him. There was a strange echo in her voice, though, her face was narrow and the flesh of it thin like a transparent sheet of horn, and her eyes were wide and shifting and saw much more than he did. It hurt to look at her. "You seem to be trying very hard to get yourself killed," she went on, lines deepening between her eyebrows as if it somehow hurt her to speak, "and they don't like some of the people you're running around with."

Aron turned to look over his other shoulder—a sickening, dizzying motion—at the two wanderers linked with Toria. They were the same ones he'd seen outside the city gates, no doubt, though he hadn't paid them much notice before. A madman was a madman: all rags and brightly colored things worn to ribbons, hair tangled in braids and dye and string. Elzith was not quite so disheveled. But Aron met their eyes, something he'd never done before, and saw that they were weird kaleidoscopes of green and gray and blue, and they were at the same time wise, knowing, and utterly mad. Aron shivered and looked away. Elzith's eyes were still green, weren't they? They'd always been green. The sky whirled as he turned and he stumbled again, and Toria wrenched hard at his arm.

"Are you trying to impress us with your little trick?" Toria was saying to the wanderer at her side. Aron thought she must be clenching his hand just as hard as she was clenching Aron's arm, and wondered if wanderers felt pain, if they got angry.

But the wanderer's answer wasn't really an answer. "You're Thessa," he said. "I've been given blessings to give to you. You know him. Karinalitarinaril."

Toria—Thessa, whatever her name was—turned purple with rage and choked with silence. "You've shut her up," Aron rasped, clenching his teeth against the swimming of his stomach. "Good show."

Then the last wanderer, an old woman at the end of the chain, answered, but it seemed she was speaking not into the air but into Aron's head, her voice bleeding through the joined hands to throb at Aron's ears from the inside. He buckled over, hands on either side of him roughly holding him up. "You laugh, boy, human. You have forgotten so soon. You think this is a joke now, you are afraid to look at power, you tell yourself it is something else, as if you've never seen it. You cannot even see the power in your own hands, so you lie and say ours is nothing."

"Irisith," called Elzith, "it's no use. He only lives in a straight line. There's none of the blood in him at all, he's nothing but human. And not a very bright one at that."

Aron was furious but could not stand or draw the breath to scream. "You lie to me," he spat, hoarse with nausea, "you leave me, and now you insult me?" But he could say no more, because bent as he was, he was able to see the ground. And it was moving.

"Bloody hell," he uttered, then the dizzy consciousness he was trying to hold on to left him, and not even the pain of his strained shoulder joints could keep him in the world that had inverted itself so badly.

When he opened his eyes he was lying on his back, in grass. There were no rocks or scrub, no mountains, no guards with guns. The wanderers were gone. Toria was not.

He sat up too fast, clenching his head to stop it from going into that spinning world again. "What in hell happened?"

"They moved us," she said simply. "They put you out so you wouldn't be frightened."

Aron seethed, to hide the traces of nausea. "You're lying."

Toria smiled, a thin, ugly, smug smile. "You don't know everything, now, do you?"

He struggled to his feet and ran, in some direction, he didn't know which, until he came to a road. There was a carriage on the road, and though he looked like some dirty beggar, without a suit coat or a wig, his velvet vest and breeches caked with mud and his hair grown out in a filthy shock, still the carriage stopped for him. When he told the stunned occupants his name, they believed him. No one would be so bold as to lie about being the Lord Justice's son. They took him in, gasping about what kind of brigand would have attacked and robbed a gentleman, of course he can't remember what happened, he must have been stricken unconscious by the villain, and certainly they'll return him to his home, Origh is only a half day's journey away. They poured water from their silver flasks so that he could clean himself, and gave him fresh clothes from their own luggage. Aron held his breath as the carriage began to move, but it was only the wheels rolling. The world had almost returned to normal.

It was strange and disconcerting, not having language, and it made Rayner angry. Not having control over his body made him angrier. He lay in bed for a time that he was painfully aware of but could not find the words to count, helpless as an invalid. One of his operatives—one of the mutes, thank his rotten fortune—spooned into his mouth water and gruel that he could not swallow. He held Rayner's hand when he had trouble breathing, like Rayner was a child who needed comforting, and he lifted

Rayner over his shoulder to strip the bed of its soiled linens when Rayner lost control of his bowels, as if he needed any further indignity. When the operative settled him back into the bed Rayner's throat seethed with screams he could not find words for.

When he was alone in his room, he would pull back the top sheet and move his legs. His left leg was unaffected, and after a few painful days, he had command over his right. His right hand was useless. His left was as strong as it had ever been, and he used it to quickly cover himself up whenever the door to his room opened again. Only two people came into Rayner's room: the operative who played nursemaid and Kerk. Kerk was there to look for money. For the first several days, Kerk watched Rayner like a nervous hound dog, wondering if he should attack or if the bigger dog would attack him first. Now that nervousness was gone; Kerk had decided Rayner was toothless and harmless, and he went boldly around hunting for Rayner's stores. Obviously he had not found the portions of money that Rayner kept hidden in the side trails of the labyrinth under the hall, or he would have taken it and run, never needing to darken Rayner's door again. But he was here again, day after day, opening drawers and sifting through wardrobes, as if Rayner were stupid enough to hide his cash somewhere so easily accessed. It was that, even more than the mutiny of his body, the assumption that his mind had crumbled like his worthless right hand, that enraged Rayner most of all.

So he lay in bed like an invalid and waited. The

cacophony of meaningless noise and confusion that had troubled him when he first woke had resolved into a furious clarity, made even sharper by the silence of his own voice. He was ready, then, when Kerk turned toward him, lying in the bed like an empty suit of clothes, and made an insolent face at the man who he thought could not see or hear him. "Now, what does this little thing go to?"

Rayner hissed. Dangling from Kerk's hand was a key. Where had he found it? Where had Rayner put it? But the questions did not matter. Rayner would not let Kerk use the key. When Kerk turned his back—a foolish mistake; no operative of his caliber should have made it—Rayner threw back the linens and leapt to his feet. In an instant, only an instant, he was at Kerk's back, and with a dinner knife nicked from the nursemaid in his left hand, he caught Kerk from behind and held the knife to his throat. Rayner had regained control.

Now, to regain power in the world. With the knife at Kerk's back he marched him through the hallways, trying to find something that would say what he could not. He climbed up through the Great Hall, above all the minions that he still dominated, above the city that he was still the head of, no matter what his pathetic body could not do. He strode—did not stumble, did not limp, but *strode,* he was certain—into the antechamber of the man whose name he could not articulate, to the inner chamber with its darkness. At the prick of his knife Kerk threw open the door. The chamber was empty. Rayner cut through one of the hangings that muffled the window. There was no sign of the wanderers or the Lord Councilor. The alcohol lamps had burned dry. Rayner hunted through the room, searching for anything that could carry his meaning. Kerk made a move as if toward the door and Rayner grunted, gesturing at him with the knife. He would not leave. Then Rayner's eyes fell on a bottle, a single remaining bottle full of alcohol. He tucked the knife into his belt and lifted the bottle in his hand.

"Jannes?" Kerk said.

Rayner nodded his head furiously. He threw down the bottle with a wet crash, seized the knife again, and pointed with it to the south.

He did not let go of the knife as they rode together in the carriage; being unarmed around the mercenary would be unwise. The mute, who was driving the carriage, was fortunately trustworthy; Rayner did not know why, as the operative was as unable to tell the melodramatic story of his life as Rayner was unwilling to listen to it, but whenever a Justice needed to be assassinated, the mute was a reliable tool. Concealed in his walking stick, in fact, was a fine specimen of a blade. He would be only the second line of defense, though. Rayner had to remain prepared to deal with Kerk himself.

When Kerk said something that Rayner could not grasp, he tightened his grip on the blade, looking at the man with suspicion. Kerk began to root through the bag he had hastily packed, but he brought out no weapon, only a stub of pencil and one of the many forged travel documents Rayner kept on hand. On the back of it he drew a picture, badly: a figure in a skirt, obviously meant to be a woman. He sketched bare breasts and a head with two faces, each turned in opposite directions.

"Tanie?" Kerk said again, and Rayner tried to recognize the picture in the jagged shape of the word. He knew what the man was asking, though. What would they do with her? He snagged the pencil out of Kerk's fingers, and in the awkward scrawl that was all he could get from his left hand, he drew in a rope and made a noose around the figure's neck.

Jannes would not be at his house, Rayner knew. The house was not empty, though. The yard in front was filled with a mass of people, gossips. If he could have heard their words he would have gathered the story of Aron's assault on the road from District Three, how the Lesser Justice who found him, scraped and muddy, had been fortunate enough to recognize and rescue him, how the Lesser J had had a dreadful time convincing the locksmith—dastardly commoner—to cut a new key and let the Lord Justice's son into his house. None of the gossips noticed Rayner walking into that house where the door stood open.

The household had left, whether in Jannes's company or dismissed from his service Rayner did not know. The rooms were dark and the furniture was dusty, and the door to Jannes's office was ajar. One individual only was inside the house, and that was Jannes's son.

He was pulling drawers from his father's desk and rifling through their contents. With his ill-fitting borrowed clothes and lacking his lost wig, he looked like a ruffian or a thief, and when he heard an intruder's approach he looked up with a mixture of guilt and anger. The sight of the old man, stooped and shuffling, his mouth wet at the drooping right corner, was as distasteful to him as his own image was to that old man, but in the next second his brows pricked up. "You're Rayner?" he asked.

Rayner growled and nodded with as much superior dignity as he could find.

In a rush Aron sifted through the papers and ledgers he had found, pulling this and that, saying things about them that he seemed to think were terribly important. Aron pushed the papers into his hand and Rayner batted them away, knocking them on the floor. He didn't want those things, he didn't care. The game was larger than that now, larger than any of the simple details of Jannes's crimes. Rayner was past threatening the man. Any fool could make threats. It was time for greater action, one that only a man of Rayner's power could take.

But he could not make the stupid boy understand. He uttered and waved his one good arm and shouted with his eyes, but Aron only shook his head like an idiot. Rayner stormed out into the corridor, looking for Kerk, but the man had vanished, probably upstairs to loot the rooms. Rayner's eyes fell on the shelf in the foyer where the statue of the scales of Justice stood, and he seized it and carried it to the office, the plates swinging on their chains. Aron looked at him like he was mad. Rayner shrugged out of his jacket and covered the scales.

Aron shook his head in confusion, uttering senseless words. "Where is justice?" Rayner heard him say.

Where is Justice, that was an amusing little joke. There was no justice. But the silly boy finally understood. "Where is my father?"

Rayner shouted inarticulately.

Aron laughed roughly, seizing the papers from the floor again. "Somewhere," Rayner caught him saying, "one of these places." Rayner could not read the words on the pages, they must have been too small or too blurred, but he read the expression on the boy's face infallibly. All such dysfunctions were the result of parents. Aron's father had abandoned him, and he was angry. He wanted to get him back. He wanted to find his father, and he would lead Rayner there. Rayner smiled, feeling the left half of his face tug upward. He had Jannes's son.

4

WINTER WAS COMING TO THE ALAÇAN REGION.
It was late fall in Dabion, but the mountains of
the southeast met the season early, and within a few
weeks the paths to Mount Alaz would be impassable until after the turn of the year. It was a bad time to under-
take a military strike, Lord Justice Frahn knew. He would
rather have moved earlier, weeks earlier, but when Frahn
sent his first strike out he'd had only a few hundred Public Force to spare.

After the news of the secession of Mount Alaz, Frahn
had tried to contact the Lord Councilor for advice on
how to respond, but Muhrroh could not be found. He
went to the Lord Councilor's chambers and found them
nearly empty, only one mad wanderer there to deliver a
bizarre message about Muhrroh having gone on holiday.
Frahn had called a meeting of the Circle then, but
though he waited in the underground chamber for
hours, none of the other Lord Justices came. Trying to
contact them through their secretaries yielded the news
that Marsan refused to leave his district, Wirthir was occupied with business in Azassi, Nosselin hoped all the

country went to hell, and Jannes was missing. All of them except Jannes had recalled their contingencies of Public Force to their home cities, leaving Frahn one-third of the country's complement of guards to draw his first wave from. He could not even send all of these, since news of the secession had stoked the rebellious tendencies of commoners across the Five Countries, and no one but Frahn was left to take hold of the problem.

By the end of autumn, though, he had raised something that more closely resembled an army. Rebels were easily pressed into service when prison was the alternative. The village factories in Cassile that busied themselves making velvet, a job they had done since Mandera was in power, were now put to work weaving uniforms, building weapons, and making ammunition. Velvet was a luxury that was now of no use; the crises of the times would not tolerate the hypocrisy of those who enjoyed all the wealth that Mandera once had and called it the reward of the Just. Frahn took in the taxes due to both Districts One and Two, as Jannes was not available to collect his, and funneled them to the war effort. He went to the School of Bioran Science and gave the students the old books of history, instructing them to devise plans for building the siege engines therein described. Those professors who objected that Bioran philosophy abhorred war as an affront to rationality were dismissed. The times could not bear dissent; there was enough dissent in Dabion as it was and, as Frahn had built the school to begin with, it was he who had the authority to change its curriculum. Some of the students at the Insigh School were so prodigious at the science of war that Frahn appointed them officers in the new army, swelling the ranks. By the time he led his second wave to Mount Alaz, late in the season though it might have been, he had a viable force.

Lord Justice Frahn led the army himself. There was no one else to do it. For his entire career he had been only one spoke of the wheel, and not even the most notable one. He had struggled against the rejection of his school, suffered condemnation by his fellows, and when the Bioranism he championed was finally accepted, it was only on the word of Muhrroh, a higher authority. Now, though, there was no higher authority. Now preeminence was his. Command was needed and he was the one who grasped it. Fortune had suddenly rewarded him with an unexpected boon. Frahn had kept the law as well as any of his peers, but he had been singled out. Some great design was meant for him, and he would rise up to meet it.

Fortune was not being kind to Zein. Folklore had no bearing on the world, and things did not go as the stories would have them. The old kings had withstood sieges in their mountain castles, they had turned away invaders and survived long seasons behind their walls. They did not face shortages in their stores. When Zein went to the storerooms to assess his weapons and supplies, he found the numbers were even worse than he'd feared. Mount Alaz had neither the weapons to turn away an assault nor the food to support its people through the coming winter. The city's only hope was that Dabion would not amass an army and would give up the fight soon.

Folklore might have had it that the Alaçans were blessed by fortune, but Zein's lookouts said differently. They could not even open the gates to go out and seek more supplies without facing Public Force troops ranged at the foot of the mountains. A few scouts were sent out the other way, over the peak behind the city and into Azassi to find what they could, but there was little to gather in that direction, and no way to bring more than a little back through the difficult mountain passes in any case. Before long the early-winter storms would come and close those passes, cutting off what thin trickle of supplies came in that way. The same winter storms that threatened the mountain peaks would certainly intimidate the small contingent of soldiers, though, or so Zein hoped. He watched the plain below the city, and waited.

This world that paid no heed to stories had more in store for Zein. He'd heard the rumors of the plague that was simmering in the keep, in the kitchens below him, but had dismissed it as the idle talk of people too frightened to speak of the war itself. Now he could no longer ignore it. One of the clerks came to his door and reported forty-eight deaths of the plague, and twenty-three people currently infected.

Those rumors also identified as the source of the infection one of the retainers that Zein had brought from Tanasigh. Forty-eight deaths were laid squarely at Zein's feet. "Why didn't Carra bring me this report?" he asked with a sticking voice. The clerk could not answer him.

Zein would not allow himself to think of the most obvious reason.

Zein's fortune did not improve with time. He watched the Public Force on the plain, a scatter of tiny gray dots in his spyglass. He watched the numbers on the plague rolls rise, and he watched the sky and the almanacs for the coming of winter. Finally, he could wait no longer. If the plague were not removed from Mount Alaz, he would be fighting for a city of the dead. A camp for the sick would be established at the mountain's foot, a quarantine for the plague. It would not be in danger from the enemy, Zein told himself; only barbarians would kill the sick, and in time even barbarians would not need to bother. He ordered the sick to be lined up on their feet or in stretchers and readied to move, under the watch of caretakers he selected for a suicide assignment. They had to be ones who lived on folklore, the elders who remembered when Mount Alaz was built, or their faithful progeny weaned on stories, people who believed passionately that the Alaçans would be free and who were willing to die in seeking that freedom. Zein lined them up and opened the gates to march them out.

It could not have been poorer timing. The gates were opened in the early morning, to give the sick camp time to be set up before nightfall. Zein did not know until the gates were opened that Frahn's army had arrived, moving in during a darkness that had hidden them from his spyglass. When the gates opened the front ranks charged.

Fortune, when it was kind to Zein, was perverse in its

kindness. The caretakers lunged forward to meet the advancing army, wielding poles meant to build tents, eager to fight the battle that had been foretold for ages. The sick were too ill to recognize the danger and followed their leaders without hesitation. The entire party was through the gates in moments, and the gates were shut and barred before the army was halfway up the mountain.

A clerk offered Zein his spyglass. Zein refused it. The lookout came to give his report and Zein brushed the boy away. He did not want to hear how the party fared outside the city's gates. He did not want to contemplate whether the plague would spread to the attackers, as if the sick themselves had been a weapon that Zein had cannily created and launched. The only thing Zein wanted to do as he descended to the kitchen where servants were hastily scrubbing everything with vinegar was apologize to his niece. Carra was among those he had sent out, he knew, and whether she was ill at the moment or not was now irrelevant. She was not here, and that was what he rued. He had hoped for her to be here with him, sitting at his side in the free city that he would lead, helping him build it, managing it with her wisdom. Now his wishes grew even simpler, and he imagined himself sitting at this table, never having left the city, never having become Lord Justice, feasting Carra at the celebration of the wedding she would never have.

5

HE WAS NOT GOING BACKWARD, ARON TOLD HIM-self. He was progressing farther ahead than he had ever hoped to; it could be called his first and only success. He had carefully analyzed every piece of paper in his father's desk, finding things that he had overlooked before, and had drawn up a map as accurate as anything in the history books. He had laid out a route, a plan to investigate every distillery identified in the records, and it was being followed. He was going to find his father.

Progress required strange company, though. The freakish mute carriage driver would have been enough, but then there was Rayner. Aron still had no idea who he was, other than Toria's highly untrustworthy employer; how he could have commanded Toria or arranged anything like his mother's supposed murder, Aron could not imagine. He was an old, shaking, slavering man, unable to speak except in grunts, absurdly clutching a steak knife like a weapon.

"He thinks he has control over you, holding that ridiculous knife," Kerk, the third member of the strange company, told Aron. "You can humor him if you want. I only did it to get him out of his rooms. Now I'm going back to get his money, then I'm going to get the girl." And he narrowed his eyes, expectantly, at Aron.

"What girl?" Aron murmured.

"Don't try to play me, boy. The spy. The one who went with you to District Three. Where is she?"

Rayner could not have hurt Aron, but Aron had no doubt that Kerk could. "I left her on the road south out of Origh," he said, chafing his hands. "She was with some wanderers."

Kerk made a very small, very cruel smile. Aron averted his head so he would not have to look at him. His life had been at risk, he said defensively to himself. It wasn't his fault, what Kerk did with the information. Aron had only answered a question. That he could have lied to protect someone else's life was a thought he pushed down with the bile in his throat.

Kerk, thankfully, left with that bit of information. Only Rayner and the mute driver would accompany Aron on the journey to Karrim.

He felt he was in control for the first few days. He was even able to shut out the freezing anger that usually gripped him when he thought of his father. His heart beat fast and he felt the anticipation burn in all his fingers. He stripped the bandages and the splint from his hand and found he could move it again—so strong was the power of action. But they did not find his father at the first distillery, or at the second. They could not find the third one at all. Aron was no longer the son avenging himself on his father's abandonment and betrayal. He was an angry little child screaming and kicking his legs at nothing, chasing around the countryside surrounded by madmen, lost. He dug at the scars on his hand with his nails, trying to rip them open again.

"Where in hell are you now?" he whispered out the carriage window, at the woman who might be following him, still thinking she could come back to him. "Elzith? You know where he is, don't you? You could tell me." If she had not betrayed him like everyone else.

The sound of Aron's voice bothered Rayner, and the old man shook his knife in Aron's direction. Aron turned his head and pressed his face to the glass of the window, feeling it grow cold as night came. The carriage rolled on.

More distilleries, more dirty Karrimian villages. Still there was no sign of his father. They came to the end of his planned route. The carriage stopped. Rayner climbed out and attempted to have a conversation with the mute and some gin-soused criminal. They were in Karrim, and a fever was going around. Aron wondered if he could go out and catch it. But the thought of death still made Aron's stomach clench in resistance. He would fight it, like Julian would. No, nothing like Julian would. Aron moaned thinly, his heart in his throat, catching the sound.

Then Rayner clambered back into the carriage, grunting and gesturing wildly. The carriage began to move again, not doubling back to the east and Dabion, but turning south. As if there was somewhere left to go. Aron did not believe it; if he shut his eyes he could be-lieve they were going east. But when the carriage finally pulled to a stop they were not in Dabion. Rayner pushed at Aron's shoulder to wake him, then shook him until he reluctantly opened the door and stepped outside. In front of them stood a large barn, in the center of a parcel of farmland. Aron stared at it, uncomprehending.

Then the driver was behind him, pressing the handle of a walking stick into his back. Aron was to walk forward. He took a few steps and stopped, tired of the game. But the stick prodded him again, forcing him toward the door of the barn. Aron had to go. It was a long time, twenty, thirty steps, before he guessed why. Then the anger came. Ice filled up his throat, thickened his legs, stopped his breath. Only the pressure of the driver walking behind him kept him going, up to the door. He could not feel his own hand as he watched it, pale and twisted, make a fist and pound on the boards.

Lord Justice Jannes had struggled to find a place to relocate to. He had sought his contacts in the north of Karrim first, the alcohol manufacturers, men accustomed to evading the authorities. It was not a satisfactory choice, though. Rayner would certainly have discovered the ring and identified its members, and he would look for Jannes at their residences. Jannes regretted having visited them at all, thereby leaving a trail for Rayner to follow. Men accustomed to evading the law were not known for their fidelity, and they were likely to point Rayner in Jannes's direction. He needed to find another place.

Then indecision had nearly crippled him. He had

nowhere else to go. He knew Dabion and that was all. The other countries were lines on a map, reports filed neatly in his desk. He couldn't live in one of them. In his haste to escape unnoticed he had brought the barest frame of his household and none of his clerks. He had not wanted to trust anyone who had been in the courtrooms or offices or anywhere Rayner might have tainted them. Once he'd gotten to Karrim, he found he hardly had enough staff to keep himself alive. He knew the office of Lord Justice and little else. Alone he would literally starve.

But Jannes was fortunate in always having been a good judge of character. The estate manager for his parcels in the southern fields of Karrim had been in his service since Jannes was a Greater Justice, and that manager was a quiet, honest man with no great love of profit. Jannes went to him at once. Parcel eighty-seven was a small square of wheat-producing acres, neither the most fertile nor the least. It did not boast a tavern or a post office, and as it was not on any major route, it saw very little traffic. The parcel was inconspicuous in every way. Jannes arrived at the estate manager's door and the man asked no questions, merely instructed twenty of his farmers to clear the upper floor of the barn and ready it for their guests' living space.

It was something like living space, Jannes thought on seeing the results. Sheets were hung for walls, creating rooms for him and his servants and an office that housed a worn but serviceable desk. He needn't have brought the cook, since there was no kitchen available to them; still, the woman was one of the soundest minds in his household and he was happy to have her. Dal, his manservant, was put to work at once organizing the books and papers Jannes had brought. It was not the best match, as Dal did not read, and he was so old it was almost unbelievable that he was still on his feet and strong, but he had been a faithful member of Jannes's household for years and was one of the only people Jannes felt he could now trust. With his help Jannes soon had offices established in parcel eighty-seven, and he was ready to return to work.

He did not know what that work would be, though. Correspondence with Dabion—correspondence with anyone, in fact—was dangerous. It would allow him to be traced, and he could not risk it unless the need was severe. His governance of District Two was for all intents over. There might not even be a District Two any longer, for all Jannes knew. Dabion was falling apart, and there might be no place for Justices in the world that was left. There might be no place for him at all but within the insubstantial walls hung up in this barn.

For some time Jannes occupied himself with writing in his books, looking at his old letters and documents, scanning the columns in his ledgers. Then he closed out all of his accounts. He drew heavy black lines to mark the end of his register and dated his final entries. He sketched notes of dismissal on correspondence he had not been able to answer. He filed it all in precise order in his new desk. Then he stood back and looked at his work. It was done. He might as well set fire to it all.

But there was no sense in such actions. He had been

trained in rationalism, whether or not it had been called Bioran science at the time of his training, and he would address his situation rationally. He had a new district, a new seat. He had a new home. He had to devise a new position and life, without profession, without family.

For some time Jannes stared at the desk with blank eyes, no idea what to do.

Then he went downstairs where the estate manager and his workers were putting up winter stores in the barn. There was work being done here; Jannes would find some place in it. He climbed down the narrow steps and found the estate manager near the wide front doors.

"My lord!" the manager exclaimed. "I was about to come up and give you a message. Your son is at the door."

Jannes was stunned. He had nearly resolved himself to pursue his new life, void of anything he once knew. Now a curve in the road threw him backward. His son— he was supposed to be in Mount Alaz, safe from danger, freeing Jannes to find shelter for himself without worrying about Aron. When had Aron left the city? As Jannes analyzed the question, he began to doubt that it was Aron at all and grew suspicious that a trap was being set for him. Even more troubling, Aron might be used as part of a trap, in which case Jannes could not trust his own son. But this was doubtful. With a lack of further evidence, the only course of action was to open the door and see who was truly there.

It was with some astonishment that Jannes found Aron at the door.

News of the seige of Mount Alaz had broken after Jannes had gone underground; he did not know enough to wonder how Aron had escaped the city. Fleetingly, he did wonder how Aron had arrived, a question quickly resolved when he saw the carriage parked some distance away. Then he saw who stood next to the carriage. His throat tightened. His hand clamped on the door, muscles drawn to throw it shut, breath gathering to shout at the farmers and tell them to bring everything they could lift to barricade the door.

But he hesitated an instant. And saw the man who stood behind Aron, some operative, some fiend of Rayner's, raising his walking stick like a sword. The sun caught a flash of something. Jannes stared at the man with the walking stick. Then every question, every fear vanished. His mind was filled with a single urgent need. He motioned to his son, reaching toward him. "Aron," he shouted. "Come here!"

But Aron did not obey his father's command. He could not, because faster than he could move, faster than he could even think, his arms were taken and he was tugged out of time.

The world did not spin this time, and Aron did not see the ground slide past beneath his feet as he hunched over, unable to clutch his stomach with hands that were pulled severely to his sides. What he saw this time was a terrible, unmeasurable *weight,* a slowness and heaviness of everything around him. His ears throbbed, the pulse of his blood raging inside them but the air outside pressing and smothering him.

"What are they doing?" Aron gasped, unable to feel the air move into his chest.

Elzith did not answer his question, of course. She'd gone mad like the rest of them. Her voice was so distorted by the impossible stillness of the air that he couldn't tell where in the chain she was standing. "Julian was right. You did make the wrong choice."

What do you know about Julian? he wanted to shout, if he could get enough air. He struggled against the hands that held him, tugging at the heaviness in the joints of his shoulders.

"Child wants to get away," another voice said, maybe the old woman wanderer, maybe the one holding his left arm. "Do you want to die so soon, little human? Those of your blood don't come back."

"Go to hell," Aron croaked.

"You don't understand," said Elzith, Aron thought. "You never did. Look past your own anger. Did Julian teach you how? Humans die, in more ways than one." The chain pulled to the right, tugging him down, and in the corner of his watering eye he saw Elzith crouch beside him. "Look up, Aron. Look up."

It was hard to see through the wind. They had turned it opaque, sheets like thick spiderweb hanging in the air, sliding at an infinitesimal rate. Blurrily figures appeared through it, the barn, the open door, the two men. His father, reaching a hand out toward nothing. And the mute driver, the shaft of his walking stick in his left hand like a sheath, his right hand drawing out a blade from within, inch by painful inch, the scrape of it vibrating the air at such a low frequency that Aron could hear no more of it than a tremble in his throat.

"We are Sage," the old woman whispered at his left side, through his hand. "We do not regard time."

Through his other side, another voice churning: "You have been given a second chance. You are lucky. Most never get one. Choose again, Aron. Which one?"

Fruitlessly, Aron tried to pull away again, throwing his balance. "Which one *what*?"

The thickness of the air kept him from falling, and he swayed in the bonds of his arms. "Which path do you take?" the voices flooded. "Step inside with your father, or step aside and let him die?" He felt himself lifted, wrenched to his feet, moved forward through the curtains of wind. "Which one? Rayner or your father?"

Aron pulled back with all his strength, though his movements meant nothing. He was hot with dread, so full of it that it was unbearable. He closed his eyes against it and the steam rose from them. He would burst. But then, the anger. His father. Cold fury, ice in his veins. The fear subsided into paralysis. And he could not step forward on any path.

Then, suddenly, the air cleared. For an instant he saw Elzith's face, frowning. "Too late," she said. "You took too long." And the world began to move again.

He fell to the ground, rolling backward. The wanderers were gone from his sight, but he felt the inaudible pounding of their feet, moving too quickly across the grass, their wake tugging at him, hands that no longer held his reaching to grasp a new target. The driver winked out of sight. Aron squinted, sure he could see a shadow of the man, but his eyes were dry and cold. He let himself fall back on the grass.

In the doorway of the barn Jannes blinked in complete confusion, but only for a moment. An inarticulate shout stirred him, and he saw Rayner approaching him in a wildly erratic limp. Hastily he shut the door. Barred from within, it was not opened by the terrified farmers for the better part of an hour. No one saw Rayner disappear from the field.

Some distance away, the Sages set Rayner down on the ground near the mute operative, whom Irisith was holding in place with her eyes fixed on his. Zann kept Rayner still while Elzith went to the mute. "You are scarred," Elzith said, leaning close to whisper in his ear. "Terribly, terribly. Do you even see it anymore? But I won't make you remember. It would be too cruel." Then she lifted the blade and its stick sheath, thrusting them back together with a burst of noise that made the man's eyes flare wide for just an instant. That was her entry. She stopped the man's heart and that was the end.

Rayner was angry when Elzith approached him. The wanderer Zann was holding him down, with a single hand that he could have smashed if he hadn't been so frightened of it, and fear made him angrier. "You're too dangerous even without your tongue," Elzith said softly. Her eyes darkened as she read him, and though he could not tell what she was doing, he still railed against it. "I see what you're afraid of, who you've been running from all your life. You're scarred and you do remember, but you will not admit it." Rayner's eyes narrowed and he hissed through his nose, but something went hollow in his face. "We could trap you there. You would see it over and over again, that face you see only in dreams. We could leave you there, in your prison. Which one was it? Prison 15?"

That was when Rayner's eyes, so blinded with anger and arrogance, finally widened with shock and opened into his center. That was when his guard was breached and his life blown out in a breath. "But I think that is too great a punishment," Elzith murmured, "even for you."

The third figure lying on the grass, they left alone. Aron did not open his eyes as they dragged the bodies away toward the river, nor did he open them when they returned. When they started to leave the second time, though, that was when he sat up, dizziness and sickness still shaking him. "Where are you going?"

"You are free," the wanderer Irisith said, a weird irony twisting her features. "Nothing binds you, not even what should."

"You're not going to take me back?"

"Back where?" Elzith asked him.

Aron could not answer.

"Your father would have saved you," Elzith said, her mouth pressed close. "Are you going to see him?"

But the ice had not thawed out of his throat. "No."

"Well then," she said, and turned. The three wanderers took hands again, then they were gone.

6

THE WOMAN KNOWN AS T WATCHED ARON JANNES run up the road, away from her, and ground her teeth angrily. He'd won again. She couldn't win anything. He was the prize she was going to bring Rayner and now he was gone. She wanted to scream, if anyone had been there to hear her.

But someone was there and she jumped as that person spoke. "I thought you were nothing like me," the female wanderer said, the younger one. T had thought all three of them had left. "You are always angry, getting angry at everything, letting it move you rather than moving yourself. You don't think, you do things without knowing why." The Sage nodded as if this was some grand revelation, something T should listen to instead of just the musings of a madwoman. "But maybe you are like me."

T frowned and tried to stand. For someone who had grown up on the uneven ground of Dabion's open fields, she was pathetically clumsy, able to find any hole in the earth and sink her foot in it, and on the short piece of land between here and Mount Alaz that they had actually walked with their own feet, she'd managed to turn her ankle again. "Why do you care?" she spat at the Sage.

Then the woman said something unexpected, not just something mad, but something that shocked her. "Rayner's looking for you."

For a second T's heart stopped, and she held her breath with excitement. He was looking for her. Her father. He wanted her after all. But the hope did not last. Sages didn't bring good news, and Rayner had no love for anyone. He was looking for her and she was worried. Before she could ask the Sage any more questions—as if Sages could answer anything clearly—the woman was gone, disappearing into the distance, going west.

It would not be wise to go back to Insigh. Too much time had passed and T didn't know what had happened in Dabion while she was gone. It was an unstable situation, as any spy had to know. She should be briefed before going forward. Mandera was close, just across the river here at the southern border of Dabion, and she could go to Anamaril station, find the operative who worked that town. That operative would know what was going on, could tell her if it was safe to go back. But she did not cross the river. She clambered to her feet and began to walk north.

It took her longer than usual to cover ground, limping as she was. She could have begged her way onto a carriage or a wagon—she saw enough of them on the road, rolling by like dots pulled by horses shrunk in the distance to the size of dogs. She kept to the grass, away from the road, and limped on. Night came. When she saw the tiny village that served as a travelers' stop between capitals, her feet pulled her onto the road and into town, deciding on their own that they refused to carry her any farther. She hobbled into town and toward the inn. What she would do to pay for a bowl of stew, a room or a space on the floor to sleep, she didn't know and she didn't think about.

Then, in the window of the inn, lit from inside and stark against the dark night, she saw Kerk.

She froze, terrified. In the open street there was nowhere to hide. But she realized he was inside the building, behind brightly lit glass, and would be unable to see her in the darkness. The fear ebbed and sank down into the pit of her stomach, and in its place came anger. She began to chew on her lip, but this time not in frustration.

She had been trained by a master of spies. By two of them, in fact: her father and the man who treated her like his daughter. It wasn't formal training but it was training enough. She could follow someone and not be seen, track him into the stable behind the inn, and wait silently until no one was watching and Kerk began to search the saddlebags and carriages for anything valuable that might have been left behind. She slipped out of the shadows and watched him, his head stuck through a carriage door, rooting around under the seat cushions, his back defenseless in the belief that he was alone in the stable. Her feet made absolutely no noise as she moved forward and clasped her hand around the handle of a rake that stood against the wall. She watched Kerk and she began to tremble with laughter, biting the inside of her cheek to silence herself until blood pooled on her lip. She was sure she could feel it pulse in her mouth, that blood, and in her ears, and in her hands and feet, throbbing in mad pride and fury. Here was the man she hated most in the world and he was defenseless before her. With a single blow she could destroy him, and with him destroy the terrible operative she had been and the bastard child of the mad village harlot she had been born and the wanderers' mouthpiece she had never wanted to be. She could win. She pulled the rake from the wall and clenched it in her two hands.

The tines scraped against the floor. Kerk jolted at the sound and backed out of the carriage, closing the door smoothly, pulling himself upright and looking toward the stable door. He had prepared for someone to enter and see him. He had not prepared for T standing behind him. By the time he looked around and saw her, widening his eyes in surprise and disgust, she had brought the rake down on his head with such force it cracked the handle in two.

The laughter, the proud rage, burst out of her in a shout. She was not expecting anyone to enter the stable then, but she knew what to do. She always knew what to do. When the man—the inn's proprietor, or a village constable, it didn't matter—came in and saw her, saw Kerk lying on the floor, and opened his mouth as if to ask questions or shout an alarm, she stepped in on him and covered his mouth with hers. He turned her around and bent her over the railing where saddles were perched, and when he was finished he grunted, "Go on, get out of here," and she was free.

She ran out of the village, heedless of the pain in her ankle and not caring about the dinner she had missed or the bed she had left. She could live on pride and fury. Kerk was dead, she laughed to the sky. Her arms still shook with the impact of the rake. When she finally ran out of breath she collapsed on the ground and savored the trembling in them, the taste of blood on her lip, the breaths raging in and out of her. And they began to slow and caught in her throat, choking her, turning to hard, horrible sobs.

They knifed through her, stabbing her sides, echoing the pain in her ankle, turning the fire in her arms to rivers of agony. She couldn't breathe. She tipped to the side and lay with her face in the dirt, sucking mud and grass into her mouth as she cried.

Somehow she knew that one of them was watching her. She raised her head and saw the Sage called Elzith. Not caring how embarrassing it was, she dropped her face in the grass again and cried on. The Sage did not say anything and did not stop her.

Later, when she could almost breathe evenly, she looked up again. "Why are you here?" she rasped.

"I'm on my way home."

T wanted to scream but the thought of it hurt too much. "You know, don't you? You know everything. So tell me, where is home? That's what I want to know, isn't it? The question K said I don't know how to ask? Where is my home?"

Elzith said nothing.

T's breaths came faster and angrier, short and stabbing between her ribs. She was almost angry enough to stand. Biting her lip with every twinge of pain, she rolled up to her knees, leaning on her hands as she tried to catch her breath.

Then she looked up, glaring at the Sage, but over the woman's shoulder was something else. Against a sun she hadn't seen come up was a figure, stumbling out of the village. Kerk.

His face was mottled in shadow and contorted with hatred. Blood made a black stain on the side of his head, and there was a knife in his hand. T had no voice to scream with. She was frozen on hands and knees, helpless, failed. Pride slipped out through her mouth with the drops of blood. She whimpered like a dog.

And Kerk stopped. The Sage had done something, made some noise, startled him, shocked him into motionlessness. His eyes were wide and he strained against some barrier, but he could not move. The knife fell out of his hand. T watched it fall, hit the ground, bury its point in the grass and tip slightly.

The Sage did not move, tense and trembling as she held Kerk. Without releasing his eyes she turned her head in T's direction and spoke through clenched teeth. "You don't have long."

Mad panic bubbled in T's throat. "Kill him," she hissed, staring at the knife where it bobbed, almost in her reach if she were able to move her arms. "Kill him!"

But Elzith shook her head tightly. "That choice isn't mine. You don't have long."

Then T saw. The Sage wasn't saving her. The Sage was making her choose. She could kill Kerk, or she could run. The fear that had lain in her stomach seethed up again as the anger bled out. She couldn't kill Kerk, she'd tried that and she had failed. The knife finally overbalanced itself and fell to the dirt, away from T's hand. With a sob she lurched to her feet and ran away from the sun.

She evaded him for some time. For a while she thought the Sage might have killed him after all, or that he'd killed her. After running for hours, she begged her way onto a transport into Insigh and slipped off at the outskirts of the city. She sneaked past the yard of a smithy there, where the smith or his apprentice was cooking a bird on a spit over the fire in his brazier. She reached out a hand and snatched the bird and the spit both. She would need a weapon. Creeping into the shadows behind another building, she ate the bird and hid until nightfall.

When she came out again, the woman was there, alive, and with none of Kerk's blood on her. "I'll be running now," T hissed in a whisper, not turning her head toward the Sage as she hurried past. She had no time to lose. "I'll be running forever. Where am I running to?"

Elzith did not hurry to follow her, and T almost missed her answer as she put distance between them. "Nowhere," the Sage said. "I'm sorry. This is your home."

"Who is he?" Tod asked again. He still hadn't given up hope, foolish as it was, that sometime one of the Sages might answer his question.

Tod had been there for days, the longest time he'd ever spent in Sor'rai. "We have someone who wants to see you," the Sages said. As it turned out, that was a ridiculous thing to say. The someone in question couldn't see much of anything. The Sages might as well have told Tod, "We have someone *you* should see." Tod was all but blind, and this man was all but dead.

"He's on holiday," they told Tod, and that was the closest thing to an answer he could get from them. Not much of a holiday, Tod thought. The man was unconscious, only stirring occasionally to murmur something inaudible. He wasn't aware of any of his surroundings, much less of Tod. When the light was good Tod could tell he was quite old, without much hair but dressed in clothes that seemed to be well cared for. Sometimes he put his hands on his stomach and made a sigh of pain. He was dying.

"They can't do anything for him," a voice said close to Tod's ear. "He thought they could cure it. They didn't. But they thought it would make him happy to bring him here, so they did. It's no risk to them. It's cancer, he won't spread it, and it's not as if he'll go back home and tell anyone what he's seen here."

"Are you back?" Tod replied to this answer. He didn't doubt the voice belonged to Elzith. It was Zann and Irisith who had come for him suddenly, after almost two years of hearing nothing from them, and brought him back to Sor'rai. Seeing Zann and Irisith always meant seeing Elzith. They said nothing about their absence, though, or about Julian, or about the gate that they passed through so quickly this time Tod didn't see or feel it. They hardly said anything at all. They brought him to Sor'rai, left him on the grass beside the old man, and wandered away.

"He's the Lord Councilor of Dabion," the voice said finally.

Beside Tod the old man stirred in his sleep. He'd been tending the old man, in a way. He couldn't do much but pat his forehead and try to share a little of the food that the Sages brought him. The old man never quite woke enough to speak. Tod could hear his breaths, thin and uneven. He would be able to hear when they stopped. Death made no exceptions for Lord Councilors. There was nothing Tod could do. "Is he happy?"

"Are we changing subjects, Tod? You'll sound like a madman if you keep that up. You were asking if I was back."

Tod let out his breath in something like laughter, and he felt Elzith lie down on the grass near him. "Are you?"

She paused for a long time before answering, and when she did speak her voice sounded terribly fatigued. "I don't know where I am."

"Where did you go?"

"To find something," she said without hesitation.

"Did you find it?" Tod asked. He wanted to ask whether she'd found Julian, but the question caught in his throat.

"Yes," she answered. "I did, unfortunately. He's as bad as I expected him to be."

Tod couldn't remember her talking about Aron, but he knew that was who she had seen. "There's still a chance. It's not finished. You'll see him again."

"How do you know, Tod? I can't see that. Have you seen him? Have you had any more dreams? Do you know how long he'll be alive?"

The Lord Councilor coughed, held his breath for a lurching moment, and let it out again.

Breaking the silence, Tod said, "I haven't had a dream. I haven't seen anyone die. Not even the old man."

"Have you seen me?"

The tightness in Tod's throat sank into his chest and weighted on his heart. "Are you waiting to die, Elzith?"

She sighed, a thin sound almost indistinguishable from the breeze, but then she stirred a little on the grass and turned toward him. A braid of her hair fluttered and came to rest against Tod's arm.

Tod cleared his throat. "I haven't seen you, Elzith," he said. "I think I would have, though. I'm sure I would dream about you. I don't think you die."

And then Elzith laughed. It was a sound Tod hadn't really heard before, a laughter that was not bitter and was not false. It stirred the leaves above them and Tod reached out, hoping to find her face, to feel the lines around her eyes that would tell him she was truly smiling. But before his hands reached her she moved, toward him, into the ring of his arms, and she let him draw her close. He pressed his face against her hair, and she smelled of the outside.

7

WHEN THE WEATHER CLEARED FOR ONE EARLY, unexpected week, the army was ready. They had been entrenched all winter, at the base of the mountain where they could be seen from the sick camp only a little distance away, and they could move no more than the camp could. Like the strange hospital, though, they were not without contact with the world. Back at the Insigh School, the students had been attacking the problem of the weather, and they had devised ways to send couriers, bundled against the cold, with light and tightly packed supplies that would keep the army through the winter. The students went on to build new siege engines, sturdier ones that could weather the difficult journey to the mountains, with stronger mechanisms that would better aim their missiles over the city gates. These engines were rolled across from Tanasigh and waited in the snows beneath the mountains, and when the winter storms cleared for just a few days at the start of spring, the siege force went up.

Lord Justice Frahn rode at the head of his army himself. By this time he had trained a complement of officers; this time he did not ride because there was no one else to do it. This time he rode because he would see his victory with his own eyes. There was no doubt in his mind that he would see victory. Looking out across the field below Mount Alaz, he could not have been surer of himself. His army was arrayed before him in formation, its siege engines at the ready, thousands of men that Frahn himself had assembled through his own force of will. They could not help but succeed.

Not long ago, Frahn would have attributed his success—something he'd regarded as a tenuous and fragile thing—to fate. Now he saw that fate was not the ethereal and untouchable entity he'd thought it was. Fate was not the hand of the gods, as heathens would have it, but a rational progress of cause and effect. Frahn would succeed not because of random chance but because of his own deeds. The outcome was a logical progression of his actions. He had done the correct things to assure victory and victory would be assured.

He felt no fear as his led his army up the slopes, ordering men and machines into their places. He watched the trebuchets launch their ammunition, the ladders scale the walls, the artillerymen load their weapons, all with the greatest calm. It took twelve hours to breach the walls of Mount Alaz and Frahn marked the hours, neither feeling them rush fearfully nor drag in agony.

He felt no guilt as he ordered the executions of the rebels within the walls. The old books prescribed such actions as a matter of course, part and parcel of a successful campaign. Frahn owed his success to carefully following the lessons of the historical warriors, and he was not going to fail to take this measure. It was necessary to act with harsh consistency to maintain power. The books detailed these actions without fail: Men were killed, women raped, children enslaved. Mistreatment of the prisoners, Frahn believed, was an excess on the part of his less civilized forbears, and he discouraged these excesses among his soldiers. The books described unusual treatment and methods of executing the men; Frahn likewise discouraged these activities. He would act efficiently and rationally. The rebels of Mount Alaz were killed neatly by firing squad.

Some of the men pleaded for mercy. They were not Alaçans, they maintained; they were clerks and Justices of Lord Justice Zein's court, brought from Tanasigh. They were faithful Dabionians. But Frahn would not relent. They had not resisted Zein, they had not acted against the rebellion, they had not fled Mount Alaz before the gates closed. They were traitors and they would be treated as traitors.

Then Frahn looked for the ringleaders of the rebellion: the so-called royal family, the household of Guérite. He could not find them. In fact, he found far fewer Alaçans than he expected. Army lookouts who had spent the winter below Mount Alaz suggested that a good deal of the loss could be explained by the sick camp; Mount Alaz had lost much of its population to the plague. But it did not explain all. It certainly did not explain the disappearance of Zein and all of his kin. And though Frahn's officers employed every reasonable method of extracting the truth from the remaining Alaçans before sending them to the firing squad, none would reveal what had happened to the erstwhile Lord Justice.

None would have revealed Zein's actions in the days leading up to the fall of the city, and none would have spoken of his state of mind. They would not have told how their leader hid in his chambers, refusing to look over the walls as the army grew in size, refusing to listen to the reports of his clerks, refusing to consult with his men. They did not see themselves how Zein fretted and despaired, and no one witnessed the long hours he spent in a paralysis of fear, staring at an empty wall with an old copper bracelet clutched in his hands. It was said to be the last relic of the king, that bracelet: not a crown, not a sword, but a circle of jewelry so thin it bent in Zein's hands like a switch from a supple young tree. No, not a young tree, he thought—something old and lifeless would be more appropriate. He didn't even know if the legend was true. The bracelet could be a lost trinket from some now-dead child.

Once during his miserable vigil a servant entered his chambers, heedless of the guards Zein had stationed outside his door. This servant was the eldest member of Guérite, more an advisor than a serving man, though he brought food and made his circle of the room to clean it. He gave Zein no counsel, not even addressing or looking at the Lord Justice, until the very end of his ministrations. Then he raised his head with authority and spoke the words, "The city will fall, but the Alaçans shall be free."

What does that mean? Zein cried to himself. The
question had run circles in his mind since his first days
of training in the foreigners' justice. It was the question
that had never been answered by the old tales, never by
all Zein's hours of fretting. He was certain it would not
be answered now. In his mind's eye he saw himself sitting in his chambers as the army surged into the keep,
still staring at the wall as they struck him down, an old
battered bracelet clutched in his stiffening hands.

Then the sentries cried out, in voices heard across the
city. The walls were breached. Mount Alaz had fallen.

Zein found himself on his feet, fears and thoughts
alike having vanished from his mind; he walked only by
instinct. Striding through the halls of the keep he gathered his men, his retainers, all his blood kin who still
lived. He led this party through the streets in the distant
part of the city, into the slum quarter, to the tinker's
shack. In a voice so powerful it admitted no dissent, he
ordered the man to open the gate to the king's tunnel.
The gatekeeper could do nothing but obey. When the
last of the Alaçan royal blood had vanished into the
earth and the passage toward safety, the gatekeeper
buried the mouth of the tunnel. He buried it so thoroughly that when the soldiers came to kill him they did
not even recognize it as a means to escape.

So the soldiers of Frahn's army left Mount Alaz and
descended the slopes of the mountain, and Julian saw
them come. By the time the city fell he was almost the
only one left in the sick camp. The camp had its contact
with the outside world in the form of Sages, who took

away the bodies of the dead. That number had remained mercifully small. The plague had not spread as Julian had feared, and the caretakers who had come down from the city, but for a few sad exceptions, had not fallen ill. Carra had mixed a tincture that could be applied to the wounds of the sick, and it kept the disease from spreading, though it did not help those who were already afflicted. It was the last thing she did before she died.

Her death was a sadness Julian only felt in the lowest reaches of his heart, curling out like tendrils of smoke and filling him in the dark when he sought his few short hours of sleep. Waking, he knew nothing but his work. He was the keeper of the sick camp and every man and woman in it was his charge, as long as they remained or lived. The sick were his as they lay in their fevers and ranted with their delusions. The living caretakers were his to teach and foster. Most of them were young, impulsive souls—no matter that some of them had more years than Julian. They heard the army as it gathered on the slopes throughout the winter, and watched it with fear and eagerness through the flaps in the tent walls. They gossiped and speculated and sang old folk songs of fighting and victory, soothing their fears and rallying their passions. Julian feared for them. On those rare occasions that he turned from his patients to look outside, he saw an army far larger than the entire population of the city, with strange, fearsome weapons, growing each day as the weather cleared. When the Sages came, he began sending the caretakers away with them. The sick numbered fewer and fewer and so many caretakers were no longer necessary. By the time Frahn arrived to lead the charge up the mountain, Julian had dismissed the last of his caretakers. They walked from the camp hand in hand with the Sages, and before they could be seen by the army they melted into the air like a cloud of dust dissipating with the wind.

Light did not touch the Sages, Julian thought. They would never question the nature of it. They spoke to it as one deity spoke to another, never crossing paths if they did not wish. He expected he would not see Sages again.

He was alone now in the camp with two men, the last of the sick. On the day that the army made its strike against the walls, Julian was with them, oblivious to the chaos outside. One of his patients was in his death throes, crying out and tearing at himself, and Julian held his arms. As the walls of Mount Alaz were surpassed and its gates beaten down, the sick man finally quieted, and made his pleas for forgiveness. Over the sounds of battle that drifted down the mountain Julian leaned in close and whispered absolution.

But the man did not die; his throes passed and he lay in near sleep, neither waking nor speaking, fever overtaking him silently from within. The other man was equally quiet. Early in his illness he had allowed one of the caretakers to bind his arms, and as the delirium took him he strained within his bonds but did not test them. He had been a caretaker himself, and had led the sick out of the city. Now he lay as if mute, only crying out once, wordlessly. He turned his head away when Julian came to comfort him; whatever guilt he faced in his fever dreams, he met alone and without fear. When the army came down the hill, then, two days after overtaking Mount Alaz, the tent was silent and Julian could hear them.

The first wave of Frahn's men left the city with the blood of rebels fresh on their hands. The tidy executions of the firing squad had not satisfied them; bloodlust was a scent that drove them like fire. They saw the tent in their path and surged toward it, waving their long guns like swords, splitting the air with the same cries of warriors in Biora. Julian heard them and came out of his tent. The sight of him spurred the soldiers on faster. Julian stood and watched them come.

He had no weapon. He wondered what good it would do against these soldiers if he'd had the cavalier's sword or Davi's knife. He did not wonder whether he could outrun them. He stood before the tent, and he would not be moved. He stood with back straight and head erect, his feet firm against the ground. As the soldiers neared him he could see one in the front, then another one, falter, their eyes widening, faces gathering confusion as this single unarmed man, white-haired and pale, stood and did not give ground.

Then from behind them mounted men came, maneuvering their horses and herding the foot soldiers away from the tent. A voice shouted "Hold!" at a great volume, and the men stumbled to a stop. The bloody charge was halted. The cavalry moved aside to let their commander approach and the footmen dropped their heads. The commander rode more slowly, not accustomed to the saddle, but he wore authority in his bearing and his voice. "Record these men," he ordered one of his mounted officers. "They will be reprimanded for their disobedience."

As the soldiers began to move away, the commander shook his horse's reins and approached Julian. He looked down on the Bioran with faint curiosity on his stone-hard face. His blond wig was cut short and tied back with a ribbon, out of his way. Though his clothes were soiled from the fight and his face showed the gray of sleepless-ness, that ribbon was smooth and shining. "You stand your ground," he said to Julian, raising his chin toward the tent. "How many souls are you defending?"

"There are two left," Julian answered, loudly and clearly. "They are the last of the sick."

Lord Justice Frahn raised an eyebrow, as if he still knew humor and kindness. "The sick? Death is coming for them anyway. Why risk your life defending them?"

Because I could not save Davi, Julian wanted to say, if this Justice could understand. "They will die by the hand of the plague," he said. "Not yours."

Frahn regarded Julian for a long moment. Then he nodded, and called two of his officers. "Guard this camp until his charges have passed. Then help him dismantle it." And Frahn rode back to lead the rest of his men down the mountain.

Julian withdrew back inside the tent, where no one witnessed him fall to his knees in a fit of trembling. His charges had already passed.

Dismantling the camp meant burning it: the tent, the rough cots, the bedding, anything that might have harbored infection. The soldiers allowed Julian to recover the last of the tincture and his few belongings before they set their torches to the structure; they scattered his things on the ground a distance away and let him gather them up. He paused as he chased a sheet of paper, the recipe for the tincture, tossed by the wind down the hillside. From a distance he could see the whole of the blaze, rising up toward the sky, silhouetted by the mountain behind it, a hot and violent beauty. He paused to watch and felt someone else watch it with him.

"You smelled it, didn't you?" he asked. "It called you."

The footsteps that brought Aron to Julian's side crunched heavily in the dirt, sullenly. "How did you know?"

Julian smiled. "I know you. Hold this for a second." He handed Aron a sack he'd been filling and a notebook he hadn't yet tucked into it, and hurried to catch the paper before it blew any farther away.

The notebook was Julian's journal of the sick camp, where he'd tracked the progress of the illness. Aron was reading it when Julian returned, sitting cross-legged on the ground, his head inclined away from the fire. He read it through with a wrinkled brow, and finally said, "But you didn't get sick."

"No," Julian mused, taking his bag and slipping the paper into it. "I didn't."

Aron frowned up at him. "No symptoms at all. And you were exposed to it longest. Why didn't you get sick? It doesn't make sense. What is it about you that kept the plague off of you? Is it that you're Bioran? Are you immune to it?"

Julian shrugged. The question, in the end, did not matter. He stood for a moment more, watching the fire as it began to die.

Aron looked back down at the book and flipped more pages. "Carra isn't here," he said after a long breath.

"No," answered Julian quietly.

It took Aron a moment to remember to be rude again. "Did you bed her once, at least?"

Julian turned toward his friend, letting his eye echo a little of the wicked light as he shook his head scoldingly, but he did not answer the question.

Aron watched Julian gather his things and pack them away for a few more minutes. Then he cleared his throat, awkwardly. "I've been told I made the wrong choice," he announced.

Julian continued about his work.

"It's going to be bad, you said."

"Yes," Julian answered. "It's bad already."

"And we have to fight it."

Julian turned then, to look in his friend's face. "We have to fight it."

Aron frowned and shook his head. "You still haven't told me why you care. And I haven't told you why I don't." He looked at Julian's bag, watched him sling it over his shoulder. "You're not coming back in my direction, are you?"

"No. I'm going back with the army. Some of the soldiers have the plague. They were taken away as soon as it was seen, sent to a camp near Tanasigh where the weather's been milder. The commander is sending me to tend them."

"And you're going," Aron scoffed. "You're mad. Absolutely, thoroughly mad." Then he turned away, his eyes on the fire that was now crumbling into ash. "And I'd give anything to be needed that much."

"Anything but your life, you mean?"

Aron looked back at Julian, trying to answer caustically. He could not. "Anything but my life," he repeated.

The officers on their horses rode up then. It was time for Julian to go. Aron sat still on the ground. Julian paused, just for a moment.

"I won't go with you," Aron said suddenly. "But I'll find the plague. I'll find what causes it. I'll find out how to stop it."

Julian smiled. "Why do you care?"

"Because I won't be outdone by a Bioran," Aron growled in reply, but Julian could hear the weight in his voice. He would find something, Julian's dark friend— he would find somewhere he was needed. "Thank you," Julian murmured, then, because Biorans did not know how to say good-bye, he turned and let the officers lead him away, following the army transport on the road toward Tanasigh.

THE END

About the Author

MICHELLE M. WELCH is an Arizona native, a historical re-creationist, a musician, a reference librarian, and author of short stories and the novel *Confidence Game*.